Manufactured in the United States of America
ISBN: 978-0-9844348-9-3
First Edition
Cover Design by A.M. Wells

AN IMPERFECT LIFE

BY

DYANNE DAVIS

Dyanne Davis TITLES:
       Hitting The Right Note
       The Affair
       The Critic
       Another Man's Baby
       Many Shades of Gray
       Two Sides to Every Story
       Forever And A Day
       Let's Get It On
       Misty Blue
       The Wedding Gown
       The Color of Trouble
Anthologies:
       Continental Divide (Lotus Blossoms Chronicles 11)
       Anthology
       On My Knees (Destination Romance) Anthology
Novellas:
       Santa Baby
       Flight 22
       It's The Little Things
       Taming The Bad Boy
       Rebound Love
       Just A Taste
Titles under F.D. Davis:
       In The Beginning
       In Blood We Trust
       The Good Side of Evil (Carnivale Diabolique)
       Anthology
       Lest Ye Be Judged

The rage was building in him as he thought of the things he'd given up for his family.

Damn it, he and Sadie were having the hardest period of their relationship because of his hunger to be Poppi's obedient son. Sadie had seen through the manipulation and Poppi was aware of it. That was the reason for the animosity between them. He stopped talking to his father and turned toward his mother. "Is this the way you feel about it too?"

"Yes, Dominic," she answered him, holding his gaze without fear of repercussion from her husband. She was truly angry with Dominic.

"Listen, you think because she is your mother her answer would be different. You owe your life to me, Dominic. Your mother wanted to kill you. I stopped her." Poppi laughed out loud for several seconds then he stood smiling at Dominic.

The smile on Poppi's face was more sinister than anything Dominic had ever seen in his life. It would be wise to leave before the words that would really destroy him could come out. But he didn't move. He couldn't.

AN IMPERFECT LIFE

The smell of lemon oil brought a grin to Dominic's face. Glancing around the courtroom he took pride in the tidiness of the place, including the gleaming, fresh polished desk he was sitting behind. All of it was part of his dream come true. He gave a light pat to the shoulder of the man sitting next to him. His client Antonio Remeris glanced at him, his gaze showing the fear of possibly not winning the lawsuit. Dominic gave the man another pat and a nod of confidence. When he saw his client was catching the win fever Dominic shifted his attention to his woman and co-counsel on this case. Sadie Hawkins

Desire instantly curled through him and he swallowed in an attempt to tamp it down. It was damn near impossible. From the moment he'd met Sadie she'd set his libido on overdrive and it had never changed. She had legs that stretched to heaven and back, long, silky, soft hair that he loved running his fingers threw. He especially loved when she'd used the curling iron to curl it and he'd coax her into a hot shower to make love, turning her massive ringlets straight once again. She'd fuss and complain about him making her have to get a perm twice as often as she should. But she'd yet to refuse to make love to him. Her skin was the exact color of warm honey and tasted even sweeter. And her big brown eyes sparkled with little flecks of gold when she was horny, and red flecks when she was angry. And the way she curled just right into his arms was nothing short of magical. She'd been put on this earth with the specific purpose to love him. He was eternally grateful to the creator. Glancing in her direction he moaned and the arousal came.

Catching Sadie's eye as she sat on the other side of their client, Dominic's grin widened. Sadie was impatiently tapping a pencil on the polished desk, her trait when she was edgy. He knew it couldn't possibly be worry over losing the case. Mr. Remeris had a strong discrimination case. So did the ten others they represented in this one lawsuit. The payoff would be a big haul for each of the clients and an even greater haul for the law firm. Both he and Sadie would be assured of bonuses. For Dominic it would put him one step closer to landing the junior partnership that would be handed out in a few months.

While Sadie's pencil tapping became more pronounced his grin grew wider. The side door opened and the jury filed in. He didn't have to read their faces to know they'd won, but Sadie sure enough turned toward the jury. A deep but soft chuckle was his way of letting her know he was aware of her actions. He knew she was scanning their faces. That was his woman, she liked to be sure of the outcome. Though confident, still Dominic listened as the jury Forman read the verdicts, each in their client's favor, each a multimillion dollar win against Novellan for blatant discrimination.

"Yes." He heard the strong but softly spoken word from Sadie. That was her trademark each and every time they won. He wondered what she'd say if they ever lost. Why worry about that now, they'd never lost, not once since they'd been paired together, and he had all intentions of making sure they remained paired.

It was all planned out, every second of their lives. He'd make partner in December and on Christmas Day he would give Sadie the ring he'd bought for her months before and miracles of miracles he'd managed to keep hidden from her. He'd ask her to marry him. They'd marry in June and by the following Christmas they'd be working on their first baby. After the third baby he'd persuade Sadie to quit working. Then they'd buy a house in the suburbs and live happily ever after. Their lives were perfect now and their future would follow suit.

Snapping her fingers in his face Sadie pulled on Dominic's arm to get his attention. "Why do you have that silly grin on your face? You didn't hear a word I said."

He gave her a full grin feeling confident and a bit cocky. They were winners and this win was but another diamond in the collection. "I was thinking of our future."

"If you want that future you'd better take care of our present. We won."

"Of course we won. You talk as though you had doubt." Grinning broadly Dominic translated the verdict for his client then turned to the gallery where the remainder of the clients were seated and gave them two thumbs up and laughed.

There was justice in the world after all and he was proud to be on the winning team that had secured it for so many of the firm's clients. Shaking hands with his clients, accepting the hugs and thanks he tried unsuccessfully to keep his eyes from wandering over Sadie's behind or glancing at her beautiful silk encased long legs. Her whispered 'stop it' had the opposite effect she wished on his libido. Yep, a hard on, right there in the courtroom. Sadie had that effect on him, add the huge win and there was no way that wasn't going to happen. A raised brow from Sadie and he slid his briefcase into position

"Is that better?" he asked her as they began walking out of the courtroom surrounded by their clients. "You know you're feeling the same way. You're just lucky enough that you don't have outside proof. Why don't we make a quick run to our apartment and have a special celebration before we head back to the office?"

At that moment Sadie pulled a little away from him and took out her cell. She liked to play it professionally. But even she wasn't immune to what this win meant for them. She wasn't fooling him in the least, a stickler for details she was calling the boss to let him know of the win and that they were going to celebrate before returning to the office. He snickered wondering if she'd said they were going out for drinks or taking the clients to lunch. When she came back and faced the clients instead of him he knew the answer. Not only had Sadie told the boss they were celebrating by taking the clients out for lunch, she was actually following through with it. With a growl and a smile he moved closer to Sadie in order to translate. Turning toward her he asked, "Do we get to celebrate privately?"

"Of course. I explained to the boss that the two of us would be celebrating the rest of the day." She smiled. "This was a big win for all concerned. No one cares that we're not coming back to the office. We got the job done. Besides, Dom, you gave me what I've never been able to resist. An offer to ah …" Sadie raised a brow and laughed teasing Dom, giving him the quick look that always turned him and her own. Why not give in and go home and make love?

Keeping his hands to himself was a challenge but one he was sure he could handle. Considering that Sadie had positioned herself between two of the clients he was left with little choice. Every few second he'd catch her gaze, teasing and sensual and he fought his erection. A couple of hours celebrating with the clients would be worth it if it meant Dominic got to celebrate with Sadie alone for the rest of the day. Grinning he glanced at her and found her brown gaze set firmly on him. Everything he needed was in that look. The world was theirs and would only get better.

***

Sudsy water sluiced over them carrying the vanilla spice scent to the shower drain. What an absolutely perfect beginning to what would be a picture-perfect weekend. If their lovemaking last night was anything to go by they would be using the fragrant body wash several more times.

Lips, demanding, rough and soft all at the same time claimed her own. Dom pulled her even closer while using his free arm to provide a cushion for her back to lean into. His erection strummed with life making her stop at the wonder of it all, of them. They had always been good together a big win somehow always gave them an invisible extra boost. Accepting the knowledge without question Sadie smiled as her body was lifted and she was filled with Dom.

"Um," she breathed drowning in his kisses and his flesh. This man was her life, only one thing was missing, a wedding band that she'd have soon enough. Just a few short months and Dom would propose. He would be her biggest Christmas gift. No matter how perfect a relationship was, legalizing it for the world to see their commitment was always uppermost in a woman's mind. In their case it had been Dom who'd first uttered the 'M' word.

Rational thought left her as magic invaded her body. God had created love and making love just so it would be perfected by them. With a guttural groan from Dominic, her cue to hold on tight Sadie allowed herself to let go. It felt as though she was flying without a net beneath her to catch her in case she fell. But that didn't worry her. Dom was her safety net and would never allow pain to come to her. That was the last thought she had before bliss wiped out everything else. Pressed against his body they both trembled with the force of their release deciding to remain locked together.

Ever so slowly she uncurled her legs from around his back and smiled as Dom held her around the waist sliding her slowly down his torso creating delicious after waves of pleasure.

"Sadie, my love, you're my oxygen."

With a smile she glanced at him struck as always by the love in his gaze. "And you're mine," she finally answered. "Dom, sometimes I feel as though I should pinch myself. I'm so happy. I hope it's always like this for us."

"Considering that I would not be able to stop loving you even under threat of execution, I don't see things changing." He laughed. "Sadie, I can hardly wait until December. I have never been more excited about Christmas in my life."

"Why?"

"You think you know me so well, and maybe you do. But you're not going to spoil Christmas for me no matter what you might think I'm getting you."

"Would you like to know what I'm getting you?"

Curiosity pulled at him but he wouldn't give in. Sadie only wanted him to admit to the fact that he was using the holiday to finally make things official. As much as he knew it wasn't a surprise to anyone that he was asking Sadie to marry him, he still wanted to hold it to himself a little longer. After all he'd shopped for her engagement ring with her father. The man hadn't told Sadie in actual words but the beaming smile on his face every time they were in his presence was a dead giveaway.

Dom had threatened him that if he didn't stop hugging him when they went over they would cease coming to visit until after he'd asked Sadie. He laughed softly to himself remembering Sadie's looks after her father's continued display of affection. She'd joked that her father was in love with him. True to his word her father had not told Sadie no matter how much she'd prodded him for the information. But being a woman, his woman, he already knew she knew. And unless he'd missed his guess she'd found the box. But the wrapping was undisturbed and even if it wasn't Sadie loved when he surprised her and would wait for him to present the ring at his own good time.

Sadie was holding out the bath gel. "I don't intend to spend the entire day in the shower. At least let's have breakfast."

"And then?"

"And then we can continue the celebration."

Showering hurriedly Dominic turned Sadie so he could wash her back and other places, laughing when she swatted his hands away.

***

If the smile adorning Dom's face had been any brighter Sadie would have needed shades to cover her eyes. She smiled standing a little to the side as her man took his victory stroll through the office. She glanced at Paul noting that his head was tilted a tiny bit in her direction and he was observing her. When their gazes met they both smiled and he moved closer to her.

"Sadie, Santiago didn't win those cases alone. Why aren't you strutting?"

"That's not my style."

"You're giving him the spotlight."

"He looks good in it."

"You'd look better."

"Paul, you are definitely good for my ego. And one day Dom is going to beat you to a bloody pulp because of that." Paul's easy smile turned into a laugh and Sadie found herself laughing right along with him. Naturally it had to be that moment when Dominic turned toward her. He blinked as though he couldn't believe what he was looking at and it only made the two of them laugh harder. Bad move.

"What did I tell you?" she grinned up at Paul. "If I were you I'd run for cover," she whispered behind her hand as Dominic strolled up to the two of them.

"Okay, what's so funny that has the two of you laughing so hard?" Dominic inquired irritably.

"We're laughing at you," Paul said without hesitation.

"That's a lie," Sadie objected. "I told Paul that one day you're going to beat the crap out of him." Dominic stared at her for a moment longer than necessary she thought then he glared at Paul.

"Dom, we're kidding around."

"Santiago, I was asking Sadie why you get to do all of the boasting. There were two lawyers on the cases. You always strut and she always move to the side."

Embarrassment colored Dominic's cheeks surprising Sadie. Her man was cocky and he had reason to be. He was as he'd put it— a winner. It was time to put an end to the teasing. "Baby, don't listen to Paul. I love to see you do your victory stroll." When he didn't answer but gave her a questioning look instead, she could have kicked Paul and herself.

"Seriously, Dom. Paul just likes to annoy you. He's teasing and wishing he was in your shoes right now."

"Now, that statement is true, Sadie. I do wish I were in Dominic's shoes, perhaps in his..." Paul drawled leaving the rest to the imagination. Though his playful leer at her gave no such out. Sadie took Dominic's arm and turned from Paul before she laughed again.

"Dom, you have got to stop taking the bait every time Paul needles you. He does it just because you can't take it."

"I hate him flirting with you."

"It's harmless."

"You like it."

"Of course I like it. I'm a woman. But for God sake, Dom, when you get angry that's another win for Paul. He loves it. I'll bet he spends hours thinking of new ways to make you explode."

Dominic turned back to glare at Paul. "So, what's your excuse for laughing with him?"

"He's funny. I like him and he's my friend. He's also your friend, and even if he wasn't you can't tell me who to have as my friend. And you can't tell me when to laugh. So stop trying." Sadie stopped walking to look at Dominic. The hint of sadness she saw in the depths of his eyes prompted her to soothe his ruffled feathers.

"But you're my man. Listen, if you want that partnership you're going to have to put a lid on that temper of yours. You have to stop biting Paul's head off every chance you get."

"He makes me crazy."

"Don't let him."

"Maybe I wouldn't if I didn't know how much you like him."

Sadie smiled.

"You like making me crazy too don't you?"

"There is no way I'm going to win this. Telling you, showing you how much I love you seems to have no effect. You're more concerned with this pissing contest you have between you."

Walking into the conference room Sadie thought for a moment not to sit in her usual spot next to Dominic. Paul was baiting her, laughing still. He was forever teasing that her man had her on a short lease. Sometimes it did look like it. But that wasn't it at all. There was something about her and Dom being in close proximity to each other that gave each of them more power and confidence. She felt as invincible as her man when they were seated alongside each other, as if nothing and no one could ever come between them. With a smile and a slight negative shake of her head toward Paul, Sadie slid into the seat next to Dominic. She held her breath on noticing Dominic had been watching her.

"You could at least stop encouraging him." Dominic growled then sighed and pulled out the chair next to his for Sadie

Turning on every ounce of charm she possessed Sadie smiled at Dominic. "When we get home I have something very special for you." She saw the flare of interest as he leaned toward her to whisper into her ear.

"The same special thing you did before we left home?"

"With a bit of extra." Running her tongue over her lips in a suggestive manner she touched his leg lightly making it appear to any observer that it was strictly an accident. Only she and Dominic were aware of what she was doing. "There are conditions though. You have to behave for the rest of the day, like an adult, like a successful lawyer who's about to become the next junior partner. Like the man I'm in love with, who is cocky and confident and knows he's the only man I want in my bed."

"And Paul?"

"A friend baby, just a friend."

All eyes turned toward Mr. Secret and the folders in his hands. He was forever trying to keep the lawyers off balance. Some days he'd have folders and hand out random assignments, other times he'd put the cases in a basket tell them was what they were and allow them the opportunity to choose whatever interested them. Today was not going to go that way. He would be passing them out. Sucking up her feelings on all of the discrimination cases being given without questions to her and Dominic, Sadie waited. Her parents and Dom had said she shouldn't complain. After all they always received hefty bonuses with their wins.

Still something niggled at Sadie. Dom wanted that damn partnership probably as much as he wanted her. She wished she could think he wanted her a bit more but that would be naive. Sure he loved her, but he was trying constantly to impress his father, and in some ways, her. The only impressing she needed from him was knowing how much he loved her.

The thought that they were practically excluded from most other cases didn't bode well for him to make partner. She'd tried to tell him that over and over. She'd even brought it up several times to Mr. Secret, both in private and in meetings. All the lawyers at the firm were crossed trained in all manner of law. No one really specialized in any one type, though they might do certain cases more than others. It was beginning to appear more and more that while the other lawyers at the firm were encouraged to take on cases outside their comfort zone, even expected to do so, discrimination cases had been relegated to them. Sure they were good at winning them, but they could, and should do more. That was all she was asking for.

So now she sat with her fingers crossed beneath the table praying there were no new discrimination cases. When Mr. Secret turned in her and Dominic's direction and smiled Sadie's abdomen tightened.

"It looks like the two of you are in luck. You don't have any cases."

"Excuse me," Sadie said, "we need billable hours. Pair us with another lawyer."

"There's only one case that could possibly use a second lawyer." The boss turned slightly. "Paul might be able to use some assistance but you know the rules, the lawyer with the case choose who he wants to work with. The case definitely isn't big enough to justify three lawyers. So you and Dominic wouldn't be working together."

"We've worked separately before."

With a determined look Sadie glanced at Paul. He was watching her curiously. Dominic touched her leg under the table pressing his fingers against her followed by a quick caress, a signal she'd said enough. And she had. Her face was burning making her feel embarrassed as though she'd done something wrong, cried foul when there was no problem.

For a long moment Sadie stared at her boss. She was making him and everyone else in the room uncomfortable and she should stop. But she didn't. Then Paul gave her the tiniest of smiles and she knew with his next words he'd make things better and worse for her.

"Sadie, I'd love to have you help me with the case. We work so well together."

Paul glanced briefly at Dominic and Sadie swallowed. "Thanks, Paul." Defiantly Sadie turned her attention to her boss. "Problem solved?"

"Well, everything's settled. Dominic, enjoy your free time. Believe me, you've earned it."

The meeting continued but the tension that she'd invoked was still felt. Sadie kept her eyes on her legal pad not looking across the table at Paul and definitely not looking at Dominic. He was no longer touching her, instead he was writing on his legal pad as well. Only he was writing in

Spanish. She glanced over briefly, yep he was writing curse words.

Chapter Two

Reading over the sketchy notes on the case she was now sharing with Paul, Sadie pulled her pencil from behind her ear and began chewing on it until she noticed Paul staring at her transfixed.

"What?" she asked.

"Nothing."

"You weren't looking at me like that for '*nothing*'."

"I like the way you do that." He pointed at her pencil. "I like the way you chew on a pencil when you're concentrating. By the way I'm glad you're working the case with me. You're the best researcher I've ever known. Most of us are content to have the office staff gather the info. But not you. That's one of the many reasons I like you so much. You're not only smart and determined, a fantastic lawyer, but you're a damn fine researcher. And..." he lowered his voice several octaves. "You're beautiful."

"Thanks."

"Sadie, why did you make such a fuss about not getting a case today? Not all of us receive a new case each day. Besides, you're just coming off that tremendous win. Are you sorry that you didn't share the spotlight with Santiago?"

"You're a smart lawyer. You know the reason why."

"You want Santiago to make partner and you don't think he will if the two of you continue to be lumped together and considered the discrimination lawyers."

"Bingo." Sadie closed her eyes briefly. "You get it. So, tell me, why is it so hard for Mr. Secret to get it?"

"He sees green, Sadie. You and Santiago are among the highest paid lawyers at this firm. He just thinks you should be satisfied with that."

"And you… what do you think, Paul?"

"I think I'd love to have you defending me against anyone you believed wronged me. I'd be grateful for you to have my back like that."

"But?"

"But there's a fine line you're treading when you're trying to help your man. Especially in public. I think you may have crossed that line today. Santiago didn't even lose his temper a tiny bit. That tells me he's seething."

"It's not just about Dominic. I don't want to be labeled. Like you said, I am a good lawyer. I'm a damn good lawyer. I want to work in every area of the law." She thought over her remarks. "Well, I want to do more than discrimination lawsuits. Even when we win the cases I feel disappointment and sadness that the world hasn't changed. It's ironic that I would be fighting discrimination lawsuits yet feel that at the same time Dom and I are in some small way being discriminated against by being given only those cases." She brought her eyes up and smiled at the way Paul was observing her.

"Stop looking at me like that. If Dominic walked in here right now he'd kill us both."

"It's not lust."

"I know. That's why he'd kill us."

"I can't help how I feel about you, Sadie. When you hurt I want to hold you and make it better. The same as you do for Santiago. I have your back as you have his."

This was a very dangerous game the two of them were playing and they both damn well knew it. "I know. And thank you for having my back in the meeting, for asking me to work with you and not leaving me hanging"

"I'd never do that. Is there anything else I can do for you?"

"Yes," Sadie laughed and tapped him with the file. "Don't you dare look at me like that around Dominic. I don't want to have to visit my future husband in prison for murdering you."

***

Stopping to stretch and give her eyes a break Sadie looked up to see Dominic staring silently at her. Pouring over law books for hours had given her a bit of eye strain.

"How long have you been standing there?" she asked wondering what was on his mind, hoping if he was angry they could wait until they returned home to fight it out.

"A couple of minutes."

"Anything wrong?"

"A couple of things, but I'm trying to remember the deal we made earlier." When Sadie didn't seem to know what he was referring to he smiled. "You promised me something extra when we return home. And it was contingent on my managing to control my temper for the rest of the day."

When the look in his eyes softened Sadie pushed the law books away. "Dom," her words came out all breathy and soft. "You're a damn good lawyer. You deserve to be made partner."

"I know."

"But?"

"But... I'm not going to do or say anything to stop whatever surprise you have in mind."

They both laughed and the tension between them eased. Dominic sat down and took the abandoned book. "You're tired. Give me the file and I'll help you with the research."

"You're going to help Paul?"

"I'm going to assist you." Dominic smiled. "It can't be helped that Paul will benefit from that."

"Thanks."

Dominic held Sadie's gaze wondering if his temper had really gotten the better of him. Didn't Sadie know that he'd always have her back no matter what? He gave her a smile thinking she definitely couldn't read his mind.

"Sadie, I love you. Regardless of what might be happening I'm always going to be there when you need me. You've been at this for hours. I saw you were tired and knew you could use my help. That's why I'm here. It's why I will always be here. That doesn't mean that come morning the two of us are not going to have one hell of a fight."

***

The ride home was pleasant, the talk easy with them joking about things that held no importance to either of them, as though an unspoken agreement had been reached. Neither of them wanted to fight, at least before they made love. And it appeared that wouldn't happen if they talked. Glancing at Dominic Sadie allowed herself the pleasure of perusing his body and enjoying the view. She sighed in pleasure at his chiseled good looks, his rippling muscles that spoke of his physical strength. She smiled when her gaze landed on his thick brown hair and his unusual green eyes which were the color of a well-worn piece of jade she owned. Dominic looked so different in appearance from his siblings, matter of fact from his entire family. Of all the things she loved about her man most of all she loved the way he looked at her. He had an expressive face, his eyes and lips spoke volumes to her. She could damn near read his mind by being very observant. And she'd read it often enough to know she was firmly in his heart.

Sadie sighed softly and smiled in Dominic's general direction. She loved him, plain and simple, and there weren't many things about him she didn't like. His temper was probably the only thing. But even that she knew was brought about by childhood insecurities.

From the moment she'd met his family warning bells had gone off. Something was wrong with the family dynamics. There were things between Dominic and his father that she'd tried piecing together for years. The man manipulated his son, which went without question. Why in the world he was shelling out over two thousand dollars a month to a father that wasn't disabled and was working, was a mystery. The bigger mystery remained her man's reaction. Anytime she'd tried to talk about it he'd bitten her head off. There was a wary truce between her and Dom's father. She suspected Poppi didn't like her any better than she liked him.

With thoughts of Poppi Sadie was suddenly overcome with weariness. She turned her head to look out of the window. She wanted to get married but the thought of shelling out a good portion of her income to Dom's family wasn't sitting well with her. She wanted the partnership for Dom probably more than he did. She wouldn't have to worry about the money that was going out so rapidly. As it was, they shared things. But she maintained her own accounts and more than likely always would.

That wasn't what she'd thought her marriage would be like. It wasn't the way her parents took care of their money issues. All money earned went into one pot. She'd spoken to her parents about her concerns and for once they'd been on her side. Thank God. They loved Dom. But she was their daughter and they wanted her secure.

In the end it hadn't mattered. She'd they'd to Dominic. He'd never intended that her money be used to take care of his parents. He'd been honest about his plans not even giving her a chance to ask questions or voice her opinions. He wasn't going to stop taking care of his parents and that was that. And he wasn't going to marry her until he was making a hell of a lot more money.

The thing of it was Sadie would have gladly contributed after marriage if his parents needed financial assistant. But they didn't. Dom just doled it out each month and Poppi not only accepted it as though it were his due, he expected it. So yes she prayed day and night for her man to get that damn partnership.

She wasn't viewing the upcoming partnership through rose colored glasses. She was looking at it realistically and always had. As good a lawyer as Dominic was, she knew Paul was also in the running. And he was very good. To her way of thinking Paul had another advantage. He was not stuck doing only one type of cases. Because of that Sadie felt forced to speak up about their being given all of the discrimination lawsuits. What would happen if companies started treating their employees fairly? Would she and Dominic be out of jobs? Admittedly the likelihood of that wasn't going to happen. It was just part of Sadie's nature to plan her life out to the second if she possibly could.

***

From time to time Sadie would give him a look and he'd answer it with only a smile. Dominic had no intentions of fighting before they made love, or even before they had dinner. When Sadie gave him a seductive smile and sashayed up the stairs to shower he added wine to the crock pot, gave it a stir then joined his woman in the shower. Despite his intentions to feed Sadie first, her succulent, naked flesh called for him. And being a man in love he had no choice but to answer it. Dinner would have to wait. A quickie in the shower was but an appetizer he realized when they were done and he was lifting her wet and soapy from the shower to carry her to the bed.

"Dom," Sadie purred. "I thought you said you were hungry."

"I am." He laughed and positioned Sadie quickly entering her, before she could take her next breath. He gave her a grin before taking her mouth. When she moaned he moved them both to the main course.

Dominic pumped harder riding Sadie with passion and lust, looking at her with love, wanting her for always. When the urge to come made him feel as though he would burst he pulled back and did a slow three count. Her body burned him as though it were molten lava. He wouldn't be at all surprised to find ash in its wake. Would he give up the feeling for even one millisecond? Hell no. He loved it.

Feeling Sadie's hips gyrating and pushing into him as though she couldn't get enough, it only served the assumptions he'd always had about the two of them. He'd known from the beginning that they were mated…meant to be. He was certain Sadie had been born just to love him and he to love her. Kissing the corners of her lips he whispered. "Te amo, Sadie."

Closing her eyes Sadie sighed, moaning the entire time as she moved with Dominic inside her, taking what she wanted from him, moving so she was on top, positioning him where she felt the most satisfaction. A shudder rippled over her flesh and she eased up.

Too soon, she thought, much too soon, but Dom always felt so good buried to the hilt in her that she could never last long. She wondered if when they were in their eighties if she could hold out a bit longer. Good thing, Dominic had a lot of stamina. His laughing startled her out of her thoughts.

"Dom, are you laughing at me?"

"Three strokes max. That's all it would take when I slide into you, Sadie, if I didn't concentrate. Something indescribable happens. I feel as though I'm on fire. And I think to myself, I'm going to go up in flames. I'll bet you never knew I talked to myself. I do. I have to in order to make our loving last. So I talk to myself to remain sane, to…"

Swallowing, trying to turn his own internal flame down a bit Dominic waited. With the pad of one finger he moved slowly downward. The timbre of his voice dipped even lower as lust clouded his reasoning. He could feel the tiny quake began again in her womb. He gave her a quick glance and noted her eyes were glazed, clouded by desire.

He trailed his hand along the ridge of her shoulder following with his lips, his tongue, nipping her lightly, licking her skin in circular motions, sucking her tongue into his mouth, pulling her closer, holding her tighter but never ever taking control.

"Your skin is so soft, Sadie. You taste delicious and you smell…Um…yummy." Sadie moved up and down on the base of his erection and a low moan slipped out of him. His eyes clenched tightly. Resisting the urge to thrust upward to just grab her buttocks and go at it hot and heavy Dominic concentrated on not having an early climax.

He'd helped her to delay her climax with talk and look at the thanks he'd gotten for it. Sadie was toying with him now. She was deliberately killing him. With one hand he braced himself while with the other he flipped Sadie onto her back.

"Show mercy," he whispered. "Sadie, you're so not playing fair."

"And you're thinking the way you're touching me is playing fair?"

"But I was attempting to be helpful darling."

"How? By burning me up?"

He heard the delight in her and once again leaned into the hollow of her neck breathing in her essence, laving her repeatedly. His hands twisted in her hair and he held her as longing and love vied for dominance.

All was lost when she wrapped her legs around his back and held on, her pelvis tilted also giving just the angle he was looking for. He was thrusting into her without mercy, faster and faster and…

"Yes, yes, that it's baby, yes. Oh, Dom."

All thoughts of his annoyance from earlier in the day slithered out of his mind as he claimed his own release.

It was hours later before they made it downstairs to eat. Still they avoided the conversation they must yet have, preferring to return to their bed and their loving. Falling asleep in each other arms would be the best way to start the conversation in the morning.

***

The smell of coffee pulled Sadie from her sleep. Waking completely she sniffed the air and pulled in a deep breath. There was something else going on besides coffee. She was hoping Dom had made cinnamon rolls. Like a kid she bounded from the bed and made a beeline for the bathroom doing the necessary grooming in record time and rushing back to bed. She knew Dom would bring the coffee to her on a tray. And she knew her lying in bed would soften his mood. Smiling she thought of their lovemaking the night before. In fact she didn't think he'd want to fight for too long.

Gathering all of the pillows when she heard Dominic coming up the stairs she put them all beneath her head. Dom walked in the door gave her a look then smiled.

"You look so appetizing lying there like that. But put my pillows back. I'm having my coffee in bed."

"What did you make?"

"Cinnamon rolls. I thought they'd put you in a listening mood."

"And I stacked the pillows to put you in one."

"Hmm. Should we have our coffee downstairs?"

Dominic put Sadie's coffee and pastries on her bedside nightstand and came back to his side of the bed. "We're not going to fight this morning, just talk."

"You're too willing to be agreeable, why?"

"Sadie, you're too suspicious." Dominic took a sip of his coffee then slid beneath the covers and leaned over to kiss her. "Poppi called this morning and invited us over for a cook-out this afternoon. I didn't think we had anything on the calendar so I told him we'd come by. The whole family's going to be there. I don't get to see my sisters as much as I'd like."

And I don't get to see you as much as I'd like, Sadie wanted to tell him, but took a bite of the flaky cinnamon roll and said nothing.

When Sadie said nothing Dominic turned to stare at her. "Do you mind?"

"For the last six weeks Poppi has called wanting us to come over. I do have family, Dom. And I miss the way we spend our weekends alone. So asking me if I mind might not be the question you want to ask. How about one fight at a time?"

"Will you go?"

She smiled. "Like I said, I want to spend time with you and I know you're going regardless. So yes, I'll go."

Her tone of voice screamed loudly that she didn't want to go. Shaking his head slowly Dom put his cup on the nightstand then placed his head in his hands and took a couple of breaths. Hell, he didn't want to go either. "He's my father, Sadie? What am I supposed to do?" After no response he decided to move to the reason they were fighting civilly and not screaming.

With a sigh he began. "Okay, new topic. I know you understood me yesterday when I tried to get you to stop. But you chose to do exactly what you wanted, like always. Just in case you're wondering, you didn't get respect for us with your hissy fit. If anything, you got pity and you made everyone in the room uncomfortable."

"Tough."

"And you don't care."

"I was right."

"I didn't say you weren't, but there is a time and a place for everything."

This time it was Sadie who was placing the coffee a safe distant away. "I can't believe you're going to lecture me on keeping my temper. You fly off the handle if Paul so much as smiles at me."

"That's different. That's personal."

"And our jobs? I think that's very personal. People in the office are beginning to think we're one person. I don't want that. We're not joined at the hip. We do not share one brain. And the discrimination lawsuits are not the only things we can handle. I'm serious, Dom, this is not just me ranting. I'm going to start taking other cases. I want to do more."

"But we're so damn good at winning them, Sadie. And we're making a ton of money."

"Enough to get married?" *Shit. Why had she said that?* "Scratch that one, Dom. Just forget I said it."

With a deep sigh he brought her into his arms. No way would this be a fair fight today. "Baby, I know you're doing what you think you need to do in order to help me get that partnership. I'm just asking that you try not to call the boss out in front of the entire staff of lawyers. We're trying to succeed, not get fired. Can you at least concede to that small point?"

Sadie knew Dom was offering an olive branch. She didn't want to waste the few hours they had alone fighting either. "Okay. But I'm serious about working on other cases."

"Does that mean you're going to continue going after cases to work with Paul?"

"I like working with Paul, so yes. And I'll work with any of the other lawyers in the firm and alone."

"And me?"

"I'll always work with you. The two of us together are magic."

"If you believe that," Dominic asked softly, "Why are you so willing to dump me?"

"Get it straight, Dominic, I never said a thing about dumping you. We are my main priority. We are the reason for the magic."

"You're right. How about making some magic right now?"

"Our coffee will get cold."

"So what? I'll make another pot."

Sadie finished off her cinnamon roll and licked the crumbs from her finger before giving Dominic a leer. "Take the phone off the hook so your father can't call." Sadie gave a shrug. It was as close as she planned to get to an apology she didn't mean.

"I'm way ahead of you baby."

In less than a second the phone was off the hook and beeping and Dominic was plundering Sadie's mouth with his tongue. She was his love and his anchor. They'd not really taken care of anything but he didn't want to waste their precious hours fighting when he could be making love to her.

Chapter Three

In Dominic's opinion the day had gone pretty well. They'd spent most of it making love and just relaxing in bed. But he should have known when he'd attempted to pull Sadie into the shower once more and she'd begged off saying she needed to take care of a few chores that trouble was brewing. When he heard the shower running in the guest bathroom he couldn't help but wonder why she'd prefer to shower alone. *Poppi*, he thought and sighed hoping she'd let it go, taking much longer in his own shower in order to give her time to cool off. Still when he reentered their bedroom it was a surprise to find her dressed but sitting there as though she were deep in thought. He almost didn't ask but shrugged his shoulder and took the plunge. "Are you okay, Sadie?"

"How long do we have before we have to leave?"

With a quirk of his brow Dominic dropped his towel. "We have time."

"Not that." Sadie gave him a half frown before reaching down to rewrap the towel around his waist. "I was thinking I'd like to go and visit my parents."

"Today!"

"Why not?"

"Sadie, they live in Downer's Grove."

"And?"

"How are we going to go to Downer's and come back to the city and make it to my parents on time? We can visit your parents tomorrow or next week. Sadie, you said you were okay with going to my parents."

"I didn't really say I was okay with it. I wasn't given a choice before the decision was made. And considering I like

spending time with you, what I said was, in order to do that, I
have to go where you're going to be."

She raised a brow and quirked her lips as though she
was suddenly tasting something gone rancid. Thinking it over
for a moment Sadie realized it was actually the way she was
feeling. "I want you to think about it. Like I said, Poppi has
been planning things and calling you early in the mornings
deliberately.   Everyone knows our routine.   You make
breakfast for us and for the most part we spend our weekends
together." She shrugged. We've always spent at least three
weekends at home. We've saved the weekdays for visiting our
parents and once a month rotating going out with friends and
alternating weekend visits with our parents. He's been slowly
trying to change that for the past six months. He's trying to
come between us and make it seem like it's all a coincidence."

"Sadie, you can't really believe that."

"I do. Plus I don't like how I behave when I'm around
him."

"That's partially your fault. You don't have to call him
on every little thing you know."

"And he doesn't always have to spout a bunch of
chauvinistic nonsense," Sadie defended her actions.

"He's of a different generation."

"I get that and I wouldn't get so crazy if he wasn't
trying so hard to make you and your brother into the same kind
of macho jerk." Dominic tilted his head and Sadie paused.
She'd crossed the line. She didn't believe in playing the
dozens. It was a one way ticket out of a relationship, besides
being extremely disrespectful. "I'm sorry. I'm not calling
Poppi a jerk, just chauvinistic."

"Sadie, I thought we were good."

"I thought so too," Sadie answered turning away from
him. They had been good but the thought that they would be
spending another weekend with Poppi and she'd have to watch
as he manipulated her man yet again was giving her very weird
vibes. If it were in her nature to be silent it would probably be
okay. But that wasn't in her nature. She always fought with
Poppi then Dom afterwards. Why would she want to spend yet
another weekend there?

"Sadie, come on. You're a smart woman. You're a lawyer for God sake. Why in the world if you know what Poppi is doing would you succumb to it?"

"I can't help it. He works my nerve when he tries to manipulate you."

"Be reasonable, please. I already told him we'd come. How will it look if you don't show up? Can't you do this for me? Please, Sadie. Will you go today and try to have a good time? I promise you, I will be the one to cut Poppi off when and if he goes on a tirade." Dominic waited a moment trying to gauge her reaction. She still wasn't happy. "Do we have a deal, Sadie?"

She didn't want to capitulate but who knew what Poppi would talk Dominic into if she wasn't at least there to be a buffer. She sighed heavily. There was no such thing as a relationship without problems. They were definitely proof of that. But she was melting from Dom's touch. He knew exactly the things to do to bring her out of her worst mood. When he whispered he loved her and asked her once again to go she knew she was lost. She'd go and she'd do what he asked. She'd not rise to the bait. Should Poppi attempt to start a fight, it would be without her. She'd allow Dominic to handle it." Yes, I'll go. Just don't forget I have family also."

Pulling Sadie to him Dominic was determined to repair the minor riff. His hands slid over her hips and rose to encircle her waist. He pressed against her reaching around to undo the zipper of her dress. As his towel again fell to the floor he buried his lips in creamy brown flesh. "Te amo baby. I don't want to fight. "

"Dom, we don't have time for this remember."

"We'll make time."

He heard her audible swallow. If he didn't know better he would have thought she was swallowing unshed tears but that couldn't be right. Sadie didn't cry. Turning her to face him he tilted her head and gazed into her eyes. "I know you do the things you do for us. And I know I should stand up to Poppi. I want you to know I'm aware of what he's doing. I am. I would never let it get to the point where it affected us." When she tilted her head downward he narrowed his eyes wondering if he'd allowed things with his father to go farther than they should.

"I'll take care of things, Sadie, with my father and at the office. I'll talk to the boss. Just give me a chance to handle things and I promise I won't go ballistic. I will do it mano e mano. Comprenda?"

Before she could agree he'd moved her backwards on the bed, entered her and smiled at the look of pleasure that washed over her face.

"No fair," Sadie moaned.

"All's fair in love." He made slow sweet love to her, his strokes giving them their special connection and his kisses reclaiming her heart, sealing their love. Life was so unfair Dominic thought as he picked up the pace. He and Sadie were paused on the edge of everlasting happiness and always a tiny pebble threatened to shove them over. They should be making love because they couldn't stand the thought of not doing so, not because they were keeping ghosts at bay.

***

Two blocks from the home of Dominic's parents the smell of barbeque wafted toward them. When they parked it grew stronger until it reached out and grabbed them by the taste buds. The smell permeating from the grill put Sadie in an instant good mood. No sooner had they parked Dom's family was rushing out to greet them. As much as Poppi annoyed her the rest of the family was fun much like her own noisy family. Before she could say two words a piece of lechon was popped into her mouth by Roberto. "Um delicious," she licked her lips and went in search of more ignoring Dom laughing at her.

After consuming a massive amount of food she was finally sated and enjoying herself. She stretched in a double wide lawn chair with Dom lying beside her, his arm around her. A constant smile played across her lips because he was giving her stolen sweet kisses. Everything was mellow, Poppi was in a very rare mood. Thank God for that that.

"Elena, what would you like for Christmas?"

Sadie came to attention wondering what the heck was going on. Christmas was two months away and never once in her memory had she ever heard Poppi asking his children what they wanted him to buy for them. She was guarded but not overly concerned as Elena answered. As each of Dom's sisters then Roberto answered Sadie remained on the alert.

"So, Sadie, what would you like?"

His smile was blazing. She felt touched. Could this be a new beginning for the two of them? She felt Dom lightly caressing her arm. Sadie could tell he was smiling without having to turn in his direction. "Poppi, I don't really want anything."

"Come on, Sadie. We want to buy all of our children a nice gift for Christmas."

Okay, now she smelled a rat. This time she couldn't help it. He'd never referred to her as one of his children. Turning her head she allowed her gaze to connect with Dom. The look in his eyes confused her, there was such longing. She narrowed her eyes wondering exactly what he was trying to convey to her. Then his eyes changed and she knew the look well, one of pleading. Was he pleading with her? Was she that awful that Dom worried about her blowing up and embarrassing him every chance she got? She thought of what she'd done yesterday at the office. Perhaps he had reason to worry.

"Sadie?"

She returned her attention back to Dom's father. "Poppi, a black sweater would be nice. Thank you."

By the time everyone had finished with their wish list Sadie was on pins and needles. When Elena asked Poppi what he wanted in return Sadie waited for his answer.

"I'd like a new Cadillac Escalade with all the bells and whistles."

Knowing where this was going and before she could stop herself, Sadie said, "But, Poppi, you have a Hummer with all the bells and whistles and it's only three years old."

"And now I want an Escalade."

Poppi's voice no longer had a hint of the syrupy sweetness he'd used when asking what she wanted for a gift. There was a harshness underneath.

Sadie watched as Dom's siblings all turned toward him expectantly. So this was the plan. They'd been had.

"Bro, you're the one with the money. I guess we know what you're getting Poppi for Christmas."

The pressure of Dominic's fingers on her shoulder was a warning. Swallowing a retort Sadie lay back against the chair cushion. An ambush, pure and simple. Dom was giving his parents, both working, two thousand dollars a month and now they expected him to spend more than sixty thousand dollars for a new car. That was the most selfish thing she'd ever heard of.

"What color do you want, Poppi?" Elena asked edging him on and proving beyond a shadow of a doubt to Sadie that all of them with the exception of Dom were in on it. Closing her eyes and laying back she brushed Dominic's fingers from her shoulder. His message was received loud and clear. This was his family, he'd handle it. She only hoped to God that he would. His father had his tentacles wrapped so deeply into Dominic that Sadie didn't hold out much hope. She turned a bit from him wondering if her resentment was showing. Of course it was. She and Dominic weren't married because he didn't think they had enough money. Perhaps if he kept more money in his pocket they could get married.

His finger brushed the side of her face. She kept her eyes closed not wanting to look at Dom, afraid she'd be unable to mask the bitterness that lay in her heart. Another brush was followed by a kiss on her forehead. She was beginning to melt. Then his voice was whispering in her ear… and there was no hope. They were partners; he needed her in this, not to talk, not to take over his battle, but to assure him that he wasn't being forced to make a choice between his father and her. To tell the truth she didn't know if she pushed it if she would win. Opening her eyes she stared at Dom. And when he brushed her lips with a soft kiss she returned his affections.

***

Dominic listened in stunned silence to his father's Christmas request. Sadie had been right to be suspicious. She was so tense now that he wondered how long his touch and easy kisses to keep her silent would work. She loved him. That much he was certain of. But she had no idea what bound him so tightly to his father. More than likely she'd spout off some nonsense about him wanting to earn Poppi's love. And while some of that might be true, a big part of the things he did for Poppi was out of gratitude. Poppi had been there his entire life while his biological father had wanted nothing to do with him. Yes, his parents took advantage of him. And he allowed it. But he owed them.

When Sadie finally opened her eyes to look at him he stared at her for a long moment and wondered for the millionth time if what he owed Poppi should be paid at the cost of Sadie's happiness. Or his? More than anything he wanted to marry Sadie and give her a safe and secure future. That partnership should do it. Then he'd parlay that into doing the things needed including raising capital for a full partnership when the time came. She'd never understand his need to take care of her. She was too damn independent. There were times he loved that about her, when it didn't interfere with their relationship, and times he hated it—when it did.

He could tell she was seething with rage and wanted to confront his father but that wasn't her job. It was his. And what needed to be said between him and his father, would not be done in a public arena. It irritated him a bit that Sadie didn't think he was aware that this little, *'what do you want for Christmas'* hadn't been planned.

Guilt was a powerful inducer, so was love and gratitude. But he wasn't about to jeopardize his future with Sadie by indebting himself even more to his father. The money he gave him each month would have to pay for a new car if that was what he wanted. Dominic wasn't buying it. He'd bought and paid for the hummer.

The idea that the entire family plotted against him was like a knife to his heart. It hurt almost as much as Sadie's thinking him weak. He tilted her chin to peer deeply into her eyes hoping that she could read the message he wasn't giving to the rest of the family. *I love you Sadie and I'm not going to do anything to jeopardize our future.* Eventually the time would come when Dominic would have to discontinue the monthly payments to his parents. He'd known for some time now that the bribery was coming to a close. His father called it a gift but he called it what it really was. A payment in order to be a part of the family, a payment to remain Poppi's son.

Dominic leaned into Sadie and kissed her, knowing that because he wasn't saying no to the Christmas request she'd think he was saying yes, knowing they'd fight about it later.

***

The drive home was accomplished in almost total silence, the same kind of silence that Sadie had sported for the remainder of the time they'd stayed at his parents. She'd pretended to be asleep but there was no way in hell she was sleeping with the noise around her. She didn't want to bite anyone's head off. They should all be grateful for that. Sadie rarely backed down, especially, he'd learned, when she thought she was protecting him. The thing of it was though it was a bit sweet and a bit irritating he wasn't in need of her protection or coddling. He was in control of his faculties. What he did, he did with clear knowledge of why. Something he didn't feel he had to tell Sadie.

Still he didn't want the silence that existed between them so he decided to end it. "The food was really good wasn't it?" he asked as he pulled the car into the garage, turned off the engine and waited for a reply. Getting none he took in a deep breath and slowly released it. "Sadie," he called her name softly.

"Sorry, I was thinking about something. Yes, the food was very good. It always is."

Hmm. Sadie was being agreeable. This was definitely not what he expected. He glanced at her over his shoulder as he made his way to the kitchen door. She gave a half assed smile then looked away. He could push it now or wait. He decided to wait to see what Sadie was up to. When they entered their apartment it was like a breath of fresh air. For several moments all he wanted was to relax in their home, enjoy the freedom of not being pressured. Resentment pressed in on him but with a deep breath he released it. This was his life and he'd always known his life was far from perfect. In fact perfection had seemed a long way off until he'd met Sadie. Being with her was as close as he ever hoped to get to a state of perpetual happiness and that wasn't happening anytime soon. Dominic strode into the kitchen and reached for glasses to pour them wine. He had a feeling they were going to need it. When he saw Sadie head for the phone he waited for the detonation of the powder keg she'd sat on all afternoon.

"Hello, Paul, it's Sadie."

Dominic paused, glass in hand, and turned in Sadie's direction. She was looking through him as though he wasn't even there.

"Listen, I think we need to go over that case before Monday. Why don't you come by for lunch tomorrow? Dom will grill steaks and we'll make a day of it."

He listened as she laughed at whatever remarks Paul had said, more than likely flirting. So that was her plan, to piss him off with Paul, to remind him she had options. Taking a sip of his wine he held Sadie's glass out to her and studied her as she toyed with her top lip with the index finger of her left hand.

She'd issued a challenge, that much was obvious. She wanted to fight. He didn't. He'd made plans for the both of them without asking her and she'd done the same.   Fair exchange, right? But there was more to it. There was a message for him in her actions.

"Do we have steaks?" he asked.

"I'm not sure. If we don't I'm sure you won't mind going out to get them tomorrow while Paul and I work."

Oh hell no. She'd just pushed it a bit too far.

"Sadie, you are aware that this is a different situation aren't you?"

"How so?"

"I can't stand Paul."

Sadie smiled.

"You didn't do the cooking today"

Still Sadie smiled.

"Maybe the similarities are the same and maybe I owe you this one, but, Sadie, don't push it. You're my heart and I love you madly. But I won't sit passively by and allow you to walk all over me. And you're not going to guilt me into doing things I don't want to do. I already have my fill of doing things because of guilt. If you take this farther, as much as it will kill me inside, I'll walk away, Sadie." He took another sip of his wine realizing he'd not just given an idle threat, he meant every word.

Holding Sadie's gaze he waited in vain for her to offer more, but she didn't. Instead she took a sip of her wine and renewed the challenge in her eyes. Checkmate, he thought he read in her smile.

'Sadie, I'm not stupid. I'm aware that today was a setup."

"Are you buying the car?"

"I haven't decided," Dominic lied.

"Can we afford it?"

We, she'd said 'we.' She was acknowledging they were a team. If she could give a little so could he. "Probably," he answered still not admitting that he had no intentions of buying the car. "How tired are you?"

"What do you have in mind?"

His lips twitched. "I thought we could take the phone off the hook, get under the covers and watch a good movie. And whatever else we might like to do."

"I think I can handle that."

"So are we done?"

"Done?"

"Fighting."

"I guess."

"Was that really Paul?"

"Yes."

"And you expect me to cook for him and to sit quietly by while he flirts with you and looks at you like a hungry wolf." She was grinning; apparently she liked the description. Perhaps he should have said, rabid dog, that picture wouldn't be a bit romantic.

"I expect you to cook and treat Paul like a guest. I expect you to behave and not embarrass me. Before you ask, yes your jealousy does tend to embarrass me. I suppose I could avoid that by not doing things to make you blow, but who knows what will set you off. And frankly, I have no interest in living my life under such a restricted regiment that I can't talk to a male let alone a friend."

He remained silent. This was Sadie getting things off her chest. She wasn't the type to just let things go without having her say. He wasn't sure if it was the lawyer in her or the woman. Either way for now he'd wait until she was done.

"We've been fighting more than usual, Dom. That damn partnership has been making us way too tense. And we haven't had as much time alone as either of would like," Sadie conceded. "Yeah I think it's a very good idea to spend the rest of the evening in bed."

"I know babe. I agree. It's that damn partnership."

"As nice as it would be, would it really be the end for us if you didn't get it?"

"Sadie, having it means we can really and truly begin our lives together."

"I thought we were doing that when we decided to move in together."

"We were, we are. Come on, Sadie, let's get back to our plan for the rest of the night. Us, the two of us alone and undisturbed."

With a smile she changed the conversation. "With the leftovers we brought from your mom we don't have to worry about cooking later."

"Yeah just what I was thinking about. Food." With a laugh he took both their wine glasses and placed them on the kitchen counter then he smiled at Sadie a moment before claiming her lips. He was wishing they had spent the entire day at home making love. But it wasn't too late, they'd make up for his error now. Bending a bit he lifted Sadie into his arms and headed toward their bedroom.

Chapter Four

The weekend hadn't gone as badly as it could have. Paul's visit hadn't set him off and in the end they'd actually enjoyed themselves. He'd even put in a couple of hours helping them on their case. They'd been too tired for smart remarks or flirting in Paul's case. It reminded him of the three years they'd been friends before Sadie joined the firm and they'd both fallen for her.

So on Monday morning when they arrived at the office Dominic couldn't help but do a double take as Sadie moved smoothly pass the chair he was holding out for her to sit elsewhere. *What the heck was going on?* He ran the morning conversation through his mind trying to identify something that may have irked her. He came up with nothing. He wondered if it could be his playful boasting about their recent win that had her annoyed.

He caught her gaze and she smiled pointing at Jillian, another lawyer indicating she was staying put. For some reason he'd thought she was kidding when she'd mentioned to him a few days ago that she thought they should work a bit harder to be friends with the other lawyers in the office. Did that mean she couldn't or wouldn't sit next to him in the morning meetings? He started to move toward the vacant chair on the other side of Sadie when common sense ground him. He'd look like a possessive fool. He could just imagine what his father would say about him playing the puta for Sadie. He gave her a look, their gazes held and he looked away. Her voice rang out with laughter as she chatted with Jillian.

The stacked requests from clients sat in a basket waiting for Mr. Secret to call out the cases and ask which lawyer if any wanted it. Sadie was hoping for something different, as much as she enjoyed working with Dominic she didn't want the reputation the two of them appeared to have been stuck with, the lawyers that handled the discrimination lawsuits. They were both aware it was because of their both being considered minorities the reason they'd first been given the cases. With Dominic being Puerto Rican and her been an African American female it was a perfect slam dunk. After they'd won the fifth such case they were given all discrimination cases because they were damn good. Still Sadie wanted a change of pace. She wanted the boss to know both she and Dom were ready for more and varied cases.

"Father's rights," Mr. Secret's voice boomed slapping the manila folder on the highly polished cherry table.

Sadie's hand was about to go up when a snicker from one of the partners stopped her in mid wave.

"This one's a bit different. It's the stepfather who's suing for rights."

"Is the mother dead?" a voice asked.

"No, he's married to the mother. He's suing the biological father," Mr. Secret answered.

"Come again," Sadie said before she had time to think.

"The stepfather married the mother while she was pregnant. The biological father wanted nothing to do with the mother or the child. Eleven years later he's had a change of heart. He wants joint custody."

"You're kidding, right?" Dominic asked.

"Not kidding," Mr. Secret replied tersely. "In the beginning it seemed the father wanted visitation. When the stepfather refused he decided to sue for joint custody. Now the stepfather is suing for full custody with no visitation."

Sadie was getting a bad feeling about this case and didn't know why. Her intention had been to keep silent and listen to the opinion of the others but as per usual she found herself opening her mouth and asking questions. "He's listed as the stepfather? You said he was married to the mother at the time of the child's birth. So shouldn't he be listed as the father?"

"Actually on the birth certificate he's listed as the biological father. But here's the rub. A few years ago when the biological father contacted the mother with some sob story about needing the child to help him with some illness she consented. The father of record," he nodded at Sadie dismissing the word stepfather. "He tried to talk his wife out of having their son tested, she thought she had to, she couldn't just allow the man to die if the child could save him."

"DNA?"

"Exactly, what she'd been determined to keep a secret he'd found out with her help. The child was his. He had his proof. Apparently she's allowed him to see the child a few times without her husband's consent or knowledge."

"The child knows who his biological father is?" Dominic asked.

"No, she allowed him to see the child and told him the biological father was a friend of hers. He doesn't know the man he believes is his father really isn't."

"So the adults are playing tug of war over this kid. No one is even wondering what it will do to him to find out his parentage."

"That's not what's at issue, not for the moment. The father of record believes since the child bears his name he is the father and most jurisdictions uphold that. Since he's listed as the father and was married to the mother at the time of birth the child is his. The biological father insists the mother terminated his rights without asking his permission. In essence she lied to him. She told him she'd gotten an abortion. When he finally saw her with a child he did the math."

Dominic gave a disgusted grunt. "And it took him years to decide he wanted to be a father?"

"He still has rights." Paul looked at Dominic squarely. "The child is his son."

For less than a second Sadie's gaze swung between Paul and Dominic. Both men were having strong reactions to the case. Something was up. On this one she was in agreement with Paul. "I agree with Paul. In essence the mother and her husband perpetrated a fraud on the law and on the biological father."

"And what of the man who raised him? What about his rights? The biological father doesn't have a right to disrupt the boy and destroy his home, his self-esteem, his self-worth, he doesn't have that right," Dominic yelled snatching the folder. "I'll take the damn case. I'll do it pro bono."

"That won't be necessary, Dominic. They can well afford to pay."

"I still want the case."

"It's going to be a lot more work than you think. There are lots of studies you're going to have to delve into."

Dom turned from the boss to glance toward Sadie. "Are you in?" he asked.

Pulling her bottom lip between her teeth Sadie looked away wondering why Dominic couldn't have waited until they were home. Why did he assume she'd feel the same? Hadn't she just stated that she didn't? Eventually she'd have to turn back to face him. As it was she felt his glare on the back of her head. Doing as she had to do Sadie pulled in a breath and faced him doing her darnest to send him a silent message to let it go. Stupid, she knew. When her man felt passionate about something there was no waiting for him. For whatever reason, he was feeling passionate about the case, and she wasn't.

"Sadie, are we in this one together?" Dominic gritted out the words, his voice nearly a bellow.

She glanced quickly around the room before allowing her gaze to land on Dominic once again. Did she need to remind him she was already on a case with Paul? Hell, she might as well pick up a cannon and blow a hole through his heart if she were to do that. While she procrastinated he was waiting, his jaw clenched in anger. Refusing him in front of the others would feel like a betrayal. She wanted an out that wouldn't hurt either of them. She wanted a case she believed in and she didn't believe in this one. The biological father had rights, and the child deserved to know his biological father. Sawing her teeth she pointed toward the basket. Sadie finally had an answer she was hoping Dominic would accept.

"I'm waiting to see what the other cases are, Dom."

"We're a team, Sadie."

Trying for a smile she decided to be a bit firmer in her refusal. "We can also work cases alone," she finally answered.

"This is going to require a lot of legwork, research hours that could best be done by two lawyers working on the case."

End this Dom, she wanted to plead with him. *One of us should,* she thought. "Dom, I'm up to my eyeballs in research already. Maybe Paul can spare some time to help you on this one." Sadie turned a hopeful eye in Paul's direction. For a nano second she wished she'd thought to name one of the other lawyers, Paul was busy with his own case. The same case she'd known not to mention less than a minute ago. Why had she mentioned Paul? Better yet, she wished she'd not said anything.

"Don't look at me, Sadie," Paul spoke up, "I'm with you on this one. I meant it when I said I believe the biological father has rights. I'm not up for this one."

"I didn't ask for your help, Paul. I asked Sadie."

Dominic was speaking to Paul but it was Sadie whom he was glaring at. Why was he pushing this? *Why couldn't he just let it go?* Sadie wondered. "Let's talk about this later, Dom. Maybe give me some time to think it over."

"The boss needs to know now who's going to take the case," Dominic insisted refusing to glance away from Sadie.

Clearing his throat the boss looked first at Sadie then Dominic. "You're taking the case, Santiago. I marked it down. I don't need to know who will be assisting you at the moment. You can fill me in later."

"I need to know." Dominic answered the boss glaring at him then glaring at Sadie in turn. *What the heck was going on?* He and Sadie always teamed up together, especially with cases that required a lot of legwork and two lawyers. "What's it going to be, Sadie, are you in or out?"

"I can't help you with this one, Dom. I think every parent has a right to know his child. Unless the man is some kind of child molester or he abused the mother or child. Other than that I think it's unfair that the parent child relationship is severed."

"In that case I don't need your help, Sadie. I can and will do it alone. Besides, if you don't believe in the client's right then I don't need nor do I want you on my team." Dominic pushed his chair back and left the room his jaw clenched in anger.

The tension in the room was mounting. *Damn,* she thought, this was in no way helping them in their desire to have Dominic named the new junior partner. Just a few days before she'd caused a minor uproar now her man had done the same thing. Everyone was looking at Sadie wondering what the heck had just happened to Dominic Santiago and thinking she had the answer. After all they'd been a couple for four years and had been living together for one.

This time looking to her for an answer as to what was bugging Dominic wouldn't work. She had no idea what had come over her man. To yell at her in front of everyone was so out of character for him. Her face was flushed so she pulled her yellow legal pad to her and began writing as though she was making notes. She continued until the conversation returned to normal. When Mr. Secret had given out all the cases he looked at Sadie.

"Nothing interested you here, Sadie?"

"Not today, maybe tomorrow." She smiled ignoring the knot in her belly.

"Are you thinking about working with Santiago on his case?"

"No Sir. I really don't agree with the father of record."

"Why is Dominic taking this case so personally? Got any ideas?"

"Not a one. But you're right, it does seem to be special for him."

"You sure you don't want to help him out on the case?"

"No. I disagree with him on this one."

Smiling, Mr. Secret reached out a hand and gave Sadie an awkward pat on her left shoulder. "You know I've never said anything about your relationship with Santiago but now I feel I must warn you not to allow your differences to create a negative distraction in the workplace atmosphere. Surely you felt the tension in the room when Santiago left."

"I felt it. But I can assure you, Dominic and I are consummate professionals and we'll be able to handle this disagreement without having it spill over to our work here at the firm." The look on the man's face required more. She smiled hoping to take the frown away from her boss's face.

"Well, any more than it has already. I'll make sure. I'll talk to him."

"His pride is hurt that you went against him in public."

"That wasn't what I was trying to do. I wanted us to handle it in private.

"I'm aware of that but that man of yours has an explosive temper at times, especially when he's working on one of his causes. He wanted you in his corner right or wrong. He didn't expect you to go against him and especially not in front of the rest of us. What he wanted from you today was your total acquiescence."

Sadie stared hard at her boss trying to read him before she spoke. She wondered if he too thought she should have supported Dom regardless of her feelings on the matter. Even she had wondered why she'd not done that. It would have been the easiest thing to do. Later at home she could have given him her reason for not doing the case. A part of her wished desperately she'd done it that way. But it was too late for wishing. Her boss was still waiting for an answer. "That's not me. I have my own thoughts on things," she said at last.

"Well said, Sadie. Good luck with Santiago."

Damn Dom, Sadie fumed. How dare he do what he'd done. They'd both worked hard for their good reputations, and with one action he'd pushed them back. If he thought he was going to make partner like that he'd better think again. He'd better learn to control his temper if he wanted to remain at the firm. Besides that, he didn't just jeopardize his own career, he'd put hers in jeopardy as well, she thought while fuming silently. As for her own little tantrum, that was different. Besides, she'd not shouted and walked out of the meeting. She'd merely been asking for what she thought was fair.

She heard the footsteps behind her, felt him before his hand reached out and touched her. Another thing that would upset Dom if he saw her talking privately with Paul. She swiveled her head to peer over her shoulder. "What's up?" she asked.

"Can I talk to you privately?"

If she could have groaned she would have but enough of looking unprofessional for one day. "Sure, she answered and followed Paul back to the meeting room they'd just moments ago vacated.

She anticipated what he was going to ask before he had a chance to, and she answered. "I don't know what's gotten into Dom so I can't help you if that's what you wanted to ask me about." She took a good look at Paul's face. "Tell me why you took your position so strongly?"

"Why did you, Sadie?"

"It's just my opinion. It's the way I feel."

"I'm adopted, Sadie. I love my parents like crazy. They kept the information from me my entire life. My grandmother died two years ago and in her will she left a letter for me with her lawyer. She thought I should know. After about a year I agreed with her. But initially I didn't think she had a right to interfere with my life or my parents' wishes. I was so angry with her for telling me. She hurt my parents and me not to mention she put a huge riff in the family. There were those who understood why she'd done it and those that thought she didn't have the right. I was angry with all of them. Why hadn't anyone told me? Then I went through a bout of depression while I attempted to pretend I didn't care. I'm an adult. My life is already mapped out and finding out something like this shouldn't have had any effect on me I thought. But I was wrong. It took me a little over a year to realize that my grandmother had done me a favor. She'd really given me something I had a right to. She didn't do it out of malice, but love for me, and her belief that I had a right to know."

"Have you contacted your birth parents?"

"No, but I've begun searching for them. I haven't shared that information with my parents and I won't unless I find them."

Sadie didn't know what to say to an adult that was just now beginning to find there were secrets in his life. She blinked at the look in Paul's eyes wondering what had made him seek her out. Somehow she didn't think Dominic was really the reason he'd asked for the private talk "Sadie...Are you adopted?"

"Me?" Sadie laughed. "Why?"

He shrugged. "I don't know, maybe it's because of your reaction to Santiago. You two never seem to disagree about anything and it would have been so easy for you to have gone along with him then changed your mind when you got him home. But you didn't do that, so I wondered if maybe it was because you were adopted."

"You thought we had that in common. Is that why you told me?"

"No."

For a moment Sadie studied Paul. She really did like him and regardless of how much he went out of his way to annoy Dominic he was a good guy. She thought about him saying he'd had a bout of depression and wondered why she hadn't known. If he were truly her friend shouldn't she have been able to tell?

"Paul, I'm sorry if I was so self-absorbed that I didn't even notice you were hurting."

A smile lit up Paul's face with an internal fire making him more handsome than he already was. For a moment Sadie wondered if he'd been teasing when he'd told her about his depression. He sure wasn't behaving as though he'd ever known a second of despair.

"Sadie, how were you supposed to know? Do you think I wanted to win your affections with pity?" He laughed and shook his head. "Actually being around you helped to lift my spirits. There's just something about you that…makes me happy to be alive."

"Yeah, but we're friends. I'd like for you to believe you can come to me when you're hurting. Or just to talk. I'm always coming to you."

"Then two minutes after you come to me Dominic comes and tells me to stay away from you."

"Dominic can't choose my friends for me, Paul, nor can he choose which cases I want to work on. You and I are friends, remember that. And friendship works both ways. But it would seem I haven't answered your question. No, I'm not adopted. Do you regret telling me?"

"No, Sadie. You're aware of my feelings for you. I've never hidden any part of myself from you."

"Paul."

"Yeah, I know, you're with Santiago. I just don't know if you'll be with him forever. He's a stubborn, foolish man. He should have married you long ago. I would have."

"But it wasn't you I fell in love with. It was Dominic."

Paul smiled. "To be honest, Sadie, I think you fell for both of us. There was just something about Santiago that pushed you a little more his way. I have yet to figure it out

"Uh… love."

"No, not love. Pity perhaps."

Paul grinned and walked away leaving Sadie in stunned silence. What the heck was wrong with Paul? Why would he ever think she'd pity Dominic Santiago? He was one of the most brilliant men she knew and sexy as hell. She loved him, all of him, even his macho bullshit and the vulnerability she'd sensed beneath the surface. *Pity*. The word surfaced again and she wondered.

There was no good that would come from thinking about this. The thing of it was she loved the man. She was annoyed with him now but she still loved him. She walked away from the conference room and did her job the rest of the day ignoring Dominic who was glaring at her every chance he got as he called the client, made arrangements to see the couple and began pouring through the law books in hopes of finding cases to support his position. He was doing exactly what the boss had warned Sadie of. He was loud and very verbal about the case, talking about it to no one in particular just spouting off out of anger. She thought over what Paul had said and wondered if perhaps Dominic or maybe his brother Roberto or one of their sisters could possibly have been adopted.

By the time they were heading out of the door Sadie was more tired from trying to put on a professional face the remainder of the day than anything else. The drive home was quiet, neither of them wanting to be the first to speak. They would have it out at home behind the privacy of closed doors, the place where it should have stayed in the first place.

***

Finally home Dominic paced back and forth through their apartment stopping to glare ever few seconds at Sadie who'd promptly ordered take out the moment they'd come in the door and had plopped down in front of the television tuning him out. His anger was misdirected. It wasn't Sadie's fault that he'd never told her that he was not Poppi's son by blood. It was hard enough dealing with that knowledge himself. He sure as hell didn't want Sadie to pity him. He knew her well enough to know she'd want to fix things for him, feel sorry for him. And then she'd insist he needed to know his biological family.

That was Sadie's way. She'd try and tell him it was for the future of their children, that he had a right to know his biological father, biological family. But he didn't want to upset his life. He'd worked a long time to earn his father's respect and his love. He wasn't going to do anything to chance losing it.

The best way to go at this would be to go on the offensive so he did. "Okay, Sadie, why would you go against me like that in front of everyone?" He turned to her, saw her stance, hands on hips and a look of disgust for him on her face. She wasn't backing down. She was ready to fight. He hated when she did that, just looking at him as though he were a stupid male, not answering.

"Sadie," he cautioned, "you know I don't like you looking at me like that. Cut it out and answer me. Why did you ask Paul to assist me? You know I can't stand him and you know we're both fighting to get that partnership."

"I have a question for you. Why didn't you let it go?" Sadie asked. "I gave you every opportunity to, but nooooo you insisted on making it personal."

"It was personal."

"Damn it, Dom, we were at work. You made both of us look like fools. If you want to present that face to the office then you do it. As for me, I don't. I don't want people looking at us and thinking anything other than we're good lawyers who know how to behave in a business setting. I don't care about your Latin temper. You had no right to lose it today. And you definitely didn't have the right to speak to me in the manner that you did."

For a moment Sadie paused in her tirade clenching and unclenching her hand trying to get a handle on what was going wrong in their relationship lately.

"For your information Mr. Secret had a little talk with me. He gave us a warning that we'd better keep our personal lives out of the office. I think they all thought we must have had a fight before coming in. Why not? You were acting crazy, like a man possessed, storming out of the office like that, demanding that I support you in a cause I don't believe in. Help me out here. Tell me what's going on, Dom."

"What's going on is that we made promises to each other and you broke them. First you continue to flirt with Paul knowing how much I hate it. Then you pick a fight with our boss and attempted to pick one with my father. Today you refuse to help me with a case that you know requires at least two lawyers, yet you're all gung ho to help Paul."

Could he really mean the things he was saying? Sadie breathed in an out before tackling the problem once more. "There is something more going on with you and I want to know what it is." When Dominic merely stared back at her not answering she narrowed her eyes.

"You're not adopted are you?"

"I believe in something, I want you to have my back and you think that's the reason?"

"What else could it be? Seriously, I could see that. Besides, you don't look a thing like anyone in your family. Tell me, Dom, is that it?"

"It could be that the two of us are building a future and I shouldn't have to explain. You should have my back as I have yours. You should not ever open your mouth to ask Paul to help me in anything."

"What is this thing you have against Paul?"

"You."

"Me?"

"He wants you, Sadie. He tells me every chance he gets."

"He's kidding you."

"He's not kidding."

With a sigh of frustration Sadie wagged her finger at Dominic amazed that after four years he was still insanely jealous of Paul. She was getting tired of dealing with it. Taking a look around their high tech living room she groaned. As a couple they had what every young couple dreamed of, well almost. The trust issue was a sticking point and she'd done nothing to cause it. Well, almost nothing except a bit of light hearted teasing with Paul. Drawing in several breaths Sadie prepared to revisit the same old ground. "I'm not with Paul."

"Not now you're not."

"God, Dom, you're becoming impossible.   You're making me crazy."

"You think it's too much to ask you, to think you'll have my back?"

"This is stupid. I don't have any plans to ever agree with you on matters that I'm against. Now, I'll do my best to keep those feelings between the two of us. But if you press it like you did today then the same thing will happen. You're my man, not my conscience. You can't tell me how to think."

Lucky for both of them the take out arrived at that moment giving them a chance to control their tempers, to not say words that couldn't be taken back. Dominic took the bags from Sadie's arms and carried them out to the kitchen. Pulling two plates from the cabinet he filled them with food and carried them out to the living room. As he handed one over to Sadie he allowed his fingers to lightly caress her.

"Sadie, I'm sorry I yelled at you like that. You know how crazy Paul makes me."

"I know but you were acting crazy before I mentioned Paul."

Taking several forkfuls of the food Dominic waited until he could think of a different avenue to take the conversation. Sadie was still pissed and he couldn't blame her. He'd had no right to treat her the way he had. He'd been floored by the case and had no chance to moderate his feelings. He's exposed much more than he wanted. Turning toward Sadie Dominic asked, "Did Mr. Secret really scold us?"

Her head tilted to the side and Sadie stared at Dominic trying to figure out what was going on. She was aware he was using subterfuge but decided to ignore it. She was as anxious as he to change the topic.

"Yeah, he did. And baby that's going to be the last time I'm scolded by the boss. Do you get that?"

She was running out of steam. Darn Dominic for looking so sexy. She watched him as he ran his hand through his thick hair. He wanted to be in the right and couldn't find a way to pull it off. Now he was sulking like a little boy. He looked so cute that she wanted to hug him until he smiled, ease his pain. *Pity*. Paul's word now haunted her. She didn't pity Dom but she hurt when he hurt. Breathing deeply she put her plate on the coffee table, reached for the remote and turned off the movie that neither of them had been watching. "Baby, I'm done eating how about you?" He grinned and she continued. "Let's go to bed and fight later."

***

Running his hand over his woman's body, deep satisfaction pierced his heart. Dominic loved touching Sadie's body. The faint sheen of perspiration on her beautiful brown skin glistened. He dipped his head to taste the moisture and heard the catch in her voice as she tried to keep him from knowing how close she was. He chuckled.

"Mi amour you're greedy."

"I'm not greedy," Sadie responded hating that her breath was wispy and without strength, knowing that as well as Dominic knew her body he knew what he was doing to her. They were good together, had been good together for four years and she knew they would be good together for life. Matter of fact, if Dominic didn't ask her to marry him soon, she was just going to buy him a ring, drop down on her knees and propose to him. And if he didn't say yes…well she'd just have to kill him. She was a lawyer. She'd be able to find some legal reason to keep from going to jail.

"What are you thinking?" Dominic whispered softly.

"Wouldn't you like to know?"

"Tu eres mi vida."

"No swearing," Sadie admonished.

"I wasn't swearing. I said you're my life. By the way, I don't like you becoming distracted when I'm making love to you."

"Then maybe you should stop taking so long."

Dominic couldn't believe his ears. His once shy woman had changed. He pulled a little away from her to peer into her toffee brown eyes. Warmth spread through his body at the look he saw there. She loved him. And he planned to keep that look in her eyes for the rest of his life.

He was going to ask her to marry him on the anniversary of their first date. December twenty-first. Just as soon as the new partner was announced at their law firm. Dominic was a shoe in for the position, so much so that he didn't even have to think about it. He and Paul had been hired at the same time. They both were excellent lawyers and they both worked a lot of the same cases. Still, there was just the knowing in him that allowed him to be so sure. One thing he was glad of: Sadie wouldn't be angry at him for getting the partnership. She'd even strategized with him on ways to make sure it was offered to him. They were the only two minority lawyers at the firm and they were working on a ton of discrimination cases.

It only stood to reason given the current situation at the company that they'd offer the partnership to Dominic. He didn't care if people thought he was only a token, given the fact they'd never had a Latino male as an associate before him, much less one as a partner, didn't matter. What mattered was that with a partnership under his belt Dominic could offer Sadie the stable life he wanted for them.

"Now who's distracted?" Sadie asked.

Her voice was soft and running over Dominic's skin like a caress. "I am baby, and it's deliberate for your trying to take over and do my job. Yo soy el hombre, not you. Eres mi mujer. Got it?"

Sadie moaned as his hand flicked at her, making her draw him closer. Right now she wasn't in the mood for arguing with Dominic, not about any macho bull. Right now she wanted him to stop taking it so dang slow and just make her body come alive. She grinned. "You're the man, yada,yada, yada. I'm your woman, more yada, yada, yada."

Pulling away Dominic looked down at her, frowning. "That wasn't exactly the way I said it."

"What? I said you're the man."

"But you said it like, I'm-the-man-but-not-the-boss."

As her eyes clouded over with lust her hand reached down and squeezed his hardness. And she smirked. When his flesh jerked in her hand a tug of satisfaction touched her. Sure he was the boss. She wanted to laugh but instead she wiggled her behind against his fingers that were pressed against her flesh. When he growled, game, set and point—she'd won.

Then he flipped her over on her back and entered her, and all thoughts of winning completely left her mind.

"Te amo, Sadie."

"I love you too. Te amo," Sadie mimicked.

***

Sadie was sleeping, her body wrapped around him, her head on his chest, her right hand thrown over his belly. Dominic kissed the top of her head thanking God they'd found each other, that he didn't have to wonder if he'd have the life he'd longed for.

From the beginning they'd never had the usual problems many of couple found when they were dating outside their race. No family problems, no one not accepting the other. Both Dominic and Sadie had friends in both races and they both had several family members who had married outside the race. Parties were always a little United Nations affair. Even if it hadn't been that way there was no way in hell anyone could have prevented him from falling in love with Sadie. Even the fact that Sadie and Poppi didn't seem to like each other didn't faze him. He knew his father believed he'd someday tell Sadie the secret he'd sworn never to tell another living soul. Sadie's dislike of Poppi was more practical. She resented the hold Poppi had on him financially and emotionally. Once both had figured out no one was going anywhere they'd formed an uneasy truce.

The moment he'd seen her it was love. In less than a nanosecond he'd taken in her toffee brown eyes, long shapely legs, and that she was built as the song said, like a brick house, nice round behind and ample bosom. She'd grinned as he's stood there obviously checking her out. His eyes locked on hers and he watched as redness flooded her caramel coloring turning it a warm burnt orange.

His heart had thumped in his chest and he'd felt flushed. Sadie claimed it was lust when he told her about it. But he knew she was wrong. After his initial perusal of her it had taken at least two full minutes before he'd gotten an erection. For a minute fifty nine seconds he'd merely stared at her tongue-tied as he'd drowned in her eyes, loving everything about her, picturing them married and with babies. He'd wanted her in his life even then, but the thought of babies lead to the making of them. That's when the erection hit hard and fast. He'd swallowed and hurriedly thrust the folder he was holding in front of the bulge, glad that he had something to hide it with. His eyes had sought Sadie and she'd grinned wickedly at him with a knowing, and he'd grinned back like a fool. He'd known then that he wanted her. More than one lawyer at the firm besides Paul had hit on her, but she wasn't interested. And good for them that she wasn't. He would have fought off all contenders for her love.

Her five-five frame was perfect for his height. At six three Dominic loved the feeling of protecting his woman. Taller women just didn't appeal to him. Sure she'd called him a chauvinist but so what. He liked what he liked. Her eyes that were a bit slanted always made her look as though she had an incredible secret. Later he'd found that she did. When she loved it was with everything she had, it was in her soul. When they made love her eyes would change from the toffee coloring and become imbued with streaks of reds that he so loved. It meant he was the cause for the change. She was beautiful inside and out. Lips half way between full and thin, lips that he'd classified as just right.

An immediate bonding had taken place between them, no games. Just yes, I'm your man and you're my woman. There had been no need for discussion, just as there had been no need to say one day they would be married. Everything in their lives had become centered on the time they would marry. For three years they'd maintained separate apartments spending time at both places until one day at the supermarket they'd looked at the shopping cart filled with cleaning supplies for both places and put half of them back. No talking it over. They knew it was time they had one place to call home. And why not? Everything they did was together. So what was the point in living alone?

Their perfect tune went so much farther when they'd moved in together over a year ago. He'd helped her to perm her hair and she'd shaved him, surprising him with the ease with which she'd done it. She hadn't nicked him once, not once.

A raspy moan filled the quiet room and Dominic smiled. Sadie was searching for him, needing him he knew, wanting to make love. The more she moved the more turned on he became not wanting to take it as slowly as he had the night before. Besides Sadie had become impatient with him taking it so slowly.

"Dom, baby, where are you?"

Sliding his hand between her thighs, he drew her even closer. As the moan started low in her throat he pressed his lips to the spot. She was still half asleep but responding to his touch.

He couldn't help but feel the pride in that. He loved Sadie with everything that was in him. He'd never had to wonder if she felt the same. She loved him. It was that simple. What crazy fool wouldn't love a woman like that? Just a few more weeks and he would make it official.

He'd discounted Sadie's words that the two of them should pool their resources and take the final plunge. And while they did it now somewhat, he didn't want to have to depend on his wife's salary. Besides, he had other obligations he knew wasn't fair to burden Sadie with. He wanted to take care of her and the babies they would have without them wanting for anything. He wasn't there just yet.

Dominic wanted to make enough money so Sadie wouldn't have to work. His dream was to be able to afford to have her stay home and raise his bambinos. Of course he hadn't mentioned that idea to her. Why do it when he didn't yet have the means? Starting a fight with her over something that hadn't yet happened was a real waste of time in his opinion.

"Dominic."

Dominic moved his fingers inside of Sadie feeling the juices that were starting to flow. He'd touched her initially to tease her into waking up. Now he felt the hunger rise in him to have her, as though he'd not made love to her repeatedly a few hours before. It didn't matter, not now. Now Sadie would be accurate in talking of his lust. He would admit it freely. He lusted after her in his heart, his head and his body.

A smile broke out on his face as Sadie wrapped her hand around his hardness. He didn't have to be content with the lusting from afar nonsense. She was his woman. Her beautiful body was his for the taking. Heat pooled inside his body and his erection grew swiftly as he bit her shoulder lightly. He wanted her fully awake. He wanted to see the love in her eyes, the wanting of him.

Soon baby, very soon, he thought to himself as he began to make love to her. In just a few weeks they could begin making plans and stop playing house. For now he'd let go of the craziness, ignore the secret he couldn't believe he was keeping hidden from Sadie and he'd do what she'd asked. He wanted that partnership, had worked hard for it for over seven years. And he wouldn't screw it up over some macho bullshit.

So what if he wasn't Poppi's blood. No one else had ever stepped up to the plate. He belonged to Poppi and no one had the right to take him away from his father, just as no one had the right to take his client's son from him. Blood was blood but it still didn't beat the day to day job. Where was the gratitude in that? Dominic knew where his gratitude laid, with his father, more than likely the same as this kid if anyone had bothered to ask him.

When Sadie's moan intensified Dominic stopped thinking about the origins of his birth and just loved his woman in earnest.

Chapter Five

The days flew by quickly once they'd made it through Thanksgiving. All the excitement of the holiday and his upcoming plans culminated in one grand moment. Finally the day he'd waited for more than a year was at hand. The new partner would be named at the annual Christmas party. There was a sense of peace that permeated his being.

Dominic was holding onto Sadie's hand so tightly that he was aware he had to be hurting her. He eased his grip and grinned sheepishly at her. "I'm sorry, baby. I'm just so damn nervous. I want this night to be over. I want to…"

He stopped. He'd held the words back this long, a little longer wouldn't kill him. Besides, he wanted to do it right, the way Sadie deserved. He wanted to buy her flowers, take her out for dinner, then bring her home and make love to her. After he made love to her he would drop to his knees beside her sated body. And he would ask her to marry him. He already had the ring buried in his junk drawer. He'd at first put it in his underwear drawer until as usual Sadie prepared to put fresh underwear in the drawer and he'd almost tackled her to get her away from the ring. He'd nearly gone into a panic trying to find a safe place where she wouldn't look.

"I thought you weren't nervous," Sadie teased.

Dominic allowed his gaze to travel over Sadie before lingering on her lips. He couldn't wait until they could make it official, he wanted the permanency. He wanted her to have his name. "I wasn't until just this moment."

"What happened? Why are you looking at me like that?"

"Te amo."

Sadie's face broke into a grin as he'd known it would. A shiver of want raced up his spine. She touched him and desire pooled in his belly. "In this moment I've never loved you more, Sadie. I want this for you, for us."

"Baby, calm down. You know you have it."

"What if I don't?"

"Then the partners are just plain crazy." Sadie saw doubt creep into Dominic's eyes. She blinked, suddenly afraid as her line of vision followed Dominic's across the room. She observed the little scene. Paul was playing up to Mr. Secret. There was no doubt in that. She watched for a few seconds more before returning her attention back to the man she loved.

Her heart froze at the look in Dominic's eyes as he watched Paul with the boss. For the first time she worried right along with him. The sight of her empty ring finger gave her the words she sought. Nothing and no one was going to stop Dominic from proposing to her. She inhaled taking in newfound courage along with the much needed oxygen before she began naming the reasons Dominic would be given the partnership. She named the facts for him and repeated them for emphasis, and for herself.

"Listen, you're a damn good attorney and they know it. You've been working hard on the discrimination cases. We both heard the questions from the justice department asking why the firm didn't have any minority partners."

"But they can't make them offer me the partnership."

Dominic troubled his upper lip with the tip of his tongue finding it hard to continue staring into Sadie's intense, honest gaze. He looked over her head. He had to in order to tell the lie he was about to tell. "Besides, I don't want it that way. I don't want anyone making them give me anything. I want the job because I've earned it, because they think I'm good enough for it."

In actuality that wasn't altogether a lie. The reasons he'd given to Sadie were true. Dominic wanted to make sure Sadie knew she wasn't settling for him, that he was good enough to compete and win on his own merits. He wanted her to know he would always take care of her.

Glancing around the room Dominic squeezed Sadie's hand absently. "Paul's still talking to Mr. Secret."

"So what, babe?"

"He wants to make partner also."

For a long moment Sadie stared at Dominic. She wasn't used to seeing him unnerved. He was generally cocky, sometime a little too much, but she loved him and ignored it. "Paul's not going to be named partner tonight, you are," she soothed looking into his eyes and holding his gaze. "You don't have to worry about Paul tonight." She traced his lips with the tip of her finger and grinned. "I'll take care of Paul and you go talk to Mr. Secret," she whispered.

"Sadie, what do you have in mind?"

"Never you mind. Listen, if Mr. Secret doesn't appoint you, we'll walk, both of us."

"You mean that don't you?" Dominic smiled.

"Of course I mean it."

A sigh escaped his lips and he attempted to smile. "I'm sorry to be behaving like this. It's so..." he shrugged his shoulder. "It's the most unmanly I've ever been. This partnership means so much to me, to us," he said squeezing her fingers, this time gently. "With it I can give you everything you deserve."

"I already have everything I want. I have your love." Sadie smiled at Dominic then returned the squeeze he was giving her fingers.

"But you deserve so much more. I love you baby," he whispered then gave her a quick kiss before glancing once again in Paul's direction.

"Paul's not going to get it," Sadie repeated.

"He's been here just as long as I have. Why not give it to him?"

"He hasn't been working as hard as you have on those discrimination cases."

"So what?"

"He's not as smart."

"Paul's a very good lawyer babe."

"I know that, but he's not as good as you."

Finally Dominic swung his eyes back toward Sadie. "Are you just telling me what I want to hear?"

"No way. You're the right man for the job. The firm knows that. They love you, babe, almost as much as I do."

Sadie stepped back from Dominic. "Now start mingling, both of us. We're standing here in a corner like we're afraid. This is our office and our party also. Let's act like it, okay?" She reached her finger up and gently wiped away her lipstick from his lips. He caught her hand. "Te amo," he said.

"Yes, I know. I love you too." She walked toward the corner where Paul was still talking to Mr. Secret knowing that Dominic was watching her. If all her man needed was for someone to take Paul away from the boss then she would be that someone. She had his back like she promised.

***

For a moment, anger stirred Dominic as he watched Sadie sashay over to Paul. She was fighting his battle. He knew she thought of it as having his back, but not in this case. Now it was a very thin line that she was about to cross. He wasn't a puta. He didn't need nor did he want her to fight his battles. Have his back, yes, but there was a difference.

When Sadie linked her arm through Paul's and walked away with him, his anger turned to jealousy. Paul was in love with Sadie, he'd never tried to hide that fact. Dominic walked toward them ignoring Sadie's look that she casually tossed over her shoulder, a look telling him to go and talk to the boss.

Hell no, he wasn't about to have her selling herself to Paul even for a little inane conversation. He didn't give a damn if he never made partner and that was the truth. Sadie was more important to him than any promotion. He stalked angrily toward her only to be stopped two steps from her by a hand landing on his shoulder. He turned intending to brush away the intruder.

"What?" he growled.

"Why are you biting my head off?"

Dominic caught himself. This wasn't the way to speak to his boss. Then he noticed the man was teasing. He stood for a second tapping his shoe slowly against the highly polished tile while Mr. Secret shook his hand and pounded his shoulder. Despite his intentions Dominic couldn't keep his eyes from following Paul and Sadie. A low growl was emanating from his closed lips. Catching himself he licked his lips.

"I'm sorry sir. I'll be back in a moment. I need to speak to Sadie."

"Don't worry, Dominic, she doesn't want Paul. Everyone in the office knows she only has eyes for you. You don't have to pull a macho caveman routine.

"You mean Latino caveman." Dominic couldn't stop the quick spurt of temper. He hated being stereotyped but right this moment he was behaving like every bad Latino stereotype there was.

"Stop being so touchy, Dominic. She's your woman. I've got it. But it doesn't mean that I meant that as a slur. You're not the first man to not want his woman to talk to another man, Latin, Black, White or Asian. We're all the same on that score. But you have nothing to worry about. You know as well as I do why Sadie came and took Paul away. She thought he was taking too much of the boss's time and she wanted you to have your turn."

Dominic could only stand there with his mouth open slightly. There was nothing to say.

"So…since she went to all of this trouble why aren't you taking advantage of it?"

"I didn't ask Sadie to do that."

"I didn't say that you did. But can you deny her reason for doing it?"

"Sadie's not using her body for me to talk to you."

"No, she used her brain. She knew that Paul wasn't going to get out of my face until someone came and took him away. And she did the job." He smiled at Dominic. "Relax, you two are fine. When are you going to marry her?"

Without blinking Dominic looked intently at his boss. "Just as soon as I know we're set financially."

"Then you should be asking her very soon. Money's not going to be a worry for you after tonight." He smiled, clapped Dominic on the shoulder and walked away.

For a moment Dominic remained where he was, stunned. He couldn't believe the old man had just told him he was getting the partnership. He wanted to jump up and down like a little kid. He wanted to…he wanted to tell Sadie and kiss her and ask her to marry him. He resumed his intended destination heading toward her and Paul, annoyed that she'd continued talking to him even after Mr. Secret had left. If her purpose had been to give him time to talk with the boss alone then she should have ditched Paul by now.

"Hey." Dominic reached his hand out to Sadie, clasping her fingers in his he moved to stand alongside the pair. Sliding his free arm possessively around Sadie's waist he maneuvered her away from Paul. "What are you two talking about?"

"Nothing much."

Paul smiled lazily making Dominic want to hit him.

"I've just been asking Sadie for the millionth time what she sees in you." Paul continued grinning boldly downward at Dominic before he turned toward Sadie. "If you ever get tired of Santiago, I'm waiting." Before Sadie could object he leaned in and kissed her on her cheek then walked away.

"Don't, Dominic, you know he's trying to irritate you." Sadie pushed against Dominic's chest to stop him from going after Paul, thinking that keeping the two of them apart was getting old. For four years she'd been in love with Dominic. There was no need for him to doubt her. Sure Paul flirted with her. She couldn't really tell Dominic that he didn't mean it because they were both aware that he did. But what did it matter? She didn't want Paul. She enjoyed his friendship but Dom was her man. He was the one she loved. She really wished he'd get over his jealousy. If he was going to be made partner in a couple of hours he had to learn how better to control his temper, especially where her relationship with Paul was concerned. They were only friends and he couldn't allow that to jeopardize either of their jobs with the firm. Sadie sighed as she felt Dominic slight push against the palm of her hand. She turned so that she was facing him.

"I would never cheat on you, you know that. So don't go getting all macho."

Dominic continued to glare after Paul until Sadie's hand turned his face toward her. "What's up with you? You don't usually act like that when I talk to Paul."

"You don't usually touch him the way you were doing tonight."

"I don't believe you." She put her hand on her hip and started to walk away. "Damn, Dominic. I don't believe you."

"I'm sorry, Sadie. I saw you touch him and I went crazy."

"Too crazy to know why I did it? I wanted to give you a chance to talk to Mr. Secret, and you did."

"I don't want you peddling your flesh for me."

"Dominic, would you stop, Please? Just tell me how it went with Mr. Secret. What did you talk to him about? Did you get a feeling of his plans?"

That stopped him. Dominic shook his head slightly letting go of his sudden anger. He now remembered his mission and pulled Sadie away from the crowd behind a potted plant. He grinned at her then held her face between his hands and kissed her. When they came up for air he was smiling. "I got it baby, he told me. We're going to be okay."

"We were always going to be okay," Sadie answered, pulling Dominic to her. "Baby, don't let this promotion define us okay. I loved you before the promotion and I'll love you after. I don't want this to change us. Promise me, you won't let it."

"Only for the better I promise you that." He hugged her to him. "I can't believe it, Sadie. Partner." He touched her face. "You're so beautiful. I can't wait," he said.

"Wait for what?"

"Our anniversary."

"That's two days away. Make it now. Why can't you just do whatever it is you want to do now? Why are you making me wait?"

Sadie was pressing a little, knowing that as much as she wanted him to he was going to carry out his plan and propose to her on the anniversary of their first official date, knowing that he had the ring and that he'd hidden it in his junk drawer. With every cell of her being she'd wanted to see the ring yet resisted the temptation to take a peek at it until he gave it to her. She trembled wanting him to ask her to marry him now. Ring or no ring she wanted to be his wife.

***

Two hours later Sadie stood pressed against Dominic, his arm around her waist. They'd danced, eaten lavishly and now the moment they'd been waiting for was here. Dominic was trying to play it off, act cool, not wanting anyone to know how excited he really was. But she knew. He'd kissed her so often tonight that she wished the night would never end.

The sound of the knife hitting the side of the crystal glass was their signal to come to attention, the boss was making his speech. He stood at the podium looking suave and confident behaving like Santa Claus knowing he had the power to make dreams come true, to deliver to a little Latino boy the crown jewel he wanted. Hell they'd dangled that carrot long enough in Dominic's face. It was time he had it. He gave her waist a squeeze and she smiled.

"Okay, okay, settle down. You all know why I'm up here. You have all been waiting for the announcement of our new junior partner. I'm sure it won't come as a surprise to many of you. The firm has been doing great and the swarm of discrimination lawsuits has only added to it. Which, by the way, will mean a bonus for all of us this year. We're also going to be able to have a real vacation. Everyone is off until one week after New Year." He waited a moment for the ohh and ah's and claps to subside.

"This will of course be with pay." Again he waited for the applause to subside. "Now that that's taken care of we only have one more piece of business, naming the new partner. It gives me great pleasure to announce our new partner to the firm of Jackson & Secret, Sadie Hawkins."

Dominic had taken a step away from Sadie to walk toward the podium. He froze in his tracks and turned toward Sadie wondering if he'd heard right. He blinked rapidly on seeing the confusion in her eyes then a glistening of tears and panic. He'd heard right. Sadie was suddenly holding him whispering in his ear.

"I won't take it, Dom. I'm so sorry, baby. I'm so sorry. This was yours, it should be yours."

The clapping grew louder as Mr. Secret bellowed for Sadie to come up. Dominic was trying to push her toward the podium. "Go, Sadie," he urged.

"No, Dom, this is your job, I'm not going to take it."

"You go to that podium and take the damn job," he hissed in her ear. "Everyone is staring at us. Don't treat me like I'm less than a man, Sadie. If you have my back you'll go now. Don't make me feel like a fucking invalid with you clinging to me." He unwrapped her arms from his neck. "If you love me, you'll go now," he commanded his voice rough.

Sadie moved toward the podium in disbelief, she wet her lips. She'd never thought about the promotion being given to her, not that she didn't think she deserved it or hadn't worked as hard. It was because she hadn't coveted it. She liked her job and she made a good salary. It was Dominic who'd been bucking for partner, him who was holding out on asking her to marry him. It was him they'd planned on getting it. He was the one who wanted the job.

Damn, she couldn't help but think as she stood there pasting a smile on her lips trying not to look at Dominic. She didn't have to in order to know there was hurt in his eyes. But she wouldn't be able to take it if he wasn't clapping along with everyone else. *What a mess.*

"Sadie, Congratulations. You deserve this."

For a long moment Sadie could only stare at her boss in shock trying to keep her hands from trembling. Mr. Secret kissed her on each cheek and handed her an envelope that she knew would contain a hefty bonus. In spite of her pain over Dominic not getting the job, joy filled her. The boss was right. She did deserve this. She'd worked hard and she was a very good lawyer.

At the moment she was running on automatic pilot, accepting the envelope, giving her sincere thanks to the boss and finally making a little speech before withdrawing and making her way toward the crowd, accepting their good wishes, their kisses and their handshakes. Paul was grinning at her. He held his arms out enfolding her in his warm embrace, his grin genuine.

"Mr. Secret couldn't have chosen a better or prettier partner," he declared hugged her again, releasing her a moment before Dominic came to her.

"Dominic, I didn't know," Sadie whispered when he stared at her his eyes flicking toward Paul then back to her.

"I know." He hugged her quickly. "You deserve it."
Try as he might he'd been unable to conceal the tone of his
sentiment. His voice was thick with emotion but that couldn't
be helped.

"I thought Mr. Secret said you had it."

"He did."

"Then why?"

He touched her to stop her from talking as the boss
walked toward them. With nothing more than a softly muttered
plea for him to remember he still needed his job Sadie walked
away.

"Now you can afford to ask Sadie to marry you,
Dominic. You're set financially."

He was trying to remember Sadie's warning. To deck
their boss would definitely put a damper on what was a big
night for her. "Mr. Secret, is this truly what you thought I
meant?" Dominic was furious. "Do you think I want Sadie
taking care of me?"

"You said financially set, you're set. Sadie will make
enough money to more than fit your needs."

"I don't want Sadie taking care of me. It's my job to
take care of her."

"For God sake, Dominic, lighten up, that's such a
macho attitude. Money is money. As long as you have it and
you're married, it's yours. Besides, it's not as though you're
making peanuts. You make a damn good living in your own
right. Get over this attitude and don't you dare say that I'm
stereotyping. I'm going to go and get a drink. You'd better get
with the program and be genuinely proud and supportive of her
or you'll lose her for real. And it won't be because of Paul."

***

Sliding his key into the lock Dominic told himself for
the hundredth time not to rain on Sadie's parade, to be happy
for her. He held the door as she entered knowing that he'd
taken away the joy from her getting the promotion knowing
that he'd never meant to. It had just happened so fast, it had
snuck up on him so unexpectedly. It was like a whammy but
something he should have been thinking of. Sadie did deserve

the job as much as he. She'd worked long hours on the cases and was an excellent lawyer.

Once inside they stood in the dining room staring at each other. For a long moment they remained silent until Dominic noticed the rapid blinking of Sadie's eyelids. She was trying to hold back tears. He fell like hell for doing that to her.

"Baby, I'm happy for you, congratulations." Dominic moved to bring her into his arms to kiss her and do the things he should have already done but she shoved him and moved away.

"Liar."

"I am happy for you!"

"Is that the reason you gave me the cold shoulder for the rest of the night after the announcement was made? You barely came near me, not even when Paul danced with me three times. Before that you were ready to tear his head off just for talking to me."

"Why did you dance with him three times? Were you trying to make me jealous?"

"I was trying to have fun. You were trying to prove that you weren't disappointed and that I didn't exist."

"So you danced with Paul?"

"This isn't about Paul and you know it. I told you I would not take the position but you pushed me up there. You insisted."

"And you were happy about it."

"Do I look stupid to you? Of course I'm happy to have made partner. I wasn't looking to make it and I wasn't bucking for it, but yes, I'm happy."

"They were looking for a token you know."

Dominic spread his legs apart in defiance and waited. He wasn't stupid either; he knew the words he'd just spoken would cut into her psyche the same as they'd cut into his. Still he'd spoken them. Before he could issue an apology fire blazed from Sadie's eyes. Then she turned from him and shook her head. She was angry that much he knew. When she turned slowly back to face him he held his breath. Now she was livid.

"And if you had gotten the job would it have been as a token?" she asked.

Dominic had decided to ignore the look of pain in Sadie's eyes ignoring also that it was he who'd put it there. "They gave it to you because you're Black and female, kill two minorities with one stone."

"And your being Puerto Rican and male, that wouldn't have meant anything?" Her voice caught. "I would have never believed this of you, Dom. I would have never behaved like this if you'd gotten the job. I wanted you to get it, remember? You said our future was riding on it. Is it still?"

When Dominic didn't answer she walked away from him stripping her clothes from her body, putting her dress across the chair for the cleaners, dumping her undergarments in the hamper. Sadie was deliberately going through her normal routine, anything to stave off the inevitable. What had just happened wasn't a fight. It was only the precursor to what she knew would come. She showered quickly refusing to listen for Dominic opening the door. When she went to their bedroom she had expected him to be there but he wasn't.

Still sulking, she thought sadly as she slid beneath the covers. A tremor went through her. This couldn't be happening, not to them, not to their almost perfect relationship.

***

Ribbons of light caressed and transformed the golden color of the cognac as it twirled in the crystal glass reflecting back toward Dominic trying to entice him out of his foul mood. He sat on the coco brown leather sofa sighing as he bent his hand back and forth to create more patterns of light in his glass. He pulled in a deep breath hating the way he was acting and feeling. Sadie was hurt. He'd hurt her. *Damn.* And all he'd wanted when they'd left home tonight was to come home and make love to her. He'd watched her walk away from him, listened as she ran her shower. He could even hear the sound of the bed as she slid into it. He thought of her lying there naked and warm. *And hurt and angry.* Yet he didn't move. He took a sip of the liquor disappointed that when the first hurdle hit them he'd behaved like a macho jerk.

He shuddered wanting to hold Sadie, make it up to her, knowing that the longer he waited to go to her the worst it would be for them. He swallowed and reached for the phone.

"Coma esta," he said when it was answered.

"Sacaste la promoción?"

"No, I didn't get the promotion."

There was a few seconds of silence on the line as his brother searched for something to say. "Thanks for the card. I liked it." Dominic almost smiled knowing his brother would deny sending him the card as he'd done for the last twenty-three years. His big macho brother had never failed to send Dominic cards with words of encouragement or love just when Dominic found himself in need of it. It didn't matter that his brother refused to take credit for the cards or that he called him loco. His emotions were made clear and the cards were always signed your brother, or from the family. He'd play it his brother's way for now just as always. He wondered what kind of card his brother would find to send him for him not getting the promotion. Sighing Dominic returned his focus to his brother. "Like I said I do appreciate it, your sending the cards. This one was…it was really nice."

"Don't do this again, Bro, you know good and damn well I don't send you no damn cards so stop that nonsense. Now what's up? Did they give your promotion to that prick Paul?"

"They gave it to Sadie," Dominic said low. "I understand the reasoning." He waited.

"But you don't sound happy for her."

"I really am."

"You could have fooled me, Dominic."

Dominic's sigh filled the room. "I want to be happy for her. I really do. But I have been planning this moment for months." He sighed again. "You have no idea how long I've planned how this was going to go down, the way I would ask her to marry me. I've planned it out to the very last second. And now…"

"And now what?"

"How can I ask her to marry me now?"

"The same way you would have asked her in the beginning. You love her and she loves you. What are you going to do with that ring you bought, take it back?"

A lump of pain formed in Dominic's chest. "Damn, Berto, this is just so fucked up. I had everything planned out. When Sadie and I would get married. When she'd have our first baby. That promotion would have given us our future."

"Dom, you said you wanted to be financially secure that you wanted to make sure you had enough money before you married Sadie. Now you have enough."

"Sadie has enough."

"Dominic, man, don't go there. It doesn't matter to Sadie and it shouldn't matter to you."

"It shouldn't, you're right and I know that. But somewhere deep inside of me it does make a difference. Tonight she looked at me with pity. She's never done that. There was something else she did tonight that I didn't like."

"What? Took the job?"

Dominic ignored his brother. "No, she used her body thinking I would want her to do that."

"What the hell are you talking about? Are you saying she was flirting with the boss that she maybe did something hoping you'd get the job?"

"No, sangana. Paul my rival, you've met him. He kept talking to my boss and Sadie knew I was anxious to talk to him. So she went over grabbed Paul by the arm, smiled up into his face and walked away with him. Then she gave me this look like we were in on it together."

"You're telling me Sadie did this so you could have a clear field in talking to your boss?"

"Yes."

"And did you?"

"Yes."

"So why did you get angry at Sadie?"

"I didn't want her to think she ever needed to do something like that."

"Man, she just talked with a guy, moved him out of the way for you."

"You don't understand Roberto and neither does she." Running his hand through his hair Dominic sighed and took another drink of the liquor. "I don't even know if I understand it. All I can say is that I didn't like her touching another man, smiling at another man. And it didn't matter if she was doing it for me. I didn't like it. And now…"

"Now what? You're wondering if she'll change because she's now a partner. You can't possibly be thinking she'll start screwing around. Don't tell me that you're worried about that or about having Sadie disrespect you. You're loco. Sadie got that job man. Do you realize what a big deal that is? She's a woman and she's Black. She just succeeded in a man's world. You should be proud of her instead of acting like a little puta. Sadie's your woman and you're acting like she stole your job. It wasn't yours until the boss gave it to you. He didn't give it to you so it wasn't yours."

"You don't understand what I'm trying to say. You can't begin to know how I feel."

"I do know. Maria makes more money than I do. She doesn't rub it in my face. We both have direct deposit and it was her suggestion. I knew it was so I wouldn't have to look at it every week. But still I know it's there. Hell, I'm just glad the money's there to pay the bills when I need to pay them. I'm proud of her man. I love her. Besides, Dominic, we both know you'd have more money if you'd stop giving half of it away."

"I'm not talking about that now. The raise I would have received from the partnership would have more than made up the difference.

"Still, Dom—."

"Like I said that's not my main concern. It's this thing with Sadie."

"It shouldn't be a thing with Sadie. You should be proud of her hombre."

"I am proud of Sadie."

Then start acting like it bro. Instead of talking to me on the phone you should be making things up to your woman. Go man, I'll talk to you later."

The phone clicked and Dominic closed his eyes knowing his brother was giving him sound advice. He'd called Sadie a token, told her she'd only gotten the job because she was a woman and Black. Oh yeah he needed to make up for that remark. He looked toward the stairs and thought of moving but he didn't, instead he took another sip.

***

A token. Sadie couldn't believe Dominic had called her that. For several long minutes she lay in bed wondering how she could kill him and get away with it. She heard his muffled voice on the phone and did her best not to listen. She didn't like that he was talking to someone other than her. He should be in their bed begging her to forgive him, telling her how much he loved her, assuring her that nothing had changed. But it wouldn't be true. She knew that everything had changed. With one act their relationship had been fractured. Closing her eyes she prayed for sleep.

***

Looking around the home he shared with Sadie he had the good sense to think about what losing her would mean. He'd done and said things to her he'd never thought he would. And now their feet were firmly planted on the path of destruction. The only option open to him was to make amends. Rising from the chair he sighed and emptied the last of the liquor into the glass, not wanting to deal with the damage he'd done, the pain he'd caused the woman he loved, or the thought that he'd shoved her away knowing another man loved her, and had been begging him for years to screw it up.

Well, he'd definitely screwed up, and wanting to do it or not, he didn't see how he could remain downstairs for much longer. Sadie wasn't asleep, he'd heard her restless tossing and turning. Deciding to man up at last another sigh was expelled before he made a move toward the stairs.

Walking up the stairs Dominic prayed that Sadie would fall asleep by the time he reached their bedroom. He didn't want to talk to her right now, didn't want to see what kind of look would be in her eyes when she looked at him. It wouldn't be a look of love that much he knew. Maybe later, but not immediately. Taking a shower as quietly as possible he took a moment to listen at the door. He was being a childish coward. He'd be lucky if Sadie didn't cut off his balls and feed them to him. When he'd dawdled as long as possible he pushed the door open with a bit more force than he intended then walked slowly toward the bed and climbed in beside Sadie. She was breathing easily; she wasn't asleep, just pretending. He slid his body around hers, holding her tightly, pressing his lips against the back of her neck.

"I'm sorry baby," he whispered into Sadie's ear just as he heard her light snoring. He almost woke her just so she would know he'd apologized. They'd broken one of their rules, never go to sleep angry. Twenty seconds earlier and he could have prevented that. With a sigh he breathed in her warmth and settled more closely against her wishing he'd had the common sense to have thought of Sadie as being in the running. *Damn*, he thought just before he fell asleep.

Chapter Six

For over an hour Sadie had been cooking. To put it more accurately she'd been slamming pans and burning food. None of it mattered. She needed something to do to rid herself of the myriad of emotions swirling around in her head. She was thrilled to have made partner. True, she'd not been expecting it. But she couldn't lie and say she didn't want to shout it from the rooftops. Yet, she had held in the urge to call every member of her family out of loyalty to Dominic.

Slamming another pan on the last burner she dropped spicy hot sausage links into the pan. Dom was the real reason for the way she was feeling. She totally understood his pain. She'd hurt for him when the announcement was made. Why wouldn't she? She lived with the man. Of course she knew how much he wanted the job, had counted it as his…but still. She sighed. Did he have to treat her the way that he had? If he truly loved her he wouldn't have done it.

A lump formed in her throat and the tears she's been trying not to shed ran down her cheeks one at a time. Sadie had never been a crier. She much preferred taking care of things, doing what was necessary to get the job done. And tears didn't do it. She loved Dominic with her whole heart and until last night she thought he felt the same. But now she wondered. She'd waited for him and he'd taken his time coming to bed, avoiding talking to her. The real kicker had been him taking his shower then coming to bed and holding her, but not saying a word. She'd waited for him to apologize. Nothing.

With a flick of her wrist Sadie turned the pancakes over stacking them on a plate and covering them to keep them warm before shoving the plate into the oven.

Anger flared again at the knowledge that Dominic had broken his promise. They'd both promised never to go to sleep angry. He should have apologized. Sadie swallowed not liking where her thoughts were taking her. Surely this morning they'd be able to get over this. She'd allow him to vent and she'd vent and then they'd make up.

But the memory of what had happened the night before would linger. A chill followed the thought.

***

The bed felt strangely empty. Dominic moved toward Sadie reaching his arm out to her, opening his eyes when all he came away with was bed linens. Sitting up in bed he wiped the sleep from his eyes and looked around the room. All was in place. Sadie's things were right where they were when he'd fallen asleep. She hadn't left him. Thank God.

Then his other senses kicked in and he smelled coffee and burnt food. Cocking his head to the side Dominic wondered what was going on. He always made breakfast for the two of them on the weekends. That was their thing. On Saturdays he made a huge breakfast and brought it to Sadie. Then they would eat, shower together and make love. Sometimes all day, sometimes stopping in the late afternoon if they were going out.

Despite the fact that Sadie was a horrible cook on her best days he couldn't imagine what she was doing in the mood she was no doubt in. Thoughts of running a defense swarmed in his head while slipping on his pajama bottoms knowing that the reversal in roles didn't bode well.

***

A microsecond of time passed as he entered the kitchen and gazed across the room at Sadie. She glanced up but didn't speak so he made the first move knowing it was what he should do. Pretending it was any other morning he walked directly to Sadie and stood in front of her before slipping his arms around her. "Morning babe."

"Morning," she answered moving away.

"You're still angry at me?"

"Shouldn't I be?"

Dominic stood back and watched her for a moment. Sniffing the air he decided to turn on the charm hoping teasing her would work. "Why didn't you wait for me to make your breakfast?"

"I was hungry."

"I always make breakfast for you on the weekends."

Sadie stopped in her tracks and glared then she grabbed two cups and poured coffee. "Is it that hard for you to say you're sorry?"

"I said it last night."

He watched as sadness filled Sadie's eyes and she blinked rapidly as though she were trying not to cry. She'd never cried, not once since he'd known her.

"Baby, I'm sorry," he said reaching for her, ignoring her pushing him away. "I'm sorry I acted like a jerk last night. I did. I know I did. I was rotten to you. Please, can you forgive me?"

Before he knew what had happened she was bawling, great sobs racking her body making him feel panicked. He couldn't believe he'd made her cry. "Hush baby," he soothed. "I didn't mean to hurt you."

As he rubbed his hands along her body he felt like the heel that he was. "Don't cry, Sadie. I don't want you feeling bad about something so great. I'll do my best to get over this. I promise." He heard her pulling in air, gulping as though she couldn't remember how to breathe then she pushed from his chest.

"That's the problem, Dom, you have to try and be happy for me, to get over how you feel about my getting the promotion. I would have never said the things you said to me last night. I would have never thought them. All this time I've had your back. I wanted you to get the partnership."

Sadie took a step away and glared at him. "You want to know something? I deserve that partnership. I work just as hard as you do. I've worked my tail off on those accounts. If I'm a token so be it. I'm a token that now has a bonus, a huge raise and corner office. I think I can live with being a token." She turned to walk away and Dominic caught her by the arm.

"You're right, you did deserve the job. But you have to admit, Sadie, you never thought of it either. You can't blame me for being surprised. You were surprised. I didn't just want the partnership. I wanted it for us, Sadie. I wanted to give you all the things I've been dreaming of for the past four years. I wanted us to be a family."

"And now we can't. Is that what you're saying? Something this stupid is going to break us up?"

A cringe of regret filled Dominic at his choice of words. "I didn't mean it like that. I know my attitude is archaic and I'm being a macho jerk, you don't have to tell me that. I already know it, Sadie. Just give me a little time to lick my wounds, okay. Be patient with me."

Dominic words were the death knell to their relationship. Sadie knew it was much as she knew her own name. She should just tell Mr. Secret she didn't want the job. But what would that prove, that she was an accomplished liar? She did want the job. Even if she did that Dom would protest and not take it anyway. And like she'd told him, she deserved the job as much as he did.

"How much time do you need to lick your wounds?" she asked.

"Sadie?"

"No, I'm serious. How long will it take?" She brushed his arms from her and went to the phone.

"Mom," she said as soon as her mother's voice came on the line. "Guess what? I made partner."

***

Dominic drank his coffee as he listened to Sadie talk to her mother, then her father. He stayed where he was until she'd called every friend and relative she knew. That would be his penance for what he'd done to hurt her. Then she turned to him. He chewed on his lips and tried to smile.

"I guess I'm through licking my wounds."

The look Sadie was giving him had lost a bit of the frost. This time when he smiled at her, she returned it. Pulling her into his arms he kissed her thoroughly. "Forgive me baby," he said again holding her tighter.

"Sangana."

"You're right. I'm a jackass," he agreed. "Forgive this jackass." He could tell she wanted to remain angry but she was melting. He blew on her ear lobe then pulled it into his mouth and suckled it as his hands roamed her body. "Perdóneme mi amor. Forgive me, my love."

"Let's eat breakfast then we'll talk."

"I'm not hungry, Sadie." He neglected to say he wasn't hungry for burnt food.

"I am."

He ran his tongue along the side of her neck paying close attention to the spot that made her lose all inhibitions. He pressed her behind bringing her in line with his erection. "Food can wait a little while can't it?" he asked. "Besides most of it is uneatable."

When she didn't answer he lifted her into his arms and buried his lips against her throat. "Don't be mad at me anymore, please. You're not a token. You're a brilliant lawyer, a wonderful, beautiful, brilliant lawyer and you're going to make a great partner. Mr. Secret was wise to have chosen you. Now let's celebrate the way we should have last night."

Before she could protest Dom carried her back up to their bed. "I love you so much, Sadie," he moaned into her neck. Placing her upon the bed he kissed her trailing his tongue along her neck, lapping her ear lobe and suckling the bud into his mouth. His hand roamed over her, removing her clothes, preparing her. His arousal came quickly as blood flowed into his engorged flesh. This was what he should have done earlier.

"Sadie," he moaned moving from her throat to suckle her breast. "You're so beautiful baby. I love you so much."

"I don't know if I believe you anymore, Dom. How could you talk to me the way you did, say the things you said if you loved me?"

"Let me show you," he whispered moving his hand between her thighs, touching her where he knew she wanted to be touched before sliding a finger into her wetness. "Let me love your body, Sadie, then you'll know. I can't lie to you when I make love to you. I'm only alive when I'm inside of you. You know that, don't you, Sadie? Tell me you know it baby."

"I know it, Dom. I know you love me." Sadie's voice was low and lust filled.

Dominic looked heavenward and whispered a silent thank you. He didn't want to lose Sadie. He'd do whatever it took to make things right. He felt her hand twisting in his hair tugging harder than she normally did. He knew this was called payback. She wasn't even close to coming.

Wetness covered his finger making it easy for him to slide another finger into Sadie's heat and then another. She rocked her hips against his caresses moaning as her pulling of his hair changed from the tugging meant to cause him pain to the insistent way she had of trying to force him into position. "Not yet," he whispered knowing he owed her a lot more than to just enter her and take his pleasure. No, he needed to make sure his woman was well satisfied before finding his own pleasure within her body.

"Baby," Dominic felt a tremble of desire rip through him bending his spine in half and causing him to clutch her to him. He held her and felt the shudders of lust that came from her.

He slid even farther south until he was where he wanted to be. Then he tasted her and sighed with pleasure as her body relaxed and became accepting. Now what he was doing was for his own pleasure. He loved the taste of Sadie on his tongue. He loved feeling her pleasure in the most intimate of ways.

His hands wrapped around her hips and he lifted her slightly wanting more access. He could feel what he was doing to her, the ripples of pleasure going through her belly, her legs tensing and thrashing. Dominic twirled his tongue deep inside her body feasting like a drowning man. His erection became painful as he heard the little sounds she made in the back of her throat. The hum of Sadie's impending orgasm always affected him that way making him proud that he was the one she'd chosen to love, that he was the man in her life bringing her pleasure.

He'd die to insure he kept that position in her life. He continued loving her body and loving her. When she came, Dominic pulled her even closer holding her until she was done. When her pleasure diminished he felt a different shiver go through her body and he heard her soft cries.

Moving upward he wiped his mouth with the back of his hand and gathered her into his arms. "It's going to be okay, Sadie. Baby, I promise, it's going to be okay."

***

Sadie lay with her hand on Dominic's stomach running her fingers over his rippled muscles. "I'm sorry you didn't get the partnership," she whispered.

"I know," Dominic answered her trying not to think about it trying to ignore the sudden catch in his throat. He was doing his best to ignore all the old insecurities reaching upward to strangle him.

"Do you want me to tell Mr. Secret that I don't want it?"

Dominic laughed at that. "Of course not. And if I did what would you say?"

"That you're being selfish."

"Would you do it?"

"I'd think seriously about it."

"That I know. But would you do it?"

"No."

"So why are we having his discussion?" He leaned on an elbow and looked down at her. "Look baby, I know how much you wanted me to get it. Without a doubt I know that it was never an issue. And yes, it was damn short sighted of both of us not to have thought you were in the running. I'm not going to lie and tell you I'm not disappointed. But can't I be a little disappointed for me and proud of you at the same time?"

"If you're sure that's all it is."

"That's all it is. I promise." He sighed and lay back on the pillow. There was no reason to tell Sadie that he was still pissed, that he believed the boss led him on. That comment about him not taking everything as a racial stereotype, then wham, right in his face giving his job to his woman. That was...Dominic stopped feeling her eyes on him. He blinked wondering why Sadie was staring.

"You haven't heard a word I said."

He thought for a moment trying to make her words come to him but they wouldn't. She was right. He hadn't heard a word she'd said. "Sorry," he murmured choosing to bring her down to meet him, to kiss him. "I was daydreaming," he explained yet not elaborating, kissing her instead.

For a moment Sadie hated how easily her body betrayed her when Dominic touched her. A sliver of hurt remained and she wanted to stay angry with him. She almost did but his whispers in her ear broke down her resolve and she returned his hungry caresses. Still, underneath it all she wanted to comfort him, take away his pain in not getting the partnership. Between kisses Sadie's mind wandered. She thought of the ring he had hidden away in his drawer and wondered if he'd still give it to her. She felt a tremor race down her spine as Dom moved between her thighs. He entered her and her eyes closed. Dominic definitely knew which buttons to push. Sure, Dom had been daydreaming, and of course he'd not heard her. This one hurt to the core to accept, but accept she must if they wanted to work through their problem.

God, please don't allow this to take over our lives, she prayed while succumbing to Dominic's touches.

***

Christmas morning came and went with visits to both families. For once Sadie had planned it so the bulk of her time would be spent with family, knowing she'd need the camaraderie of her cousins, aunts and uncles, and her parents to get through the day. They exchanged gifts and bless their hearts no one asked her about her missing gift.

Being with her big noisy family was almost her undoing. Dominic was in seventh heaven playing with all the kids, teasing her and telling anyone within earshot that they planned to have an entire baseball team of kids. Right. Like that was going to happen. Glancing across the room at her cousin Sierra, Sadie renewed her promise not to have a child out of wedlock. Sierra had been shacking with Leon for more than ten years. They had four kids and still he hadn't married her. Her gaze fell on one cousin after the other. They were all shacking, all with babies. Her friends were in the same situation. She'd always promised herself she'd never shack. She'd gone back on her word. Her stomach clenched. She was something she'd never thought she'd be. She was a failure.

Her bright idea to spend most of the day with her family was akin to being in a torture chamber. She could no longer believe she was too smart to fall in the age old trap but there she was just the same. She'd compromised her beliefs to be with Dominic Santiago and he'd left her with a huge gaping hole where her heart used to be. No one asked if she were engaged to Dom. And when the day was over she was almost able to pretend that her heart wasn't broken, that a stupid job wasn't the reason she wasn't engaged.

Of course all of her relatives and Dom's had called her privately to question her. She'd given little explanation, just told them that no, he hadn't proposed, and no she wasn't sure when he would. She could swear she could feel them gloating over the phone lines, glad she'd been taken down a peg. That she had no more control over her life than they'd had over theirs. Now they were the ones lecturing her, telling her what to do about Dominic, what things not to accept. And she took it. It was well deserved payback for the many times she'd tried to run their lives.

Every single time a call came in Dominic glanced at her with a plea in his eyes. She wasn't sure if he wanted her not to answer the calls or if he was simply hoping she'd come up with another story.

Never before had Sadie been so glad to see the end to a vacation. She'd received a tremendous gift that had started the bricks of her perfect life to crumble. One could only hope the foundation had a sturdy base.

Chapter Seven

Rearranging the picture of Dominic on her desk Sadie looked around her new office before turning to the window and smiling. She had her own secretary now. She actually had an office instead of a little door-less cubicle. She wanted to jump for joy.

Gazing out of the window she stared transfixed at the scene below. Of course she'd known what existed outside, but now she could look at the snow covered streets and just people watch. She ran her hand down the side of her shoulder. For the first time since she'd started working at the firm she felt toasty warm in January. She had bought her own little heater for her office. Now no one could complain about how hot she'd made it when she dared to turn up the thermostat. She hugged her arms around her.

"You're enjoying this aren't you?"

"I was just looking out the window." Sadie toyed with her lips biting down then blowing out several short pants of air before turning wanting to wipe away some of the joy from her face. It annoyed her that she hadn't heard the opening of the door. "Good morning, Paul."

"Good morning." He glanced at her hand. "Where's your ring? I thought for sure over the holiday Dominic was going to propose to you."

"How do you know that he didn't?"

"Because if he had you would be wearing a ring."

"Maybe the ring didn't fit."

"Maybe, but I don't think that's the case."

"Maybe we don't believe in rings. Or maybe I don't want to wear it to work."

"Ha! A woman with a diamond and she doesn't want to wear it. Come on, Sadie, not even a ten year old would buy that. What happened, the big macho guy couldn't take it that his woman got the partnership and he didn't?"

Sadie glared at Paul. She tilted her head and leaned back. "But you didn't get it either and you wanted it too. You wanted it bad." What did he think, that he could come in her office and crap all over Dominic and she wasn't going to defend him?

"Damn straight I wanted it. I've kissed every partner's ass to get that job. I don't know why Dominic and I didn't figure you'd be up for it also. You're a good lawyer. Congratulations."

"Do you really mean that?"

"Of course I mean it. It's funny though that the two of us who wanted that job and were fighting like dogs over a bone to get it never saw that we weren't in the running. It serves us both right," he laughed. "Nice going, Sadie."

"Thanks, Paul."

"Now seriously, what happened? Didn't Dominic ask you to marry him?"

There was no way she could get around answering Paul's question. As much as she wanted to Sadie couldn't prevent the sigh that escaped. But she did manage to look away feeling the pain as intensely as she had for the past two weeks. She'd lived with the hurt in private knowing that as soon as they returned to work it would become a public affair. She'd known everyone in the firm was going to ask her about it. She'd practically announced it to everyone. Oh God, if she could keep tears from coming to her eyes she would be forever grateful.

"Sadie," Paul said softly, "Dominic loves you."

"I know that."

"Give him some time."

"But you said you're happy for me. Are you really?"

"I am but we both know I'd have been happier for myself. Don't worry about it, Sadie. Things will work out."

"How come you can say all of the right things?"

"I've had two weeks to get used to it. Beside, I'm not sleeping with you," he leered at her. "But who knows. If

Dominic keeps acting like a jerk…" He allowed the sentence to drop.

"That's never going to happen—not unless he no longer wants me."

"Then like I said, you have nothing to worry about. He'll always want you. He claimed you the moment he saw you."

"Claimed me?"

"Well yes. I remember the speech he made two weeks after you started. He was going to quit if interoffice dating wasn't allowed."

Sadie smiled remembering. Dominic hadn't even asked her out at that point, just stood up one morning and looked at Mr. Secret and asked straight out if interoffice dating was frowned upon. When he'd been asked why, he'd turned to her and said, "If it's a rule, it's one I can't keep. So I thought I might as well put my cards on the table. I would have to quit now."

Sadie could feel her skin warm at the memory. The entire room had turned to look at her. It seemed that it had taken forever for Mr. Secret to answer and when he'd said no that there was no rule against it Dominic had smiled at her and sat down. Paul was right he'd claimed her. And she'd allowed him to claim her.

Dominic's voice outside her door brought her out of her reverie. "Don't tease him okay," she asked giving Paul a pleading smile.

"You're kidding right? He would do it to me."

"Please don't."

"If I don't you're going to owe me."

Dominic entered the room looking at Paul then Sadie. "What's Sadie's going to owe you?"

"I think that's between the two of us." Paul smiled at Dominic then turning on all the charm he smiled at Sadie. "I don't see a ring on her finger," he teased before turning once more in Sadie's direction. To rub it in he quickly gave Sadie a peck on the cheek and darted past Dominic before he could react. Laughing he left the room. Getting under his rival's skin was just too easy.

***

Damn. Regret settled in Dominic's chest. He should have thought of what Sadie would have to go through when they came back to work. He'd been preening for weeks before the announcement, telling anyone who would listen that he and Sadie were about to start their future. He'd even told their boss that he was asking her to marry him as soon as their future was financially set. He knew Sadie was watching him. He wanted to be able to give her what she wanted. One day he would, only not now.

"What was all of that about?" he asked going on the defense instead. "What favor did you ask of Paul? Why do you owe him?"

"I don't owe him." Sadie sighed. "I had asked him not to mention the fact that we're not engaged. He mentioned it. Therefore I don't owe him."

"Sadie."

"I'm not going to break down and cry, Dominic. You don't have to worry about that. Naturally, today will be hard, but I'll live through it."

She lifted her eyes and stared at him. If he thought she was going to absolve him of the pain he had another thought coming. She was an adult. She'd live through the humiliation and the disappointment.

Her gaze fell on her naked finger and she couldn't help the tiny hitch in her chest before she found the strength to pull her gaze away, rubbing her teeth against her lips. Right now she wished he would leave her office and allow her to deal with all the questions. If he really cared she'd be wearing that engagement ring he'd hidden. She'd almost begged him to just let her see it. But she had too much pride for that. Since it was apparent that he wasn't going to give it to her she'd satisfy her curiosity and look at the ring the first chance she got, when he wasn't home. The only reason she'd resisted before was because she wanted there to be genuine surprise on her face when he gave it to her. Now it didn't matter.

"Sadie."

"Would you please stop calling my name like that?

"I love you, Sadie."

"Yeah, I know." She sat down in her chair and plopped open a folder. As she ran her fingers through her hair she begin making notations on the paper in front of her while avoiding looking in Dominic's direction and not telling him she loved him, or that she understood. She didn't understand.

***

It was obvious Sadie wasn't going to talk to him. He couldn't say that he blamed her. He wanted to take her in his arms and whisper to her that he was sorry. He wanted to ask her to marry him. But he couldn't, not right now and not like this. It didn't feel right. Dominic gazed at Sadie. He'd blown it.

Walking out of Sadie's office he looked back at the closed door trying as hard as he knew how to let the envy pass him by. Pain he could deal with, his anger he didn't know if he could and still have a job at the end of the day. He looked past his boss knowing the emotions he felt would be reflected in his eyes. He needed time to sort this out. But, like everything that was happening in his life, he wasn't going to get that time. He knew it with a certainty the moment his boss spotted him, grinned and started walking toward him.

"So, Dominic, did you and Sadie set the date?"

Dominic couldn't have prevented the glare he threw his boss even if he'd wanted to and he didn't want to. "We're not engaged," he said after a two second hesitation, two seconds when he'd debated hurting the man he blamed for Sadie's tears.

"You said you were only waiting to be financially set. You are. Sadie's making a lot more money now."

"Sadie's making a lot more money. Until I'm making a lot more money…"

"You're a young macho fool. I know you were expecting the partnership but I never thought you would behave like this. I guess I choose the right person after all."

The look of disgust thrown his way didn't escape Dominic. So what? He was also disgusted by his actions, by Mr. Secret and by Sadie's talking with Paul, going behind his back and asking the man to not mention things, to keep secrets from him. It was a weak excuse and he was aware of it. But it was the only one he had.

Walking back to his cubicle Dominic shied away from his co-workers. He didn't miss the curious looks tossed his way or the hushed tones. When he saw a couple of the secretaries huddled together staring at Sadie's closed door he glanced at them then stared at Sadie's closed door before sitting behind his desk. What a mess. Hoping coming back to work would decrease the tension had been nothing but a fairytale. It was almost worse than the holidays had been.

The holidays had been bad. Both of their families had been expecting an announcement. When Sadie had shown up without a ring the looks on everyone's faces had been enough to almost make Dominic give her the damn ring. He'd hurt her twice. She would eventually get over his reaction about the job, but he didn't know if she'd get over his not asking her to marry him. That was more personal.

Reading through the papers on his desk he swallowed the disgust filling his throat. It was killing him not to ask her, to not have asked her, for her to have to go through all the prying eyes. He picked up the phone to order roses and put it down before it was answered. Roses wouldn't make up for what he'd done.

***

Her first day as a new partner should have brought more joy. It hadn't. She'd barely been able to look at Dominic during the morning meeting. Her face hurt from smiling all day trying to reassure everyone that she and Dominic were just fine, that their not being engaged was as much her idea as his.

Ha! She'd not been able to pull that one off. And each time she's had to repeat that lie she'd wanted to scream.

"You ready to go?" Dominic asked poking his head in through the open space.

"Sure, give me a minute."

Sadie needed a minute to take in a deep breath. It would be needed to be able to continue the façade and walk out of the office arm in arm with Dominic and pretend that all was right in her world. When he closed the door and came into the room she looked up. There was a question in his eyes, one she didn't have the answer to.

She stacked the folders neatly on her desk before shoving other papers into the drawer. "I'm ready," she announced and marched out of the room doing her best not to touch him. "Goodnight," Sadie called cheerily to the employees still there. A step away from freedom and Paul rounded the corner. She'd thought all the lawyers had gone home long ago.

"Good night, Paul," she glanced at him hoping that for once he wouldn't give his usual response.

"Goodnight, Sadie. Remember if you ever get tired of Santiago, I'm here waiting for you."

She should have known he'd say it. "Sure thing, Paul. I'll remember." She saw his lips twitch in a half smile. They'd played this game for nearly four years and never once had she given him that answer. She'd never joked or even hinted that there might be a chance with her. Now she had and the three of them knew the reason she'd done it. Dominic and that damn promotion. Trying her best not to glare at either Dom or Paul she shoved the door open with more force than necessary, walked out into the hall pushed the elevator button and waited.

"Were you trying to make me jealous?" Dominic stood alongside Sadie waiting for her to answer.

"Nope."

"Then why did you tell him you'd remember?"

"Because I will," Sadie answered and stepped into the elevator. "I have a good memory. I always have."

"I know today was hard," he attempted to explain.

"You have no idea. Save it okay. I should have seen this coming. Let's just go home. I'm tired."

"I thought you wanted to go to a movie."

"Not tonight."

"Maybe grab some dinner?"

Leaning against the elevator Sadie tried, she really did. She didn't want to sulk but she was tired of pretending that all was right in her world. It wasn't. And Dominic of all people should know that. When he reached for her hand she pretended she didn't know what he was doing and moved away. When they walked out of the building she still refused to look at him glancing instead down Michigan Avenue pretending her interest was in the Chicago transit bus that was coming at a moderate pace down the street. If she didn't love Dominic so much she would do what she was fantasizing about and shove him in the path of the bus.

"Are you angry at me because I didn't ask or because you're embarrassed?"

Did he just ask her that? Sadie nearly stumbled as she glanced at him. "Leave me alone."

"Sadie."

"You have been calling my name all day and I'm tired of hearing you. Just leave me the hell alone, Dominic."

"Are you going to keep trying to make me jealous with Paul?"

"I've never done that."

"What about the party?"

She sighed, that didn't deserve an answer. She kept walking, stopping only when Dominic's strong hand gripped her stopping her in her tracks.

"Sadie, you know we're getting married."

When, was on her lips. "It doesn't matter," were the words that came out of her mouth. "You don't have to keep looking at me as though you think I'm going to commit suicide. I'm not. I'm okay. Give the office a week or so and everyone will stop looking at me as though someone has died. Listen, Dominic, I'm a big girl. You didn't put a gun to my head to get me to agree to share an apartment without benefit of marriage. Getting married was never meant to be a payoff. I know the old saying, 'why buy the cow when you can get the milk for free.' I understand."

"You know you're blowing this way out of proportion."

"Gee, thanks. If you hadn't told me how I should be reacting to this I would have never known."

He wanted to be angry with her, the typical response of the person who'd done wrong. Instead he slid his arm around her waist and walked with her to the parking garage.

"I want to give you everything," Dominic said once they'd gotten to their car. He unlocked the door and waited for her to climb inside. "We just need a little more money."

"We make enough money."

"No me refiero a nosotros. I don't mean us. I mean me. You're not going to take care of me, Sadie, I'm not a pendaho. You're my woman. I'll take care of you."

"Dominic, you're being crazy."

"I don't care what you say. It's how I feel."

"You don't care what I say? Do you really think this is the way for us to end this argument? Because I can tell you it's not."

"Just give us a little time, Sadie. Give me a chance to come up with plan B."

He counted to ten as he waited for her response. Her silence was not unexpected nor was her glare. But when she turned to look at him it was the single tear that slid down her cheek as she tried to maintain her calm, that greeted him. It was that which melted him. "Sadie, baby, marry me." Dominic begged. "Marry me now. You're right. I'm being a macho jerk."

"No!" she shouted.

"No? But I thought you wanted me to ask you."

"Not like that, not with you being blackmailed by my tears. I want you to want to marry me because you can't live without me."

"I can't."

"I want you to want to marry me because you can't stand the thought of our not being married."

"I can't

"And I want it not to matter that I make more money for now."

Dominic pulled away from her and started the car. He'd asked and she'd said no. He wouldn't ask again until he was the one earning the most money.

"Dom, why does it have to matter?"

"It just does, Sadie."

"A few weeks ago we were happy and making plans. I can't believe how fast everything's changed for us." Another tear slipped from her eye and rolled down her cheek. She looked at him. "I'm scared for us. I love you... but I'm scared for us."

"Nothing's changed in our feelings. I still love you and I asked you to marry me. Now you don't have to worry about being embarrassed. You can honestly tell everyone that I asked and you said no."

"Asshole," Sadie whispered, glaring at him and letting the lever of her seat adjust until she was almost lying down. What was wrong with Dominic? Did he really think she wanted a proposal at the point of a gun? When he turned on the radio, she shook her head and gazed out the window. *Was this partnership worth it?* she wondered.

Sighing softly Dominic turned and stared for a long moment at Sadie before returning his attention to his driving. He wanted more than anything to give the words to her that would erase her pain. He loved her and he knew she knew it. She was thinking his behavior was some Latin macho bullshit. He knew that also.

He sighed again allowing his right hand to drop down on Sadie's body, ignoring her when she shoved his hand away. This wasn't them, this fighting. The hostility was driving him crazy. Since the party things hadn't been the same for them no matter how much he tried. They were out of sync. Sadie was either angry or crying. And loving?

Yes, they made love because there was no way they could lay in the bed with each other for long and not make love. It was as natural to them as breathing. What wasn't natural was for Sadie to roll away from him as soon as they were done. Knowing what that would do to them Dominic hadn't allowed it. He'd merely curled his body around hers and prayed as he held her. He was doing more than his part to get through this and it annoyed him a bit that Sadie wasn't trying as hard as he was.

Out of the corner of his eye he saw Sadie swipe the tears with the back of her hand. There was far too much of that lately. Sadie's heart was broken. And she was right. He was the world's biggest asshole for daring to hurt her like he was doing.

Another ache stabbed Dominic, a hurt as deep as any pain Sadie was going through now. But he'd made a promise to his father not to ever tell no matter what. Swallowing hard he glanced once more at Sadie wondering if she'd forgive him if she knew the reason for his refusal to have her take care of them financially. He wondered how his father would react to knowing he'd broken his promise. He didn't think his father would forgive him. He remembered a couple of years ago when his father had taken him aside and asked his intentions with Sadie. He'd thought that was obvious. When his father waited patiently for an answer Dominic told him without any hesitation that Sadie was his soul mate and would be his wife.

Their conversation replayed itself now in his thoughts. "I love Sadie, Poppi, much more than I ever knew I was capable of."

"More than me?" his father had asked.

"Poppi, why would you ask me that?"

"Because I need to know."

"Poppi, it's different. You're my father. Sadie is the woman I've given my heart to. There is no way for me to compare the two."

"Would you go back on your promise to me because of your love for her?"

Even now Dominic could remember the pain in his father's eyes and the hurt in his own chest. He'd wanted to forget what he'd learned at ten. Knowing had only caused him pain and a truck load of insecurities.

"Well, Dominic, will you betray your father?"

"Never, Poppi," Dominic had answered knowing that he should have tried to tell his father how much the lie was hurting him. Now he felt forced into a position he didn't want to be in. Now he had to lie to Sadie by omitting a very important truth about himself to her.

He blinked rapidly as he watched Sadie wiping away the ever falling tears. *I don't think I can keep putting her through this without telling her,* he thought and swallowed his own pain. *I love you Poppi. I never thought I would be forced to make the choice, but I love Sadie more.*

Worrying his lips with his teeth as sigh out of sigh came from his lips he reached for Sadie's hand and gave her fingers a squeeze. She was his world. She was the reason he wanted success, to make her proud, to give them the life he'd envisioned.

Don't forget your promise Dominic. He heard the words as clearly as if his father had been there in the car and had spoken them.

Guilt. He knew it for what it was. This was a mess. He'd try to keep his father's secret as long as possible. He'd promised to take that secret to the grave but…

Chapter Eight

One more shot, that's all Dominic needed. He couldn't get his father's tearful plea from his mind. Nor could he push away Sadie's tears. Still he would try once more to keep his father's secret.

Sadie had dried her tears but she was still hurting. They'd decided instead to pretend as if he'd not broken her heart. It wasn't working for either of them. Two weeks and things had barely improved.

Now Dominic found himself in one of the most expensive jewelry stores in the city. Sadie wasn't materialist but he also knew she was a woman and loved bling. He was hoping the sparkle of diamonds would put the sparkle she had for him back into her eyes.

Eyeing the jewelry case before him, he let out a whistle of amazement wondering why he'd not thought once about the price of the engagement ring and was hesitating on buying her a gift to make up for his wrongs. What had changed? That's right he didn't have that big fat raise he'd counted on. Damn. *Let it go*, he admonished himself. If he didn't let it go no wonder Sadie was unable to look at him the same way she had for the past four years. Of course he saw fear cloud her eyes whenever he poked his head into her office. That damn promotion was chipping away at their relationship.

With a sigh of resignation he pushed away the thought of going into his savings to buy her a gift. Then he thought of the strained look she'd worn since the night of the party and the choice was made for him.

Trailing his fingers over the immaculate glass case he stopped the groan. The bracelets were way too expensive now.

But still he had to buy her something. He swallowed and moved toward the case that held the earrings. Damn, he muttered as he looked at the glittering gems.

Each pair of earrings appeared to be more expensive than the one before. He couldn't help but groan at the impracticality of what he was about to do. What if Sadie lost an earring? Women did that all the time.

His hand shook just a little as he drew his MasterCard from his wallet. Two thousand dollars for earrings that she might lose. He handed the card over to the clerk who had her fingers on it staring at him as if to say, let-go-you-cheap-skate. He smiled slightly trying hard to breathe correctly.

"Can I get insurance on those just in case of loss or something?" he finished.

"Sure," the clerk answered immediately reliving Dominic of some of his distress. Trying hard not to mentally deduct the amount from his bank account Dominic bit down on his bottom lip. He wouldn't change his mind. The decision was made. His hand shook again as the clerk handed the now gift wrapped velvet box to him. He'd have to stop worrying about the cost or worrying about Sadie losing them. He'd been screwing up royally lately and knew he needed to do something big to make up for it.

***

"Dominic, oh, Dominic, I love you. Yes, yes," Sadie screamed throwing her arms around his neck when he handed her the small wrapped jewelry box. "Yes, I'll marry you," she said through tears of joy kissing him every place she could reach. She was talking so fast so grateful that Dominic had come to his senses. They were getting married.

"Sadie."

"I've got to call my mom," Sadie screamed attempting to hop up from the bed.

"Sadie, baby, open the box."

The look of panic on Dominic's face stopped her for an instant. Then she looked at him on his knees besides the bed and at the velvet box in her hand. She glanced at the gaily colored foil wrapping paper and paused. She didn't remember that her ring had been gift wrapped. A moment of hesitation touched her but she ignored it. It couldn't be anything else. She kissed him trying to still her rapidly beating heart.

Flipping the lid open she blinked at the sparkle of diamonds. She stared for a long moment. Earrings, diamond earrings! She bit her lips rocking her body slowly back and forth.

"They're beautiful, Dom. They're truly magnificent," she said taking her gold hoops from her ears and putting them on the nightstand. She took the earrings from the velvet cushion and put them in her ears brushing away the tears with the back of her hand. "How do I look?" she asked Dominic as she held her head up for his appraisal.

"Sadie, I—"

"Don't, Dom. They're gorgeous, let me go look at myself in the mirror," she whispered practically running for the bathroom. Closing the door she leaned against it and allowed the shudder to invade her body as well as her spirit. She wouldn't cry. She wasn't a crier. She should have opened the box first. That would have been the thing to do. Oh God, but it hurt.

***

Dominic stared at the velvet box Sadie had dropped on the carpet in her haste to run to the bathroom and away from him. He picked it up then glanced toward the closed bathroom door. He'd hurt her. He'd spent two thousand dollars to hurt her. He couldn't believe it. How could he have been so stupid? Shaking his head he lifted the box. It was about the same size as the box her engagement ring was in. It was a mistake any woman would have made.

Why the hell don't you just get it over and done with? Give her the damn ring and ask her to marry you seriously this time, without the attitude. You know you want to marry her and you sure as hell know she wants to marry you. Go ahead do it, he scolded himself.

"Sadie," he called as he walked toward the bathroom door. "Come on out baby, we need to talk." After several tries the door opened and Sadie came out with a phony smile pasted on her face.

"I love them, Dominic, thank you."

He took her hand in his. "Come on baby. It's time I told you. It's not just some macho bullshit that's stopping me from asking you to marry me. It's a life lesson, baby. One I promised my father I'd never tell."

It was time Sadie knew the truth, maybe then she'd understand, or at the least maybe she wouldn't leave him.

Taking in a deep breath Sadie sat on the bed and stared at Dominic. His look was serious, his eyes pain filled. Finally he was going to share what had made him so crazy.

"What's going on?"

For a moment Dominic stood where he was gazing down on her. *The sins of the father*, he thought. "Sadie, I need to hold you." He moaned softly getting in the bed behind her so that she was positioned against his chest. "Just let me talk and you listen, no questions until I'm done."

"When Roberto was about eight years old my parents split, filed for divorce."

"Why?"

"You're going to let me finish okay."

"Okay."

"I didn't learn any of this until I was ten. One day my parents were fighting in the bedroom, really loud and really angry. My father was swearing, saying things that I didn't understand. They thought I was outside playing. I'd come in for a drink of water and heard them. Their voices were so angry it frightened me. I'd never heard them going at it like that before."

Taking in several deep breaths he steadied himself. This was going to be harder than he thought. The remembered pain was raw, as though it had just happened. In a flash it was as though Dominic had been hurled back through time. He could hear the voices of his parents shouting as plainly as if they were in the room with them. And he was once again the ten year old boy listening at the door.

"He's my son. You're not going to let him come in and take my son."

"Dominic has a right to know his real father."

Real father? Dominic froze outside his parents' door. What were they talking about? His real father?

"*I am his real father! I've been his real father since the day he was born. Now you want another man to come in and take him away from me. I'd kill Dominic first before I allow you to take him away from me. I'll kill all of the kids and you. Then I'll kill myself if you ever allow that man into your life again.*"

"*You don't say that every month when the check arrives.*"

It was then Dominic heard what sounded like a slap followed by his mother's cry of pain.

Dominic shivered out in the hallway.

His mother was crying. "Carlos, he doesn't want to take Dominic from you. He just wants a chance to get to know his son."

"*Know him? Where was he for the last ten years of Dominic's life? He wasn't here was he? And he didn't love you or Dominic or he would have married you and raised his son. It's too late. Dominic is my son. He's always been my son. He'll always be my son.*"

"*He was there, Carlos, and we both know it.*"

In that moment Dominic burst through the door of his parents room without knocking, a definite no no. He ran to his father and threw his arms around him. "Poppi, Poppi, what are you talking about?" he cried, fat tears were racing down his cheeks. "Are you saying you're not my real father?"

"*Tell him," his mother chided his father. "Tell him the truth. He has the right to know, to choose for himself. He's old enough to make that decision, Carlos. It's unfair of you not to tell him."*

"*Tell me what, Poppi?*"

His father fell to the floor bringing Dominic with him. He was crying, the first time Dominic had ever seen his father cry.

"*You're my son, Dominic, and I'm your father. Do you love me?*"

"*Yes, Poppi, I love you.*"

"Then make me a promise, Dominic, that I will be your only father."

"Carlos, that's not fair."

Dominic glanced over at his mother, before bringing his gaze to rest on his father.

"Not without telling him, Carlos."

"Poppi, I don't care what happened. I only want you for my father always and forever."

"There's a man who wants to take you away from me, to have you call him Poppi. He wants to steal you and your love, Dominic. I don't want to let you go. I was the one who raised you. I don't want you calling or thinking of another man as your father."

"Carlos," his mother had said quietly from the corner still crying, *"You're being selfish. Think of Dominic, think of your son. He'll always be your son, Carlos. His knowing won't change that."*

The memories of that day were whirling fast and furiously. He'd never told anyone what transpired that day, not even his siblings. He'd done as Poppi had asked. For a moment Dominic couldn't speak. He tightened his arms around Sadie and leaned his chin on her head.

"I love you, Sadie. I have since the moment I first saw you. I've never wanted anything but to marry you and take care of you, to have a bunch of babies with you."

"What happened, Dom?" Sadie asked softly.

"My mother had an affair. She left my father and filed for divorce. She became pregnant with me. The man wanted nothing to do with her or the baby. My father found out. He'd never stopped loving her. My father offered to continue in the marriage, and make me his son in every way, including legally. So they went to counseling, renewed their vows before the priest and tried again a few months after I was born to live as man and wife. Everything was pretty good more or less until I was ten and the man my mother had the affair with came back into my mother's life. He told her he'd made a mistake, that he was sorry, that he regretted how he'd treated her and me that he wanted a chance to make it up to me. He wanted to be my father."

"Dom," Sadie whispered softly turning to hold him. "Baby—"

"You weren't going to speak, remember, Sadie? Just let me get it all out."

He sighed and kissed the back of Sadie's neck before pulling her to lie again on his chest. Her warmth was the impetus that was enabling him to break a twenty-three year old promise to his father. He sighed again and continued.

"My mother had met this man, a doctor at the hospital where she worked. She was impressed by his money and position. My father at that time couldn't get any decent paying jobs. My mother was the main breadwinner. She lost respect for her husband because he couldn't provide. She fell in love with someone she could look up to."

He paused and glanced at her reflection in the mirror, studying her face. "I would rather lose you than for you to stop respecting me."

"Dominic, I'd never…"

"Sadie, let me finish. I promised my father that day that I would never go looking for this man. I never even asked my mother his name. My father and I had a long talk and he told me everything that had happened, things my mother refused to talk about. I promised him and myself that I would never allow the woman I love to be the breadwinner. I will never be put in that position"

"Dom," Sadie whispered softly finally turning around. "That's crazy. I know Maria makes more than Roberto. He doesn't let this bother him. Why should you?"

"My father made me promise that I would never tell my sisters and brother about my heritage. Roberto isn't under the same burden I'm under. He belongs to Poppi and no one can come in and take him away. Sometimes I've felt that a very thin line has kept me as Poppi's son, that if I broke my promise to him I would lose him and lose his love. I would lose myself. I'm Dominic Santiago. I have no idea how to be anyone else. I like who I am." He sighed and closed his eyes. "Now you know."

"At least I know why you behaved as you did about the case at the office. But I can't believe you'd think it would have made a different to how I feel. Dom, I can't believe no one else in your family knows about this."

"Believe me, no one knows, only my parents and me. And now you," he murmured barely above a whisper. "I broke my promise to my father because I want you to know this isn't about macho bullshit. This is who I am, Sadie. I can't marry you until I can take care of you. Do you understand?"

"No, I don't understand. Dom, this is crazy. What happened with your parents isn't going to happen to us. I'm not going to look at you any differently."

"That's not true, Sadie. You're already looking at me with pity in your eyes. I didn't tell you this to elicit your pity. I told you because I never want you to doubt my love. I've never meant to hurt you, but you have to understand that I can't ask you to marry me just yet." He stroked her face with the pad of his thumb. Then he swallowed saying what he didn't want to say but he was forced to continue.

"Sadie, when I can take care of us, I'll ask you to marry me, I swear. But until then, baby, you just have to be patient. Try to understand. As much as I want to make you my wife, I can't, not right now."

"Then why don't we both quit the firm and strike out on our own? We'll be on equal footing."

"We'd be broke and that would be stupid. I don't want you to quit your job, Sadie. And I don't want to quit either. I just have to find a way to make it happen so that I can marry you."

"I'm beginning to wonder if you're using that as an excuse. You tell me this isn't about macho bull and I tell you it is. You're so afraid that marrying me with my having made partner is going to diminish you somehow, that your net worth will go down in value. That you're going to have to cut off your cohoonies and give them to me in a bag. You're so worried about appearances. Dominic, I don't want your cohoonies. I want you."

"You're right. I am worried about appearances. My mother made a fool out of my father and she tried to do it twice. How do you think that makes him feel? It felt like she was attempting to castrate him. She called him selfish. It was she who was selfish. Why couldn't she have left well enough alone? I could have lived the rest of my life just fine without knowing that Poppi isn't my biological father."

"Your mother wasn't trying to be selfish. She was trying to do what was right by you."

"What about my father?"

"That was probably a harder decision than you can imagine, her child's welfare versus the pride of her husband."

"What do you think everyone would have said to my father if this had come out? How do you think this would have made him feel?"

"So he forced you to give him some stupid promise."

"Sadie." Dominic said in warning.

"Don't Sadie me. I'm tired of you doing that as though I'm some little kid and you only have to call my name and make me be quiet. What will happen if I keep talking? Will the world fall apart? Will you leave me? Your mother was right. You had a right to know your biological father. When we have kids we might need to know the medical history. Your father was wrong to put some foolishness in your head. Look what he's done to you, to us."

"You're just angry with me."

"You're damn right I'm angry with you. And then you have the nerve to tell me that I pity you. I pity the ten year old Dominic who had to hear all of this. And yes, maybe I even have some pity for the man I love who thinks he can't be happy because of what one man went through. Stop worrying about being embarrassed about the world's opinion, Dom. It should only be our opinions of each other that matters, no one else."

She attempted to rise from the bed but he held her in his arms. "Sadie, baby if I could I would. You wouldn't have to beg me."

Beg him? Was that what he thought she was doing? Hell Naw! She groaned low. Damn. That was what she was doing. She was begging Dominic to marry her. That had to stop. Marriage was only a piece of paper. They were already committed to each other. She couldn't love him anymore than she already did. A marriage license wouldn't change that, she thought ignoring that little voice that women have tried to ignore for centuries. *But if he married me it would show the world that he loved me enough to make a permanent commitment. It wouldn't be another case of him not buying the milk when he was getting the cow for free.* Now look who's worried about public opinion, Sadie thought shuddering.

She had to get herself under control. "The earrings are beautiful," she said to Dominic accepting his kisses, his caresses. He was holding her so tightly that he was hurting her and still she wanted him to hold her even tighter, anything to push the pain of not being his wife away from her. Dom, don't worry. We're going to be fine. When the time is right we'll get married. Besides, what difference does it make really? I love you and you love me. That's enough. I promise."

And she'd do her best to not bring up the subject. That was a promise she was making to herself.

Chapter Nine

Stacking up the last folders Sadie looked around her office, noted she wasn't nearly as happy to have a corner office as she'd been initially. Even the small heater failed to produce a response, because she didn't use it anymore. Who would have thought adults would tease her for so long, calling her '*boss*,' asking if she were hot enough, any dumb thing they could think of. Normally she would have taken their good natured ribbing in stride but their jokes were like pins in her relationship. Dominic was tense and irritable, snapping at their co-workers, their boss, most especially Paul and a couple of times at her. They were both trying, but the trying was eroding their life.

The fact was hammered home in one way or another every single day that their perfect life wasn't so perfect. The only bright spot was the new discrimination case she was working on with Dominic. In the courtroom he was almost his old self, cocky and self-assured. Jokingly she'd told him they could turn their home into a courtroom. He'd merely looked at her, not smiling, not commenting.

With one last sniff of the lavender plant she glanced at her watch deciding to leave her office and go to Dom's cubicle. Sure he was aware why she was doing it. But if it meant she wouldn't have to witness the pain that still came to his eyes when he came into her office, it was worth it.

An immediate groan came from Sadie on spotting Paul waiting outside her office. His grin would be a problem. On the one hand she had to admit he was fast becoming her bright spot in the office. That wasn't right. Her bright spot had been Dominic for the past four years. Yet, Paul was the thorn in her side because he was the thorn in her man's side. He never failed to send a stinging barb toward him. Regardless of how many times she'd pleaded with her man not to allow Paul to get to him Dominic always rose to the bait.

"So shall we go and collect Dominic from his cubicle?" Paul asked.

Paul's words brought Sadie to an abrupt stop. "This stops now. I'm sick to death of this juvenile behavior. Hear me and hear me well, Paul. One more barb, one more raised brow in Dominic's direction and I swear we're no longer friends. I will not and I promise you that, I will not speak to you ever again. Try me if you think I'm kidding. Without so much as another glance at him she walked away.

She was sick of Paul pushing Dominic's buttons. And she was fed up with her man pouting like a like a kid. Fed up didn't begin to describe how she felt.

"Good night boss."

Sadie turned with a glare toward the person who'd dared to utter those words yet again. "Last time, Mark, understand. The jokes are stale." She continued her trek. She felt Paul's hand on her arm tugging on her to get her to stop. Sadie turned and glared at him. "You started this nonsense getting everyone in the office to hassle me. Now I want you to put a stop to it."

"I'm sorry, Sadie."

"Those are just words. Do something about it."

"It was only meant to be a joke. I thought you'd get a kick out of it."

She rather doubted that. She continued to glare. "You thought my life was a joke?"

"Sadie."

"Paul, if you're really my friend you will end this nonsense. Now leave me alone. I don't need another thing for Dominic to get upset about." Did she really just say that? It was not something she'd wanted to make Paul aware of. But who was she fooling? Paul already knew he was upsetting Dominic. That was his purpose. She walked away with a snort of disgust.

Pasting a smile on her face she stood beside the entrance to Dom's cubicle. "Hey babe you ready?" When he glanced up at her she wanted to cry. *God, please can't we have our old lives back?* Waiting as he gathered his things and joined her they made their way to the elevator, not talking, not touching, just two very emotionally drained people.

Reaching the car Dominic opened the door for her and stood behind her allowing her to feel the soft whisper of his breath on her neck. Then he whispered in her ear. "So, where was your shadow today?"

Should she answer that or ignore him? Sliding into her seat she decided to ignore him. She was tired.

Too tired to fight.

Too tired to make him feel better.

Too tired to try and convince him that he should ignore Paul.

Too tired to pretend that she was happy.

Sliding into the car she took in a deep breath and allowed it to seep out in a prolonged sigh. It felt good so she did it again. She could feel Dominic's eyes on her but she refused to acknowledge him. She needed a moment.

"I'm glad we're able to continue working on cases together. I worried about that.

This time Sadie did turn toward him. "Me too. We're a winning combination. I don't think the firm can afford to mess with that."

When he grinned broadly at her, she knew he meant it. It should have made her feel better. But somehow it didn't make her feel the joy his smiles usually did. She felt a sense of loss, a great sadness and tremendous foreboding of a dark omen for their future. Not wanting him to question her Sadie returned his grin and reached for his free hand to give it a squeeze. Then she settled into the cushions to wait out the ride home.

Was this really what they'd been reduced to? If so Dominic didn't like it. Telling Sadie his secret had not helped them in the least. Sure, she didn't say anything about their not being engaged but there were little things like the way she went out of her way to keep him out of her office. He knew she was doing it so as not to rub his nose in her partnership, but it irritated him. Just as the idea that they used the conference room to strategize on their new case when they could have a lot more privacy in her office. Hell if he'd gotten the partnership they'd damn sure be using the space.

He was also irritated at the way she was glaring and snapping at the people in their office when they teased her about the promotion. He was beginning to feel as though she thought he was someone who needed protecting, weak, frail, not a man. He'd not done as he'd wanted and proposed to her because he didn't want to look weak to her, not a man. And here he was in that position anyway.

Dominic did his best to remain focused on the road instead of Sadie. She wasn't happy and neither was he. He was determined to at least do something to get them out of their slump. With one last glance in Sadie's direction he turned on the DVD loaded with Sadie's music. He saw her smile. Her eyes remained closed but the smile was genuine. Yeah they had to get back on track.

***

Their gazes were locked. After dinner and a little TV with less than a little conversation it was time for them to regain them. Sitting on the bed as Sadie came from the shower he mentally calculated how long it had been since they'd last showered together. A month. Was it really that long?

"Sadie, what happened? I asked for you to wait until I cleaned the kitchen so I could shower with you?"

"I was tired."

What the hell. Since when had his woman become too tired to shower with him? "Sadie, we can't keep doing this, baby. We're drifting so far apart. Is that what you want?" He waited until she lifted her eyes to look at him.

"No, Dom."

"Then why won't you talk to me?"

"It seems that anytime we talk lately it turns into a fight. I'm tired of fighting."

"Sadie, come here." Closing his eyes tightly he rubbed at his throbbing temples. With a groan Dominic opened his eyes and shook his head at Sadie who hadn't budged. "My bad, baby. Would you come here, please?" She was moving toward him so slowly that he half expected her to stop before reaching him.

"I love you in the towel." She smiled so he continued. "Tell me something you like about me."

"I love the dinner you made."

Progress. Not much but a tad. "Thank you. So are you really tired?"

"Yes.'

Sadie had dropped her head when she answered making Dominic wonder if she was tired or just tired of him. Lifting up her chin he gazed into her eyes until she stared back at him. "Come on babe, are you too tired to let me hold you for a little while?"

He threw back the thick down comforter and removed most of the pillows then held his hand out to her. His eyes closed automatically when she took it and crawled into the bed with him.

"I'm not giving up on us, Sadie."

He pulled one of her fingers into his mouth and suckled it while grinning at her. A moment later he pulled another of her fingers into his mouth and sucked on it hungrily, waiting for the look in her eyes to change to love then lust. When she closed her eyes he knew why. She wasn't going to refuse him her body but she wasn't planning on enjoying it either. He'd have to change her mind about that.

"Counselor, you're withholding."

Sadie blinked. She was in no mood to play. She didn't care that Dom's dimple was so darn deep that she could hid things in it. Usually, her tongue. He grinned wider thinking he had her. And as his dimple deepened she would be a liar if she said she wasn't weakening. That was the problem. Dominic Santiago was her weakness.

"I need to see your briefs." Dominic said.

"Objection," Sadie finally murmured. "You're trying to use undue influence."

"Is it working?"

Sadie smiled getting into the game. "You're out of order."

"Out of order? Why? You are withholding and I do need to see your briefs."

"Counselor, my briefs are my business. Let me see your briefs." The giggle couldn't be contained when Dominic let go of her hand and dropped his pants.

"So you want to see my briefs. Are you satisfied?"

"Too little evidence. I think I'll ask for a continuance."

"Objection."

"What are you objecting to?"

"I'm here and ready to perform."

"Once again I see so little evidence of that."

"Objection."

"Overruled."

Dominic laughed taking her in his arms. "How can you say you see little evidence of my love for you?"

"That's lust, Dom."

"I love you, Sadie. Don't you believe me baby?" His voice had turned low and husky and sadness tinged his words taking away the momentary reprieve of playfulness. "Don't let the things that have happened in the last few weeks make you doubt my love. Nothing has changed about my feelings for you." He caressed her cheek. "Tell me, you believe me."

"I do, Dom…I do believe you." Sadie averted her eyes. "I've never meant to pressure you. It was never about that. Let's forget it, okay." If only he'd keep it light and continued the joking. Now, things were tainted for her. As much as she loved him and loved his touch, making love was the last thing on her mind. But they'd sworn never to use sex as a weapon and it would feel too much like that was what she was doing if she refused him.

Dominic was watching Sadie closely. "You okay, baby?" he asked. He'd felt her pull away from him emotionally. Still he was determined to unearth a response from her, a true one. He felt a hard shudder wrack her body and pulled back. He knew every emotion he produced in her and this wasn't desire. "Sadie," he said softly holding her a little away from him so he could better gauge what was going on with her. He looked at her hard. She was fighting back tears.

"Let it go, Dom. Just make love to me. We're going to be fine. Just let it go."

"But, Sadie—"

"Please stop talking."

Her voice, so pain filled scratched at him. Dominic entered her body needing to feel connected to her, praying it would work. He thought of his father's face. Sadie was right. His father should never have asked such a promise of him at ten years of age. He'd been much too young to know what it would mean to his future happiness. But he had asked and Dominic had given his word.

He ran his hand over Sadie's satiny smooth body keeping his eyes closed so he wouldn't see the look in hers. Desire quickly overtook all other thought and he continued stroking her, giving her all of his love with each thrust. The moment his orgasm took on a life of its own he clutched Sadie to him. Too late to stop his explosion, his heart withered a little. Sadie had not reached completion. She's not been there with him and he'd felt so alone.

Breathing hard Dominic lay back on the mattress glancing over at Sadie who lay next to him, her breathing even. It had not been a ruse, she'd not enjoyed it. She'd faked her responses to his touch.

"What if I give it to you as a promise?" Dominic said softly, not believing the words that had come from his mouth.

"I'm not twelve."

"Sadie, I want to make this right. I love you and I don't want to lose you."

"You're not going to."

"Is it going to continue like this, with you pretending?"

She didn't answer and he swallowed closing his eyes knowing he was mere moments from doing something he'd sworn never to do. He'd accept that his woman was making more money and he'd ask her to marry him in spite of it. Losing Sadie was more important than what he was trying to hold on to. Maybe they could reach a compromise.

"Would we have to set a date?"

"You don't have a gun to your head and I'm not going to put one there. Listen to me, Dominic. I don't want any more of these stupid, lame ass proposals from you. I held back from hitting you the last time you did it. I don't think I could keep from doing it a second time."

For the first time in hours Dominic found himself smiling. "We promised no hitting."

"We promised a lot of things," Sadie said low then pulled the covers over her body and turned on her side away from him.

Thoughts of the conversations he'd had with his father concerning women came to him. He glanced at Sadie's back aware she wasn't going to push him. She was accepting his decision. But she wasn't happy about it and neither was he. He wished it didn't matter to him, that she really understood all he was trying to do was keep from losing her. The thought flitted across his mind. *What you're doing now is a sure way to lose her.*

Dominic watched Sadie's back move with her breathing knowing within moments she'd fall asleep. Then he moved as far as he could away from her. He wanted to know how it would be to not feel her heat, not to lay with his arms around her with the roundness of her hips pushed back into his groin, not to smell the different things she perfumed her body with while underneath it all her own sweet essence was there for him.

"Sadie, if I could I would." She ignored him as he'd expected she would. Her breathing changed to a barely audible snore evidence she'd fallen asleep.

A tremor shimmed through his soul. He didn't want to live like that, not without all of Sadie, not even for another second. Moving back toward her he knew the decision had been made. He'd give the ring to Sadie and he'd ask her to marry him. Just not right away. They'd wait a little while until they made sure that Dominic was the one making the most money. When he could support the both of them they'd get married. He ignored the words he wouldn't say, the words that Sadie would hear regardless of him saying it. When he made more money than she did they would get married.

Now he'd just have to think of a way to present it so that Sadie would be okay with it. If he screwed up again not only was she liable to deck him, but she just might leave him.

The presentation was extremely important. He wasn't just going after a yes from Sadie. He wanted the sparkle in her eyes when he gave her the ring. He didn't want acquiescence. He wanted the look that his soul couldn't live without.

***

Taking a breath Dominic waited for the knot of tension to ease from his shoulders. He was doing the right thing. Swallowing he bit back the silent prayer he'd said for more than a year. *God, let me make her happy.* His proposal would be a start but it wouldn't make her completely happy. Closing his eyes he maintained a firm grip on the jeweler's box in his hand. She was waking up. He watched as her hand reached behind her searching for him, forgetting for the moment her disappointment in him. Dominic smiled as Sadie not finding him near her moved backwards, wanting his heat. Dominic knew this and he smiled at the knowledge. Her hand moved a little more frantically and when it finally registered that he wasn't in the bed she woke.

While she was blinking the sleep from her eyes he walked toward her. His gaze connected with hers as he knelt by the side of the bed. He was feeling a rush of emotion and breathed deeply to calm himself. *This was the right thing*, he repeated to himself. He brought his eyes up to rest on her beautiful face then he opened his hand and held out the jeweler box. His hand shook just a little but it was the only decision he could make.

Her eyes opened fully and she glanced at him curiosity quickly filling her tawny brown eyes. He didn't speak but opened the box and held it toward her watching as she looked down. Her eyes quickly came back to rest on his face and the look he was seeking was there. The love his soul required.

"This is for someday, Sadie, the moment I know it's time. Is that okay with you? This is more than a promise."

She shook her head vigorously.

"Sadie, will you marry me?" Dominic asked. When tears filled her eyes he almost left off the most important word but he couldn't. "Someday, Sadie. Will you agree to marry me someday?"

"Yes," she said holding out her hand. "Yes."

Dominic slid the ring on her finger then kissed her hand.

"It's so beautiful." Sadie gushed unable to take her eyes from the ring. "I knew it would be beautiful."

"You never looked at it."

"No, but I wanted to a hundred times, Dominic it's…it's…"

"It's someday, Sadie."

"I know. But do you mean it? Are you really asking me to marry you?"

"Of course I mean it. You knew I always meant it."

"But you said last night that you couldn't ask me to marry you, not even someday. What changed your mind?"

"I tried to live without you in my life and I couldn't." He smiled at her confusion. "I love you, Sadie, that's all you need to know."

"Can I tell my family?"

"Yes."

"And my friends?"

"Yes."

"Can I tell everyone at work?"

"Yes," Dominic said. "Just remember it's someday."

"I don't have to tell them that," Sadie said bouncing from the bed kissing Dominic quickly and rushing for the phone, screaming the moment she heard her mother's voice. "We're getting married," she screamed then dialed number after number telling everyone. "You should see my ring. My God, it's the most beautiful ring I've ever seen. He asked. We're getting married."

Dominic went to stand in front of her to remind her it was someday but she was ignoring him. He stood there as Sadie gushed to whatever family member she was talking to.

"We haven't discussed a date yet," she said. "We have time for that," But we're getting married," she shouted. "We're getting married," she said again more softly then looked directly at Dominic. "We're getting married," she said a third time then went into his arms dropping the phone on the floor.

With her lips glued to his and the taste of her in his mouth he felt her joy. Yes, they were getting married.

Someday.

Chapter Ten

The high polished wood glistened. The fragrance of flowers filled her new private office as well as the lobby. Glancing at the huge pot of lavender that set beneath the window, she breathed in its calming effects. A smile crept across her face. Sadie didn't attempt to wipe it away. She was almost happy. For the tenth time in the past hour her gaze landed on her engagement ring. Now if only Dom would stop working himself to death she would be truly happy. They'd just nailed another major discrimination lawsuit and they'd done it in record time. She'd been so proud of Dominic as he strutted about the courtroom doing his thing. His passion was something to behold. Once again they'd received a nice bonus all of which went into their joint savings. For a moment she wondered how much it would take for Dom to think they had enough money to walk down the aisle.

Turning off the light Sadie walked from her office saying her goodbyes to the few stragglers. It was much too late for anyone to still be around. Mr. Secret had peeped in on her over an hour ago when he'd left and told her, jokingly she hoped, that she didn't have to work so hard, the partnership was already hers.

She'd merely smiled at him as she rearranged folders on her desk. She wasn't about to tell the man she wasn't working. She was merely trying to kill time hoping Dom would not be seeing one of the many clients he'd taken on in the past week.

Sometimes Sadie wondered if he'd taken out a billboard. Their office was pretty upscale and the clients Dominic had been working with hadn't appeared to have the funds the firm usually charged. She'd hesitated to ask because she was aware of what he was doing.

Walking toward the bank of three conference rooms the firms lawyers used she tapped lightly on the closed door knowing Dom was in there. When he told her to come in she entered and stood there for a moment attempting to smile but couldn't. He looked so tired. She rubbed her finger over her ring. This was the reason for him working so hard. He was determined to bring in more money than her, to be the man, to support her. Sadie's sigh slipped out before she could stop it.

"Ready, Dom?" she asked.

"I've got one more client coming in." Without looking up he chewed on his lips and braced himself for her disappointment. "Sadie, I'll take a taxi home."

He'd heard her sigh of annoyance. He'd also seen her run the tip of her finger across the ring he'd given her. She was blaming herself for the late hours. That couldn't be helped he thought. He'd tried telling her his reasons for not wanting to ask her to marry him just yet. But all that had done was cause her pain. Now they were engaged and he had to ensure he would be able to take care of them. He had no plans now or in the future to depend on her working to support them. Sure, now they shared some of the expenses, but once they married he planned to change that nonsense.

He tensed, this was the fourth time in a week he was staying at work late. A fight was coming on that he wanted to avoid. "You go on home, I'll see you soon."

Sadie stopped at the door, she was tired. And she was hungry. She wanted nothing more than go home and have dinner then cuddle with Dominic. But she saw the look of determination on his face. Asking him to stop working so hard was not going to do one bit of good. She kissed him and left without a word.

Less than an hour later Sadie was listening for the sound of a client with Dominic. Just to be sure she pulled out her cell and called. "Are you alone?" she asked.

"Yes, the cleaning people left five minutes ago but I still have one more client."

Just what she'd been hoping for. Opening the door she pasted on a smile.

"I thought you went home. What are you doing here baby?"

"I brought you some dinner."

"You didn't have to do that."

"Sure I did. I was hungry and I wanted to have dinner with my fiancé. The only way that was going to happen was if I brought it here so we could eat together." She walked into the conference room closing the door behind her. "How much time do we have before your next appointment?"

Dominic glanced at his watch. "About ten minutes." His stomach growled and he looked toward the bag in her hand. "Enough time for at least a couple of bites," he said cleaning a space for them.

"If your client comes while we're eating, you can take him into my..." Sadie stopped. "I'll delay him and give you a couple of minutes to get rid of things." She smiled grateful she'd not mentioned that Dominic could just use her office.

The stew was good. Dominic had made it in the crock pot that morning putting in a cup more wine than the recipe called for making the broth rich. She smacked her lips as she shoved the last bite of corn muffin into her mouth. Dominic had not stopped eating from the moment she'd uncovered the dish. When he was done he looked at her, grinned and wiped his lips with the napkin. Then he looked toward the door at the sound of his late night client. "Just in time," he murmured going to greet the client. "Thanks baby."

But it was the look he gave her that made Sadie grateful she'd not started a fight but had done something more positive. If Dominic wanted to work late into the night to make more money so that they could get married, so be it. She brought her left hand up and gazed for several minutes at the ring. She swallowed back the longing to plan. *Just a little longer*, she thought. *Just a little longer*.

***

Rubbing the stiffness from his neck Dominic glanced in the reception area. Sadie was thumbing through a magazine. "I'm done. We can leave now. Thanks, babe."

"You're welcome."

There was something on Sadie's mind. He decided to wait

"How much are you charging the clients?"

"Whatever they can afford. Why?" he waited.

"You have to charge enough so the firm can see a profit."

"Are you talking as one of the partners?"

"I'm talking as the woman you love who doesn't want to see you getting in any trouble. The cases you're taking…Dominic they have to be enough to justify keeping the office open.

"They're easy cases. Ones I don't even have to go to court for."

"But, baby you can't be making that much money."

"Are you judging my clients' ability to pay based on their names?"

"Don't make this about race, Dom. You know I'm not going there. But Mr. Secret will if you keep it up." She pursed her lips. "He's here in this office because he takes clients that have big bucks."

"And the ones that don't, they don't deserve a good lawyer?"

Sadie wasn't going to fight with Dominic over his choice of clients instead she took the bag with the dirty dishes and went to wait by the elevator for him. A hundred bucks here and there was not enough money for him to work so damn hard. They weren't that hard up for money. Hell they weren't hard up at all. They both made more than enough to take care of all of their needs.

"What?" Dominic asked coming up alongside her taking the bag from her hand and pushing the button for the elevator. They rode the elevator in silence both saying an automatic goodnight to the security guard in the lobby.

"What's wrong?" Dominic asked again. "You said you would stick this out. I'm trying to make a living."

"You already make a living. You're trying to work yourself to death for…"

"For what?"

"That's your bag, Dominic. I came down to have dinner with you not to fight about your clients. I'm just stating the obvious. Be careful, baby." She slid her hand into his. "That's all I'm asking. Besides, we just received that bonus."

***

Since he'd proposed to Sadie he'd avoided visiting his parents. But they'd made a big deal out of going to Sadie's parents and showing her mother the ring. Now it was time to submit to the disapproval of his father. There was no way around it. It had to be done. Walking up the cobbled driveway his steps slowed. He stood for a moment watching the smoke from the grill rise over the roof of his parent's home. He took in a breath savoring the charcoal cooked meat. Then he listened to the sounds of his family, the laughter, the teasing. Swallowing down his disappointment he turned to answer the question in Sadie's eyes.

"I wanted to savor this moment before Poppi says something to spoil it."

"Why are we worrying about your father? Will his disapproval make you take back the ring?" She slid her hand in front of his face. "You'll have to kill me and then cut off my finger to get this ring back. I love it and I'm never taking it off not even if you demand it of me."

She tilted her head and grinned while watching Dominic hoping her teasing would lessen the tension he was now carrying in his shoulder. *Poor Dominic*. It was easy for her to think he could and should just get over it. It wasn't her life. She wasn't the one adopted, or the one who was struggling with it still. She could tell he was worrying if his father would somehow magically know he'd spilled the beans. She'd promised him she'd say nothing with look, glance or word that would give it away, but he didn't seem to trust her. 'Oh yea of little faith,' she'd said to him as she playfully swatted at him.

An hour later it was Sadie's stomach that was tied in knots. She couldn't believe the archaic thinking of the Santiago men. Scratch that. At least Roberto was on their side; at least he said he was. Hell, his wife made a lot more money than he did and he seemed to be okay with it. But there was a look in his eyes when his father said he had sanganas for sons. There was a jackass in the house alright but it wasn't Roberto and it damn sure wasn't Dominic. As far as Sadie could tell Poppi was the biggest jackass she knew for propagating such foolishness.

Chattering from behind her caused her to divide her attention. The women in the house were scrounging for more bridal magazines to include with the ones Sadie had brought. The talk was of gowns, patterns, colors and food. That should be the conversation she was a part of. It had been until she'd decided to walk to the patio and try to get the men to join them. If only she hadn't head Poppi's angry words to his sons. She'd been aware for years that Poppi didn't care for her. That knowledge didn't bother her for the feelings were mutual. But to try and convince Dominic that marrying her would be a colossal mistake had stopped her in her steps and struck her mute. She was now eavesdropping on a conversation she shouldn't be listening to. She wanted to move but found herself rooted to the spot waiting for Dominic to put his father in his place, tell him he loved her and they were going to get married, that it was their business.

"Dominic, you do not marry a woman who makes more money than you. Is that clear? Sangana."

Again with the sangana, Sadie thought as she slid behind the door making it obvious to anyone that might see her that she had not just happened upon the men talking but was purposely invading their private time.

"I'm disappointed in you. I don't know if I will continue to claim you as my son."

She couldn't believe the emotional blackmail the man was using on his own son. Yet at the same time she thought, 'well played Poppi.' Holding her breath she waited for Dominic's answer.

"Sadie and I are not getting married immediately, Poppi. We're getting married when I am the one making the most. I learned that lesson from you. I have no intention of marrying Sadie until I can take care of her."

"You're a fool," Roberto sneered.

"Sadie has always known this," Dom snapped. "We're getting married someday."

True she'd known it. He'd said it when he'd given her the ring but somehow this felt like a betrayal. Enough so that she couldn't continue hiding, eavesdropping on their conversation. Taking a step from her hiding position Sadie walked toward the women, halted, turned abruptly and walked onto the patio right into the hornet's nest. *I have a card too Poppi,* she thought as she walked to stand in front of Dominic. She stared at him until his eyes lifted. He shook his head a tiny bit wanting her to leave but she refused. They were waging a silent war, one she knew she couldn't afford to lose. Her eyes narrowed and she allowed the disappointment to take over her features.

When sorrow filled Dominic's eyes and he moved to touch her she moved away still holding his gaze. Her eyes filled with tears and she blinked rapidly as though her intent was to stop them. When one fell Dominic reached out with his thumb to rub it away. She closed her eyes suddenly as she realized she was no longer acting. The tears were real. She bit on her lips until her vision was no longer blurred by tears. She was switching tactics. Now she was glaring, knowing how much he hated it when she did. But she also knew because she was in the right her glare was going through him and cutting him to the quick. Anger suddenly filled his eyes. Still, she held his gaze. There was more for her man to do. His jaw was clenched his breathing faster. He looked at his brother then his father.

Dominic swallowed and looked at Sadie tilting his head to the side asking her once again silently to leave. "Berto is right, Poppi. It's a foolish macho thing that we men have, believing we must be above our women." He'd broken; he'd given her what she wanted. He saw her smile in triumph. Sadie had played him and he knew it. The anger melted from his bones and flew from him. This time when he reached out for Sadie she relented and allowed him to take her into his arms.

"Now will you leave?" he whispered in her ear.

After a few moments Sadie pulled away stared at Berto who was laughing softly, stared until he swallowed and apologized then she turned her razor sharp gaze on his father daring him to make with the wisecrack. She gave a grunt, a toss of her hair over a shoulder in an, I-thought-so manner.

When Poppi dared to look away without an apology she stopped. "We're going to look at wedding gowns. I'll leave you guys to finish your conversation. Poppi, if you're not careful I may not chose a color for you to wear at the wedding that you will not like." Smirking at Dominic she decided to do as he wanted and leave. At least she'd shown Poppi she was aware of his manipulations and was not without weapons in her own arsenal. Grinning Sadie flounced away with a, 'carry on,' tossed carelessly over her shoulder. The thought that neither of them should be manipulating Dominic crossed her mind. They were both wrong for doing it.

For a moment all three men remained quiet waiting for Sadie to return.

"Sadie is going to kick your ass when she gets you home hombre," Berto laughed.

"Sadie has your brother's cohoonies in a sack," Poppi sneered and spit.

"You'd better be careful she doesn't hear you, Poppi, or you might find yourself in a pink tux for the wedding."

There was a feeling of gratitude for his brother turning the episode into a joke. Despite the laughter and the change of topic Dominic was fuming inside. He was angry at his father for reaffirming his reason for his not marrying Sadie as quickly as they could pull off a wedding. He was angry at Sadie that she'd busted him in front of his father and brother. And he was most angry at himself that he'd had to be busted at all. First his father had punked him. Then his woman. If he didn't love both of them so damn much neither would be allowed to get away with it. As angry as he was he realized that beneath Sadie's display of temper there had been real hurt there.

***

Bridal magazines were spread across the top of the antique glass table and pretty much covered the hardwood floor. Taking a glance around the cozy room Sadie wanted to bolt and run. The mood was ruined. She no longer wanted to look for gowns or plan a wedding for someday. God how she wanted to smack someone, just up and knock some sense into the Santiago men. She wanted badly to question Maria to see if she had any problem with Roberto. Did he care that she made more money? Did he just pretend he was okay with it? Were his feelings really wounded? Why the heck did she have to be so nosey and listen in on what was meant to be a private conversation?

"Sadie, come here look at this gown you'll look beautiful in it."

What could she do? She took the magazine from Dominic's mother's outstretched hand. She didn't want the women to know what had just happened. She sat on the floor between Dom's sisters and pulled one magazine after the other into her lap trying to laugh, trying to feign excitement. When it didn't work she shrugged and got up dusting her behind before sitting on the couch.

"You're tired already, Sadie?" Dom's mother asked.

"Not tired, but we don't have a date. So, it's much too early to be looking at gowns."

"That's not true. It's never too early to plan a wedding. What changed your mind?"

"Nothing. To be honest, I'm hungry. That barbecue smells so good, I just want to eat. You know how much I love your cooking. It's all I can think about."

She looked up as Dominic came in carrying a chunk of meat on a napkin, heading for her. Everyone laughed at him praising him on knowing how to keep a woman happy. Sadie took the proffered meat thanked him and daintily wiped her lips. She wanted to strangle him. Instead she ate his peace offering preferring to wait until they were home to have it out. When his fingers began to massage her neck she leaned back into his hand wanting to strangle him a little less.

***

"I didn't lie, Sadie," Dom began the moment they stepped inside their apartment. "We are getting married someday. You agreed."

"You knew the reason for the celebration. You knew your mom and sisters wanted to help me with wedding plans. You could have stopped me from taking the magazines. You could have asked me not to. You could have went alone and told them I wasn't feeling well and you could have stood up to you father and told him to mind his own business."

"How many times have you told your mother or father to mind their own business?"

"I haven't had to because they already do."

"Sadie, we need to do some research for our new case. Right now we don't have time to fight." He left her standing there and returned with his appointment book. "I have Tuesday at 2:A.M. available to fight. What about you?" She laughed as he'd hoped she'd do and came into his arms apologizing for her actions at his parents.

***

For two months things between Dominic and Sadie was on the right track. They'd worked hard on two more cases together, winning both in record time. Things at work were even beginning to even out. When he strode into the morning meeting it was with confidence. That should have prepared him that something was going to change that. The meeting was basically routine, cases being assigned, reports taken, nothing out of the ordinary until his boss glanced over some papers in his hand then turned in his direction.

"Santiago, are you doing pro bono work?"

"No more than usual." Here it comes, Dominic thought, keeping himself from looking in Sadie's direction not wanting to see the, I-told-you-so look that would be in her eyes. "Why? Is there a problem?"

"Well, I've had a chance to go over your balance sheet and I've noticed that you've picked up a great deal more clients and none of them have been charged our going rates. Actually they've been charged a great deal less. Is there a reason?"

"Yes," Dominic answered without hesitation. "They can't afford our normal rates."

"There is legal aid."

This time Dominic couldn't help looking in Sadie's direction. At least she wasn't pleading with him not to continue. She was looking at him with curiosity as much of the others in the room were doing.

"I thought they deserved more."

For ten long seconds Mr. Secret pondered his words tapping his fingers on the table, frowning as he looked at Dominic. "Well, you're the lawyer on the case. If you want to work for peanuts so be it. Paul, how's that pharmaceutical lawsuit going?" he asked changing the subject.

Dominic was embarrassed for having been called out like that, for having taken penny anty cases that were not making money for the firm. He was more upset and insulted that the boss had let him off the hook without even a reprimand, as though he was throwing him a bone. Instead of being grateful Dominic was angry. His boss was right. He was taking far too many cases from people who couldn't pay. He was actually getting a reputation. While his words were true and he did think everyone deserved a chance at a decent lawyer that wasn't the reason he was working these crazy hours. He was working like crazy so he could make more money. And so far his bank account had only increased by a few hundred dollars. At this rate Sadie would be a hundred before he could afford to marry her, well past the child bearing years. This plan wasn't working. He had to do more.

***

With a look around the courtroom Dominic's attention was focused on the client chatting with Sadie. She'd told him there was going to be a partners meeting and she had no idea what it was about. That was a lie. They both knew what it was about. *What to do with Dominic Santiago?* He made too much money for the firm for them to let him go. And besides, if they tried he'd bring a hell of a lawsuit, and who was better than him in the entire state of Illinois to battle a discrimination lawsuit? He'd win hands down. He cringed realizing he'd completely forgotten about Sadie and the truth of the matter was it had taken both of them working together to win those cases.

He loved working with the woman he loved. She was fantastic in the courtroom. At that moment she turned and smiled at him and his heart lurched. He would definitely miss working with her. *Where the hell had that thought come from?*

He would be working with Sadie for a long time to come. There would always be discrimination lawsuits and he and Sadie were the golden team. He shivered as though someone has walked over his grave. A cliché but true. Suddenly Dominic wanted to do something to ward off the evil eye. He thought to call his mother. *You're being crazy*, he chided himself. Sadie's meeting could be about anything. He watched her for a moment as her gaze left the client and she stared intently at him. There was sadness in her gaze and fear he realized. She was worried, as worried as he was. With a sigh he turned away from Sadie. They would only make each other crazy with worry.

A few minutes later Sadie's fears came to the surface. He waited patiently as she shook hands with the client.

"Dom, let's grab some lunch before we go back."

"You're worried aren't you?"

"Would you like for me to lie?"

"I never want you to lie. Have you heard anything?"

"They don't really confide in me. And if it pertains to you I doubt I'll be the one they talk to."

"Do you think I'm about to get fired."

Sadie shrugged her shoulders. "I don't see how they can and give a reason that would stand up in court. You have made a ton of money for the firm."

"And for the past couple of months I've turned the firm into an unofficial legal aid. Sadie... I just want to—"

"I know baby. What do you want me to do?"

"Don't lose your job. One of us needs to have one." He tried to smile to pretend he wasn't worried but Sadie knew him too well for that. "Listen, Sadie, I know your instinct will be to fight for me, to beg for my job. Don't do it. If I have to leave the firm I'd rather do it with pride, not with my woman groveling for me okay."

"Dom."

"I'm serious, Sadie." He rubbed his thumb over her ring. "We're going to be okay."

If only he could go back a few months and not care that Sadie had gotten the partnership. If only he'd not become crazed and mouthed off to his boss, or started packing clients into the firm after hours who couldn't afford to pay their high rates. Maybe if he wasn't intent on paying Poppi for being his father, for giving him an identity. There were a dozen 'if only' but if was too late for self-recriminations now. They'd just have to wait it out.

Leaning over he kissed Sadie. When her worry hadn't lessened he kissed her again. "I'm the man, Sadie. Remember that."

***

The Woodridge office needs a new manager. Any suggestions?" Mr. Secret looked around the office at the partners. Sadie could tell everyone was waiting for her to speak. This was a set up plain and simple. The other partners had talked and the obvious solution for the preservation of their décor was to get Dominic out of the office and someplace where he would not cause any harm. But she was supposed to be the one to suggest it. Then it wouldn't seem like what it was. They didn't want the lower paying cases at the firm.

Dominic had warned her not to plead for his job. Okay, she wouldn't do that, but she had to try something. The boss wanted suggestions, she'd give him one.

"Millie would make a great manager. I'd hate to lose her as my secretary but I know she'd love the promotion and I'm confident she can do the job."

Sadie saw the amusement in Mr. Secret's eyes and stared as the other partners made small choking noises, some scraping their chairs as they moved around in discomfort.

"I was thinking of putting a lawyer in charge."

"But if you put a lawyer in charge is he or she supposed to do bookkeeping and everything else that's involved with managing an office?"

"It's a promotion, Sadie. That means a lot more responsibility will be expected. Promotions are very different than firing."

She got it. Dominic's head was on the chopping block, either he would be fired or he would be moved. Her choice. *If I have to leave the firm I'd rather do it with pride, not with my woman groveling for me okay."* It didn't matter that Dom

more or less had told her not to fight for him, she still felt that
what she was about to do was a betrayal.

"Maybe Dominic would like to do it," Sadie offered
looking directly at Mr. Secret. She saw the instant smiles.
She'd played the game, done the right thing and sold her man
out. She felt sick, her head pounded. She'd sworn to have
Dom's back always. The partners were staring at her trying to
see if she'd fold, if she'd cry. Hell no she wouldn't cry. She'd
at least like to salve her conscience by working out a good deal
for him.

"I think he should be compensated for the travel as well
as a substantial raise in pay," she said not batting an eye. At
least she felt a little better for what she was doing.

A quick agreement followed.

"Do you want to tell him?"

"No," Sadie answered Mr. Secret. "This was your idea
so I think it will be best coming from you." She doodled in her
notepad, her ring flashing 'traitor' at her. If inwardly she
hadn't breathed a sigh of relief she might have been able to
convince herself that she was doing this strictly for Dominic,
that she had his best interest at heart. But she couldn't lie to
herself. Things were still a little tense between them at work.
Before, they'd always enjoyed working together now she felt
as though every word, every look was being analyzed. Every
time she turned Dominic was there watching her and there was
something unreadable in his eyes. She'd tried many times to
push it away, flashing him a smile and glancing at her ring. At
least he hadn't taken it back.

When the meeting was adjourned Sadie stood for a
moment as Mr. Secret had his secretary call Dominic into his
office. "Are you going to tell him I suggested it?" she asked.

"I don't see the reason in that. It was a decision made
by the partners, a very good decision. This is a good
opportunity, Sadie. He'll be in charge of the office and I'm
going to give him a good size raise to compensate him. You
don't have to worry about that."

"Will he make what I'm making now?" Sadie asked
hopefully.

"Is there a problem, Sadie?"

"No, no problem," Sadie smiled wishing she had not
said that. "I was just wondering."

She rushed to her office brushing Dominic's arm as he walked past looking at her. "Anything wrong?" he asked.

"No, baby, nothing's wrong," she answered and rushed past him. *Not unless you call me selling you out wrong,* she thought and closed her office door leaning against it for a moment before she felt the hitch in her throat. *It's going to work out,* she thought.

Chapter Eleven

"So this is my punishment?" Dominic shook his head as he finished his coffee. "I should have listened to you."

"Don't look at it as a punishment. After all you got a nice raise and you're in charge of the Woodridge office. It's a promotion."

"Raise. Yeah right? I've been banished and we both know it. Damn, it's going to take me more than two hours of travel time. You may as well get used to my coming home late, Sadie. I'm not coming into the city until the rush hour traffic is over."

Sadie opened her mouth to say something but didn't. She hadn't thought of that. "Perhaps you can have dinner with my parents until the traffic calms down."

"Should I request a bed at their home also?"

"Dom, I'm just trying to think of a way to make things better for you."

"Don't bother, Sadie. This isn't your fault. I got myself into this mess. I'm just warning you not to wait dinner for me. I don't know how the hell we're going to do this. We definitely can't have you making dinner. We'd more than likely die of food poisoning." He stopped and smiled. "Don't worry, Sadie. I'll think of something. I'll just use the crock-pot a lot more and we can order in.

When Dominic took her in his arms Sadie held on tight praying inwardly for forgiveness. This wasn't what she wanted at all. All she'd wanted was to marry Dominic. That should have been simple enough. She clung to him even tighter as tears streamed down her face. She could practically see the cracks in their future. She had to think of a way to repair the damage she'd done.

***

Two weeks later Dominic was so tired he was almost falling asleep in the shower. Time was of the essence. Dominic had spent several evening with her parents preferring to make the trek to Downers Grove rather than fight the traffic coming back into the city. They loved seeing more of him and actually her mother had solved one of the problems Dom had fretted over. Since he was having dinner with them she always sent a plate home for Sadie. While the effort was appreciated, and the food delicious, Sadie missed Dominic cooking for them. She missed the two of them sitting down together to share their evening meal. They were out of sync and she didn't like it.

She was going to have to do something about that. She'd gotten him into this mess. She may not be able to get him out of it but she was definitely going to find a way to lighten his load. She owed him that much. She had an idea that might prove to be just what they needed in more ways than one. If things went according to plan they'd be closer to her parents and farther away from Dom's. Making a brief appearance in the office for the usual morning meeting she told her secretary afterwards she'd be out for the rest of the day. For once she'd caught a break. There was nothing on her planner that needed her attention. Besides, Dominic was her immediate concern and she believed she'd found the answer to their problem.

The drive to Woodridge was making Sadie feel better. They needed a completely new start and renting a house with option was just the thing to allow them to put down roots.

"Sadie what are you doing here?" Dominic asked opening his office door to allow her in. Did Secret send you here to check on me?"

"No, baby. I have to tell you that this wasn't the reception I was expecting."

"Why aren't you at work?"

"Why are you interrogating me?

"You didn't mention not going to work and you definitely didn't say anything about coming to Woodridge, so I'm a bit puzzled. Tell me the truth, Sadie. Why are you here?"

This was going to be harder than she'd thought. Not only wasn't Dominic excited or even curious to see her, he was suspicious. She couldn't help it; she went to her telltale and used her tongue to play with her lips. It was only then that Dom moved toward her to use the pad of his finger to lift her chin so he could stare into her eyes as though he were a truth machine.

"Something is going on, Sadie."

"Nothing's going on. I came up with a solution to our problem. I came out to discuss it with you."

"Our problem? I didn't know we had a problem."

"Dom, you act as though you don't want me here." She raised a brow, suddenly she was the one suspicious. "Is there a reason you don't want me here?" She held his gaze. "Is there someone here in the office—"

"Don't be ridiculous. I'm not even going to dignify that with an answer. And don't think I don't know what you're doing. You're not going to make me go through a song and dance and forget you haven't given me a reason for being here."

"Are you angry with me?" Sadie asked.

"No."

"Why are you behaving like this?"

"Because you're stalling. And because you didn't go to work. You never miss a day. You hate driving and yet you drove all the way from the city to Woodridge. I know you, Sadie. You're stalling. If you came out to tell me in person that I've been fired just get to it. I'm a big boy. I can take it."

Sadie wanted to jump for joy. For now she'd forget that things had deteriorated between them. And though it really wasn't a victory she'd rather he thought the boss was making his life miserable rather than her. Still it hurt that his first thought was she'd been sent to bring him bad news. Poor Dom.

"Baby, you've been so tired since your promotion." She ignored his raised brow meant to say what he was doing in Woodridge was definitely not a promotion and he was right.

"I miss you," she said softly and brought her hand upward to caress his cheek.

"To put your mind at ease though, I did go in to work. I went to the morning meeting and since I didn't have anything urgent on my calendar I decided it was time to implement my idea."

Dominic was eyeing her suspiciously. "I had this idea that maybe we should we rent a house out here? With all of this driving back and forth and your putting in so many hours it would be the perfect solution."

"A house? What are we going to do with our apartment? Or are you suggesting you stay in the city and I live out here?"

"Of course not. Why would I ever suggest that? No, Dom, I'm thinking that we should find a house to rent with option to buy and rent it."

"We can't afford that, Sadie."

"Sure we can. You've got the raise."

"What about our rent on the apartment? We still have another six months to go on our lease. Besides, what are you going to do, drive into the city every day?"

"No, I'll take the train."

"How is that fair to you?"

"Dominic, how is this fair to you?"

"I'm the one who screwed up." Dominic held her gaze and then shook his head before glancing away. "You told me to be careful and I wasn't. I'm the one who got myself stuck way out here."

"Come on; don't look at it like that." Sadie couldn't keep looking at Dominic. She turned to observe his office. "This is very nice and Woodridge is a very nice community. We'll be okay. I've set up a couple of appointments for us to go and see houses during your lunch hour."

"You should have asked me first."

"Haven't you ever heard of a surprise?"

"Yeah, I guess I have. You do always have my back don't you, baby?" He moved behind her, nuzzling her neck with his lips. "We'll go and see the houses you've lined up but if we can't afford it, Sadie, we're not going to do it."

He turned her so he could kiss her. "God, I love you," he said crushing her to him. "I'm sorry for the inquisition. It just seems since December everything has turned sour for me."

"Even us?"

"No, baby, not us, never us. Maybe you're on to something with the idea of renting a house. I tell you I wouldn't mind finding us a little house out here. Maybe you're ready to stop working for a while, get pregnant."

"Not without a wedding," Sadie teased but meaning it. She grabbed for Dominic's hand. "Why would we have enough money to get married if I were to quit my job."

"I didn't say anything about marriage. I asked if you would want to have a baby."

"You already know I have no plans to have a baby without our being married. If I were ready to have a baby would that make a difference?"

"We both know it would make a difference. But we're using birth control and we're too smart to have a baby until we're both in agreement. Besides, you know I was kidding."

"Perhaps. But I don't have as long as you do to have a baby. You know when a woman is thirty the risk to the mother and baby goes up."

"Sixty year old women are having babies."

"I don't want to be sixty." Sadie made a face at him.

"You know that ring is making you awfully damn bossy. First you decide we need a house in Woodridge and make arrangements and now you're talking about babies. No more surprises." He gave her a stern look then ran his hand over her flat belly. "You're not pregnant are you, Sadie?"

"No. But you're the one who brought up having a baby don't forget."

"And you're not planning on it, are you?" he asked, ignoring her comment.

"Trust me, baby, I'd never do something you don't want." She cringed inwardly and leaned in to kiss him, running her tongue over his lips. When his hand grazed her breast his phone rang and he lifted it with his free hand and smiled at her.

"We'll have to continue this later. I have a client."

"What time are you taking lunch?"

"One."

"Then, I'll see you at one."

"What will you do until then?"

With a grin, Sadie raised a brow. "Why shopping of course. Bolingbrook has a new mall I've being dying to check out."

"If you're thinking about renting a house you'd better watch the shopping."

"Don't worry about it. Haven't you ever heard of window shopping?" Sadie smiled and walked out. She was determined they would find the perfect house. Dominic didn't deserve to have to come home so tired. It had been her who'd suggested he be given the assignment. It should be her who had to travel. And it should be her who found a way out of their latest problem.

***

Walking through the house for the second time the stars appeared to be in alignment. The house was perfect for them. The moment the agent left them alone Sadie allowed her excitement to show.

"I love it."

"You've loved them all, Sadie." Dom smiled at her, not wanting to burst yet another bubble for her. If they didn't continue saving they would never have the money they needed.

"Dominic, baby?"

The sound of her voice pleading with him was going to be his undoing. She definitely had a hold of him and he knew it. He would give her whatever it was that he had it in his power to give.

"Fifteen hundred dollars, plus the eighteen hundred we're already paying for the apartment, Sadie, that's way too much."

"Dom, you do know if we stopped giving so much money to your father every month we wouldn't have to worry about covering our bills. That's two thousand dollars. Maybe you could decrease the amount you give Poppi each month."

Sadie watched the stubborn set of Dom's jaw and the sheer defiance that came into his eyes. She'd crossed a line now. She'd have to backtrack. Damn Poppi for screwing over

Dominic like this, for taking advantage of him. Then she thought of the ways she'd taken advantage of him and changed direction.

"Don't go there, Sadie. You know my father depend on the extra money I give him. I can't just take the money away. Look, maybe we should forget the house." Dominic glanced away hating to use blackmail on Sadie. She was right. If he wasn't intent on supporting his family they wouldn't have money worries. Hell, he wouldn't have to be constantly telling her what they couldn't afford. It wasn't her fault that he was trying to honor a debt and a promise to his father.

"Baby, all I'm saying is, we both work hard. We should be able to enjoy some of the fruits of our labor. I know you don't want to stop helping your parents so we'll think of something else. We can tighten our belts a bit more. Your raise will more than take care of the rent for the house. We'll still be able to save. Besides it will only be for a few months. Then we'll just have this house and maybe later after we're married…" Her voice dropped an octave and she was almost whispering. "Maybe it can be ours."

He heard the longing in her voice and mentally calculated the cost of keeping up two homes plus helping his family. It was going to take a lot.

"Sadie."

"We'll do it together, baby, please don't fight me on this. We're a couple. We have to start thinking like that. It's our money Dominic."

He groaned. How was he supposed to think when Sadie was kissing him like that? He didn't want to tell her no again, he saw the hope in her eyes. "Okay, okay," he acquiesced. "Okay, baby if you want this house we can rent it. But please tell me what we're going to do for furniture. We can't buy more right now."

"Just a bed."

"Just a bed?" Dominic sighed.

"You do know we'll need a mattress right?

"Of course, but that's it. A bed and mattress. A cheap mattress. We can bring over a few items from our apartment and maybe my mom has some furniture we can use.

"Or mine," Sadie added.

"Good, this may not be too bad. We're in agreement. We'll rent this house and buy a new bed and a mattress."

"And maybe a chair."

He kissed her then to stop any further requests. If he'd thought he'd lost his heart to Sadie before, now he definitely had. Since he'd placed the ring on her finger it seemed his cohoonies had taken a vacation. He lifted Sadie onto the kitchen counter imagining when the house was theirs how he would make love to her there. He grinned and looked around the house. This was a good idea. A home was just what they needed.

***

The short two months in their new rented house and they both knew they would let go of the apartment as soon as the lease was up. The house in Woodridge was just what the doctor ordered. Going into the city didn't faze her in the least, not when she came home every night to Dom, their house and the peace and quiet they'd found. She used the train ride to get a ton of work done. And Dom went home during his lunch hour to rest and check on whatever dinner he was making in the crock pot. It was beginning to seem as if Dominic's move to Woodridge had been ordained by God.

A smile lit Sadie's face as she sashayed into the office. Everything was working out in spite of what she'd done. She swallowed it down. She'd more than made it up to Dominic for her betrayal though she still didn't want him to know

"Sadie, how's it going?"

She turned toward Paul noticing the devilish twinkle in his eyes as though he had a secret. She started to walk pass him then turned back. "What's up, Paul?"

"I think Mr. Secret should be the one to tell you."

He gave a coy half smile and walked down the hall toward the elevator. A tiny thump in her chest alerted her that something was wrong. If she'd not just talked to Dominic before she came in the door she would have thought it had to do with him. She sucked in her breath trying to tell herself the feeling was just her imagination.

***

"Sadie, good, you're here. We have a doozy of a case. I want you to work it with Paul;

"What is it?" Sadie propped her hip against the door not coming into the room trying her best to calm herself. She would be a fool if she didn't know the doozy of a case was a discrimination lawsuit.

"Mr. Secret," she paused and stared straight into his eyes. "Skip the buildup, what's the case?"

"You're getting yourself worked up, Sadie. It's just a case, a big case, but nothing preplanned."

"What's the case?"

"Discrimination."

"And you want me to work with Paul?"

"Well, you being a partner will carry some weight so why not team you with Paul?"

"Because Dominic and I have done almost nothing but work on these cases for years, now you're putting me with Paul. You know how Dominic feels about Paul working with me. What are you trying to do to him?" She eased away from the door feeling sick.

"Come on in, Sadie. It's not as bad as you might think."

"Please tell me why it isn't. Why can't Dominic work the case with me?"

"Dominic's in charge of the Woodridge office. Did you forget it was your idea that we transfer him there?"

A groan came up from her soul and she almost whimpered out loud but caught it in time. Oh God she thought, *what have I done?* "You didn't tell me he wouldn't be able to work on any more cases with me."

"Who's supposed to do his job if he comes here? Listen, Sadie, it's merely a matter of revenue. The firm is not trying to punish him."

"Why does it feel like it? It feels like you're using me to stick it to him. Is that the reason you gave me the job instead of him? You need to fill a quota so you took care of two things at once. Make a black woman partner and all would be well?"

She forgot for a moment how to breathe and thought back on the words Dominic had said to her out of anger and jealousy. *Oh God, he was right.* She took a step into the room her gaze on her boss not wavering. "Listen, tell me the truth. Is that the reason I made partner?"

"Even if that were true do you think I'd be fool enough to say it?" His eyes bulged out of their socket and for a moment he appeared as angry as Sadie.

"I did not give you a promotion to fill a quota. If that had been the case I would have given it to Santiago. He wanted the damn job. You didn't even think about it, and that was the reason I chose you. You're a great lawyer and a team player. At least you were. Now I can't say two words to you without you biting my head off. If you hadn't wanted Santiago to have the move to Woodridge you shouldn't have suggested it." He glared at her. "If you don't want him working there you tell him to come back here. We gave him a hell of a lot more money. I thought that was what he wanted, what you wanted, so that he'd have more money to marry you. Sure, tell him to come back here and his salary goes back down."

He stopped walking before turning toward her on his way out the door. "Is that what you really want, Sadie? Do you really want to be the one to take away Santiago's pride? We both know his making less money than you is a sore spot with him. But you do what you want. I can get someone to cover Woodridge."

"He's going to blow a gasket."

"Why? Because you're doing your job?"

Sadie rolled her eyes upward. Dominic was going to blow a gasket because she was working with Paul. She pressed her lips together to keep from blurting anything else out. The more she talked the worst she was making him look. She didn't want to emasculate him to have anyone thinking that his pride was so wounded that he couldn't take Sadie doing her job. But his pride was wounded.

Damn, she thought and walked toward her office. She rounded her desk barely glancing at the lavender plant. One thing after another, when would it end? Just when she'd thought their lives were getting back on track, wham. Why were the fates trying so damn hard to wreck her relationship? Why did it seem they'd chosen her man to be their personal punching bag? And why was she chosen as their instrument of destruction? The more time passed the more it was beginning to look as though this partnership was not a good thing.

A tap on Sadie's door alerted her that what was coming next would be something more she wouldn't like.

"'Sadie, can I come in?" Paul called out.

Counting to ten Sadie marched to the door and opened it with the intent to unleash her frustrations on Paul, to make him the fall guy for the misery of the past few months. She stared at him for a moment having the good sense to reign in her tongue. He wasn't the culprit, fate was. Still she didn't like that as her friend he hadn't given her a heads up. "You knew this when I came in this morning. Why the hell didn't you warn me?"

Paul raised his hands in the air. "Hey did you really think I had a death wish? I knew you weren't going to like it. Come on, Sadie, you know this wasn't my idea. I work here and I do what I'm told. I may not have made partnership in December but the next time one is going to be given out I plan to be in the running."

For a long moment Sadie stood where she was and glared at Paul. He grinned at her and she glared even more before sighing. "Paul, what's happening to my life?" she whispered loudly. "This should be a happy time. What am I going to do? How am I going to handle this?"

"Sadie, you're going to hurt my feelings. I like working with you. I think we're good together. The way you're behaving it's as though you think I'm a third rate attorney."

He was teasing but when she met his gaze she saw hurt. "I like working with you too, Paul. And you know I think you're a fantastic lawyer." Tilting her head she laughed. "Even Dominic has commented on your skills as a lawyer. But that's not what I'm talking about. You like to needle him and things have been pretty rough for us."

"Sadie, I had no idea. Are you saying it still bothers Dominic that you got the partnership?"

"There's a lot going on but I'm not at liberty to tell you about it. It's not about the partnership per se, but about his urgent need to be the main provider. It has nothing to do with his love for me." She sighed. "Neither of us has made this easy for him with our friendship or our flirting." His lifted brow made her smile.

"Paul, I wish I didn't like you so much or enjoy working with you. I wish I could complain about it when I go home at night. But it would be a lie and Dom would know it. We were going to have a cookout in our new place and I was going to invite you. The house is so nice, we were thinking of buying it maybe." A tear fell and she wiped at it. Then Paul was pulling her into his arms to comfort her and she was accepting it crying out her tears of frustration. When she was all cried out she moved way.

"Thanks."

A look filled with longing and a half smile was Paul's answer. She had to ignore that or get in even more trouble. She gave him a stern look. "You're going to have to behave. Is that understood? No teasing Dominic about this. I'm not kidding. If you do or say anything to him I'll never forgive you."

"Are you going to tell him?"

"I don't know how."

"Sadie, you know he's going to find out somehow and it's going to look as though you were hiding it from him. If it were me, I'd want to know. Tell him."

That was so easy to say. And it was good advice but she didn't think she'd take it, not just yet anyway. They needed more time to heal.

Chapter Twelve

For over a month Sadie had kept her secret. If Dominic hadn't been so happy and more like his old cocky confident self she would have felt the burden more sharply. But they were making the rental house in Woodridge into a home.

Walking into the living room she ran her fingers across the sofa her parents had given to them. The entire home was now furnished with hand me downs and a few new pieces mixed in here and there. Dom had been on several shopping trips finding the odd and end pieces to make their new home cozy.

"Hey babe," Dominic called out. "You look good in here. This was a good idea you had. I hate that you have to deal with being the one to go into the city every day."

"I love it. It gives me time to work on my case."

"What are you working on?"

Sadie tilted her head and smiled. "No work talk, okay." She arched her brow and gave an invitation. When Dom smiled broadly she heaved a sigh of relief.

"Do we have time before your parents come over?"

"We do if we make it a quickie in the shower."

***

"Sadie, you know you're asking for trouble not telling Dominic you're working on discrimination cases with Paul."

"I know, Mom, but we've fought so much in the past few months that I'm afraid to say anything to him. Paul's name sets him off automatically. And if he knew we were working on what's supposed to be our cases. I'm just hoping…"

"You know you're lying to him."

"Not really."

"Don't give me that. You know the difference. And you know it will be worse because he's going to imagine all sorts of things."

"I think I may have waited too long already. Just a few more weeks and the case will be over."

"And what about the next case you have to work with Paul and the one after that?"

"Mom, please. I just want to enjoy a stress free day with the people I love. I can spend more time with you and daddy now."

"Don't think we didn't notice you haven't invited Dom's parents over and you've had us over twice. Whatever you have against his father you're going to have to get over it. How would you like it if Dominic didn't want to be around us?"

"I like most of his family."

"Sadie, that's his father."

Sadie was trying to think of an answer to give her mother but noticed Dom staring at them. It was time they ended their hushed conversation. Kissing her mother on the cheek she went to stand by Dominic taking the food from his hand and eating it, kissing him when he laughed. Life was good today. She had no plans on spoiling it.

***

Dominic couldn't help but notice the pinched look around Sadie's mouth or the constant fear in her eyes. Had he done that to her, to their relationship? They were trying so hard to get back to normal that most of the time it appeared their actions were frenzied with a false note. For more than a month Sadie had been jumpy, not wanting to mention work not even to say if she'd had a good day. Something was off. For the most part he'd decided to ignore it. He was tired of fighting, tired of seeing Sadie unhappy. So he was deliberately pretending that things were as they should be. They'd always shared everything and he wanted them back to normal. He knew Sadie wasn't telling him things in fear that he'd blow up. He would definitely have to work on that.

He stared hard at Sadie and her mother; something was going on with the two of them, another thing Sadie didn't want him to know about. But he loved her parents and knew they loved him. He was holding out hope that one day things between Sadie and Poppi would be as they were with him and her parents. He'd not mentioned that they hadn't had his parents over to their new rented home. Nor had he mentioned that she'd refused all the offers of furniture that his parents had given them. Sadie had a good relationship with his sisters and even with Berto and his mother. It was Poppi she had issues with. And since he'd told her his secret it seemed her dislike of him had intensified.

For now he was letting it go, but it couldn't continue. He was the man he was because of Poppi. He was his father and Sadie would have to learn to accept that. Today though he would be satisfied with just having Sadie be happy.

When she turned to find him staring at him there was that strange flicker of fear in her eyes before she grinned and came to him. He decided to let this go also. Sadie was happy and he would be also. They'd deal with whatever the hell was going on when Sadie got ready to tell him. He was tired of fighting.

***

Pulling up in front of the house he took a moment to admire the changes he'd made. His father had questioned him about putting so much work into a place he didn't own but he was beginning to think Sadie had the right idea. Maybe they would actually buy the house. One day he'd love to have a home built just for them but until then he could see living here for a few years. The neighbors were nice. The community was quiet. And it was giving them a sense of peace. They were finally finding their way back to where they should be.

With a smile he walked up the drive and collected the mail leafing through it as he went to check on the meal he'd prepared in the crock pot. A card with no return address but familiar scrawl caught his attention. As always it brought a smile to his lips to get a card from his brother. Opening the card he was puzzled at the words and had to read it a second time.

"Hang in there, Dominic. I'm sure everything will work out for the best. Just to let you know I was so proud of you for the work you did on those discrimination cases. I'm sure Sadie will miss working with you. I hope she has success with the lawyer she's now working with. I can't get to see you as often in action but I still know you're doing great things. I need to ask a very important favor of you. It's a family emergency. I wouldn't bother you if it wasn't extremely important. Meet me tonight at 5:30 P.M. at McGinnis on sixty-third. I know you usually leave the office by five. I hope you come. Take care little brother."

What the hell? Dom read the letter once more and looked at the card. A part of him was sick of this stupid game his brother continued to play through the years going to the point of getting angry and denying he was sending the cards. Even when Dominic had shown them to him he'd knocked the cards from Dominic's hand and told him to get the fuck out of his face with his nonsense. That last time he'd almost convinced Dominic that he had not been the one sending the cards. And if he didn't have the physical proof he would possibly have thought he was loco. Despite Berto's denial he was touched that his brother cared enough to always know just what to say.

In disbelief his eyes scanned the paper once more. This time Berto had it wrong. Sadie wasn't working on any discrimination cases. Those were theirs. Surely just because he'd been transferred to Woodridge he wouldn't be cut out. A hollow feeling swept through him and he cringed. The little things he'd noticed with Sadie for the past month, the fear in her eyes, her not wanting to discuss work. It was all beginning to make sense. He reread the letter again then slowly he pulled his cell from his pocket and called Sadie.

"Where are you?" he asked the moment she said hello.

"Dom, I'm on my way to court."

"What's the case?"

"It's no big deal."

"Tell me, Sadie."

"Later when I get home we'll talk, okay, baby."

Baby, he thought as the feeling of a knife being plunged into his body came to mind. "Sadie, who're you working the case with?"

Her silence was his answer. "When the hell were you planning on telling me?" Dominic struggled for calm but the best he could manage was a low growl. "Sadie, what the hell is going on?"

"Okay, baby, love you too." Then click. He couldn't believe his woman had just played him and why he wondered. She was with Paul, his gut told him that. Damn she was behaving as though she didn't want Paul to know what she was talking about. Was she protecting him? Oh hell no. Now, she thought he was some weak little punk that she had to shield.

Pacing back and forth he checked the food and paced some more. When he realized he was not accomplishing anything he headed back to the office. For over an hour Dominic fumed slamming folders on the desk while trying to reach Sadie. When she got home they were going to have the mother of all fights. Two hours later Sadie was still on his mind. Barely giving his secretary a good night and no excuse, he left, determined to find out what was going on.

Walking in the door of the law he Dom stopped and stared before ordering his mind to calm down. It didn't work. With deliberateness he strode to Sadie's office ignoring her secretary wanting to announce him. Screw that. He didn't need any announcing. He opened the door and stared as many thoughts raced through his mind. Well, he'd found the trouble he sought. He stared for a nanosecond longer at his woman with another man's hands all over her body, A growl came up from his throat like that of an animal startling Sadie and Paul as well as Dominic.

Two steps that's all it would take to choke the life out of Paul. But what about Sadie? What would he do to her? In the blink of an eye he ordered himself to calm down a bit, murder wasn't in his plan, at least not at the moment. No, at the moment he needed an explanation. Shoving Paul away from Sadie, Dominic stood there glaring at them.

"What the hell's going on?" he asked Paul. "Why are your hands on Sadie?"

Then his attention turned to Sadie where it should be. She was his woman, his heart, his life, the woman he was engaged to marry. If only the slight trace of guilt wasn't in her eyes, but it was. He acknowledged it and swallowed needing to know what was going on.

"Sadie, why was he touching you?"

Dominic would have given anything to have kept the hurt from his voice but he was hurt and it seeped out. He blinked shaking his head slowly. Not Sadie. Sadie wouldn't cheat on him. Sadie had his back. He opened his mouth to speak but no words came. He narrowed his eyes and just stood there clenching and unclenching his fists praying that he wouldn't smash Paul in the face.

"Shit." Sadie groaned and moved between Paul and Dominic. She put a finger in Dom's chest then turned toward Paul. "I'll talk to you later." She moved her finger from Dom's chest and reached for his hand pulling him out of her office and through the open reception room going past his old cubicle trying to make it out the door and to the elevator, ignoring the angry scowl on her man's face.

"What was that shit about?" Dominic yelled the moment the elevator door closed. "Why were his hands all over you?"

Sadie clenched her teeth refusing to answer him. She glared at him instead.

"What the hell's going on Sadie? Answer me."

"Dom, you're not my father."

"I am your man and when you allow another man to put his hands all over your body you're disrespecting me, and now you're getting an attitude with me like I embarrassed you in front of your man or something. Is Paul your man now, Sadie? I'm going to ask you again what the hell's going on?"

Sadie wanted badly to ignore Dominic's temper tantrum but she knew better. It was a lot more going on with him than thinking something was up with her and Paul. "Dominic, I was tense, my back hurt a little and he was just massaging it for me."

"Did you ask him to?"

"No, but I thought it was nice that he did. When did you stop trusting me? When have I ever given you a reason to distrust me?" It had to be just then that the elevator stopped and Mr. Secret got on. Damn she should have taken the stairs. *Please God, she prayed, don't let Dom take our boss's head off.* As it was when the man spoke to Dom, Dominic ignored him. The boss's eyes swung immediately to Sadie. When she attempted to make a gesture Dom stopped her.

"Don't do that," he growled. "Don't speak for me. What is this?" Dom asked pushing the button to stop the elevator.

Oh shit, Sadie thought as she saw the fear begin in their boss's eyes. She had to stop Dominic before they were both fired.

"Baby, it's me your angry with. I should have told you that Paul had been assigned to work a case with me. It's a one-time thing. I'm sure of it." She glanced at her boss, silently pleading, hoping he'd know how important this was.

"Is all of this hostility because of Sadie doing her job?" Mr. Secret's eyes narrowed. "You're going a bit far now Santiago. You and Sadie are going to give me a stroke. First I had to have this fight with her about doing her job, now you. Paul is a more than competent lawyer. You're in charge of the Woodridge office. Am I going to have to consult the both of you before assigning you cases? It is my name on the firm's letterhead.

"Sadie, you may be our newest junior partner but that doesn't come with as many perks as you might think. For instance, holding me hostage in an elevator is definitely not one of your perks. Do you understand?"

"I understand," Sadie said moving past Dominic to restart the elevator. "I need to talk to Dominic first then I'll be back up."

"Santiago, if you don't like the Woodridge office you can come back here, but the salary hike goes." With that Mr. Secret turned toward the front of the elevator and waited.

No more words were spoken until Mr. Secret exited the elevator. Could their lives possibly get more complicated? If someone had asked, Sadie would never in a million years have foreseen this day coming for them. It was all her fault. She loved Dominic so much and wanted so badly to be his wife that she was screwing it up royally. She groaned as the memory of what she'd done wrong waved at her like a red flag.

"Baby, I'm sorry," Sadie said softly rubbing his arm as she did so. "I haven't been feeling well for a couple of days." She brought her eyes upward and held his gaze. "That mattress we bought..." she allowed the words to trail off knowing he would back off.

"I'm sorry, Sadie. I was just trying to save us money."

"Three months ago Poppi demanded a new bed and a deluxe mattress. We paid almost five thousand dollars for the bed and mattress alone. Then when it comes to us we have to buy the cheapest mattress made. Think about it, Dom. I'm not asking you not to help your family but what Poppi is doing to you is not fair to us. I know I promised to keep expenses down but that mattress is too darn thin."

Her eyes met his and she decided to let it go. Their only conflict was on the luxuries his father always seemed to be in need of and Dominic's inability to say no. None of it was fair to them, but it was a losing battle she'd learned. If she wanted Dom and a life with him she had no choice but to accept his father's strange hold over him. She swallowed and gave a weak smile to let him know she was ready to end the fight.

"Does your back still hurt?" he asked.

Actually it was her head that was throbbing. But if he was willing to let go of the tension then so was she. She gave him a pitiful look but remained silent.

"Turn around and I'll massage it for you," Dominic offered.

"Would you please?" Turning on the charm Sadie made her smile as bright as she could. "Thank, your hands massaging me is just what I need. God, Paul was trying but he's not you, not in any way, shape, form or fashion. You never have to worry about him."

She kissed him lightly on the lips after he was done massaging her. As they began walking she leaned her head on his shoulder for a moment. "You never have to worry about anyone. Did you drive or take the train in?"

"I drove.

"Good, we'll sit in the car and talk a bit, okay," she said in a soothing voice.

"Sadie, stop talking to me like I'm a mental case." He stopped walking to glare at her. What the hell is wrong with you? I didn't bring a gun with me and I have no intentions of buying one and coming back to shoot up the office."

"Yeah but that stunt you pulled with our boss, I have a right to be worried. I have never and I mean never seen you behave in such an irrational manner. What were you thinking?"

"That I was being shafted by him again and I didn't like it."

"That wasn't the way to go about handling it. This isn't you, Dom."

When the elevator stopped, the doors opened, yet Dominic made no move to leave. He was trying to decide whether or not to continue the fight. He was a fighter and a strategic. As he worried his lips Sadie had no idea which way he'd go only that they needed immediate privacy. She pulled on his arm urging him from the elevator and toward the parking garage. *This shouldn't be happening*, she thought, not to them. Dom was falling apart and acting crazy. This wasn't how her man behaved. She pulled in a sigh. Well, he'd always gotten a little crazy about Paul, but he'd never shoved him before.

Giving a little prayer of thanks on spotting the car she pulled out her keys and unlocked the doors before he had a chance. Again he glared at her. It seemed the smallest thing could set him off lately, as though her every move had been designed to emasculate him. The exact opposite was true. She loved his machismo. Still, there was something to be said for a time and place for everything. If they lost their jobs who knew when he'd think the time would be right for them to get married. More than likely 'never' would be his answer. So, one of them needed to be conscious of keeping a professional face when they were in public. Closing the door behind her she studied him for a moment.

"Do you want me to quit, Dom?" She watched as he blinked rapidly trying to deny the still hurt feelings. She shook her head slightly she couldn't imagine what would happen if he didn't support her if he were really selfish enough to want her to quit. "Tell me what you want."

Dom laced his hands together. "What I want is not to feel like a failure. What I want is to not feel like I've been banned from this office. What I want is to not have Paul working with you. What I want is to not come in here and find his hands all over you. You should have told me that he was going to work our cases. Why didn't you? Why did I have to find out the way I did? Why are you leaving me out of things? What's going on, Sadie? You always say you have my back, but you're making me wonder. Do you still have my back?"

His words broke her heart. Ragged sobs tore from her throat and she fell into Dominic's arms. "Oh God, Dom. I'm screwing us up and I'm so scared that if I tell you you're going to hate me. I haven't had your back. When Mr. Secret told us in a meeting that he wanted someone in Woodridge I suggested you."

Now was not the time to make excuses, to try and blame their boss, to tell him she feared he'd be fired if she had not suggested it. More than likely he wouldn't believe it. And if he did he'd be pissed that she was fighting his battles. His pride would be wounded. Through the years she'd learned the one thing not to mess with was Dominic Santiago's pride. Right now his stare was blasting a hole through her making her afraid of his reaction. Her throat ached with rawness.

"I wanted you out of the office. I didn't want you here because I couldn't bear to look at you at work every day, thinking I'd taken what you'd wanted."

For a moment Dominic was speechless. "Sadie, baby why?"

"You know why. You've been so angry at everyone since the party. Since, I got the partnership."

"I thought we were getting back to normal at work as well as at home."

"Things were better, at least between us. But you have been like a powder keg, ready to snap at everyone, taking their heads off for the least little thing. You haven't been the confident Dominic Santiago. You've been the man everyone was trying to avoid. You can't tell me you hadn't noticed the tension in the office before you left."

Taking a breath Dominic also took a moment to think over what Sadie was saying. She was right. He needed to get his shit together. He'd been trying. He'd handled the little problem of dealing with the crap at work, or so he'd thought. It was the constant noise in his ear from his father that had been getting to him, the doubts about his abilities, about what Sadie had done to get the job. Berto had mentioned what he'd told him about Sadie taking Paul away to their father and Poppi had turned it into something vile and dirty, something that Sadie had never intended. Still, even knowing her intentions, her actions and his father's words had blown the situation up and it had festered, boiling over whenever he saw Paul or their boss. He hadn't bothered telling Sadie of this. It was bad enough that he was allowing his father to have this kind of effect on him. For Sadie to know, it was unbearable. Tilting his head he refused to discard the glare. He was serious and had every intention of Sadie knowing it.

"It is not your call to make decisions for me. I don't care how crazy I'm acting. I hate to say this, but my father was right. All of a sudden our being engaged has gone to your head. You seem to think you're the man. Guess what, Sadie, you're not." He waited, mentioning Poppi being right about anything never failed to produce a fight.

"So was my mom. She told me I had no right to keep this from you no matter how I thought you'd react."

Damn if Sadie didn't surprise him each and every time. He'd expected something a lot different. Not an almost admission that she was in the wrong.

"Are you telling me you told your parents and was advised to tell me and refused?"

"You're half right. I told my mom. My dad would have told you ten seconds after I told him."

"Is this meant to be your version of an apology?"

"Not really."

"Excuse me?"

"Look what happened when you found out Mr. Secret put Paul on the discrimination case with me. You behaved worse than I imagined. And whether you believe me or not, I begged him to allow you to help me. He didn't refuse. But he made it seem like I was incompetent and that he would be giving the cases to you out of pity or something. I didn't know how to handle it. I knew you would be hurt and angry and I didn't want to tell you."

"And this is better?"

With a sigh Sadie shook her head. "No, it's much worse. This is my fault. I pushed you too hard to ask me to marry you. And I've been trying to keep the pressure away from you. I want us to go back to the way it used to be for us. But I don't know how to fix it."

"Sadie." How did he answer her? She was being sincere and he wanted not to be angry at her. There was a sadness about her. He'd grown tired of not seeing the sparkle in her eyes. She was his sunshine and lately his *sun* had refused to shine.

"Listen to me, Sadie, it's not your job to fix it. It's mine. I am not as helpless as you seem to think. I am also not so dense that I don't realize what's been going on with us. I haven't been talking things over with you because you have this irritating habit of trying to fix things, fix people. I don't need fixing. Got it?" Dom pulled in a hard breath. "What about Paul's hands on you, what was that about Sadie? No more lies. Were you really so stressed that you'd allow Paul to touch you?"

"I didn't lie to you about that. I really was stressed. I've been so worried about what I'm holding back on you. I think I may have made a comment or something or was rubbing my shoulders. I don't remember. Anyway when Paul started to massage my shoulders I didn't stop him. For a second I did wonder what would happen if you should walk in and see it, but then I thought, he's not going to, he's in Woodridge. So I just let him. And you walked in."

She pulled in a breath and wiped at the tears that were still streaming down her face with the back of her hand. "Dom, I'm not looking to replace you. Not with Paul, not with a job, not with anyone or anything. I'll admit I try to fix things. I'm sorry about that. Fixing things is a part of my nature. Why don't the two of us leave the firm and open up our own office."

"You mean quit. You want me to act like a punk and a jealous one at that. Have my woman, my wife, give up a partnership for my pride. I don't think so, Sadie, not going to happen."

"I'm more concerned about us."

"Were you concerned about us when you asked that I be sent away?"

Sadie blanched then she swallowed. There was no way for her to answer the anger in his eyes. She'd promised to have his back and she'd failed him. A low groan worked its way from her belly. Her gaze fell on the engagement ring on her left hand a sign of her commitment to Dominic. She loved him with everything that was in her. She still wanted to be his wife more than anything she'd ever wanted in her life. She should be talking, trying to convince him that her feelings were the same but the words refused to come.

"Tell me something, Sadie. And this time it would be a novelty if you'd try and answer me honestly. Don't you like the feeling of power you've received from being a partner?"

Her mouth opened slightly and she worried her top lip with her tongue. He was right. She did like being a partner. She'd never known she'd craved power or that she would even like it. But she could honestly tell Dom that she didn't completely like the heady effect. And she definitely didn't like what having it was causing her to do. Glancing down she tried to formulate an answer, not wanting to admit that yes, she did enjoy the power.   Bringing her eyes back up her gaze connected with his and she became afraid for them.

"Baby, Dom—"

"There's no need for you to answer that one. It's in your eyes. You say you're worried how I'll react, well guess what? I have my worries about you. The partnership has changed you, Sadie. You think you're in charge of US." He shook his head to stop her protest. "The house, was that so I would never have a need to come into the city?"

"No, Dom. I swear that wasn't reason." She held his gaze determined not to lose contact with him. "The house was strictly about us."

"Are you sure about that, Sadie?"

Again the twinge of betrayal before she could formulate an answer. "Alright, I felt guilty. I wanted to make it up to you. I didn't think it was fair for you to drive so far each day. But the house, I meant it about our having our own home. I love the house, Dom. We've been happier since we rented it. I can see us raising our babies in that house." Her voice became low and feathery the fear she felt in her heart slowing seeping out. "Don't you still see that?"

"To tell you the truth I don't know what I see. Sometimes it seems to me that our getting married is more important to you than us. Instead of fighting for us it seems you're fighting to keep things hidden from me. That's not the kind of life I want, Sadie." He held her gaze for a moment longer. "I think I'd better leave now."

"Why don't I go back up and speak with Mr. Secret and come home with you."

"I'll see you later at home." Before Sadie could answer Dominic was out of the car, opening her door and escorting her back to the office. He waited until she got on the elevator before turning to leave, refusing to stop and talk to any of his coworkers, wondering if they all knew why he'd been banned to Woodridge, wondering if they all knew of Sadie's betrayal.

His head hurt. But it was his heartbreak that he thought would kill him. He wondered if his brother would be able to find a card that covered this particular turn of event. He replayed the scene he'd walked in on in his mind, to see if his instincts told him Sadie was lying. He clearly saw Paul's hands kneading Sadie's flesh. He'd also seen her eyes closed. She'd been enjoying it no matter what she'd told him. Unease slithered its ugly head into his mind and he quickly pushed it away. There were a couple of things he could do to ensure that Sadie wouldn't need Paul's hand ever again to rub away her tension.

Reaching for his cell he placed a hurried call to his brother. Damn he muttered when the call went to voicemail. He'd really wanted to speak to Berto. He had no choice but to leave a message. "I can't meet you at McGinnis. I have an errand to run." That taken care of he turned the car left to head for the Fox Valley Mall and Sears. He was going to buy a new mattress and he was going to get Sadie a portable massager. He didn't want Paul's hands on his woman's body ever again, no matter how tense she was.

***

A light tap on her door brought Sadie's head up sharply. The moment Paul stuck his head in waving a white paper towel she wanted to pick something up to throw at him. He had a way of making her laugh and pissing Dom off, and the thing about it was he didn't give a damn that was for sure.

If Sadie wasn't so madly in love with Dom she probably would have admitted to the mild attraction she had for Paul. But that was just for fun, for her ego, nothing serious. He had a crush on her, lusted after her, desired her, and yes, she was a woman, she liked the way his eyes sometimes roved over her body making her feel hot and flushed. Some of the problems were of her own making. She'd flirted a time or two with him. Okay, maybe more than a time of two. And she'd deliberately used him on more than one occasion to sway Dominic when he was intent on doing something else, like if she wanted to go for dinner and Dom wanted to go home and rest. She'd mention it in front of Paul who'd jump to the bait offering to take her. And Dominic like usual would get pissed off and take her. That Sadie thought was harmless, all involved knew what she was doing, even Paul. He'd always known she was using him and always threatened one day the using would stop and she'd see him as more than a red flag to wave in front of her man.

Well that day had come. She was seeing him as something more. She was seeing him as the thorn in her man's side and she'd damn well put it there. This shit had to stop.

Damn, she thought when Paul gave her a full grin and for the first time in months it seemed she really looked at him. He was gorgeous. Marble blue eyes, and thick, silky, soft, blonde hair. He was an inch or two taller than Paul and a bit leaner. He took good care of his body. She'd seen him often at the company's gym working out and remembered even once having to turn away from the sight of him in his workout shorts and without his shirt on. He'd caught her and had laughed as though he knew he'd invaded her thoughts and had heated her veins. He had, but the heat was transferred to Dominic. She'd immediately gone to find him and had given him a passionate kiss, answering his, 'what's this for?' with, 'because, I love you and was just thinking of you.' She'd managed to push away the tiny twinge of guilt she'd felt for that temporary lusting over Paul's masculine form. She was in love but she wasn't totally blind to the beauty of a perfect male form. But it had not been serious and Dom had not been hurt by it. Now he was.

"Oh, oh, you're angry with me."

"You're damn right I'm angry. Listen, Paul, this has to stop, you and me, this twisting the knife in Dom. You know I love him and you know that I want nothing more than to be married to him. But even if he won't…" she stopped short of what she'd been about to say. "Even if we weren't getting married it would still be Dominic that I wanted. Stop baiting him."

Paul's eyes opened wide then his mouth and for the first time she'd known him, he got angry.

"What the hell are you talking about, Sadie? You had no complaints about my giving you a massage. In fact you were enjoying it. If I push Dominic's buttons then you push them ten times as hard. Admit it. You're coming on to me then have the nerve to get angry when I accept your advances. Dominic is not my man. He's yours. It's not my job to protect his feelings. You've both been aware of my feelings for you for years. Hell, I've never denied it or tried to hide it. But I would not still be holding out hope that there could be something between us if you weren't forever dangling your affections like a carrot before my eyes. As for Dominic, he came in here like a raging bull and attacked me. He's lucky I didn't flatten his little bitty ass."

Choosing for the moment to ignore the things he'd accused her of Sadie couldn't help the laugh that came out. "Little bitty? Dominic's over six feet tall."

"So what? If he's still fuming because you got the partnership, that makes him little in my eyes."

His words were swaying her. But it was his eyes that roamed over her body before focusing on her lips. She swallowed. They'd just crossed an invisible line. "Don't, Paul. I'm not going to—"

"You think Dominic is your soul mate simply because he was bold enough to come out in front of everyone and claim you. Hell, if I'd known you wanted that this would be an entirely different conversation. Damn, Sadie, I've been in love with you just as long as he has."

"No, Paul, you've been in competition with Dom."

Before she could blink or take her next breath Paul was reaching for her, pulling her roughly to him and plastering his lips against her own. She was trembling but not fighting him or his intent. Her hands flattened against his chest and for a long moment she looked into his blue eyes and waited. The kiss gentled his tongue slid into the warmth of her mouth and molten lava exploded and cascaded down her back. Her bones begin to liquefy as her mind starting spinning whirling her toward an abyss of emotions.

The kiss ended and Paul moved slightly away caressing her lips with his finger, outlining them, looking into her eyes. "I've wanted to do that forever." He moved back another inch. "Believe me, Sadie, that had nothing to do with Dominic. I wasn't thinking about him while I was kissing you. How about you, Sadie? Were you thinking of him?"

She could only stare at him.

"Well, Sadie, were you?

"I was wondering what I've done to make you think you could kiss me."

He smiled a tiny little smile that only pulled at the corners of his mouth. "Maybe the fact that you didn't slap me, that it took you," he paused and glanced at his watch before meeting her eyes, "What thirty seconds before you could talk? Did you like the kiss, Sadie? I can repeat it."

Did she like it? The question was had she wanted it? And the answer was yes, she'd definitely wanted it. She knew what she'd done to make Paul think he could kiss her. She'd stood there hoping he would. She'd flirted and she'd wondered what it would be like to be with him. Dangerous territory. Hell no, she was so far past that that she couldn't begin to think of a lie that would cover her behavior so she didn't try. When Paul began to laugh she glared at him puzzled by his action.

"My God, Sadie, cut it out. You're looking as though you think you should be executed. You're a winner, Sadie and you're just about ready to kick Dominic's sorry ass to the curb. I think you keep repeating how much you love him in order to convince yourself that it's still true. I'm your spare and you wanted me to kiss you so you could see if you'd feel any of the passion with me that you feel with him. Stop me if I'm wrong."

She could only swallow. There was no way she was going to answer that question.

"Sadie, don't be so hard on yourself. Dominic Santiago has been fucking up for more than six months. He should have gotten his act together by now. I don't blame you for checking out the merchandise."

"Are you trying to make me feel better?"

"I sure as hell don't want you wanting to commit suicide or do something crazy like telling Dominic, unless you've made up your mind. Unless you no longer love him."

"Paul, you know me much better than I'd like. This is the roughest it's ever been for us. What does it say for me that when the going gets rough I got going? Where's my loyalty?"

'I think right now your loyalty is to yourself. I think you're afraid you've tied yourself to a loser. Tell me you don't think that's true."

"Dominic has always been a winner."

"But?"

"Okay, but he seems to have forgotten that. Paul, are you sure it doesn't make me a truly awful person to have acted on my doubts? I still love Dom. I know we're going to have a really bad fight when I get home and a tense weekend. And I will admit I'm getting pretty tired of fighting. I'm sorry for pulling you into my emotional turmoil."

"Sadie, I think you and Dominic need to talk. As for the two of us. Let's just say I'd rather be your spare than anyone else."

Immediate tears sprung to her eyes and this time when Paul took her into his arms it was only to comfort her, only as a friend. "Thanks, Paul," she whispered. And though she knew this moment was innocent she knew if Dominic happened to walk in, things between them would be over. With a smile she pushed away.

"I don't think I'd better keep pressing my luck. And neither should you, or Dom's little bitty ass is going to annihilate you."

Chapter Thirteen

With a groan Dominic drove around the mall trying without much success in finding a parking spot in the general vicinity of his destination. For some strange reason it appeared people in the suburbs made a sport out of visiting the malls. Why couldn't some of them have stayed at home today? He was in no mood for this. There were only two options open to him: park in front of the store and come out to find his car towed, or go to the opposite end of the mall and walk back. Both choices made his dark mood more intense. But there was no way in hell he was leaving the mall without buying a mattress and a massager for Sadie. Readying himself to make yet another pass around the parking lot he spotted a shopper loaded down with bags and prayed this wasn't just the shopper's trip to her car to dispose of her packages. He waited impatiently until she'd loaded the bags and said a quick thank you when she finally climbed into the driver's seat and pulled away.

Wasting no time he pulled into the spot, and within seconds was in Sears. Dominic walked from mattress to mattress his mind not on the salesman or the fact that he'd come specifically for a new mattress so Sadie would not have any excuse to allow Paul to touch her. He'd become waylaid by a man that looked vaguely familiar staring at him from across the room. He was pretending to browse but every time he looked up the man's eyes were on him. *What the hell*, he thought, wondering why a man would be checking him out. This time when he looked up the man didn't look away but held his gaze. Dom began walking toward him, the mattress forgotten. It was obvious the man staring at him wanted him to know he was looking at him. He wanted to capture his attention. Now he had it. He'd picked the wrong man on the wrong day to fuck with. Actually he was looking forward to venting some of his anger. He'd love to pound the man and envision Paul's face while he was doing it. With that image planted firmly in his mind Dominic walked toward the man stopping directly in front of him readying his body to deliver the first of what he figured would be many punches.

"Why the fuck are you following me? Why the hell are you staring at me?" The reaction wasn't exactly one Dominic had been prepared for. A huge grin spread across the man's face but he didn't say a word.

Dominic was getting an eerie feeling, something he couldn't explain. He was no longer glaring at the man. He was curious as to who he was. "Do you have a problem? Can I help you?" When the man continued grinning at him as though he were a long lost relative a chill traversed his spine. He took a good look at the man, at his smile, his green eyes, his thick brown hair. This stranger looked more like Dominic than any of his relatives. Instinct told him who the man was. But his mind refused to accept it. It couldn't be. Why after all of this time? "Do I know you?"

"From a long time ago. You were about ten and I gave you a ride on my motorcycle. My name is Shawn Donavan."

Donavan. Trying as hard as he could the name didn't ring a bell. But the man who'd given him a ride on his bike had evoked memories, most of them extremely unpleasant. That was the time his father had beaten him severely for riding off with a stranger.

Shawn held out his hand and Dominic merely looked at it. "How could you possibly remember the face of a kid you'd seen once in your life? That was over twenty-three years ago. Something doesn't add up." There was a spot just beneath his left shoulder blade that always niggled at him when something was out of whack, not right, not completely truthful. "Who are you?" he demanded.

"I think you know, or at the very least I think you have a very good idea."

The man standing in front of him was beginning to piss him off. Dominic turned to walk away and was stopped by a hand on his shoulder.

"Why didn't you meet me at McGinnis little brother?"

Electrical tingles traveled from the tips of his toes to the top of his head. Dominic could feel a tremor in his body. He wanted to deny it but his mind rapidly flipped through the last twenty plus years and then he knew. The notes, the cards they'd all come from the man standing in front of him now, the one claiming to be his brother. The man who'd given him a ride on his bike when he was ten. The one who'd caused his father to beat him near senseless. This was the same man who'd given him encouragement through the years. This was his brother. A whoosh of air filled his chest and Dominic staggered closing his eyes nearly falling until caught by his brother. He stayed like that for a moment before opening his eyes to look at this man he'd never known. Yet in so many ways this brother had been his source of comfort.

"Why?" Was the only word Dominic could mutter.

"Why what exactly?" Shawn asked.

"Why did you wait until I'm thirty-three? Damn!" Dominic staggered back a foot. "You waited my entire life and now you show. Tell me why." He glared as the light that had been in Shawn's eyes suddenly faded as though his words had snuffled it out. It was replaced by sadness. Then he remembered the note, the one asking him to meet at McGinnis. It had said something about a family emergency. He should have known. It was so cliché. A dying father who'd abandoned his child, then wanted back in said child's life when he was ill or needed money. *Damn,* Dominic thought and once again walked away. This time he was stopped by a firm hand on his back and anger coming toward him in waves.

"Don't you dare lump me into some category I haven't earned. Do you think I wanted things to be like this? I've loved you almost from the moment I found out about you."

"Almost?"

"Dominic, listen, I really need to talk to you. There's a steak house on the other side of the mall. Will you go with me so we can talk in a bit more comfort and with some privacy? I can promise you, I didn't come to you for a hand out."

Staring at Shawn Dominic could tell from the way his brother was dressed he wasn't in need of money. He was dressed from head to toe in black. The clothes were expensive that much he knew. As much as he didn't want to go with Shawn he knew he would.

"I'm not hungry."

"Then we won't eat. I think it's past time we talked."

With a shrug of his shoulder Dominic started walking toward the exit not waiting for his brother but hearing him laughing no doubt at him. The moment they were out the doors Shawn pulled out his keys. "Wait, let me guess," Dominic chuckled. "The big black bronco parked in the handicapped parking." There was something about Shawn he liked. There were also a hell of a lot of questions like how did he find him at the mall. But those questions could wait until they were in the restaurant.

In a matter of minutes they were sitting behind a table, both of them having opted for coffee.

"I never knew I had another brother."

"Seriously?"

"Okay, I sort of knew. But I refused to dwell on it. I had a family and my biological one abandoned me. So why the hell would I care if I had another brother?" He saw the subtle twitch in Shawn's jaw. He'd hurt him and that had not been his intent. "I prayed for a while for my father, for my family to come and rescue me." He swallowed. "I always wondered who you were. At first I thought you might have been my father but you were much too young. I used to dream about you coming to give me another ride. Then I grew up."

Why the hell was he spilling his guts like a little kid, telling things to this man he'd only seen once before in his life? But it didn't feel that way. It felt as though he'd known him most of his life. And in a very important way he had.

"Dominic, you're not that old that you've gone senile. Don't lie to me. And stop lying to yourself. After you graduated high school Dad and I called you several times and told you who we were. You told us both to go to hell each and every time we tried to reach out to you. Even so, we refused to allow you not to be a part of our lives.

There needed to be a change in the direction this conversation was going. "You said you mentioned you loved me almost from the moment you found out about me. Why almost?" He watched as the grin returned to Shawn's face and his eyes sparkled once more.

"Yes, almost. I was eleven and not very bright about things like that, not about imperfect parents by any means. The news about you ripped my family apart for a long time. My parents nearly divorced. My father moved out for almost a year. He and I didn't speak for months. And one day I realized I wasn't alone in the world. I had a brother, a baby brother. And I wanted nothing more than to see you. I called my father and demanded to see you. I'm going to fast forward a bit here. Eventually my father returned home and attempted to explain to me why I couldn't have a relationship with you. I refused his explanations. I kept hounding Dad until one day out of exasperation he gave in and gave me your parents' number."

"Do I have other siblings?"

"No.

"But you never tried to be in my life."

"Dominic."

"Okay, Maybe I have a vague memory of calls and maybe I even remember telling you both to go to hell. But why shouldn't I? I'd lived my entire life without the two of you in it, without you giving a damn about me. I didn't need you when I was nearly an adult. You didn't give a damn about me when it would have done some good."

"That is so not true. Damn it, Dominic. I called your parents pleading with them time after time to allow me to meet you. I wanted to be your brother but always they said no. You were important to me and it was my mission to be in your life whether you wanted me in there or not.

"I badgered my father demanding to be a part of your life, asking how he could so easily have a son and not know him. That was the only time in my life I've seen my father cry. He told me he loved you the same as he loved me, that it was killing him not to be a part of your life. I challenged him to find a way and he did. He met with your mother and together they hammered out a plan. When you were a baby I was allowed to see you. When you began to talk your mother didn't want to chance your telling her husband about me. Dad told me

I'd be endangering you and your mother if I didn't do what he said. He made me agree to remain in the background until you were of age, and I agreed. But I didn't keep that promise. I already had your address and I sent you letters, cards, gifts. When I got a car I would drive there every day just to catch a glimpse of you. Your parents spotted me and all hell broke loose. Another bargain was struck and we were given limited access to you, dates and times for your games, school plays, things like that.

"For a time that appeased me. But I wanted you to know me. I called and talked to your father, telling him my intentions to introduce myself to you. I didn't give a damn about what anyone had to say. It had been too long and I'd missed out on having a brother. Your father went so far as to threaten to kill me, then later you, if I made contact with you." Shawn hesitated then took in a deep breath and let it out.

"I was arrogant and young. *What the heck*, I thought. Your father couldn't do a damn thing to me. I forgot about you, that you lived in his home and was under his control. For that I am truly sorry. I thought he was upset, bluffing until the day I dared to take you for a motorcycle ride and he beat you. I wanted to kill your father that day and I would have if my father hadn't come along. I was so angry at both men. Your father for treating you that way. And my father for not claiming you, for allowing you to live in the home with such a monster."

Dominick cringed at the memory of that day. Some things he'd forgotten, some things he'd never forget. But out of loyalty to his father he had to protest however mild. It was pure reflex that pushed the words from his mouth. "Poppi is not a monster. I'll not allow you to talk about him that way."

"Simmer down Dominic. At twenty-one that was what he was to me, but don't worry, so was my father, our father."

"Poppi is my father. He's the man who raised me, who made me what I am today. What I am is because of him?"

"Grow the hell up, Dominic. Do you really and truly think that all that you were given, school, college and law school came from your Poppi? He could never have afforded to send you to the best schools."

"My mother helped me apply for loans and grants. I got scholarships."

"Yes you got scholarships and grants, but the money was from your father and I don't mean Poppi. As for the loans, why is it that you've never been required to make one payment that you received notification that you didn't have to. You're a lawyer, Dominic. Where do you think the money came from? Dad may not have done right by you for the first few months of your life but he's been there ever since. Hell, he threatened to have you taken away from your family, he started court proceeding."

"How do I know what you say is true?" Dominic was feeling sick to his stomach.

"I've got thirty three-years of cashed checks to back me up."

"If all of this is true if he cared so damn much why wasn't..." Swallowing Dominic had to take a moment to compose himself. He couldn't allow his emotions to show. "If what you say is true why didn't he fight harder? The least he could have done was to insist on visitation. Apparently I wasn't important enough for him to do that. Perhaps he didn't want this half Latino boy in his family. Why didn't he..."

With a disgusted snort Shawn raised his hand for the waitress. "If I'm going to sit here and listen to more crap like that coffee isn't going to cut it." Ordering drinks for both of them he waited until the waitress returned to answer Dominic's statement. He took a swig of the liquor then stared at his brother.

"Dad tore our lives apart. Do you think your ethnicity mattered? If you do, you're a fool and I know you're not that. My father did the things he did because your mother pleaded with him. He loved her. He loved you. He's not a saint. That's apparent. You're the product of him not being a saint."

There wasn't anything Dominic could say to that. Finally he picked up the drink he'd had no intention of touching and brought it to his lips. "Are you done?"

"Is this the way you've been talking to Sadie for the last six months? I can understand why she's at her wits end with you."

"Leave Sadie out of this."

Taking another sip of his drink Shawn studied his brother. "You may not like it but your Poppi is a bit crazy. He swore he'd kill you and your mother this time. My dad, sorry, our dad, was finally going to give up and let it go. I wouldn't allow him to do that. Both of us met with your mother again and we devised a plan. She didn't believe he was just spouting words. She believed he'd kill the both of you if we tried for a relationship. She thought he would come after me, my mother. And as far as I know he hasn't mellowed a bit. Anyway Dad and I laid out our plan. A lot went into keeping things secret from you."

"You're saying my father was too stupid to see that the money had to be coming from somewhere?"

"You're very bright, Dominic. Yet you never guessed. I said we kept things from you. But your...Poppi was a different story. He knew exactly where the money was coming from. There were times he'd call for more. Come on little brother. It's just the two of us here. Please don't lie to me and don't lie to yourself any longer. Didn't you ever wonder how your family had access to the things they did with the amount of money they made? Didn't you ever think that maybe your biological father hadn't abandoned you?"

Dominic blinked. "There were a few times I wondered, especially after what happened when I was ten, when you gave me a ride. After he beat me, I prayed that my real father would come and take me away. When he didn't I decided to ..." Dominic stopped and took in a breath knowing this was the first time he would be admitting the truth out loud. "I decided I would be the best son ever, that I would make Poppi proud of me and glad to have me for his son. I wanted him to love me. So I guess I didn't push too hard about where all the money was coming from."

"Sometimes people feel it's better not to know too much."

Dominic saw the look that suddenly came across Shawn's face and asked, "How has all of this affected your mother?"

"About what you'd expect. For a time my father fell out of love with her and fell in love with your mother. He wasn't just using her, or out for an affair. He left my mother." Shawn swallowed. "And me, I suppose, to make a life with your mother. He wasn't in your life because he didn't love you. He wasn't in your life, because he did. He wanted to protect your mother and you so he stayed away."

"I didn't ask about my mother. I asked about yours."

"I can't very well tell you about my mother unless I speak of yours. Eventually my parents mended their marriage. It took a lot of work, several years of therapy and finally my mother accepting that her husband had fathered a child with someone else, that I had a brother I wanted a relationship with. We've both lost out on a lot, Dominic, because none of us wanted to hurt you. Do you understand?"

"I understand that I'm too damn old to fall for all of this without checking it out. What the hell do you want with me at this late date? Does your father need some bone marrow from his bastard son?"

Shawn's jaw clenched. "It's not Dad. It's my son. And he needs nothing from you, it's me. I need a miracle. He's wanted to meet you for so long. I've tried many times." He shook his head. "It didn't work out. Now my son is ill. He's in a medical coma and I want to fulfill my promise to him. I want him to meet you. At least I want you to be there in his hospital room. I think you may be the miracle my son needs. I know you're the miracle I need."

Hesitation was the first thought, guilt the second. For most of his life the thing he'd loved most about his brother Berto was the fact that he always knew what was going on with him, always had words of encouragement and love. Now to think it was this brother he didn't know who had shown him so much love. Dominic swallowed. Raising his eyes he wasn't surprised Shawn was smiling at him.

"Dominic, come on man you never really thought Roberto sent you all of those letters and cards. He's never so much as written Maria one love note."

"How do you—"

"How could I protect you if I didn't know everything there was to know about every single person in your life?"

Nothing was as it ought to be. First Sadie now this. His life was sure going to hell fast.

"How did you always know where I was, what I was doing? Are you with the CIA?" Shawn smiled without answering.

"What line of work are you in?" Dom asked again.

"Let's just say from the time I was twenty-one and saw your father beat you I knew I needed a job that would allow me to be able to protect you. You have our father to thank that your Poppi is still alive. If I'd ever thought he'd so much as hit you again he wouldn't have been. And there would have been nothing our father would have been able to do to prevent that. What I do is neither here nor there. I can watch over you. That's all you need to know. Now how about you? Are you willing to visit with your nephew?"

This was all a bit much to take in. But what was he going to do, say no? He thought to call and tell Sadie then thought not. She was keeping secrets from him so why shouldn't he have a few of his own.

"I'll go and see your son then we need to continue our little heart to heart talk. I want to know if you could come up to me and talk now, why couldn't you have done it before? Why all the subterfuge?"

Shawn smiled.

"I'm too old for you to still be trying to protect me."

Again a smile. Shawn was a bit annoying. Rubbing his hand across his face a shudder racked his body. He thought of Sadie with Paul, his hands on her body. He opened his eyes to find Shawn staring at him as though he was aware of his thoughts.

"Listen, Shawn, give me the name of the hospital. I have to go back to Sears. I have to buy a mattress first." When Shawn's lips quirked upwards Dominic got the feeling once more that his brother knew the workings of his mind. "It's important or I'd leave with you this minute."

"Go ahead and buy your mattress. Then you tell me what you need from me. What can I do to make your life happy? If you want the thorn in your side removed just say the word. As for Sadie, she loves you. The only person who can make her stop loving you will be you. You listen to me, Dominic, and hear me good. You're not unworthy of Sadie.

You are no one's bastard son. Your father loves you very much. You have my word on that."

Before he could stop him Shawn came around the table pulled Dominic up and embraced him, folded him in his arms as though he were a child. Without wanting to Dominic returned the embrace, choking back a sob. When they finally released each other Dominic pushed away and gave Shawn a stern look. "You know way too much about me. You asked what I need from you. I'm going to need you to stop spying on me. I'm wondering now if you know when I make love to Sadie. You seem to know everything else."

This time his brother grinned and for the first time in many years Shawn's grin made him wonder how their father looked. His brother's grin was so much like his own that it was downright freaky. *So many years lost,* he thought. His love for Poppi had made him miss out on having another big brother. It had almost destroyed his relationship with Sadie. He'd have to talk to his father soon, no more hiding in shadows.

Returning to Sears, his brother by his side his rational mind told him to question Shawn more. What if it were all a lie? What if he was being lead into some kind of trap? All nonsense he knew, but the real threat was there at the forefront of his thoughts. And what if when he got to the hospital his birth father was there? What would he do then?

The mattress was selected, paid for and delivery date given. He swallowed. "Okay let's go and visit my nephew."

Damn! This was all too much. This day needed to be restarted. He should call Sadie, let her know what was happening. She'd be worried if he wasn't home when she arrived and there was no message from him. Then the thought came, what will she do if she knows she has a few hours free? Will she go to dinner with Paul? Will she rush home to be alone? Running his teeth over his lips as he thought, he sighed. He didn't like where his mind was taking him, the doubts, the suspicions, worry. The sense of betrayal that was lying dormant in his belly for two thirds of his life and had begun recently to stir, had now roared to life. All the people in his life had betrayed him, no doubt about it.

No, he wouldn't call Sadie. She needed to go home where she belonged. She needed to wait anxiously for his return. She needed to worry whether he'd return. She needed some of the worry he'd had for the past months.

The ring of his cell phone jarred his thinking. Good thing. Dominic didn't like where his thoughts had taken him. He saw the unknown number and smiled a bit knowing it was his brother. "Yeah," he answered

'Is that how you answer a phone?"

"I knew it was you."

"Like I said, you're bright."

"Is there a reason you're calling me?"

"I was wondering if there are any questions you want to ask me, like am I really your brother? Am I walking you into a trap? What will you do if our father is there?" A deep chuckle followed Shawn's words. "I know you better than you think, Dominic. Any questions?"

"None that you'll answer." With a sigh Dominic asked the only question he felt safe to ask, the one that had him traveling in the middle of the night to a hospital to visit a nephew who wouldn't know he was even in the room.

"Is your son really gravely ill?"

"Do you think I'd try to trick you?" Shawn asked.

"It has crossed my mind. I know that I've done things Poppi has asked me to do even though I didn't want to. I may be losing Sadie because of the promise I made to my father."

"Dominic, does it really bother you that much that Sadie made partner and you didn't?"

How did he answer that? To tell the truth would make him the all time champion of jerks? "How do I answer that?" he finally asked.

"Try honestly."

"My brother Berto thinks I'm being a macho jerk. I don't know if I want another brother thinking that." When Shawn laughed he felt better and continued. "You have to believe me on this. It's not that I don't think Sadie deserves it, or that she's not a fantastic lawyer. I wanted her to look up to me, to be proud of me. I wanted to be able to take care of her."

"You make more than enough money to take care of a family."

"How would you....scratch that. My life's an open book to you isn't it? There are things I want to do for Sadie. I want... I want..."

"To make more money."

"There's nothing wrong with that."

"I didn't say that there was. But I do think you've allowed it to become much too important, but if that's what you want I can help you with it. You say the word and you'll have your own office tomorrow. And you can bring Sadie or leave her where she's at. Either way you'll make more. I'll make sure you're sent the best and highest paying clients."

"I'm beginning to wonder about you, Shawn. Is your business legal?"

"Some think so, some think not."

Dominic laughed recognizing the tactic his brother was using on him. Shawn was worried about his son and trying to find a way to deal with it. That was understandable and something he was happy to oblige.

Chapter Fourteen

Fear skittered across Dominic's spine. What is there to fear? he asked himself as they made their way into the hospital elevator. His life was getting ready to change. He knew that as surely as he knew his name. Taking this step meant he'd never again be able to say with all certainty that he was Dominic Santiago. How would Roberto feel about him, his sisters and Poppi. Would his father feel he'd betrayed him? And this new family Shawn was taking him to meet, despite Shawn saying no one gave a damn about his ethnicity would he sense some underlying prejudices? He licked his lips taking in a breath and blowing it out.

"You're nervous, Dominic, you don't have to be," Shawn said again as though reading his mind." I would never bring you to a place where you wouldn't be welcome. You can trust me on that."

That was the strange thing, he did trust him. He had a history with this man he'd only met a couple of times in his life. There was a hollow feeling inside him, a longing, wishing he'd known him, that they'd not wasted so many years of being family. Then Poppi's face swam before him. *Damn*, he wished he'd talked this over with Sadie.

The door to the hospital room opened a moment before Shawn's hand reached for the handle. A woman of medium height with sad brown eyes and frizzy brown curly hair that looked as if she'd not combed it in a couple of days stood before them. For a moment she merely stared then her hand covered her mouth and she let out a sharp cry.

"Dominic," she stopped put her hands on her head and began trying to smooth the matted mess with her fingers before realizing what she was doing and looking at Shawn in awe.

"Let's do this inside the room." Shawn spoke softly to his wife ushering her back inside the room. Both men stepped inside and Dominic stood there not knowing what to do or say.

"My God! You have no idea what this means to my husband. He has wanted you to meet us for so many years now. It feels like I've known you forever. Thank you for coming. This means so much to all of us."

Dominic went to shake the woman's hand but she hugged him tightly instead, and she was crying. He wanted to push her away but didn't. When he felt Shawn tapping his wife's shoulder gently urging her to release him, he felt relief. He was at a loss. He looked at the bed at the boy lying so still and white under the sheet and he shivered. He glanced at Shawn and his wife wanting to ask what it was he was supposed to do. How was he going to deliver the miracle his brother was seeking?

"I don't know what it is you want from me," Dominic said quietly. He shrugged his shoulders, "Just tell me what you want and I'll do it." Shawn and his wife both smiled.

"You've already done it. Now come on and let me introduce you to your nephew."

Glancing around the room he saw a projector and images being flashed across the stark white hospital walls. He blinked in disbelief when mixed in with pictures of Shawn and his family images of him came on the screen, random shots of him and Sadie, him at the office, at court, him with his family with Poppi.

***

"Like I said, knowing you has been my mission, even though you didn't want to know me."

Dominic tilted his head feeling anger at Shawn's words, but now was not the time. He didn't like the way Shawn had so completely infiltrated his life. But that would have to wait. For a moment he felt detached as though this was happening to someone else and he was merely watching. The weight of his brother's hand was on his back guiding him toward the bed.

"Ryan, I brought your uncle Dominic to visit you."

The emotion in Shawn's voice as he talked to his son brought a lump to his throat. Dominic had never heard that kind of emotion from Berto when he talked to his kids. Of course none of Berto's children had ever been so close to death, thank God.

Dominic blinked several times taking the chair Shawn indicated. "Hello, Ryan. I'm sorry this is our first meeting. You're going to have to get well real soon so we can have a proper introduction. Your father once gave me a ride on the back of his motorcycle when I was your age. I don't own a motorcycle but I'm sure we can find something to do."

Then he lifted the boy's hand and held it. He continued talking until he began believing his words. He was praying that somehow God would intervene and save this nephew of his he'd not had a chance to know. He didn't know what he'd expected that somehow his presence would make the child open his eyes. That would have been nice if his presence could have made a difference, if he could give something back to Shawn for his years of love. Sudden emotion was overwhelming him. He had to get himself together. "I'm sorry." He glanced at Shawn who was staring at him.

"Dominick, I didn't expect for him to wake when you touched him. It's medically induced. Encephalitis. He has a brain infection with massive swelling."

"How long are they going to leave him like this?" Dominic asked.

"I'm not sure."

For once the smile left his brother's face and the worry of a father for his son replaced it, the same worry was in the eyes of his wife. She looked as though she wanted to cry but Shawn reached for her, held her tightly and whispered into her ear. When he pulled away he held her face in his hands, wiped away the lone tear and shook his head slowly. Then he kissed her eyes before chucking her under the chin.

Dominic's heart constricted at the obvious love between his brother and his wife. It made him miss Sadie and wonder if their future was really set. Lately it sure wasn't feeling like it.

"What caused the encephalitis?"

"Chicken pox," Shawn whispered. "Can you believe it? His case seemed so mild not more than a dozen eruptions. Freak, one in a million kind of thing. We're lucky his pediatrician caught it. We'd debated back and forth about whether we should get him the varicella vaccine. Don't know if it would have helped but now we'll never know. He was tired, complaining of a headache. Couldn't concentrate. But he's in so many activities, so damn busy of course he'd be tired. The low grade fever didn't even seem to be much but Katie made him an appointment.

"God, I'm glad she did. I hate to think what would have happened." Shawn's eyes sought his wife and for a moment he was silent. "His pediatrician wanted him in the hospital immediately."

The treatment seemed to be working. He was doing so well. We were all set to take him home when he had an unexpected setback. A seizure. That's when the doctor put him into…" Shawn was visibly trembling. "That's when they did this. That's when I knew I had to talk to you face to face. I couldn't let anything happen to my son without your having ever met him. You're my only brother, my only sibling. My son wanted so much to meet you. He's begged me so many times. He's even decided he wants to be a lawyer just like his uncle."

Dominic's gaze was locked on his brother. He couldn't help the tears that came to his eyes. With the back of his hand he wiped them away while turning from Shawn and Katie. He'd never before felt so helpless. Was Shawn snowing him? Were both of them? How in the world could a person a child had never met be an influence on his life?

Suddenly he thought of all the cards and letters his brother has sent him for most of his life. Shawn's love had been a big influence in his life even though he hadn't known it. He'd felt worthy because of the things Shawn had done, part of a family, not as though he was just some lost kid Poppi had taken in. If it weren't for those mementos Dominic would have definitely doubted Roberto's love. He would have thought he was just a pesky younger brother. Roberto had never had much time for him so Dominic had held on fiercely to the cards. He glanced again at the child on the bed. If his father had filled his head with nonsense then yes, it would be possible that the child wanted an uncle in his life.

Cringing inwardly Dominic wondered if he was up to the challenge. Would he now defy his Poppi, the man who'd raised him in order to embrace this other family into his life? He truly didn't know.

Luckily his cell rang halting his thoughts but it startled him as well as Shawn and his wife. Dominic had the distinct impression they'd almost forgotten he was in the room.

It was Sadie. His battered heart was yearning for her. He wanted her there with him, but he didn't want to talk to her. He didn't know what to say, how to tell her where he was. He couldn't allow the thing to continue ringing so he answered smiling as Katie laughed about something Shawn was whispering in her ear.

"Where are you, Dom?"

"I'll talk to you later," he answered not avoiding Sadie's question just not answering it. He closed the cell knowing she would call again. "Later," he said answering the phone for the second time and clicking it off. When the phone rang again he shut it off and shrugged at the look Shawn and Katie were giving him.

"When I went to the downtown office Paul was giving Sadie a shoulder massage. She told me it felt good."

"So you're punishing her?"

"I just don't want to talk to her right now."

"But on the other hand you wish she were here." Shawn glanced at his wife and laughed.

"Enough of this. Are you psychic or what?"

"Maybe a bit, little brother but I know that's how I would be feeling if I were angry with my wife. I know how much you love Sadie. Tell me, Dominic, is that the reason you bought the mattress, so Sadie wouldn't have a reason to need a massage from another man?"

Dominic smiled hating that he was that obvious. Suddenly something akin to stark terror crawled over his entire body. Perspiration covered him a moment before he heard the strong male voice. He knew who it was. His body tensed waiting for the door to open. He could feel the slight trembling in his legs.

"How is Ryan?" the man's voice said. Then everyone in the room quieted. It was as though some magic force had waved a hand over the inhabitants. Dominic turned to face the voice, his father, at least his biological father. He wasn't breaking his promise to Poppi, he thought.

He couldn't help it. Dominic's mouth opened slightly when he gazed upon his father. It was as though he were looking in a mirror in the future. The same green eyes that had caused Dominick a lifetime of ridicule from his family. The same hair. The shape of his face, his mouth. God, if only he could stop his heart from racing, his body from trembling. There was no denying the man standing before him was his father. Shawn looked somewhat like him, but Dominic was the spitting image of this man whom he blamed for the way Poppi felt about him. It seemed they were staring at each other forever. Like a little kid he wanted to run and hide but he wasn't a punk. He would not run. He'd stand his ground. Shawn moved closer to him and slid his arm around his shoulder. Whether to hold him there or comfort him he wasn't sure. But he didn't push his brother's arm away.

"Dominic," his father said, softly. "Dominic." His eyes welled with tears and he took a step toward Dominic at the same instant Dominic took a step back. The older woman behind his father, probably his wife, laid her hand on his back. Looks passed between all of them excluding Dominic. Some secret code he assumed, some signal not to push, probably coached by Shawn. For a moment he wondered if this whole thing were a set up then a backward glance at the child in the bed and shame flooded him. Of course it wasn't. He should have expected that the child's grandfather, his father would put in an appearance.

A slight nod of his head to the couple and Dominic turned his attention elsewhere. He felt as though he didn't belong in this room with these strangers that claimed to be his blood that his own eyes told him he belonged to. *What about Poppi? What about his promise?*

The air around him became strained, the conversation forced. He wondered how long he'd have to stay before it wouldn't be considered rude to leave. Everyone's eyes were on

him there were questions on each of their faces, questions
Dominic didn't have the answers to. He stayed by the bed
dropping back into the chair and focusing on the unconscious
child. Ryan was the only one who seemed to not be aware of
Dominic, who wasn't expecting something from him that he
didn't even know and most likely couldn't give.

"Did you bring him?" Shawn asked.

"Yes, Mom has him in her bag. Shawn moved a chair in
front of the door and his wife sat on the chair. Now they had
Dominick curious as to what they were up to. For a moment he
wondered if they were staging an intervention trying to make
him remain in the room. He almost laughed at the
ridiculousness of that thought and decided to wait.

When Shawn's mother brought out a tiny dog from her
bag that couldn't have weighed more than a couple of pounds
he laughed and knew immediately they were sneaking the dog
into the room for the child. He stood and moved away as his
father carried the puppy to the bed. They all watched as the
puppy licked Ryan's face then circled around his body as
though trying to figure out what the heck was going on. He
gave a half bark and Shawn bent down and looked him in the
eye and told the animal if he made noise he would have to
leave. Dominic couldn't believe it. It was as though an
understanding had been forged between the two. A small
whimper then the dog once again licked the child's face and
curled up next to his body his eyes luminous as he looked
around the room.

"Is that Ryan's dog?" Dominic asked. His father turned
his head slowly and held his gaze before he spoke.

"No, it's his grandmother's. Ryan has a chocolate lab, a
little too big to hide. But he loves this one every bit as much as
he loves his own."

Shawn was eyeing him and for the first time since this
trip through the looking glass had begun his brother was
looking nervous. *What the hell does he want now?* Dominick
wondered as he took him by the arm and ushered him out the
door.

"Are you doing okay with all of this?" Shawn asked
with genuine concern.

"Spit it out, Shawn. What is it that you want?"

"There are a couple members of the family who would give their life to see you. Are you up for it?"

"Just a couple?" His brother was grinning.

"Yeah just a couple," Shawn replied and grinned even broader.

They both knew he'd told a lie. Less than an hour later the room and hallway filled with family, grandparents, uncles, aunts and cousin. He should have been shocked that he was friends with several of his cousins and had been for several years. He didn't think there was one person he was introduced to that he couldn't remember meeting at least once or twice.

The Donavan clan it seemed didn't know the meaning of a simple handshake; they all grabbed him up in a hug, pounding him on the shoulders, everyone trying to talk at once. He wondered how they could be allowed so many visitors and glanced at Shawn who pointed to his father. *That's right*, he'd forgotten his father was a doctor and had more than likely used his connections. And he had no doubt that if his father's connections hadn't worked Shawn would have made it happen. It was surprising that after knowing his brother for such a short time he believed he could do anything he set his mind to.

Dominic stayed for hours visiting Ryan because he had no idea how to leave. It was only when Shawn came to him and told him he needed to go home, that Sadie was probably worried sick about him that he knew it was time to go. Cringing when he glanced at his watch he worried he'd not make it home before Sadie left to take the train to work. If he wasn't so damn tired he'd drive her. Now the only thing left to do was figure out how to actually leave the room. Shawn laughed at him shaking his head making Dominic again question how he knew what he was thinking.

"Dominic needs to get home to Sadie. I'm going to walk him to the elevator."

If Dominic had thought he could leave the room without his relatives hugging him he was crazy, without Katie hugging him, totally wasn't going to happen. "Please come back," Katie pleaded.

"Katie," was the one word Shawn uttered and she backed away. Shawn's mother was looking down and his father was looking as though he wanted to sob. He was hurting to hold this son he hadn't held in years. It was written on his face. All of their emotions were taking a toll. He wanted to leave. Now.

Shawn surprised him when the elevator door opened and instead of turning to leave he got in with him.

"I'm going to go with you to your car."

"Shawn, I'm thirty-three. I'm not a little kid."

For a long moment they both laughed then Shawn turned serious. "Are you okay?"

"Yes."

"When Dad came in the room I didn't know what you were going to do. You looked as if you wanted to run, just disappear from view. I think you were a bit freaked to see how much you resemble him, weren't you?"

"That's an understatement. Now I know why the family made so many jokes about me, my birth, always asking who my real father was, saying, I wasn't Latino. And always Poppi would become furious cursing them until they said they were kidding." And always he'd ..." Hate me a little bit more, Dominic thought but didn't say.

"You should have never had to go through that."

"They were family. They were kidding." Sometimes they were sometimes they weren't. But he sure as hell didn't want Shawn feeling any sorrier for him than he already did. The look in his brother's eyes said he wanted to murder any and every one who'd ever hurt him. That made him smile. At last he had the kind of big brother he'd prayed for as a kid, the one who'd beat up the bullies for him. Only his wish had been granted many years after he'd become quite efficient at dispensing bullies himself.

"Shawn...I... I hope Ryan makes a full recovery."

"You're sounding like this is the last time you plan to see me or Ryan. Is it?"

Dominic sighed and worried his lips with the tip of his tongue knowing that a relationship with his brother would definitely mean coming into contact with his bio. He thought the situation over and knew in his heart he had no plans to go back to not knowing his brother existed. He wanted to get to know him and his family. As for his father…that would be left for another time.

"Dominic?"

"Don't worry. I like having a big brother who more than likely I'll have to go to court and defend someday." He laughed, "Besides, I did promise Ryan that we're going to get to know each other."

"What about Dad?"

"A brother, a nephew, a sister in-law and a ton of relatives are about all that I can handle right now. Will you be okay with that?"

Accepting another hug from his brother he finally was allowed to get in his car and drive away. He'd have to get used to all of the hugging. He couldn't remember ever having hugged Roberto. Laughing to himself he knew that part would be easy. He found to his amazement he rather liked it.

***

Fear had given way to panic many hours ago until common sense told her nothing was wrong with Dominic. For the first hour Sadie had been worried when he'd hung up on her then she fast forwarded into angry. Now she was worried again. She'd waited until after midnight before putting away the food. She'd waited until two A.M. to take a shower for fear he would call her and the water from the shower would drown out his call. Now it was morning, she'd showered again gotten dressed, put on her makeup and was having coffee when she finally heard the door open and Dominic come in.

Suddenly she forgot about being angry. She was just relieved. "Dominic, are you all right? Where have you been all night? I was worried sick about you. You hung up on me and then turned off your phone." The moment she said the words, anger returned. "I can't believe you did that." He wasn't answering. "Dom, baby what's wrong?" She rushed up to him and began touching him. "Tell me what's wrong. Are you hurt?"

"Here," he said and handed her a bag. You won't have to have Paul touching you anymore. I got you plenty of batteries to go with it."

"Dom?"

"We have a new mattress coming next week. You should sleep better."

"Is that all you have to say?"

"What more do you want me to say?"

"I want you to tell me where you were."

"Like you told me where you were going when you snuck off with Paul?"

"I was doing my job and you know that." Sadie stared at Dominic holding his gaze. "Tell me what you need from me baby and I'll do it." She could feel the trembling in Dominic's limbs but it was the look in his eyes that frightened her. "Dom, baby, tell me what's wrong." He shook his head and headed for the shower. "Dom, talk to me."

"Don't forget to take the massager with you when you leave. I don't want to ever find you with another man."

Did that just happen? Did Dom just spend the night out, refuse to talk to her and now was practically accusing her of cheating on him? Guilt tightened her throat. She'd done a lot of betraying of Dom lately. She'd confessed to having him sent away from the main office, but the guilt over Paul's kiss, that one she'd have to live with. She'd take that knowledge to her grave and if Paul dared to tell Dominic the truth, she'd call him a liar and hold him while Dom beat the hell out of him. The thought of that made Sadie smile. Let's see Paul call Dom little bitty while he was getting his behind kicked.

The sound of the shower brought Sadie back to reality. Something was wrong with her man. She had to find out what. She reached for her cell to call the office and leave a message that she had a family emergency and would not be in. At least that much wasn't a lie. Dom was her family and she was definitely not going to work with him in whatever mood he was in. He needed her and she needed to be there for him.

Making her way back up the stairs stripping off her clothes as she walked, Sadie opened the shower door and found Dominic standing under the water, not washing, just standing and not in the way to show he was enjoying the water but more in a trance sort of way. Peeling the remainder of her clothes from her body her decision was made. She knew what he needed. Her. Sliding in she stood under the water and waited.

Without opening his eyes his arms came out and pulled her hard against him.

"Sadie, baby my life just changed and I don't think it's for the good."

Then he held her so tightly that it hurt. And she held him just as tightly wondering what was wrong. Had Dom met someone? Had he cheated on her? What could have changed his life so completely, what could have made him stay out all night? And what could be making him behave so strangely right now. But he was trembling, hurting. She'd never seen him like this.

"Dominic, I swear there's nothing going on with me and Paul. I promise you, I'll never let him touch me again, no matter what. Talk to me baby."

"This isn't about you and Paul." He sniffed her hair and held her even tighter. "Sadie, I think this is bigger than even my love for you."

Dominic was scaring her now. Something that meant more than his love for her? A shudder rippled over her and she remembered Christmas and the partnership and the reason they were now living in a rented house in Woodridge. She'd gotten the first hint that there might be some things that were bigger for Dom than his love for her. For Sadie nothing was as important as Dominic, not the promotion, not the house, not the cases, the money, nothing. Another shiver claimed her. Not even the promise she'd made to herself more than a decade ago to never shack with a man, to not allow a man to become so important to her that she forgot herself in the process. All of that had been pushed to the background when she'd fallen in love with him. She'd become someone she didn't very much like and she'd betrayed her man.

But she'd done it all because she loved him, because she wanted him to marry her. She was fighting to save them, not to replace him. Nothing was more important to her than Dom and though she knew whatever it was that was plaguing him it still hurt that something was more important to him than she was. Couldn't he have said almost as important as she was? She would have expressed it that way.

His grip loosened as he gently pushed her away. "I hurt your feelings didn't I? I wasn't trying to. Not deliberately anyway."

That was a lie. He'd known exactly what he was saying. He was hurting and he wanted Sadie to hurt also, to hurt for him, with him. He gazed at the hurt in her eyes thinking of his brother's words to him, *only he could stop Sadie's from loving him.* He didn't want that ever. He was still punishing her.

"I just lied to you, Sadie. Nothing is as important to me as you are. I'm still pissed that you'd allow Paul to touch you no matter what the reason. I saw the look on your face, that dreamy look you get when I touch you. I thought that look was just for me. Now I know that any man can bring it out in you."

Sadie gasped. "I could swear I thought you were going to apologize."

Dominic's lips curled up a bit at the corners. "That had been my intention. But you make me crazy, and then to top it off the last few hours of my life have been so unbelievable. I don't even have the words to tell you."

"Try telling me where you were."

"At the hospital."

"The hospital, but you said you're okay."

"Not me, my nephew."

"Which one, Dominic? Stop being so vague."

"I have a nephew I'd never met until tonight. He's in a coma and he might die. I have a brother, another brother. You know all the letters and cards I thought Roberto had sent to me through the years. Well they didn't come from him. They came from Shawn, my other brother."

Dominic's voice was so low that Sadie had to strain to hear him.

"I met my father tonight, Sadie. I look just like him. My parents have told me so many lies. I have to talk to them and I have to get a few hours sleep and go back to the hospital to be with my brother. And I have to worry about you and how far you'll go with Paul today. Will you allow him to kiss you, to caress you? Will you have dinner with him? Sadie, my life is falling apart and I have to worry if the one person that I gave my heart to is getting ready to find herself someone else."

"Dom."

"My brother offered to have Paul taken care of."

"Taken care of? What does that mean?"

Dominic gave her a puzzled look as she squinted. "What? What's wrong?"

"You didn't respond to my saying what I did about you and Paul. Is that because it's happened already? Have you kissed him? Have you been with him, Sadie?"

"I'm going to ignore your dirty mind and I'm going to ignore the fact that you believe you have a reason to hurt me. You're not the first person to have his life shattered by finding out things they didn't want to know. Dom, you've known since you were ten that Poppi wasn't your biological father."

"He's been the only father I've ever known."

"And in spite of my issues with him, I believe he loves you. But he's put some crazy ideas into your head. Besides, I'm glad you made a connection with your biological father. We're going to have babies, what if there's medical information that we need to know for our children? Take this thing with your nephew for instant, what if it's a family thing? We need to know this."

"You're always so reasonable, Sadie. I tell you my life has just gone to hell and you tell me it's a good thing. On the one hand I want to kiss you and make love to you until this ache in my heart goes away. But there's a part of me that's still angry with you and want to crawl inside your mind to know what you're thinking, inside your heart to see if I'm still there. I think this new brother of mine is some kind of spy or CIA, something. Anyway he's a man with connections and he's extremely good at spying on me. I want to ask him to spy on you, Sadie, to tell me if you're cheating on me."

"If you need someone else to tell you that then we're really in trouble. I never in a million years would have thought the two of us would be here. That you would be jealous and distrustful of me, thinking I'd cheat on you, shutting me out. Dominic, eight months ago we were happy. What happened? And for God sakes make it good. It's getting damn hard for me to think you still love me."

"I'll agree with you on that issue. We're in trouble but not for the reason you think. I'm in trouble, Sadie. I no longer know who I am. I have no real identity. How can I expect you to love a man with no identity?"

That did it. Despite the hurtful words he was using she had to hold him. He was hurting for a variety of reason. Him doubting her love would be one worry she could take from him.

"Baby, please let me help you. Whatever is going on I'm here for you. I love you. I always have and always will. That's never going to change. I promise you that."

"Don't make that promise, Sadie. You have no idea what's going to happen to us in the future"

"Do you still love me?"

"Always."

He laughed slightly and held her tight. "Sadie, I wish I could explain how I'm feeling, but it's so damn hard because I don't truly know. What's going to happen to my family, to us? Should I keep pretending that I'm truly Poppi's son? Will he stop loving me now, being proud of me? Will he disown me?"

"Do you want to have a relationship with…with…you know…your other brother, your biological father?"

"My brother for sure. He's been there for me for so many years now. I'd like you to meet him, but not yet. I want to keep him to myself for a while longer and—"

"And you don't want the family angry at me for betraying them."

"I have a feeling things are going to get very ugly."

"You're thirty-three, surely your father will understand. I think you're worrying for nothing."

"I wish that were true. He never wanted me to tell you. Even after I did he still gives me looks like he thinks I'm going to betray him."

"That's foolish."

"It's about a lot of things, his sense of identity, his sense of betrayal and like it or not my mom betrayed him. He's had to endure all the jokes made about my looks, the men in the family asking if his wife slept with the milkman. His manhood is at stake here. He doesn't want anyone to know what happened. They've kept it hidden all my life. He's not going to like my blowing the lid off."

"Why would you have to blow the lid off?"

"Because of who and what I am. You know me. It's either all the way or no way at all. If, and it's a big if. If I allow them, the other part of who I am into my life, I'm not going to keep them hidden. I'm going to want to invite them for dinner, to spend holidays with them. I'm going to want a connection and the secret will be out, Sadie. This isn't something you can fix and it isn't an easy decision. I have to give this a lot of thought. My life is going to change." He saw the look of hurt on her face and amended his words. "If my life changes so will yours, so will ours. We have to be sure."

"Can I meet them before you go full steam ahead?"

"Why?"

"Like you said, it's our lives that's going to be affected. Shouldn't I get to know them, to see," she shrugged her shoulders holding his steady gaze. "I want to see if what we're giving up will be worth it."

"You want to decide if my family is worth it?"

"Why are you constantly trying to turn every word I say into a fight? You know what I meant. You said you didn't know if you wanted them in your life. This decision is bigger than you are, Dominic."

If he didn't stop glaring at her Sadie didn't know if she could take it. Her heart was hurting. She felt tremendous fear in the pit of her gut, gnawing away at her."

"Listen, until a few hours ago these people..." She heard the low growl in his throat and paused. Her intent was not to anger Dominic. "I'm sorry for saying that, but still you didn't know these people…your family existed. Now after being with them for a few hours you're treating me as though I don't matter. You're willing to part with the only family you've ever known and for what?"

"To belong, Sadie."

His eyes were so sad, brimming with tears that Sadie was aware he'd refuse to shed. "Baby, what are you talking about? You belong. You belong to your family and you belong to me. What has you thinking you don't belong?"

Without meaning too Sadie's mind traveled back through the last few months of their lives when the rift first appeared. Surely dear God it couldn't be.

She couldn't help it. She pulled away from Dominic to get a better look at him. "Tell me something, Dom,' she asked, "Before I was given the partnership, did you feel you belonged?" She watched the differing emotions play over his face for a moment. She thought he'd answer then his eyes turned cold and he mentally shoved her away by taking the bar of soap and lathering his chest.

The pain of his silence sliced through Sadie. Something this petty was derailing their life. Sure she'd contributed, but she hadn't been the one to set the ball in motion. It was obvious that if one of them didn't do something in the next few moments they may as well call it quits. She sighed heavily taking in one rapid breath after another. She didn't know if she still possessed the knowing of what would comfort her man. It appeared she hadn't known for months. That she didn't place on her doorstep. But she loved him and if he wasn't going to try and save them then it was up to her to try.

"Dom, if we don't stop right this moment there's a chance we might forever damage our relationship."

"I thought you'd love me forever, that you'd always have my back. But you're right, that was eight months ago when I took care of you, not the other way around."

"You never took care of me." Sadie paused to allow her words to register. "We took care of each other. We both contributed."

"But I didn't want or need you too."

"I'm a grown woman. I don't want or need a man to take care of me."

"I guess not, especially since you're the one with the big cohoonies. You make the money now."

"You're being stupid."

"Eight months ago you wouldn't have called me that."

"Eight months ago you weren't stupid. God, I can't believe getting that dammed promotion has done all of this. I'm trying hard to not believe you're this spiteful, jealous, little man you're appearing to be at the moment, that you're really not that big of a....sanga... Oh hell forget that. You're behaving like a jackass, plain and simple."

They were spiraling out of control and Sadie wanted desperately to save them. She wasn't having much luck. Her heart was fighting with her mounting anger. She knew her man was hurting and trying his best to push her away. She didn't want that to happen because she feared if he succeeded she'd stop loving him.

"Dominic, stop," she yelled at the top of her lungs. "Listen, I know you're hurting. But I'm not the enemy. Stop pushing me away. All I'm trying to do is help. I want to save us. I could use a bit of help please."

"Your only concern is that ring you're wearing. You want to make sure you can continue telling your friends you're engaged, you're getting married. You want everyone to know you're not one of the women who shack and never got the prize."

Sadie licked her lips taking time to think. "Are you saying I don't love you?"

"I'm saying you love that damn ring more."

"Dom, I have to tell you, you're not helping us."

"Good. I have had it with you trying to control your temper for the last few months. I'm tired of you treating me as though I have a mental condition, or I'm some freaking little boy. You're not my mother, Sadie, you're my woman. But lately I have been unable to tell the difference."

"Wow!"

"Wow? Is that all you have to say? Where the hell is your famous fire? Fight with me, Sadie. Give me that much respect."

"You're hurting. I don't want to fight with you. I want to make things better for you."

"Fuck that and fuck you." Then he did the one thing that was sure to push Sadie past the breaking point he yelled at her in rapid fire Spanish knowing she wouldn't be able to understand one word.

"Fuck me, Dominic? Fuck me? Fuck you!" Sadie was angry and hurt but not so angry that she didn't know what the next words out of her mouth would do.

"Maybe Paul really is the bigger man and not just figuratively. He wanted that partnership as much as you. But he hasn't treated me the way you have. Believe it or not he's happy for me." With her chin jutted out she stared at him. They were having a glaring contest.

"So you're going for the jugular are you now, Sadie?" Well then, let's do this. Eight months ago I didn't have to worry about you allowing Paul such liberties with your body."

"Liberties," she fumed. "Perhaps I allowed him liberties because eight months ago I didn't have to nearly beg you to make love to me half the time because you were being such a little boy about my being made partner that you didn't want to touch me."

Dominic turned in order to stand directly in front of Sadie. "Eight months ago I didn't have to worry that the knife that would be planted in the middle of my back would come from you. I didn't have to wonder if you were just like my mom, that one day you'd betray me the same as she betrayed Poppi."

Tears, Sadie wondered. Did she use tears on Dom? "Please stop. You're killing me, Dom. You're killing us. Eight months ago you wouldn't have handled this problem like this."

"How would you know? Until a few months ago you didn't know I wasn't Poppi's son. You badgered me until I broke my promise to my father not to tell."

"Badgered?" Sadie hissed from between clenched teeth.

"Yes, you badgered me to propose and I told you because of that."

The world suddenly became silent. Sadie stared at Dominic, no longer able to stop the tears that were flowing freely down her cheeks. Her body bent in half and she groaned. She felt as thought she'd been punched in the stomach. How could the two of them who were so much in love, who were always so hot for each other be naked in a shower and fighting, saying the most vile things instead of making love.

"I'm sorry I badgered you, Dominic. Consider yourself unbadgered."

She glanced down at her beloved ring, a symbol of her man's love and saw nothing but a symbol of his resentment, of his faulting her for whatever demons were chasing him. She pulled the ring slowly from her finger dying inside as she held his gaze. Then she slipped it into the palm of his hand. And he took it. That was what hurt the most.

With him staring after her she left the shower, grabbed a towel hurriedly dried, dressed, and left the house. There would be tears but these tears she didn't want Dominic to see.

***

Opening his hand Dominic stared at Sadie's ring. He'd intentionally stayed in the shower until he heard her drive away. What had he done? "Sadie, come back," he whispered knowing she couldn't hear him. What the hell had happened to his perfect life?

Chapter Fifteen

For over an hour Sadie had been crying in her father's arms. She'd barely lifted her head to swipe at the ever flowing tears choosing instead to wipe her face on her father's shirt. Her father was tugging on her hair trying to get her to sit up, to talk. She didn't want to talk. She wanted to cry. She wanted to remember that Dominic had said fuck her. How could he have been so cruel, so crude? Finally like a little child she succumbed to her father's pleas to stop crying.

"Daddy, please help me make some sense out of what's going on. Dominic is behaving so strangely. I still love him like crazy. I really do but lately I've been having dreams of a life without him and I was happy in those dreams. I don't want to be happy without him but I know I can survive without him."

"But can he survive without you, Sadie?"

"He said 'F' me."

"And what did you say?"

"I said it back. What? Did you think he'd get away with talking like that to me and I'd take it? In all the years we've been together he's never, not once spoken to me in the manner he did today. It's not my fault he's adopted. It's not my fault that Poppi is such a rotten father. And it's not my fault that I got the partnership he wanted. He's a jackass. Why can't he behave the same way Paul is doing?"

"I think you've left something out of the story, Sadie. Did you throw Paul up in that boy's face?"

Sadie refused to answer until her father looked at her in that certain way he had then she was spilling her guts. "He was being nasty."

"You hit below the belt. A woman should never throw another man in her man's face in the midst of an argument." her father scolded.

"And he shouldn't have cursed at me?'

"Sadie, what am I going to do with you? You have always wanted to win, taking no prisoners, not giving an inch. Until Dominic your mother and I never thought you'd fall in love?"

"What about Jason?"

"That boy didn't mean a thing to you and you meant even less to him."

"I was going to move in with him."

"You were talking that mess to show me you were grown. Like I said, neither of you cared about the other."

"You're just saying that because you like Dominic."

"Yes, I like him. But I like him because he loves you. You're good together. I know you've been going through some rough times but I still think you were wrong to talk to him about Paul, baby."

"Daddy, are you telling me that I should just continue putting up with his craziness?"

"Answer me this, Sadie. Do you know in your heart that you're the most important person to him, that he loves you?"

"I know he loves me. But, I don't think I'm as important to him as I thought. In the past months I've seen sides to Dominic's personality that I don't like."

"So he's not perfect?"

"No, he's not. In fact, I'm beginning to think he's totally imperfect."

Her father laughed. "Welcome to the real world baby. It's going to take a lot more than being hot for a person to make a life together."

"Daddy!"

"What? It is. There is no such thing as a perfect, life or a perfect relationship. You'd better get used to that. Dominic has flaws. You have flaws."

"But you'd think being adopted was a major catastrophe. Millions of people are adopted. Technically he wasn't even adopted. His mother just inserted Poppi's name on the birth certificate and they didn't bother to mention it to him."

"And you don't think knowing that has created pain for that boy for most of his life?" He's dealing with some heavy life issues here baby. I'm a man and I have some idea, but I'm afraid you don't. I think we may have shielded you a bit too much. Finding out you're adopted is hard. People handle it differently. I'm willing to wager there's more going on with Dominic. Someone needs to be in that boy's corner, not throwing up another man in his face when he's the weakest."

"But, Daddy."

"Sorry baby. You can't but Daddy me on this one. I think you were wrong. Being adopted is no joke."

Her father was so disappointed in her that it made her wonder. Sure he loved Dominic. Sure they'd always gotten along. But how the heck did he know so much about how Dom would feel about being adopted or not raised by his biological father? She stopped, looked at her parents and asked. "Was I adopted?"

"Would it matter?" her mother smiled. "You just said it wasn't a big deal, not a life changing event, so would it matter? Your father and I couldn't love you anymore than if you were born to us."

Sadie's face fell. "I am adopted." Tears quickly filled her eyes and her father reached for her holding her in his strong arms.

"Sadie, your mom was teasing. She wanted you to get a taste of your own medicine. Being adopted isn't a big deal for you because you're not. You're not Dominic. You can't tell him how to feel. I'm sure he'd like for it not to matter, but the heart sometimes behave in a way all of its own. Sure he's not perfect but baby as much as you don't like me to repeat myself and as much as I love you, neither are you. Look at the things you've done to Dominic in the last few months. He broke a promise to his father and told you a secret that has torn him apart for more than two thirds of his life. His siblings aren't even aware of it. But he loved you enough to share it with you. You betrayed him by telling us."

He shushed her when she would have balked. "Admit it baby, you did. And you had him transferred out of the office. I can only imagine the blow that was to his pride. Sadie,

Dominic is hurting, trying to find his way through this. It's uncharted territory for him. He's not going to behave as he wants or as you think he should. No one knows what's going to happen. And we all know that you've used Paul through the years to make him jealous. Right now the man is probably so close to being broken that using Paul is definitely not a good idea."

Sadie groaned as though she were a two year old about to throw a tantrum. "But I didn't use Paul this last time. He just gave me a shoulder massage, that's all. Would you act so crazy if you came in and a man was giving Mom an innocent massage?"

"Hell yes."

"Are you serious?"

"Of course I'm serious. And a man that tells me every chance he gets that he wants my wife and is working to take her from me, you're damn straight I'd be angry and jealous and territorial and macho. And I'd probably deck the guy." H stopped, tilted his head and stared at Sadie. "Are you beginning to have feelings for Paul? Has something happened with him?"

Sadie didn't answer. She'd never lied to her parents about important things. But there was no way she was going to tell them she'd allowed Paul to kiss her or that she'd not only wanted it but had enjoyed it.

"Sadie, are you…?"

"There are a lot of things about Paul that I like. He's happy for me that I made partner. He makes me laugh. I'm not tense around him. His ego isn't so fragile."

"Sadie, you're treading on dangerous ground."

Her father's voice was sad. He was definitely disappointed in her. His opinion meant the world to her. She'd done most of the things in her life after asking herself what would her father think. She'd not lived with Jason, a man she'd thought she was madly in love with because of her father's disappointment. Yet, she'd loved Dominic enough to live with him but the knowledge she was disappointing her father was always in the back of her mind. Perhaps there was something to what Dominic had said about her wanting to be married. But mostly she wanted to be married to Dominic because she loved him. With a start she realized she'd done the same thing she'd accused him of doing. He was tied to his father wanting his approval and she definitely wanted the approval of her father. She swallowed bowing her head low unable to look into her father's eyes.

"I know I am. It's just…this should be the happiest time of my life. Making partner Dom and I should be celebrating every day. But he's made me feel guilty about making partner. Paul just told me straight out that he'd have liked it much better if the partnership had gone to him, but he's happy for me. He laughed that neither he nor Dom thought of a third person being in the running. He really is amused and thinks they both got what they deserved." Sadie swallowed. "He didn't tell me I'd gotten the partnership because I was a token."

"Is that what Dominic told you?"

"Yes." Sadie stared at her father.

Her father laughed a bit. "Is that really the reason you stabbed him in the back, to get even with him for that remark?"

"Daddy!"

"I'm just asking. You are a fighter and sometimes you fight dirty. You like winning and I'm wondering if somewhere in your mind you weren't trying to get even with Dominic. I mean the very thing that he's been worried about, that you'd eventually leave him for Paul. Then he comes in and find Paul giving you a massage. Sadie, his life is falling apart. Don't you think he deserve some slack?"

Sadie glanced toward her mother. "I came here to talk hoping you'd make me feel better."

Her mother laughed. "You came hoping we'd tell you you were right, but you said you needed a man's opinion. You wanted to know how a man would be feeling about all of this. Your father told you and you don't like what he had to say. But it's your life. You have to make your own decisions."

With a sigh of frustration, Sadie gazed at one parent then the other. "Promise me you're not going to ever tell Dominic that I told you his secret." As she'd known he would do her father was frowning in disapproval.

"Too many secrets can definitely kill a relationship. Look what it's doing to Dominic," her father said not bothering to hide his disgust with secrets.

"Daddy, please, Dom can't know I told you"

"And we won't tell." Her mother held her father's gaze until he shrugged his shoulders in acquiescence. "But Sadie you shouldn't share Dominic's secret with anyone else. It's his business to tell people, not yours. And maybe if you had listened when I told you to tell him that you were working a discrimination case with Paul this wouldn't have happened. All of this isn't your fault of course. But some of it is."

Parents, at least hers, always gave it to her straight, no coddling to heal her bruised sprit. Then again that was why she trusted them so much. They told her the truth. As usual they were right. She had to go home and attempt to make things right with Dominic.

Her parents were right about another thing: She was a fighter. When she'd left her home she'd been so distraught that she'd not wanted her parents to see her in that condition. She'd driven to the local mall after leaving the house, parked at the farthest corner where it was empty, locked her doors and bawled her eyes out. When she thought she was all cried out she figured it was time to talk things over with her parents.

Now after taking to them there were questions that only she could answer. What had giving Dom the ring back meant? Were they done? Had she stopped loving him?

No, to both questions. In that case she needed to return home and once again attempt to get to the bottom of things. Her body ached, her chest was tight, unbearably so. What would her life be without Dom? She didn't want to know. But she did want to know one other thing or she'd go crazy wondering.

"Daddy, next week the three of us are going to go and have a DNA taken. I want to make sure I belong to you." They were laughing at her as she left. Why not? She'd berated Dominic for caring and look what she wanted. She'd have to try and be a little more understanding of her man.

***

What in the world was he doing he wondered. Sure the thought had come to him to push Sadie away, to get her someplace safe while the mess that was his life unraveled. As hard as she might want to, as hard as she might try there was no way for Sadie to ever understand what was happening to him, no way for her to understand his father and his feelings after his mother betrayed him. *It wasn't that easy,* Dominic thought. Look what he'd done merely because Sadie had allowed Paul to massage her back. The demons that plagued him, he'd made them Sadie's. He hated himself for that.

Looking through the drawer of his bureau Dominic chose black satin pajama to go over the black silk boxers. Both items Sadie had chosen for him. Both things he wore only for her. He closed his eyes tightly wishing Sadie were home, wishing he hadn't hurt her, wishing he could tell her he was sorry, that he loved her, wishing he could make love to her. He took in a breath and her scent hit him. She'd returned. Opening his eyes he stared at her for a very long moment.

"Baby, I'm sorry," he whispered walking toward her opening his arms wide. Sadie ran into his arms with such force that the forward movement pushed them backwards toward the bed he held her cradling her body tightly.

"Sadie. I've hated my biological father since I was ten. I've hated knowing that I wasn't really Poppi's. I've worked so damn hard to make him proud of me."

"He's proud of you baby."

"I'm not so sure of that. I've been presented with new facts. Naturally I will have to investigate but if—and I expect they will be proven true—then this is only the beginning. But I want to discuss something far more important. You. As for my loving you. If I didn't love you so much, Sadie, I never would have told you what I'd sworn to never mention. Don't you understand that? You are my life and today I had crazy thoughts about letting you go, pushing you away from me. But I need you. I need you in order to get through this. But I don't know how this is going to go down, baby. I'm having emotions I've never experienced."

"I can understand this is hard for you. But why didn't it bother you before the partnership?"

"Yes, eight months ago it all came to a head. But I've been heading toward this path for over twenty years. I've been afraid of this moment, but I knew it was coming."

"Just don't make me the enemy, okay. I'll do whatever you want. I'm not trying to fix things for you, Dom, just support you. If you don't want me to meet your new family, okay. I won't ask any more. But you're so close to all of this. Your nerves are raw. I was just thinking I'd see things more clearly. We've always worked together, that's all, Dom."

"What made you come back?" Dominic asked as he slowly began removing Sadie's blouse.

"I couldn't leave us like this."

"You were gone for quite a while. Where did you go?" he asked dropping a kiss in the hollow of her shoulder.

"To the mall."

"What did you do there?"

"Sat in my car."

"And?"

"And...."

"And what?"

Tears filled her eyes. "I sat in my car and bawled like a baby. I cursed you a lot," she laughed. "Then I decided to go and talk to my parents after that. After they bawled me out for letting Paul massage my shoulders I decided to ignore my broken heart and come home and try to mend yours.

"They didn't think I was overreacting?"

"Not my dad. Of course I didn't tell him that you'd bought a new mattress," she grinned. "I did tell them about the portable massager." When Dom smiled so did she. There was no way she was going to tell him about her parents knowing he wasn't Poppi's blood.

"I love you, Dominic. Forgive me for all the malicious things I said."

"You had a right to say them. I was being nasty to you. Please forgive me for cursing at you." He sighed. "Do you want your ring back?"

"Part of me does. But a large part of me doesn't. I don't think I can put it back on right now."

"Did I taint it for you?"

"Our fighting did."

"You love that ring."

"But I love you more. I think maybe we should forget about being engaged for now and try to find our way back to us." He was looking at her strangely. "Don't imagine crazy things, Dom."

"I want you to wear the ring."

"Not this moment, maybe later after...weren't we about to make love? I think we got sidetracked by talking."

Opening her mouth Sadie slid her tongue into Dominic's and moaned deep in her throat as his tongue claimed hers and his arms locked around her body. In under a minute they were both undressed and facing each other caressing as they gazed into each other eyes.

Breaking the kiss Dominic used the pad of his fingers to caress Sadie's face. "Sadie, baby I'm so sorry."

He'd been foolish and careless, extremely careless with Sadie's love. If anyone was aware how much Sadie loved her engagement ring it was him. He'd teased her about the ring being the first thing she kissed in the morning and the last thing she kissed before falling asleep. But the look in her eyes told him what she'd held back. He'd hurt her almost beyond repair. He'd hurt her to the point that she no longer loved her ring. He'd told her she'd badgered him for it. He would have to find a way to fix it. It seemed lately that was all he was doing, finding a way to fix things, to make it up to Sadie for yet another thing he'd done to hurt her.

"Sadie, let's go back to before Christmas okay."

"Why?"

"Because there was a certain way you used to look at me and I haven't seen that look since then."

Oh yeah he was hitting below the belt, playing dirty, and he damn well knew it. But he was desperate. He gently caressed the left side of her jaw line with the pads of his fingers.

"I truly miss the unadulterated look of love you used to give me. I hate that since that time your look has been colored with pity, sadness, anger, even guilt and pain. I want you to love me the way you used to."

"Dominic," Sadie cried out wrapping her arms around him. "Baby, I still love you that way. I promise I do."

"But it's not in your eyes anymore." As he said the words he realized he'd meant them. Some of the fault lay with him for taking that look from Sadie. He'd been the cause of her anger, pain and pity. It really wasn't fair to try and put this all on Sadie. But he was dying and she was his lifeline.

"I love you Sadie," Dominic pleaded. "Baby, I'm so sorry to say you badgered me into asking you to marry me. Please, Sadie, don't leave me. Please say you'll still marry me."

"I won't leave you, Dom."

He crushed her to him wanting to never let her go. Her lips slid against the side of his neck and her tongue trailed liquid fire over his skin. Perhaps she thought he wouldn't notice that she'd not answered the question about marrying him. It looked as though he'd hurt her more than he thought.

For the moment there was a more urgent need to satisfy the intense hunger that was growing between them. Sadie's hand hot, and soft, cupped him firmly, caressing him, running her fingers down the length of him, taking her liquid fire with her. He burned at her touch. The thought of not having this connection with Sadie, this heat that infused him slithered into Dominic's mind and he forcefully pushed it away.

Life for him would hold very little meaning without Sadie. He would do what he must to keep her love. He'd already done what he'd sworn not to do. The price had not been easy for him. Part of who he was depended on his word, his bond. And he'd broken that bond for Sadie's love.

And blamed her for it.

If that is true that also must be remedied.

"Dominic, baby, are you okay?"

"Why do you ask?"

"One minute you were here in bed with me. The next you weren't."

"Random thoughts, nothing more."

"While we're making love?" Sadie asked giving him a look.

"You're right. I should not be thinking of anything but how hot you are, although in all fairness my random thoughts were of you."

The pleased smile on Sadie's lips caused Dominic to chuckle. He took in a deep breath inhaling Sadie's scent. Her essence, with a bit of cinnamon and vanilla mixed in the mix did it for him each and every time. Wrapping his arms around her he pulled her firmly to him and kissed her hard, tasting her, her essence, her love and residual tears, kissing her deeper and deeper as he attempted to chase away the demons that were hell-bent on chasing him.

In the past few months so many things had happened, the woman he loved who never cried was now constantly in tears and always it was his fault. He'd better be careful of eroding her love. She was his one constant. An unwanted flash of Paul massaging her entered his mind. Another demon.

Dominic gentled his hold on Sadie and moved his hands to massage her as best he could from the position they were in. He felt the tight knots in her shoulder and a grimace of pain formed in his belly as he kneaded the muscles until they became pliant under his ministrations. Sadie's soft moan of pleasure produced many emotions in him, fear being one. He paused, his hands in midair.

"Don't stop, Dom. I know what you're thinking. I didn't feel like this when Paul massaged my back. I've never felt like this with anyone but you. I'll never feel like this with anyone but you. You are my love, Dominic, my heart."

He melted. Sadie felt like liquid silk against his skin. Buried beneath his doubts was the sure and clear knowledge that Sadie loved him in spite of his many flaws. His apprehension dissolved.

One demon down.

A million to go.

Chapter Sixteen

For several long minutes Dominic laid with Sadie resting on his chest. He moved slightly to bring her left hand in line with his vision. Placing a kiss on her ring finger he turned her face toward his. "Sadie—"

"Not now, Dom. I'm okay with it, with us returning to before I badgered you."

The slight hitch in her throat had alerted Dominic that despite his apology or their lovemaking Sadie remained hurt by his choice of words. He should let it go. "I want to give you a bath," he announced and bounded from the bed.

In a matter of moments he had the water running in the tub and had used every single bottle of essential oil Sadie possessed, being careful to only use a couple of drops of each. Then he looked for the rose petals she used and the scented bath salts. For what he wanted to tell Sadie he was going to need her to be as relaxed as possible. He checked the temperature of the water returned to the bedroom and scooped her up in his arms.

"This must be serious," Sadie said quietly.

"It is."

"Then don't try and soften me up. I'm a big girl."

"This isn't a bad thing, Sadie...not really," Dominic amended. He lowered her into the tub. Using his hand to cup the warm oil scented water, he poured it over her body touching the tips of his fingers to her nipples. "I want to tell you something, share with you things I've never told anyone. And, Sadie, I swear to God if you interrupt me or try in any manner to offer a fix for this I will not finish. Is that understood?"

When Sadie gave a slight nod with her eyes large and luminous, he kissed her lips.

"Sadie, I wasn't completely honest with you before. I knew before Poppi told me that I wasn't his son." When Sadie attempted to turn to look at him he firmly turned her head so she was facing forward. "All my life I'd felt this distance from Poppi. Sometimes he'd look at me with—" Dominic froze. "Maybe not hatred, but intense dislike. My mother would scold him, tell him not to look at me in that manner, threaten to take me and leave and never come back if he couldn't love me. Then for a time Poppi would try. But I always knew he had to try to love me. I asked Berto once why Poppi didn't love me and he told me I didn't belong to the family. He said that my real parents had thrown me into the trash and Mommy forced Poppi to give me a home, that I wasn't wanted and it would be better for all if my real family came back and claimed me. I wanted to believe he was just being mean, the typical big brother, but there was a look of utter hatred in his eyes. My brother hated me, Sadie. He knew. I don't know how but I'm positive he knew."

"Dom."

He heard the tears in her voice and swallowed realizing there had been tears in his own. That was no doubt the reason for Sadie's tears.

"Baby, you know how hard this is for me. Just let me talk to you. I've held all of this in for so long I'm going to go crazy if I don't get this out. I'd run to my mother and cry telling her what mean things Roberto was saying to me, asking her if they'd found me, if that was the reason Poppi didn't love me? I knew, Sadie. I knew."

For a long moment he couldn't continue, stopping to swallow down the childhood hurt. This had to be said, so he took a deep breath and started again.

"My parents fought about this and it only made things worst. Berto was mad at me because he was punished. I was worse off than before. I tried to do everything a kid could do to make all of them love me including Berto. I'd do anything for Poppi and my brother. I trailed around after him doing his chores, giving him my allowance, not telling when he'd done things wrong, even taking the blame for things he did and told our parents I'd done. I didn't care don't you understand, baby? I had no one, no father who loved me. I didn't even know who I was. I pretended that they loved me, that I didn't know I wasn't truly Dominic Santiago. I pretended until I believed it."

Again he swallowed. "I wanted to make them love me. I'd learned the things I needed to do to keep everyone happy, that is until the day I walked in on my parents fighting about my not being Poppi's son. You have no idea how that made me feel. What my brother had said was true. I wasn't wanted. I could no longer pretend I had a family. That's why when I began getting those cards from him..." He stopped again. "That's why they meant so much."

Dominic dipped his hands into the water and poured handfuls over Sadie. He'd done his best to keep all of this buried but it hadn't stayed there. Always he'd lived with the knowledge that he wasn't wanted. Always he'd struggled to erase the taint of his unwanted birth, to make Poppi love him as though he were his flesh and blood son.

He took a deep breath holding it then finally releasing it the same as he intended to do with his memories.

"And then the day came when the man I know now as my brother Shawn came by and gave me a ride on his motorcycle. It was one of the best days I could remember. He took me home afterwards. I was so excited. I couldn't wait to go inside and tell the family, but before I got the chance Poppi stormed outside and began punching me with his fists. When he knocked me to the ground I was pleading with him to stop. In fact I thought he would but he kept punching me, kicking me and calling me foul names.

"Poppi told me my name wasn't Santiago, that he'd allowed me to borrow it and I should be grateful. He told me I didn't have a name and a person without a name was worthless. He told me a lot of things."

So many things had happened that day when Poppi had beaten him so severely. He'd almost forgotten about the man who'd given him the ride on his motorcycle coming back, driving his bike right on the lawn, flinging Poppi from him, punching Poppi and throwing him to the ground. With a start Dominick remembered another piece of that day, one more thing he'd blocked out. He didn't blame himself. He'd been in too much pain. Now he vividly recalled an older man jumping from a car, pulling the younger man from Poppi but not before the younger man reached once more for Poppi and whispered something into his ear. From that day forward Poppi had never whipped him.

Dominic stopped for a moment reliving that day and the things that happened after. He'd shoved the memories away for so long that he'd forgotten them. The police had been called he remembered, and his mother had taken him to the hospital.

"Dominic, you don't have to tell me."

"I do, Sadie. I can't leave thing with you thinking I'm just a macho asshole. And I can't have you doubting my love. You're the first person in my life who I have ever shared this with. And I don't want you to pity me. I only want you to understand. So let me finish while I can."

"Are you sure?"

"I'm sure. I have held this in much too long. When the smoke cleared that day I ended up with a broken arm, several fractured ribs and a ton of bruises. I was placed briefly in foster care but I stuck to the story that I'd been playing in a tree with kids I didn't know and that they'd pushed me from the tree and had beaten me afterwards.

"My mother concocted the story and told me to tell it no matter what. She warned me that I'd never see any of them again if I told the truth. So I lied. And when I returned home I'd learned my lesson. I never dared to disobey. I tripled my efforts to be a good son."

Dominic bent his head to rest for a brief moment on Sadie's back. He needed a moment or he would be joining Sadie in weeping. As he thought of Shawn and Poppi he knew it wasn't his efforts or Poppi's guilt that stopped anymore beatings. It had been his brother's threats; threats that Dominic had no doubt his brother would have carried out.

It was time to get the rest of the story out. He told all of the things he remembered to Sadie, no longer trying to stop her tears.

"I think what hurts me the most is knowing my mother played as big a part in this as Poppi. She never let on. She sat in the hospital room with me, crying, holding me, begging me to do as Poppi said. She told me how dangerous it was to go away with strangers. But never once did she tell me that the stranger was my brother. So many lies."

He had to stop again for a moment. He had to breathe. He'd been made to keep it all to himself, to not talk about it with anyone, not his mother, not Poppi, not Berto or his sisters, no one. He'd never quite known what he'd done that he'd been so severely beaten. He'd never thought it was Poppi's worry that he'd ridden away with a kidnapper or someone who would have molested him or caused him harm.

Somehow even then he'd known the man had meant him no harm and that Poppi had known that also. Dominic had also known that in a way Poppi had beaten him because he wasn't his flesh and blood. He'd felt that. His efforts had only doubled to do what his family wanted. For one entire year no one in his family spoke more than a dozen words to him. When they did it was a curse. His mother was the only one who spoke to him, not conversation, just orders: *Do your chores. Finish your dinner. Poppi's home so you need to go to your room. Don't come out.*

"I hated the unknown biological father who prevented Poppi from loving me as his own." He told all of this to Sadie and more. And when she would have spoken he shushed her.

"Sadie, seeing my biological father, seeing how much I look like him, seeing the regret in his eyes, the hurt... and... God, I didn't want to see it. But I saw love in his eyes, love for me. I wanted to bawl like a baby, Sadie, right there in that hospital room with a room full of strangers. I wanted to bawl and I wanted to hate all of them for making me feel this way. I know the things I've done to you in these past months. I know I've only made things worse and not better. When I was younger I dyed my hair and wore contacts so I wouldn't look so much like a gringo. When I went away to college I found looking liked a gringo was helpful.

When I was in Ryan's hospital room with my family I thought about that time. I was so grateful that I'd given up contact I didn't need and dying my hair. I didn't want them to know I'd ever been ashamed of being a part of them. And I thought about you, Sadie. About us.

"I've tried hard to answer this question for myself. Am I really so petty as to want my wife to be beneath me? I know it has to do with my upbringing and I've been trying to let go of it. It may not seem to you that I've been doing that, but I have. Each day I'm hanging on by a thread. Each day when I wake in this house and go to work in Woodridge I am reminded why. I know you love me, Sadie, really I do. But it didn't stop you from betraying me, sending me away. And it didn't stop you from allowing Paul access to your body."

He felt Sadie tense, her muscles he'd already worked were becoming bunched.

"Sadie, just let me work through this, get it all out okay. I feel adrift, lost. And admitting this to you, even feeling this way, makes me feel less than a man. Right now I feel as though I'm saying too much. I didn't intend to say all that I have. I just wanted to tell you why this has affected me so much. I didn't know that you and Paul were bothering me so much. I don't like you not wearing your ring...and I know some of it's for the wrong reason. It says you belong to me, hands off."

Dominic turned her at last to face him. "But it also says I love you and you love me. You love that damn ring that I've made dirty for you." He sighed and dipped more water to pour over Sadie's body. "Do you understand any of what I'm trying to say to you?"

When she didn't answer he was puzzled. "Sadie, he said softly, "what's wrong baby?"

"You've been shushing me every time I tried to say anything. I wanted to make sure you wanted an answer."

Her grin touched the core of him. She was his center. She had been since the moment they'd met. Leaning in he kissed her softly. Do you understand?"

"I understand. We're human and can't always behave the way we want. We can't make our hurts go away because someone tells us that we should, that enough time has passed, that it shouldn't matter or to suck it up, let it go. You have scars on your heart, scars that I hope in time my love will erase. Until that happens I'll do whatever it takes to help you through this. I won't try and take the lead. But I will be here when you need me to be. I'll be quiet if that is what you want. And I'll talk when you need to hear my voice. I'll leave you alone when you need it and comfort you when you allow it. But through it all I will love you. Do you understand?"

"Yes, and thank you, Sadie. Do you have any questions?

"The man who pulled your brother off Poppi, was he your father?"

"I haven't had a chance to ask but I think so."

"How would he have known...I mean how could he have gotten there so quickly? Why didn't he—"

"Take me from my mother and Poppi? I've wondered the same thing. I actually prayed for it, but it didn't happen."

Worrying his lip with the tip of his tongue he sighed. He was weary from telling Sadie things he'd held inside for most of his life. He stared at her wondering if she really understood how much he needed her. Lifting her left hand he kissed it then peered at her steadily. "And your ring?"

Sadie looked away as she tried to think of the best way to say what she wanted. Dominic had enough on his shoulders. She didn't want to add to his burdens, but she couldn't wear the ring right now if ever.

"I don't want to add hurt or worry to your already troubled spirit. I swear I don't. And I'm not trying to send you a message. But I have to take care of myself as well as take care of you. Right now for this moment it wouldn't be in my best interest to put the ring back on my finger. I truly don't want you feeling pressured especially with everything that's happening in your life. I also don't want to wear it because you're feeling bad that I won't. Like you once told me when you didn't give me the ring, it didn't mean you loved me less."

Sadie took a breath needing him to understand. "I know now what you meant. My not wearing the ring doesn't mean I love you less. But I think if I put it on right now it won't be good for either of us. It's tied in with guilt right now."

"But we're still getting married, right?" Dominic asked.

"Yes," Sadie replied. "Someday."

Chapter Seventeen

Dominic woke slowly feeling disoriented. Glancing at the clock he blinked. It was a little after two. The sun was streaming through the room and he was home. Then he remembered. He'd met his other brother, his biological father and a bevy of relatives. And he'd shared all of this, well most of it with Sadie. "Sadie," he mouthed wondering where she was. She'd called in to tell the firm she wasn't coming in, family emergency she'd said. Dom laughed. How true.

Swinging his legs over the side of the bed Dominic stretched. He'd not meant to sleep so long. He needed to talk to Sadie, he needed to look in her eyes and read her emotions. She had no idea that her eyes said way more to him than her words.

The moment his foot touched the stairs the aroma of food filled the air and his stomach clenched in hunger.

"You're awake."

Sadie was smiling at him. He stared at her for a moment studying her, noticing with relief her smile wasn't forced. There was no pity in her brown eyes, only love for him.

"Your brother called."

"Berto called. Is something wrong?"

"Not Berto, your other brother, Shawn."

Dominic studied Sadie a bit more before proceeding down the stairs. "You answered my cell?"

"He called on the house phone, not your cell," Sadie said.

Dominic noticed that the look in her eyes had quickly changed to annoyance. He waved his hand dismissing his words. "What did he say? How's his son?" He walked toward the kitchen thought better of it turned and made his way back to Sadie. "Why didn't you wake me for his call?"

"He asked me not to."

Sadie was eyeing him warily. "What?" he asked knowing exactly the questions that were in her mind, the same ones that would be in his if the situation was reversed.

"Dominic, have things degenerated so much that now you don't trust me to answer a call? He called here. I didn't call him."

Her voice carried the hurt. Damn it, he was batting a thousand on hurting the woman he loved. He held her gaze a moment before answering. "I'm worried about his son."

"I know."

The annoyance had left her voice and was slowly leaving her eyes. He hadn't played her with that comment. He was worried about his nephew. "Did he say how his son was doing?"

"He said he's about the same. He wanted to check on you."

"He still thinks I'm a little kid." The thought made Dominic smile. "Did you eat yet?" he asked wanting to take them from any volatile conversation.

"I ate and I have a grilled chicken salad in the fridge for you. I used the Tyson bagged chicken. I just warmed it and added a few spices. So you can stop looking as though you're trying to figure out a way not to eat it. I thought whenever you woke you'd want to eat quickly and return to the hospital," Sadie answered and made her way to the kitchen. They were aware the inane conversation was a cover. She smiled as he trailed along after her. She was not going to ask if she could go and meet his family. He'd introduce her when the time was right. Still.

A sigh left Sadie as she reached into the refrigerator pulled out the salad and two bottles of apple juice, uncapping both before setting them on the table and taking a seat beside the place she'd made for Dom.

"Thanks for understanding, Sadie. I'm not attempting to shut you out."

But you're doing it just the same, she wanted to answer him.

Biting into the savory chicken Dominic replayed the last year of his life and shook his head in dismay. If things had gone according to his plan they would have been married months ago, shortly after him receiving the partnership. Perhaps not, Sadie would have planned for a large wedding. But they should at least be in the planning stage. Now they were trying to patch things up constantly, trying to hang on to their love. He couldn't help but groan at the way fate had stepped in and changed everything.

Gratitude could be one way of looking at his life. And he should be grateful that he had Sadie, that they'd had so many good years of an untroubled life. Life was not perfect. He was living proof of that. His life was proof. He was living an imperfect life. He lifted his eyes and found Sadie staring at him.

"If it's okay with you when I'm done eating I'm going to take a shower and go to the hospital." She gave him a look, a shake of her head and finally smiled letting him know she was aware he was trying to be nice, that she knew either way he was going.

"I'll say a prayer for your nephew," Sadie said.

And inwardly she thought, *and one for us*.

***

Indecision had pulled at Dominic for the past hour or so. He'd spent a long time in the shower debating, torn between asking Sadie to accompany him to the hospital and going alone. He wanted her opinion on his new family, yet he wanted to come to his own conclusions irrespective of her opinion. Conflicted, he tilted Sadie's face upward with his finger to look into her eyes. One decision was easy. If he saw hurt hiding there he'd take her with him no matter what he was feeling. He couldn't keep hurting her.

"Dom, why are you looking at me like that?" Sadie asked softly.

"I need to see if my leaving is hurting you." A small smile pulled the corners of her lips upwards and she closed her eyes.

"No fair," Dominic laughed and kissed her. "I need to make sure I'm not doing something that's hurting you. I'm tired of hurting you, Sadie. For four years you never cried and in the past eight months ....he shook his head. "I don't want you hurting. Do you think I'm being selfish?"

She shook her head.

"You really don't."

Again she shook her head no.

"Why are you shaking your head? Why aren't you talking?"

"Because I am hurting so much right now for you baby. It's hard for me to see you in pain and not be able to help you. I know a part of you want me to go with you. I also know a larger part of you feel the need to do this alone, at least for now. I respect that and I understand it."

"Sadie, Sadie, Sadie." Tears filled Dominick's eyes and he crushed her to him. "I love you with all my heart. I'll try to give you a call and let you know what's going on okay." It was time for him to leave. With great reluctance he pulled away from Sadie. There was one more thing he needed to say to her. Worrying his lips, an old habit, he looked down. "I don't know when I'll be home."

"I suspected as much." This time it was Sadie lifting his face to stare into his eyes. "When you return home I'll be here waiting for you. Tomorrow's Friday. I'll call in and tell the office we'll both return on Monday. That way you won't have to worry. Tell your brother it was nice meeting him via telephone."

"He really is my brother isn't he?" A grin a mile wide broke on Dominic's face. "I do feel a connection to him, Sadie. The moment he told me who he was I knew it was true. It all made sense. Some part of me always knew Berto never sent me those cards and letters through the years. But I had wanted to believe so badly that it was my brother's way of telling me he loved me that I just ignored him telling me I was loco.

"And Sadie, I know how your mind works, so I know you've been analyzing my every word and emotion. I swear I'm not looking for love, but the acceptance, the automatic acceptance and feeling that I belong to someone—other than you baby. I have blood who accepts me just as I am. I don't have to try and be anything for them. You should have seen all the pictures they have of me. They've been there all the time in the background loving me enough not to interfere in my life because they believed I was happy, not contacting me until..."

"You don't have to say it, Dom. I'm pretty good at filling in the blanks. Your father and your brother tried to have a relationship with you. You knew you had another brother. Right?"

"How did I think I could fool you? Yes, I knew. And yes, they both tried to have a relationship with me and I repeatedly told them to go to hell. I was trying to protect the relationship with my family."

"Dom?"

"They pretty much left me alone when I refused to have anything to do with them until Shawn was determined to fulfill a promise he'd made to Ryan. Do you have any idea what that means to me to feel that kind of love, that kind of commitment, to know someone had your back all of these years?"

When Sadie could only smile he smiled in return before lowering his lips to capture hers in a tender kiss that quickly turned passionate. Hunger, lust, need and love warred within him. He kissed her hard pressing her to him wanting her to know she was his everything. Then abruptly he ended the kiss. "Sadie, I love you madly. I'll see you later."

***

The weather was getting a bit chilly he noted as he parked in the garage of the hospital. Then it hit him. It wasn't the weather that had him in a pensive mood. It was knowing he was about to rip apart the very fabric of his life. He was heading into the unknown not knowing the outcome of any of it. Even him and Sadie. He could only pray they'd be okay.

He could abandon this, he thought as he rode the elevator up to the pediatric ward. He could return to his normal life and forget about this family he'd not really known until the day before. He could forget that a little boy had begged his father to introduce him to his uncle. And he could also forget about the brother who'd offered comfort to him for the last twenty plus year. Dominic let out a breath. And he could forget about the biological father who'd been the cause of Poppi's resentment toward him for more than half his life.

Stepping off the elevator he rounded the corner and the reason he couldn't abandon his brother was staring him in the face. His brother fairly wrapped around his wife was comforting her. For a moment Dominic feared the worst then as though he'd known he was there Shawn turned and his face lit up. His wife turned also and joy was reflected on her face.

Joy from strangers on seeing him, what an amazing idea. He smiled back at them. "How is Ryan?"

"He's holding on. I swear he's looking better. The doctors aren't ready to commit to that yet. But we can see it and that's all that matters." Katie put her arms around Shawn's waist and he pulled her close.

"I half expected to see Sadie with you." Shawn gave him a questioning look.

His brother was asking him many questions with that one statement and he had no intentions of lying to him. "She wanted to come." He felt his face break into a grin. "She's curious to meet all of you. And she wants to protect me." Then the smile faded. "She's a bit hurt that I didn't want her to come."

"You don't want to be influenced one way or the other about us. Is that it?"

A small chuckle was Dominic's answer. "It's not the two of you. A lot happened last night. Things that I've already done will change my life. I need to sort all of this out. I stand to lose my father over this."

The brothers held each other's gaze for a long moment before Dominic turned from Shawn. "Let's go check on my nephew."

Chapter Eighteen

Nothing much had changed in Ryan's hospital room.
Then of course Dominic hadn't expected that it would. With
the exception of an entire new batch of relatives who appeared
to have being waiting for him to make an appearance things
were basically the same. He wanted a few minutes alone to talk
to Ryan but was unsure how to disentangle himself from the
group without appearing rude. Glancing up his gaze was met
by his brother who had a knowing smirk on his face.

"Okay, everyone, give Dominic a chance to breathe.
You do remember the reason we're all here is for Ryan. So if
you don't mind I'd like for my brother to spend a few minutes
with my son."

Would it always be like this, Shawn running
interference for him? Dominic shrugged off the apologies with
a smile as he made his way to Ryan's bed wishing he could just
mutter a few words to the child without an audience. He
glanced back at the crowd and leaned down to whisper to Ryan
to get better, and renewed his promise of taking him someplace
special.

He talked to the child through the buzz of conversation
around him. When the room became deathly quietly he stood
up wondering what had happened. His father's gaze was
fastened on him. Oh Shit, he knew what was coming.

"Dominic, can I have a word with you please?"

An ambush. How was he to say no surrounded by all of
his new relatives? He stared into his father's eyes and
shrugged. Then he saw Shawn with so much hope in his eyes
that tears were glistening. He would do it for his brother.
"Sure," Dominic answered at last and headed for the door

thinking maybe he'd just flee, run for the elevator and keep on running. But apparently his father was thinking the same thing because before Dominic could make it into the hall where the elevator was located, his father had taken his arm and led him into a room closing the door behind them. Once again he was left to wonder how these people had so much access to the hospital. Why wasn't anyone telling them to clear out, asking what the heck they were doing in the private room? His mouth was dry. At first he was turned from his father in order to pull himself together. After that it was just because he felt uncomfortable. This was their first time alone."

***

"Dominic it's time you and I had a talk."

"I don't see what we have to talk about. You had an affair with a married woman, got her pregnant, left her and went back home and destroyed my mother's life. And then you disowned me?" He watched as the muscles in his father's cheeks clenched. It surprised Dominic that he thought of the man as his father. Narrowing his eyes he squinted studying him as he stood still for his perusal. It would have done no good to deny the man was his father. It was much more than the looks. It was the mannerisms; even now he could tell his father was irritated by the way he clenched his jaw. Dominic did the same thing when he was annoyed.

His father was annoyed with him for not welcoming him into his life with open arms. Shaking his head Dominic began pacing. Didn't that just beat all?

"I don't believe you," he bellowed as he paced. "You've got this look of annoyance on your face. And don't try denying it. I do the same thing. Sadie has called me on it often enough." To this his father merely folded his arms over his chest and sighed.

"You couldn't have possibly imagined this would go any other way. No man, strike that, no real father, would just abandon his son and not bother to see him. I don't give a flying fig what anyone says."

For ten minutes Dominic raged on telling his father everything he could think, calling him every foul name in the book. He'd have to give it to his father, not once did he interrupt though from the look on his face he was raring to go, anger and humiliation raced across his face but then it was always anger that came back. When Dominic ran out of steam he growled in disgust. "Well, don't you have something to say?"

"I guess I should thank you for agreeing to talk this out, or rather for you to stand there and spout off. Everyone told me you deserve to tell me off, to let out your anger and your hurt feelings. I have to tell you I didn't get an idea of hurt feelings, only rage. But I'm wondering just why I had to stand here and take this crap off of some kid who doesn't know what the hell he's talking about. A kid who thinks it's an easy thing for a father, and yes, Dominic. I am a father. A very good father I might add. It's not an easy thing for a father to do what's best for his son or the woman he loves. I'm not going to tell you that what I did was right when I strayed from my marriage. But I am going to tell you I fell in love with your mother. I was ready to destroy my marriage to be with your mother. I take it you've never questioned her about this. We ended because that was what she wanted. She'd only thought she loved me. I was her fling, her try at freedom. She cared for me, I'm sure. But she didn't love me. And she didn't want me in her life."

"That's not a good enough reason for remaining out of your son's life."

"I was never out of your life."

"A father is more than biological. Poppi raised me. I'm his son."

"You're my son, Dominic. You mother begged me to not destroy her life. She was going to go back to her husband and pretend he was your father. She promised as soon as you were old enough she'd tell you the truth. I have always reached out to you. You never reached back so I have to assume you didn't want to."

"It's not the job of the child to look for the parent. The parent should seek out the child if they're so inclined."

"So you think that's the way it is, do you? You're a lawyer Dominic, a very good lawyer. And right now you're either pretending to be stupid or thinking that I am. I have made numerous attempts to get in touch with you. This isn't a case of your mother or her husband keeping the information from you. I talked to you. And you, my son, told me to go to hell over and over again."

Cringing while he attempted to think of a reasonable comeback Dominic couldn't help but notice the smile on his father's face.

"In spite of your telling me to go to hell repeatedly I decided I wasn't interested in doing that. I've remained in your life. I wanted a relationship with you. Luckily I had one son who wanted me in his life and gave me good advice about the other one. Shawn predicted this moment between us would happen one day. He said I would need proof of my involvement in your life. Every big and small moment I've been there for you. At your school plays at your games, when you were confirmed, at each of your graduations and everything in-between."

"You have no proof of that."

"Do you want to make a bet? I think you've already figured out your brother has his ways of doing things. And the families that you've been friends with for years, your family, what of them? Did you think all the relatives you were introduced to at the hospital just happened to have been friends of yours? Come on, Dominic, connect the dots. We've always been in your life. You've never been a secret."

A pang of guilt followed by a larger pang of sadness filled Dominic. "Why didn't you try harder?"

"I was in the background because I was told that you were happy. For the most part it appeared that you were, so we remained on the fringes of your life where I prayed we wouldn't do any harm. Son, I'm sorry for the way things have gone, but I've always loved you."

"Are you the reason Poppi and Roberto didn't come to my games? Did you do something?"

"They weren't there because apparently they didn't want to be. I was there because you were my son. I'm not apologizing for that. When your Poppi took your mother back he knew damn well you had a father ready to take you. I pleaded with both of them to allow me to raise you."

"How would you have done that? Surely your wife would not have agreed to it."

"No, she wouldn't have. But it didn't matter to me. You were created in love. I loved you then and I love you now. I wanted to be your father. Hell, what am I saying? I am your father. Deal with it, Dominic."

They'd each had their say. Ignoring the look in his father's eyes Dominic turned and walked away. Grudgingly he admitted his father had finally gotten fed up and let him have it. But there was something very different in the way Michael Donovan handled things and Poppi. He'd said his piece, said that he loved him and his expression said, 'and there's nothing you can ever say to kill that love'. Dominic understood that in the deepest recesses of his heart and though he wasn't quite ready to admit it openly, he was grateful for that knowing. He saw Shawn walking toward him a question in his eyes.

"He's a good man, Dominic. You gave me a chance. Give him one as well."

"It's not the same, Shawn. He should have known how much I needed a—" Dominick blinked. "How the hell do you make me keep spilling my guts? Stay the fuck out of my head."

Ignoring his snarling, Shawn continued as though Dominick had not said a word. "What were you going to say, that Dad should have known you needed a father? I agree he should have. He should have done more. He should have raised you himself. He regrets it, Dominic, and so do I."

The brothers' gazes locked and held. "It's so much easier for me to accept you in my life, Dominic said softly. "There was something about you even when I was a kid. I used to think about you often, dream about seeing you again. Many times I thought I had and that I was just crazy. Of course now I know I wasn't crazy, you were there. I thought I saw you when I was in the hospital and I'm thinking now that Michael was there also."

"Of course Dad and I were there. Where else would we be?" Shawn's eyes clouded over with remembered pain. "I failed you that day. I should have listened to Dad. If it had been my choice that would have been the last day you lived without us. I love you Dominic. Dad loves you."

"I think the connection we made when I was ten bridged the way for me to accept you as my brother. What is it

that your father wants from me? A man can only have one
father. I already have one, Shawn. I don't need another."

"Then let him be your friend."

"The price of accepting your family in my life at this
age would be to lose the family I've known my entire life.
None of my family knows about this. How can either of you
expect that of me?"

"You're not a little boy any longer, you're a man. I'm
not going to push you and neither is Dad. Neither of us ever
has. If you want to keep us hidden then do so. But that's proof
that you need to do the opposite. If your Poppi no longer wants
to be your father or for you to be his son, remember you have a
father who's been here waiting patiently for over thirty years.
Just remember that life is too short and you never know what
can happen. Look at me. I would have never thought my kid
would be fighting for his life. He's just a boy, his life is just
beginning."

"You're disappointed."

"Dominic, don't let my feelings be what makes your
decision. This is your life like you said. Until a few days ago
you didn't have to worry about any of us. You can go back to
that and pretend none of this ever happened, that we never
made contact, that you don't have another brother, a family
eager to make you a part of our lives. Go ahead, Dominic, I'm
your big brother. I'll understand and support whatever decision
you choose."

"Shawn."

"I'm serious, little brother. I won't blame you for doing
what you need to do in order to be happy. And if you want, I'll
stop with the cards. I'll make no more contact."

Shawn turned and began walking away, hoping against
hope that his little brother would not shut him out of his life.
He'd already missed too many years with his brother. He didn't
want to miss more. He continued walking toward his son's
room not hearing footsteps behind him.

With a sigh Shawn opened the door slowly and looked
at the bed, his son then at his wife. He cringed at the murmurs
and looks from his family still gathered in the room. Then he
caught and held his father's gaze and shook his head slowly. "I
don't know what he's going to do. He said dealing with you
right now might be more than he can handle."

Tears welled in Shawn's eyes. "I don't want to lose my brother, not now. I've only had him a couple of days. We haven't had a chance to bond, to even have a beer together." Closing his eyes he took a deep breath recognizing the truth. "It looks like we'll never get the chance."

Michael Donavan had always known the day of reckoning was coming. Twice he'd lost both sons. He didn't want to lose either of them for a third time. His arm found its way around his wife's shoulder. His actions three decades ago had hurt her, but they'd done a good job of repairing their marriage. When his wife took his free hand and gave it a squeeze he choked up. When she stared at him he knew they were in this together. They would survive whatever happened. "Shawn, I'm sorry. All of this is my fault."

Shawn wanted to assure his father that it wasn't his fault, but it was. If he'd not had an affair so many years ago Dominic wouldn't even exist. And if he'd not allowed another man to raise his son he would have had a brother. He tried several times to tell his father it was okay but the words wouldn't come out. It wasn't okay. He glanced away not wanting to blame his father for the loss he was now feeling.

Without a word he walked to his mother and wrapped his arms around her. She was the one who'd suffered the most perhaps. Dominic thought his relationship with him would cause his family pain. Didn't he understand that his birth had torn Shawn's family apart, ripped a hole in his mother's heart that could never be mended? And the idea that her only son wanted a relationship with the person who caused that ache in her heart had to be too much for his mother to bear.

Perhaps Dominic was right. Perhaps they were both better off without the other. Katie came to him pressing her face against his back reminding him of the longing he'd always had in heart for his brother. His thoughts had been a lie, a way to deal with the pain. They would not be better off. Dominic would not be better without him and he would not be better without his baby brother.

***

Dominic sat in the lounge thinking over what his brother had said. A part of him wanted to go after Shawn, yet a part of him didn't know if he had the courage or even wanted to deal with the upheaval his life would take. His heart ached. He needed to talk to Sadie just to hear her voice. Taking out his cell he found a quiet corner and called home. Sadie didn't answer. He wondered where she was. He'd neglected her an awful lot lately. His mind wandered as to where she could be as he dialed her cell.

Sadie, he breathed her name willing her to answer.

"Hey baby," she answered. "Are you okay?"

"Not really, Sadie. I finally talked to my bio."

"Your bio?"

"Yeah. I can't think what else to call him."

"What's his name?"

"Michael." Dominic laughed at the simple solution before continuing. "He has the nerve to be pissed that I won't accept him into my life. He thinks I'm being a coward."

"Did he call you a coward?"

"Not in so many words, but I could tell that was what he was thinking. Dominic heard a soft laugh. "Sadie, I can't believe you're finding this funny."

"I'm not. I got this image of him and I'm thinking how DNA works. You weren't raised by him but I'd be willing to bet you're a lot like him. Baby, you don't have to make any big decisions right now. You're there for your brother. That's all you have to think about right now."

But was he there for his brother? His shoulders slumped. He'd almost forgotten the main reason he was at the hospital. His brother had supported him for most of his life without him even being aware. He wanted to be there for him now when he needed him.

"What's wrong, Dom?"

"Nothing babe. I knew the sound of your voice would make me feel better. What are you doing? You didn't answer at home so I assume you're out."

"I figured since I had no idea how long you would be gone that I might as well get a bit of work done. So I went to the Woodridge office. I'm going over some files."

"You're in my office?"

"Yeah."

"You okay with me?"

"We're good. Don't worry about us."

"You still want to meet them don't you?"

"When you think it's time. If you never think it's time then I trust that you would have made the best decision for you, and for our family."

Dominic laughed. "Just like a woman. You think I didn't notice that you slipped in that tiny little dart. That little bit of guilt."

"Hey, I'm a woman. As hard as I try it comes out at unexpected moments."

Inwardly Sadie was saying a silent prayer of thanks that Dominic had not questioned her more closely about why she was working at his office. She didn't want him to feel guilty that his secretary had called with an emergency and she'd intervened to take care of it. He was so darn touchy lately that more than likely he'd accuse her trying to fix his problems. If someone didn't take care of his clients he would soon find himself out of a job. So yes, she'd done it and she'd engendered Paul's annoyance because of not working on their case. She'd invited him to the Woodridge office to work, killing two birds with one stone. Good idea right? In Dominic's frame of mind he'd never see it that way. This wouldn't be a secret she'd keep though. As soon as it was feasible she'd tell him.

"I promise I'll introduce you," Dominic laughed.

"Promises, promises."

This was the way things were supposed to be between him and Sadie, the love, the teasing. He found himself chuckling. "I love you, Sadie. You have no idea. I'll talk to you later okay." He clicked the phone off and laughed having decided to dismiss whatever it was Sadie was doing in the Woodridge office. He couldn't worry about that now.

Softly shaking his head in wonderment at having finally figured out what the problem was for him and his brother and perhaps his father he smiled. He made his way slowly back to the hospital room glancing briefly at all the faces that were looking at him. Ignoring them he walked up to the one person in the room who had barely glanced at him. That was the person he needed to talk to. With a smile he walked directly to Shawn's mother and stood in front of her forcing her to acknowledge him.

"Mrs. Donovan, may I talk to you in private please?" He thought he saw a slight tremble around the woman's lips and knew she wanted to say no.

"You don't have to, but I think it would be good for both of us if just the two of us talked. I'll do my best not to make you uncomfortable." He glanced at his watch. "Perhaps I can buy you a late lunch."

After a short hesitation she finally said yes, no smile, no pretense of, '*I really want to get to know you.*' Dominic needed honesty about what she thought of his presence in her life. Perhaps talking to her would tell him what he should do with his own family.

Waiting until they were seated in a restaurant a block from the hospital and had ordered he began the conversation. "I know that seeing me had to be awkward for you."

"I've known about you your entire life."

He studied her, looking into her eyes narrowing his own. He glimpsed the hurt she was trying so hard to conceal. He smiled at her. "It still can't be easy. I know it won't be easy when I tell my father."

Pausing Dominic decided to be honest with the woman not to elicit sympathy, but because he was hoping if he were honest with her she'd be honest in return.

"Mrs. Donovan, can we have a completely open and honest conversation?"

"Confessions?" she asked.

"Not confessions, just honesty." He waited until he got a slight nod of approval before continuing. "My father's acceptance is something I cherish. It took a long time to win it." He noticed the sharp look the woman gave him but continued in spite for it.

"My mother's infidelity nearly killed Poppi. He loved her madly as I'm sure you loved Michael. My mother took away more than Poppi's trust. She stole his manhood when she fell in love with your husband."

Giving his words a moment to sink in Dominic waited, watched her swallow. "Raising me and giving me his name wasn't an easy thing for Poppi to do. I was a reminder of what he'd lost. He didn't want to hate me I don't think. But he did."

"Dominic, I have to confess to you that I know what happened to you when you were ten. There was a great deal of turmoil in our lives because of that incident. You should have come to live with us then. We planned for it. I thought it was going to happen. It was all arranged."

"What happened?"

"Michael had a meeting with your mother and just like that you were no longer going to live with us. For the second time Shawn cut off ties with his father. He didn't so much as speak to him for nearly a year."

Dominick couldn't believe the words he was hearing. "My family didn't speak to me for a little over a year, after that happened, not one word. I knew they blamed me for something. But I was never sure for what. Even as a kid I couldn't understand that what I'd done that would cause my entire family to abandon me, to make Poppi...."

"Did he mistreat you often?"

"How can I answer that? It was my life. I knew no other. I had nothing to compare it to. It just was. I knew Poppi didn't like me and didn't really understand why for many years. My mother threatened to leave with me from time to time when I was young if things didn't change."

"Did they?"

"I love my father. He's proud of me now. I want him to always be proud of me."

"You didn't answer the question."

"It's a hard question to answer," Dominic responded with due consideration, lowering his head for a moment taking time to think before bringing his eyes upward to meet her gaze.

"You're still not certain of his love?"

"I'm certain that he no longer hates me. I know he loves to brag that I'm a lawyer. I know he was looking forward to telling everyone I'd made partner."

The realization of what he'd said hit him square in the gut. As crazy as it was his violent reaction to Sadie making partner was tied into his father's approval. A knot formed in his belly and he stared at his brother's mother. "I'm sorry."

"Is this painful for you?"

"You might say some of the things I've done in recent months have become clearer." He watched Shawn's mother trying to make sense of the things he'd told her, trying to be objective. He could tell she wanted to treat him fairly, treat him as the innocent victim that he was of two parents who'd strayed.

"I'm sorry if my asking you questions brought up painful memories."

"I'm a big boy. I realize my father's approval comes with conditions." They stared at each other and stopped talking for a moment each trying to assess the other.

"What is it that you want from me, Dominic? Is it acceptance?"

A smile spread across his face. "I'm not sure what it is I want. I'm not asking for your acceptance. I think that would be unfair and very selfish of me to do that." He shook his head slightly, worrying his lips.

"You look so much like my husband. You have the same mannerism as he. Just now when you were looking down…You know you look more like him than Shawn. I had always hoped that you weren't really his but the older you became the more impossible it was to pretend that you weren't his son." She shook her head unable to continue.

"Mrs. Donovan, I think I know now why I asked you to lunch. It's been over thirty years and though you've known about me I wasn't right in your face."

"That's not true."

Her answer startled him. "Oh."

"In case you haven't figured it out from the pictures in Ryan's room, your father was very much in your life, going to all sorts of events. A few times I even went with him. Every Christmas and birthday we shopped together for you. He sent you checks every month, sometimes he made them out, sometimes I did."

Again the woman had surprised him. For a second Dominic could only blink. "How could you?"

"It was a bill I had to pay."

The words went straight to his heart and pierced him to the quick. To his biological father he'd been little more than a bill. To Poppi he'd been an inconvenience, a reminder. If it had not been so early in the day time the contemplation to order a drink was in his thoughts.

"Dominic."

"Yes."

"I said that's how it was for me. That's what you asked remember? It wasn't like that for your father. To him you were always his son. He loved you and wanted to be a part of your life. You were never a mistake for him, never an inconvenience."

It was so evident now. That elusive something Dominic had sensed. "That's the problem isn't it? You still resent that Michael never thought of me as the sin he'd committed." He laughed. "Don't worry. I'm not upset by that."

"You're very perceptive. I guess that comes from being a lawyer."

Smiling Dom studied the woman before him a moment then answered. "I think it has more to do with my life than my perception. I want to know how my intrusion into your family would affect you."

"Are you asking about my son or my husband?"

"Both perhaps. I'm not sure. I feel a connection with Shawn. There's a bond beginning to form between us."

"I'm not surprised. That bond you speak of has existed for most of your life. Shawn has loved you since you were a baby."

"He told me he hated me at first." Dominic waited to see what she'd say to that. To his surprise she laughed.

"Of course he did and I'm not surprised he told you. His father left us. He wanted to make a home with you and your mother. You can understand that would have been hard for Shawn to accept. I think that was the reason I hated you in the beginning. My husband loving you had hurt my son. He was inconsolable. And he was my primary interest."

"It seems the adults in Shawn and my lives may have screwed us both up," Dominic said quietly.

"It could have gone that way. Shawn was a very compassionate, giving and smart boy. He made his own decisions without any adult input. At first he hated you. He even went through a period of hating his father. I think most of it was his urge to protect me and his wanting to know his place in his father's life." Her eyes lifted. "Then he insisted on meeting you. He's loved you since that day." She chuckled. "You have no idea how many times he tried to get us to go to court and sue for custody. After he took you for a ride on his motorcycle he was consumed with guilt for what happened to you. He'd been warned by your father, but he was young, impetuous and didn't believe the threats. You were his brother and no one was going to tell him he couldn't have a relationship with you." She stopped, pulled in a deep breath and sighed. "Shawn has spent a good portion of his life making sure you're safe, making sure you felt loved. That you felt special."

"I feel so guilty for not reaching out to him, not accepting his friendship and his love. I don't understand how he could continue caring for me when his feelings for me weren't being acknowledged."

"That wasn't what he was after. You were his baby brother. He didn't care that you thought Roberto was the one who loved you beyond all else. Shawn only wanted to make sure you felt love."

A sudden lump made it difficult for Dominic to speak. "You know my brother's name."

"I know the names of your entire family."

"But…"

"Michael and Shawn refused to keep you hidden away in a closet. It didn't matter what anyone thought. The entire family knows about you as you witnessed last night. You have always been wanted by your family and most especially by Shawn. He was determined you would be safe and loved and not some forgotten secret of my husbands' indiscretion.

"You didn't answer my question though. What will it do to your life if Shawn and I develop a real relationship?"

"To be honest I can't see that it will matter. I'm not going to tell you that I envision a big happy family with your parents and us sharing the holidays. I do know how to behave in a civil manner however and if you and Sadie get married in the future and you invite us, I'll come. But that will more than likely be one of the few joint occasions you could expect me to attend."

Dominick liked the honesty of his brother's mother. They'd talked about more important things in a few minutes than he'd been able to do his entire life with his own mother. He felt in inward cringing. He had a moment contemplation wondering if he were being disloyal to his mother for his thoughts.

But he'd asked Mrs. Donavan to lunch to talk, to get her honest opinion and she was giving it. He had the feeling he'd better get all of his questions out in the open for he sensed the woman was at a disadvantage with her grandson being seriously ill, and the fact that he'd asked her to lunch in front of everyone. He'd hardly left her room to say no. He nodded a few times at nothing in particular while he wondered how to put his next question.

"Thank you for laying down the ground rules. But I was talking about a more intimate relationship with…" He paused to take a breath and decided to say it. "How will it make you feel if Shawn and I become really close, if he invites me to his home and you find me there?"

"I know what you're asking me. Can I take your being in my face in the flesh? I've lived so long with the knowledge of you, your pictures your accomplishment that it seems like you've always been a part of my family, wanted or not." She paused. "Let me check on Ryan. If things are fine when we're done here I would like to take you to my home."

After a few words with Shawn she turned back to Dominic. "There hasn't been any change. Will you come?"

In a way Dominic had known the conversation would be calm, unlike what it would be when Poppi found out. She'd had an entire lifetime of him practically in her face, her family and her husband's family knowing he'd broken his marriage vows and fathered a child. Poppi had kept it all hidden. There was no way Poppi would ever want his siblings or his friends to know of his wife's infidelity. He sawed his teeth back and forth wondering what would happen when he forged a relationship with Shawn. What kind of demons would he unleash on them all?

"Yes, I'll come. Thank you."

**

To say he had butterflies as he drove to the suburb where his father lived with his wife would have been an understatement. For the most part they were quiet on the drive with Mrs. Donavan giving directions but little else. He admired the way the woman was putting aside her resentment of his intrusion into her life.

Sadness washed over him as he compared his brother's family to his own. It seemed Shawn's family was concerned with what would make him happy. He hated to admit it but his entire life had been ruled by what would make Poppi happy.

Suddenly the what ifs started and he shivered. This was the one thing he'd tried to avoid. His life was his life. He'd never dared to wonder what if when he was a kid or as an adult. Without warning a tiny ping to his heart caused him to gasp with the memories. Occasionally he had wondered what if. Damn.

"How much farther?" Dominic asked.

"You're getting anxious?"

"I have questions and seeing your home is not going to answer them. I should be doing something to protect my relationship with Sadie and I keep pushing her away. I have so much to lose," he muttered softly then he turned briefly toward her and whispered. "And I think so much to gain."

"Dominic, don't be afraid. I think it's past time for the both of us to deal with this. I've probably dreaded this day as much as you have. I knew one day we'd meet again. Surely you have to have thought about it. Turn right at the corner, third house on the drive."

Maneuvering the turn Dominic drove through the gated community waited until he parked in the massive drive and gave the huge house a double take. From the house alone it was obvious the Donovan family had money. He thought of what Shawn's mother had said about his father paying child support and for the first time in his life he wondered how Poppi could accept money each month from a man he hated.

Michael had no legal obligation to take care of him. Poppi was listed on the birth certificate, he'd seen it. His mother had shown it to him during once of the times Berto had told him he wasn't Poppi's son. It had been his proof that his brother had lied. Now he had to at least acknowledge that Sadie was at least partially right. It seemed that Poppi had done a lot of things for money through the years. Still, where did this leave him? How the hell was he supposed to switch fathers midway through his life? And what portion of the blame would he assign to his mother, his siblings and to himself? He swallowed. *God, he'd known.*

"Mrs. Donovan, this is a bit more real than I want it to be. Can you give me a couple of seconds…?"

"What's going on, Dominic?"

He smiled at her concern. "Surely you're aware that neither of us can ever go back to pretending the other doesn't exist. What is it exactly you want to show me?"

He didn't think it had anything to do with the apparent wealth. The woman really didn't seem the type to flaunt things like that, though he'd noted the diamonds in her ears were markedly larger than the ones he'd bought for Sadie and he'd noticed the diamond encrusted wedding ring on her finger. He wondered for a moment if Sadie would ever wear her ring again, if they'd ever get married. He truly didn't know.

"Come on, Dominic, it will be okay."

He walked behind her up the long winding drive noticing the landscaping, wondering if his biological father shared his love of gardening. They had a beautiful home and well attended lawn, more than likely they had help with cleaning the place. It would be too much work for her to do alone. He was stalling and knew it. Following behind he finally crossed the threshold waiting to be assailed by the ghost of his past, waiting to sense the presence of his father in a home he'd never entered. Mrs. Donovan was staring at him, a tiny smile curving her lips her head slightly tilted. Her eyes had a sparkle of tears. She looked sad. He wondered if her sadness was for him or herself.

"Come on in, Dominic, take a good look around."

She'd brought him here to give him something she thought he needed, a sense of self perhaps. And he was standing there like a kid, a coward, afraid of what he wondered and forced himself to walk about the room.

"What the ..." stopping to gaze at the pictures on the wall he couldn't believe the number that included him, pictures with his brother, his father, the three of them. Where the hell had the pictures come from. Then she showed him a picture of his father holding an infant and a much younger Shawn grinning widely. Tears sprang to his eyes. There was a huge portrait over the mantle that apparently included grandparents and an entire group of people that resembled him.

Stunned, Dominic could do nothing more but stand there in awe his mouth agape. "How?" he finally managed to ask when he could think coherently.

"Family reunion, we introduced you to the entire family. They had all been made aware that things were dangerous for you and your mother if we pushed too hard. Your mother used to allow Michael and Shawn weekly visits with you until you were almost five and it became too dangerous. You talked about them at home and your mother was afraid."

"I don't remember the visits."

"You were young."

"Shawn didn't mention it when I told him I felt a connection with him. Neither did you."

"Shawn has been hoping that somehow you'd remember he'd been in your life on your own. He's never wanted to push you."

"But the other pictures?"

"Some of your other relatives came to your events and took pictures. You never paid it any attention. You were a kid and so good at so many things. You bubbled over when anyone wanted to shake your hand for an accomplishment you'd done. It was relatively easily to get pictures with you. You always had such a huge fan base. I will admit Shawn photo shopped you into some of the pictures. It's been so long now I don't know what events they attended and actually stood so close to you that you didn't even notice, or which Shawn worked his magic on. In any event they were in your life. No matter what you decide to do I can't allow you to think my husband abandoned you, far from it. Come on," she said and led him up the stairs. "This is your room," she called over his shoulder.

"I'm thirty-three. Why would you have a bedroom for me in your home?"

"Because it's your home too. Every home we've had since...since Michael and I got back together and decided to put our family back together we've had a room for you. I don't know why really, but it was something both your father and Shawn wanted. You stayed in our home a lot through those early years. You were allowed to stay for a couple of nights each time. I have no idea how your mother managed that. Your father and brother spent every moment with you. They didn't allow you to be alone for a second. Even when you were sleeping, one of them would lay besides you. It was very difficult when you weren't allowed to stay on overnight visits."

"What about you? What did you do when I stayed in your home?"

"Michael didn't ask me to take care of you."

"But I was in your home." He watched while it seemed she was having a hard time getting the words out."

"If I wanted to continue my marriage I was forced to accept you. I didn't really have a choice in your coming to my home." She tilted her head." Now I do. Listen, I'm going to let you look around. It's your room; everything in it belongs to you, look in the drawers and the closets. I want you to see how much a part of this family you always were. Perhaps it will make your decision easier. Either way I want you to know I'll not have any problem with you being friends and a brother to my son. And I'll not have a problem with your visiting your father. As I said this is also your home.

***

For several seconds Dominic walked through the suite. How it could be called a bedroom was beyond him. The room didn't have a dusty feel to it. It appeared to be lived in, fresh flower were on the nightstand, even a telephone. There was a sitting room complete with television, a computer and bookcases. He walked over to check out some of the titles not a bit surprised to find law books and duplicates of every book he'd ever owned. There was a humongous leather recliner with massage that Sadie had desperately wanted them to buy more than a year ago and he'd told her it was much too expensive.

He didn't have to ask how the rooms had identical pieces to the things in the apartment he and Sadie kept in the city. Wandering over to the entertainment center he laughed when he spotted the mini fridge, microwave and one of the fancy one step coffee makers. He opened the cupboard knowing he'd find the flavored coffee Sadie loved and the coffee he preferred.

Out of curiosity he began opening drawers not surprised to find each drawer stuffed to the brim with clothes for him. When he got to the last drawer he laughed out loud, there were silk pajama and a couple of gowns for Sadie. He was relieved to see the selections had not gotten a bit more intimate. Apparently they'd not had any problems buying him underwear. He was intrigued now marching over to the walk-in closet. Wow, was all he could think. It was like being in Disneyland. If Sadie ever saw this place she'd want to move in. He couldn't believe the amount of time, energy and money that had gone into the clothes in the closet he'd never worn. And the love, the unbidden thought came to him. This was about love. His father loved him. It was evident in the way he'd made him a part of his life. With a sigh Dominic knew there was a lot more to the story. He would have to have a talk with Michael after he'd talked with his mother and Poppi.

His investigation was no longer the fun it had originally been. Damn it all to hell. He'd completely stepped through the looking glass to the other side and the picture was not what he'd always imagined. He'd not been the unwanted mistake Poppi had told him he was when he'd beaten him. But why after all of that had his father not taken him in? He had to find the answer to that story. It must have been a very good reason. At least he was hoping it was.

With a rather long and drawn out sigh he saw that once again they'd not forgotten Sadie. That they'd thought to include her touched him to his core. He spotted several banker's boxes and lifted a lid, cards, letters, all addressed to him. He didn't want to open them. He'd seen too much already. With deep regret he walked from the closet and closed the door. He thought not to walk into the bathroom but again what the hell. It was as he'd known it would be. He was glad Shawn was one of the good guys. How he wondered could he possibly know so much about him. If he wasn't aware of the reason for his brother spying on him so thoroughly it would definitely feel a bit creepy.

With one last look he glanced at the array of photographs on the wall and scattered about the room on everything it seemed that had a surface. Framed photos of his father holding him. Shawn holding him. Them in a park. Him in a swing with Shawn pushing him caught his eye. Why couldn't he remember any of this? At last he walked back down the stairs and headed for the kitchen to find his brother's mother.

He knew no matter the consequences this family that had loved him for so many years was a part of him. He'd do no less than they had done. He wouldn't keep them in the closet either. As soon as things were settled he'd tell his parents.

"Mrs. Donovan, thank you. I really needed to see your home to understand what you've all been trying to tell me."

"I know you did."

"But if you don't mind my saying so, all the clothes, toiletries, it's all...it's too much."

"It's a bit creepy." She smiled. "I agree. But Michael and Shawn have gotten so used to buying for you through the years that neither of them will listen to me about it being a bit more than strange. Every year or so I box up the clothes and give them away and the two of them bring in more." This time she laughed.

"I wish I had known."

"I love my husband. Believe me if I didn't know how much he's always loved me I would not still be here. I've never been a masochist so there is no need for you to feel sorry for me. Yes, it's true that for a time Michael fell out of love with me and started loving someone else. But even during that time he still loved me. He just wasn't in love with me. I think a part of him will always love your mother. But I no longer feel he's in love with her. We've repaired our marriage.

Whatever happened more than three decades ago we've both come to accept. I do believe we're strong enough to handle whatever comes next. So you see, Dominic, the choice to have a relationship with your brother and your father," her chin lifted, "yes, your father, the decision is yours to make and yours alone."

Before he could answer their cell phones rang leaving them staring at each other once they saw who was calling. "It's Shawn he said at the same instant she replied, "It's Michael." They looked to the other with worry pushing away anymore words.

"You two need to get back here immediately," Shawn's voice yelled out.

"Ryan, is…he…is...he?"

"Just get back here now. And Dominic, don't be crazy. Drive safely if you're the one driving."

"They need us back at the hospital," he started to say when he noticed Mrs. Donovan's shoulders sag and she began to slump as though into a faint. He ran to her, steadied her and held her for a moment. "Mrs. Donovan, your grandson, my nephew," he smiled, "is going to be fine."

"Dominic, you may as well call me Kellie."

Squeezing her fingers he ushered her out of the house and as hard as it was not to break the speed laws he was more concerned that he return his brother's mother back to him safe and sound.

Chapter Nineteen

Paul's eyes bored into her. This time they weren't playful or filled with longing. This time she sensed sadness in him.

"Are you okay, Paul? You're looking so sad."

"I'm just wondering what's happened to you. Pardon my saying this but you're not looking as put together as you generally are. You look as though you grabbed the first thing your hands touched and rushed here. You're a partner now and yet you're…" He allowed the words to trail off as Sadie self-consciously examined her outfit before smoothing her hair down with her hands.

"There's nothing wrong with my clothes"

"No there's nothing wrong with them but it's not what you'd usually wear to the office. Which brings up the point that this is not your office. Why the hell did you drag me all the way here to haul a bunch of files when you could have easily come to the office where all the files are? And where by the way is Santiago? This is his office isn't it?"

"Are you really upset with me?"

For a long moment Paul stared directly into Sadie's eyes then he took a deep breath and exhaled. "How do I answer that? I used to enjoy working with you. You're such a talented lawyer and you are the best researcher I've ever known. You more than pulled your weight. For the past few months…not so much. No matter what, I could always count on your optimism, your cheery disposition, and your ready smile. Now you're either close to tears or your eyes are filled with despair. I don't like the changes in you."

There was no way she could confide in Paul what was going on. She'd received a partnership she'd never craved, but was excited at the same time that she'd gotten it. And evidently she was blowing it. Paul was right, her work habits along with her life was getting sloppy. Here she was worried about helping Dominic keep his job and doing a lousy job of her own.

"I'll be back in the office on Monday."

"Unless something else happens to Santiago. I swear he's truly beginning to irk me. I always admired and respected his work ethics and even his cocky walk when the two of you would win a case. But since Christmas I've begun to lose respect for him. Now he's bringing you down with him. Sadie, if this is what love does maybe I'm lucky you chose him instead of me. I've never been more disappointed in anyone in my entire life. I never saw this coming. I don't think I want to work with you on any more cases."

That hurt more than she wanted to let on. Opening up a file she tried her best to keep her tone cool, calm and detached. "I'm sorry you feel that way, Paul," Sadie replied hoping to hell that would end the conversation.

"It's late and you have not had one call from Santiago nor have you called him. If he loves you he sure has a hell of a way of showing it. You could do so much better, Sadie. I think it's time for me to leave now. It's going to take at least an hour to get back into the city."

Fear of losing Paul's respect gripped her making her blurt out an invitation without thinking. "Would you like to get dinner first?"

"No thanks, Sadie. For the first time since I've known you, I'm not interested."

Sadie watched stunned as Paul gathered the files and walked out the door. "I'll be in the office Monday," she called after him but he didn't answer. He didn't so much as turn his head. "Damn it, Dom," she muttered under her breath. She really liked Paul and she'd always enjoyed working with him, knowing that he admired her abilities, and thought of her as one of the brightest lawyers at the firm. This was pissing her off big time. Having Dominic's back was one thing, allowing what was happening with him to destroy both their careers was another.

Later as she was pulling steaks from the freezer she wondered if she should even bother. It was hard to make dinner for two when one may not come home at all. She had to stop pacing but nothing was working. Paul's words kept ringing in her ears.

To top that off Roberto had called trying to reach Dominic surprised when he'd not answered his cell. When he questioned her, she'd choked and stumbled realizing her mistake immediately. Part of her wanted to call and warn Dom but the other part hesitated, not wanting him to think she was trying to keep tabs on him. He was with his family, he was needed. Still, she wished he'd call. He'd been gone so long. *I wish he'd let me in,* a little voice whispered and she rushed pass it. This was without a doubt the most important thing Dominic had ever done in his life. He'd told her his reasons for not including her. She'd just have to accept it. Sadness prevailed trying to pull Sadie under. "Dom," she whispered. "I hope you're okay."

***

"Daddy," a soft cracked voice whispered as though he were speaking from a mouth filled with cotton. Bright blue eyes turned toward Dominic as he entered the room and widened to the size of a marble, the boy blinked as his family began crying and hugging him. Is that him?" he asked his father. "Is that my uncle Dominic? He looks just like grandpa."

Shawn looked over his shoulder tears streaking down his face. "Yes, that's my baby brother and your uncle." He held out a hand toward Dominic.

For a moment Dominic hesitated not knowing how to deal with the emotions churning inside him. At last he took his brother's hand and went to the bed. Sobbing prayers and pure joy flowed through the room. Relief so immense Dominic felt as though nothing in his life could ever be this perfect again. He wanted to rip the remaining tubing from the child, cradle him in his arms never let this family he'd found go. Tears filled his own eyes and ran unabated down his check as he gently held the hand of his new nephew. *Where was Sadie?* He wanted Sadie. She should be here for this. She should be holding him, helping him make sense of what was happening.

After a few seconds he was able to let go of the child's hand as his position was taken over by Michael and Kellie. As quietly as he could he left the room intent on finding a quiet place to call Sadie.

"Sadie, baby, I need you," Dom said softly the moment she answered.

"Is Ryan…did he…oh God. Dom, I'm so sorry," Sadie whispered pain filling her voice.

"No baby, I'm sorry, I didn't make myself clear. The doctors brought him out from under. He's going to be fine. I just need you here with me. I'm coming apart and I need to hold you. Can you come?"

"Of course I can come. I'll be there in twenty minutes."

"It takes thirty-five minutes to get here. You be careful baby I don't want to be worrying about your reckless driving. Promise me you'll be careful or I don't want you coming."

"I'll be careful, Dom, promise." She moved to put the steaks into the fridge trying to ignore Paul's words, trying to tell herself that Dom's not calling her until now was still a good thing. Ryan was alive and out of the medically included coma. She decided to shove Paul's words from her. "I'm glad your nephew is going to be okay."

"Me too baby." It was time he brought Sadie into this. He'd made up his own mind. There was no way he was going to let his brother or his family leave his life and if that were the case then Sadie needed to meet them as soon as possible. "I'll see you soon."

***

Racing for her purse Sadie ran for the door and nearly collided with Roberto. She stopped shook her head and blinked rapidly. "Roberto is anything wrong?"

"You sounded strange you made me think something was wrong over here. That's why I came over. Where's Dominic? Is he okay?"

"He's okay Roberto."

"Where is he?"

"Listen, I'll tell him to call you. I have to go now."

"Sadie, why can't you just answer my question? Where is my brother? Is there something wrong with him? There's something going on that I think I should know about. And where are you going so late? It's almost nine."

"I can't tell you Roberto, but I promise Dominic is fine. I'll make sure he calls you. Now I really have to leave," Sadie said attempting to brush past Roberto.

"Are you on your way to meet him, Sadie, or are you meeting someone else, Paul perhaps?"

She didn't have time for this but she stopped anyway pissed that Dominic had shared his suspicions with his brothers, both of them. Closing her eyes she prayed for patience trying to believe that Roberto was standing in her driveway questioning her loyalty to Dom out of love. If he'd shown his brother more of that love perhaps he wouldn't have held on so tightly to cards from little more than a stranger. For a nanosecond she wanted to fling the words at him but that would be a betrayal of the worst kind.

"Roberto, that was uncalled for. What I do or don't do and who I see is my business, not yours. But since you're being so damn nosey I'm going to answer your question. I'm on my way to meet Dom. But what's going on with him at the moment is not for me to tell you. I know eventually he's going to tell you but I can't stand here and debate it with you. I have to leave. Now!" she said making her way to her car putting the key in the ignition and driving off giving Roberto an annoyed wave as she did so.

Feeling like a spy she checked her rearview mirror to see if Roberto was trailing her. After she was certain he'd turned off she headed for the expressway ticked that he'd made her lose five minutes talking to him. Her hands were shaking. This new family of Dominic had nearly ripped her relationship apart with the man she loved. She sure as hell hoped they were worth all the trouble.

Later than she'd thought she'd be Sadie parked in the huge parking structure hating that she had to park on the top floor. Taking a look around the garage she dialed him Dominic. "I'm here. What floor are you on?"

"Seventh. Where are you?"

"Making my way through the parking garage."

"You should be paying attention instead of talking on the phone. I'll meet you at the visitor's desk."

"Don't hang up, Dom, it feels creepy in here, like someone is following me."

"Sadie, take out your mace right now."

His voice made caution come to the surface. She turned and looked thought, she saw a shadow and her heart fluttered. "I think someone might be following me," she whispered.

Sadie hurried toward the elevator breathing a sigh of relief when the door opened and Dominic was there. His face was drawn his eyes haunted. "You okay?" he asked.

"Yes, what about you?"

"I'm much better now that you're here." He moved over to a corner and pulled her into his arms. "Thanks for coming. I really need you."

Sadie wanted to jump for joy, run, and shout. For the first time in months she was feeling the way she had before the partnership. She looked up at Dominic's smiling face as he squeezed her fingers. *Thank you God* she murmured in her mind. She had hope again that they would get through this mess. That hope lasted as they rode on the elevator. It intensified as Dom pulled her into an empty room and kissed her then held her to his heart for a long moment after. It grew when he pulled her from the room, walked with her to Ryan's room and placed his hand on the door to open it and introduce her to the people who'd so recently invaded his life.

Then the look in his eyes changed, becoming dark and brooding then angry. The change happened so fast that it took Sadie completely by surprise. "Dom, what's wrong?" she asked.

His eyes clouded with disbelieve and pain. He opened his lips to speak, but nothing came out. She felt the way she had when she'd betrayed him. But this time she'd done nothing wrong.

"Robert, what are you doing here?" Dominic asked.

Roberto...oh...shit. Sadie turned knowing why her man was looking at her as though she'd once again betrayed him. *Hell no*, she thought, *I didn't do this and I'm not taking the blame for it.*

"Roberto came to the house looking for you. I didn't know he followed me here." She rushed out the words before turning to Roberto in anger. "Berto, why did you follow me?"

He ignored her and stared instead at Dominic. "What's going on? I've been calling you for days now and you won't answer. Then when I finally got Sadie on the phone she gave me some garbled answer so I went over and she brushed me off. What's wrong Dominic? I thought something serious was going on, that you two had a fight and one of you were injured. I thought—"

"You thought we got physical?"

"I didn't know. Neither of you would tell me anything."

"I can't believe you'd think I'd hit Sadie." Dominic's eyes narrowed almost into slits. "And it was me you thought had done something so despicable wasn't it?"

"Maybe, at least until I saw Sadie and she didn't look injured. But she was acting so damn strange like she was scared or something, scared of me. What the hell. Of course I followed her. I needed to know you were okay. You are my brother."

Dominic glanced at Sadie holding her gaze. His look had changed only a tad. He wasn't pleased Roberto was there. A darkness hovered over the three of them, ominous thoughts assailed Sadie. This should have no bearing on her relationship with Dominic but somehow she knew that it would. As their voices rose in anger the feeling grew.

And when the door opened and a man stepped out Sadie stared at him. He was perhaps ten years of so older than Dominic. He didn't speak but he looked at her and nodded his head slightly in acknowledgement, as though he knew her and then he smiled for a brief second. His senses seemed to be on the alert caused by the obvious tension between Dom and Roberto. He looked amazingly like Dominic, he had to be Shawn. Her heart pounded as she struggled to find a way to fix things, wanting Dominic not to blame her for Roberto having followed her, wanting him not to think she'd betrayed him yet again.

"You okay?" Shawn glanced at Dominic hooding his gaze before looking intensely at Roberto.

"Why shouldn't he be okay? Who the hell are you?"

For a moment no one spoke. Dominic held the gaze of his new found brother while Sadie blurted out. "He's a friend." And regretted it the moment the words were out.

Ever so slowly Dominic's turned toward her, his eyes narrowing as though he'd reached a decision then he glanced backwards at Roberto. Sadie's stomach was tied in knots. She'd done the wrong thing. Dominic wasn't a little kid. She should have stayed out of it not attempted to cover, not attempted to protect him. That alone would make him angry. She found herself blinking rapidly trying to stop the tears. Words failed her. Shawn was looking at her. He smiled then winked. At least he wasn't angry with her for sticking her nose where it didn't belong.

"Sadie's right. I'm a friend."

Dominic and his brother Shawn stared long and hard at each other and Sadie realized what had just happened. She'd stuck her foot in it again forcing Dom to make a choice. His brother had tacitly given his permission to introduce him to Roberto as a friend. The moment Dominic's eyes found her she saw his disappointment in his gaze and she groaned softly hoping no one heard. This was it. Something he'd wanted to take care of in his own time and now she'd inadvertently brought the matter to a head. It wasn't her fault that Roberto had followed her. But it sure appeared that Dom was faulting her with the crime.

Dominic turned to Roberto. "Since you're here I want to introduce you to my other big brother. This is Shawn."

"What the hell do you mean your other big brother?" Berto yelled "Are you loco? You have one brother, and that's me comprenda?"

"I'm not kidding with you. Shawn is my brother, flesh and blood just as much as you are. His son Ryan, my nephew, has been ill. I've been here visiting. I asked Sadie to keep this secret, seems like she didn't do a very good job of it." His eyes trailed over Sadie. "Perhaps I shouldn't have made her promise."

"Dom."

"Dom."

Roberto and Sadie shared a glance as well as calling out to Dominic. But it was Roberto who spoke. "Sadie didn't break your confidence. But still, what are you talking about?"

"Come on, Berto, you can figure it out."

"If he's your brother wouldn't that make him my brother also? You're trying to tell me Poppi strayed. Why did you think you had to keep that hidden?"

When Dominic glanced toward Sadie then the man staring at them Roberto hesitated.

"Why all the secrecy bro? How did you find out about this and why didn't you tell me we had another brother?" He stuck his hand out and moved toward Shawn.

There was something in the way Roberto was behaving that alerted Dominic that things were not as they seemed. His brother was nervous and he was lying.

"You don't have another brother. I have another brother," Dom said softly.

Roberto stopped in his tracks. "You're a liar, a damn liar! Roberto roared. "Take it back. Do you realize what you're saying? I'll beat the shit out of you," Roberto bellowed then lapsed into rapid Spanish.

A quick glance at Sadie and Shawn, and Dominic followed suit. They were being rude. But what was he to do. He had no choice. A sound stopped their angry words. The door opened and Michael came out and looked at all of them.

"What's going on?"

A small gasp from Sadie and complete and utter silence followed by a, 'Damn it's true,' as both Sadie and Roberto stared open mouthed at the man who'd just come into the hall. There was no doubt he was Dominic's biological father. He was the spitting image of him.

Anger flared quickly in Roberto. He moved slowly then faster across the hall, his hands out, a scream tearing from his throat. In the blink of an eye his world had changed. Battle lines had been drawn.

"Dominic, you come with me now. These people are not your family. I don't care what they've told you. I don't care about no damn DNA either. I'm your brother, the only brother you have, the one you've had your entire life. I'm leaving and I want you and Sadie to both leave with me, forget about these people. Forget these people or Poppi will disown you."

Weren't those the same thoughts he'd had? Dominic moved toward Sadie and whispered, "I'll be back. Just stay here and wait for me." He felt her tremble. She was afraid he wasn't coming back. "I swear, Sadie, I'm coming back. I have to talk to Berto. You know that." There was no time to say more, Berto was leaving. "Sadie, don't follow me." Words that had been intended for Sadie's ears alone had actually been shouted. His voice was harsh and he instantly regretted it.

Her brown eyes filled with pain and she was blinking rapidly. What a fucked up year this was turning out to be. Once again he had no time to comfort Sadie. He had to go after his brother, convince him not to tell the family. Dominic needed to be the one to break the news to his family. He'd broken his word to Poppi. But he would be the one to tell him that, not his brother. Without bothering to look at Shawn or Michael, Dominic raced after his Roberto.

***

For several seconds Sadie stared after Dominic wondering how much longer they would be together. And to think less than a year ago that thought never once entered her mind. But now she wouldn't lie, their relationship was damaged. Too many tears, too many times he'd said things to her that questioned her self-worth. Did he really think she was so dependent on him that she would go running after him come hell or high water? Had she given him that idea? Had her pride eroded to that point? Once again she thought of Paul and his disappointment in her. *Join the club. I'm disappointed in me too.*

Her attention rapidly swung back to Dominic. *Don't follow me*, he'd said. Hell, he was the one who'd called her to come to him. Now he was telling her not to come after him. What kind of nonsense was going on with the two of them? She didn't know, but she sure knew she didn't like it.

Okay, Sadie thought it was time to pull up her big girl panties, remember she was a professional, not just any professional, but a lawyer. She knew darn well how to hold a conversation. Heck she was a partner to boot, albeit a junior partner.

Pasting a smile on her face Sadie looked at the two men who so much resembled Dominic. "I'm Sadie." She stuck out her hand to both men.

"I didn't tell Roberto what was going on," she offered and stopped.

"No one think that you did." Shawn grinned and his eyes followed the direction in which Sadie was gazing. "Not even Dominic. It's very good to meet you in person, Sadie. You and Dominic have had a rough few months of it. I have a feeling they're about to get even rougher. He needs you. I hope you are aware of just how much….."

Something in his words... Sadie couldn't help but wonder if he was trying to tell her something? Damn Dominic for telling Shawn about her little thing with Paul. Paul wasn't an issue. It was her and Dominic and the things they'd gone through since she'd made partner.

After refocusing her attention she became conflicted. Was this man standing before her a good thing in their lives? Was he the one who had her man doubting her? But then she thought of the many times he'd been in Dom's life giving him love and encouragement. She didn't know whether to thank him or to be angry with him.

"Sadie, I must apologize. Disrupting your life was never intended," Shawn said.

This should be interesting, Sadie thought as she prepared to listen, surprised when it registered that he'd said her life and not Dom's. Maybe she'd find a way to like him after all. At least it seemed he understood that her life was also disrupted.

"Can you tell me how Ryan is doing?" A smile lit Shawn's face. Sadie smiled in return.

"Would you like to meet Ryan and Katie and some of the other family?"

For a moment Sadie hesitated wondering if this would be yet another thing that would cause her man to give her a look as though she'd betrayed him. Her stomach clenched that she'd even have to think about it. Yes, she wanted to meet them had wanted to since she'd first learned of them but she'd also promised Dominic she'd allow him to make the introductions in his own good time whenever that was. Common sense told her his plans were to bring her into all of it. Sadie blinked worrying her lips, sighing in exasperation.

"Dom had been so protective of his relationship with you that I swear I really don't know how he'll take it. Things are crazy right now. I'm not trying to add to it."

"I'm not going to hurt him, Sadie."

Sadie didn't answer.

"You doubt that?"

"No offense, Shawn, but you can't prevent him from being hurt. Him believing right or wrong that he was a mistake, not wanted..." she glanced then at Dominic's biological father and held his gaze. "He's been hurt and he's been dealing with it, admirably I might say." She stopped and shook her head not finishing her thoughts.

"Until you got the partnership."

It appeared Dominic was right. His brother knew every aspect of their life. She stifled a groan and answered. "Yeah, until I got the partnership."

"He loves you, Sadie."

Sadie's eyes closed.

"You're about ready to give up on him aren't you?"

Again Sadie was taken aback. How did she answer that? "I think we still love each other enough to work on our problems. I think that's saying a lot."

"But you're unhappy."

"Who are you?" Sadie asked moving away from him. "Dom said something that makes me wonder." It was that moment that Dominic's father moved past Shawn laying a hand on his shoulder smiling slightly and came toward her.

"Shawn has suffered too, Sadie. He wanted so much to know his brother and he's made the last twenty some years of his life his personal mission to protect Dominic." He held out his hand. "Surely Dominic will not be upset that we introduced ourselves. I mean I was out here in the hall when he ran off."

Wiping her hand quickly across her face Sadie made a decision. Screw Dom. Let him get angry. That was what he was most of the time anyway. She pasted on a smiled and extended her hand to the man who'd played a big part in making her man crazy.

"Seriously, I can't say how I feel about meeting you. If you didn't exist Dominic and I would be happily married by now." To her surprise he laughed.

"I can see why Dominic loves you so much. I do hope that all that I fear is going to happen to the two of you will not hamper your relationship. If anyone can make it through I'm betting on the two of you. But I saw the look on your face when he took off after Roberto. I can see you're losing patience with him. I know you love him, Sadie, that's not going to be the issue. It's how my son's family reacts to the news. Nothing that's going to happen will be your fault. You must know that going in. But all of it is going to impact your life. For that I'm truly sorry."

The decision was made. Sadie liked Dominic's brother and his father. She wouldn't allow her resentment of Poppi to color her opinion of Dominic's biological father. She held a deep resentment for Poppi's influence and manipulations. The things he'd done to an innocent boy were unforgivable. Things she now had to deal with.

Her feelings of good will remained the same after meeting Katie, Ryan and Mrs. Donovan. She liked all of them. They were Dominick's family, his blood and Dom had a right to know them. One by one, other family members strolled in surprising her that several she knew as Dom's friends were actually cousins.

After an hour it was obvious Dominic wasn't coming back. Sadie was beginning to feel much like a deserted, unwanted appendage, though the family did their best to put her at ease, wanting her to stay, wanting her to tell them things about Dominic they didn't know. She smiled knowing it was time to leave.

Driving home the words of her father played over and over through Sadie's head. This was Dom's deal. It was big and he was doing his best to get through it. She wondered where he was, but had a pretty good guess. He would be at his parents telling them what he'd learned. She wanted to have his back, to be understanding, but right this moment she needed something too. She needed someone to take care of her for a change.

Pulling to the curb she dug her cell from her purse and dialed Paul. "I know it's late. Are you in bed?"

A voice tried to warn her of the danger she was doing to her relationship, tried to tell her that Dominic couldn't handle another betrayal. Well, neither could she. She was tired of being the one to appease his ego with no thought to her own. To leave her and not call and at least tell her he wasn't coming back showed an utter lack of respect. Maybe it was time he knew what it felt like.

The voice was whispering loudly to her. *Not now Sadie not now.*

"Sadie, I didn't expect to ever hear from you again after the things I said to you."

"But you were right. I needed to hear what you had to say. I truly respect your opinion. Paul, listen, I still haven't had dinner and I'm starving. Are you busy? Would you be able to meet me someplace?"

With Paul's yes, the deed was done. There was no going back.

Chapter Twenty

"Our first official date."

"This isn't a date," Sadie replied holding Paul's gaze.

"We're at dinner. It's close to midnight. We're alone. And we're not here to talk about Santiago. If anything you should be avoiding me, especially after I kissed you and made my intentions plain. Yet you chose to call me and ask me out. This is a date and as much as I like being on a date with you, I want to know the reason other than the most recent boneheaded thing Santiago did to piss you off. Why me, Sadie? Is it because your man hates my guts?"

That should be the answer she gave. It would solve everything when Dominic found out she'd gone out with Paul and he would find out because she had every intention of telling him. But making Dom jealous, getting payback wasn't what she was after, not tonight anyway. She attempted to smile.

"I told you, Paul, you make me laugh. You make me feel good about myself and right now I find I need laughter in my life. I need to feel good. Can we have dinner and just be friends?"

"We can if you answer me one question honestly. Are you even a little attracted to me?"

"More than a little," Sadie answered honestly. "That's why I really and truly hope you don't push this. I'm extremely vulnerable right now. It wouldn't take much coaxing for me to give in to that attraction. But later I'd regret it."

"What's going on, Sadie?"

"I can't tell you."

"You just need me to be a friend to you tonight?"

"Yes, Paul, just a friend who flirts a little knowing it will end here, not pressing me for answers I can't give, not looking at me with that intense hunger that's in your eyes."

"Do you have any idea of how I'm to do away with that?"

Sadie laughed.

"You don't really want me not to look at you like that do you?" Paul teased.

"No, and that's all the more reason why you shouldn't. This won't end well for either of us if we pretend that tonight is about anything other than me wanting to lick my wounded ego."

"You do realize with me your ego would never be wounded. I'd never hurt you, Sadie."

"People hurt people all the time. If we were in a relationship we'd both hurt and disappoint the other. I've already hurt and disappointed you and we're not in a relationship."

Paul grinned. "I'd love to have the opportunity to prove you wrong,"

This was wrong on so many levels Sadie didn't attempt to justify it. That had been the reason she'd called Paul. She'd called him because of the lack of conflict that was in their relationship, for the adoring way he was looking at her, for the lighthearted flirting. For months all that had been between her and Dominic was pain. She was tired of hurting.

Paul reached for her hand and held it and she didn't pull away. When he ran his fingers over her left hand pausing at the finger that normally sported her engagement ring she swallowed down the residual hurt of not having it.

"Must be serious." He stared at her then brought her hand to his lips placing a gentle kiss on the finger before releasing her hand. Just like that he shook his head smiled at her and made an announcement.

"Don't worry, Sadie, I finally get it. You're trembling. You have no worry from me tonight. Tonight I will be your friend."

***

For several hours Dominic had pleaded with Roberto not to tell their parents where he'd been. But there was something in the way Roberto wouldn't look at him directly, something in the way he kept saying, Poppi-gave-you-a-home, that made him wonder if his brother had not been teasing when they were kids. Could it be that his brother had known all along that he wasn't Poppi's son? Could it be the reason he'd never wanted to be bothered with him until long after they were both grown, until Dominic's need of a big brother had passed.

It wouldn't really matter if Roberto called and told their parents what was going on before he could. There wasn't much hope for the outcome, but he had no choice but to tell his parents that he was in contact with his biological family.

Standing outside the door to his parents' home, a home he'd bought for them he cringed wondering if he'd be welcome after he shared the news with them. They'd both been asleep but had agreed that if Dominic thought it important enough to come and talk with them at such a late hour they would get up and hear him out.

Taking his time looking at the home, remembering the good times he'd shared with his family, he didn't want to lose them. He didn't want to lose his identity. Reason told him he should have waited until morning, instinct told him by morning Roberto would go there first if he hadn't already called. There was no way to know if his brother would give him the time he'd asked him for.

The front door opened and Poppi poked his head outside. "So, you've finally come to your senses and left Sadie."

"Left Sadie? Of course not." Dominic was stunned that would be the first thing his father would think he was there for. "Why on earth would you think I'd leave her? We're getting married, Poppi."

"I thought finally you'd regained control of your cohoonies and decided to listen to the advice I've given you for years. You're never going to be able to control Sadie."

"Can I come in?" Dominic asked with annoyance crossing the threshold and turning back to face his father. "I have no desire to control Sadie."

"Don't lie. You're a man. You're supposed to be in charge, in control. Your woman thinks she wears the pants. I don't know how you live with her after she took your job."

"She didn't take my job." Hearing all of the nonsense coming from his father Dominic realized just how badly he'd been treating Sadie for close to a year. He ran his hands through his hair remembering he'd left her at the hospital with strangers. That was hours ago.

"Dominic, if you didn't wake us because you needed a place to stay why the hell are you here this time of night?"

"Poppi, you forget I still have the downtown apartment."

Why was he prolonging this like some kind of coward? The thought to pray came to him, but he dismissed it. What would be, would be. And prayers would not change anything, not when it came to Poppi. He might stand a chance with his mother. There had been a time she'd thought he deserved to know his biological father.

Taking a deep breath he began, "Mommie, Poppi," Dominic stopped, feeling like a child. "I met my biological father and his family." He watched as the color drained from his mother's face and anger filled his father. He rushed on to tell them everything that had happened from the moment he'd met Shawn in Sears. He took a breath and waited. He should have known his wait would be short lived.

"You betrayed me, Dominic, you went back on your word. After all that I've done for you. I gave you my name."

"Poppi, you should have never asked me to make that promise."

"Why would you go looking for another family? Have I ever treated you like the bastard son?"

Bastard son. That was what Dominic had felt like without known it, the bastard son. "To be honest, Poppi, I have felt much like the bastard son for most of my life. It's such a coincidence you'd use that word. Have you always thought of me as the bastard son? What was I to you, a steady means of ready cash?"

"Dominic Santiago, you apologize to your father this minute."

Dominic turned slowly toward his mother, the reason for all of this. If she'd never betrayed her husband then he would be Poppi's son. "I have no reason to apologize. I did nothing wrong." His eyes narrowed. "Your choices are the reason why I'm standing here. I'm not a child any longer. I'm not going to keep denying that for my entire life there's been emptiness. I love you, Poppi, but the secret is no longer safe. I told Sadie."

"Sangana," Poppi shouted. "She'll tell her parents and everyone else."

"So what if she does? I plan on telling them myself. I'm no longer going to live a lie. Roberto knows." For one brief moment his parents looked at each other making Dominic believe he'd been right in his assessment that his brother had known all along.

"Roberto, how?"

His mother's voice had a false ring but he decided to let it go. "He met them, my brother, and my biological father. They're not bad people." Before another word could be said Poppi had flung the crystal vase from the coffee table. He rushed to Dominic and grabbed him roughly by the collar as he pushed him against the wall.

"Dominic, you choose right now. I am the one that raised you, put food on this table. You wouldn't be a lawyer if it wasn't for my struggles. It's me you have to thank for all that you are. Where was your biological father for your entire life? He didn't give a damn about you. Not once did he make attempts to see you, to ask about you, to send money to support you. That was me, Dominic, so you make your choice. You've already broken your promise to me. Don't make the matter any worse by forging a relationship with these people. A real man keeps his word. I have no use for a man who can't keep his word. Until Sadie you were a good son."

"Don't blame Sadie, Poppi." Slowly and deliberately Dominic pulled his father's hands from the stranglehold he had on him. "I've always done my best to be a good son to you. It was never my fault that I wasn't your blood. Even when you beat me, refused to talk for me for an entire year, I still loved you. As for Sadie, I should have never withheld this from her. She's going to be my wife. She has a right to know."

"To know what? That you were never wanted."

In this moment Domini was more grateful than ever to Kellie Donavan for taking him to her home and showing him exactly how much he'd been loved. "Poppi, you're wrong."

"Wrong? What am I wrong about?"

"My family. They cared, all of them."

"You know this because they told it to you. You're a fool."

"I know this because they showed me. They have loved me my entire life. I understand why you didn't want my father around. I do. But it wasn't the best thing for me, it was wrong, Poppi. I had a right to know. I definitely had a right to know my brother. I've thought about it, that beating you gave me when I was ten, you knew who my brother was and that was the reason you beat me. Mom, you knew as well and you never told me. It's over. I love you both but I'm not pretending any longer that they don't exist. Another thing: As soon as I talk to Sadie we're setting a date. I don't give a damn about her making more money. It doesn't matter."

Shouts and curses followed him out the door, he'd not moved as several items whizzed by his head. He almost laughed as one of his mother's favorite bowls narrowly missed him and landed on his car with a thud.

For a moment he wondered how they planned to pay for the things they were breaking by throwing them at him. Surely they didn't think he would replace them. Then again maybe they did. He thought of the money he shelled out to them each month, his reason for telling Sadie they couldn't afford to get married. He had a feeling his income had just increased.

***

The house was dark when Dominic finally returned home but Sadie's car wasn't in the drive. He wondered if she'd remained at the hospital. He should have called her hours ago. More than likely she was at her parents angry with him. He didn't blame her. For almost a year he'd treated her badly. He was damn lucky she still loved him. He called her cell and when Sadie didn't answer he called her parents.

Two hours later worry began like a slow ache to drift across his mind. *If anything happened to her.* Don't think that, he chided himself and went into the hall for the cordless phone because it was programmed with the numbers of her entire family. The moment he was about to call her parents again he heard the key sliding in the lock and Sadie coming in. She glared at him, defiance written all over her face. When she walked fully into the room he could tell she'd been drinking. *Drinking and driving.* He narrowed his eyes as he walked toward Sadie. That wasn't like her. It was then he realized he'd not heard her car.

"Sadie, I'm sorry for not calling you or coming back to the hospital. I went—"

"Save it, Dom. I really don't care where you went." She took a couple of steps, stumbled a little then took off the shoes and began walking up the stairs.

Dominic followed behind her. "Did you take a taxi home?"

"No."

"How did you get home?" Wrong question, Dominic knew that the moment she turned and glared at him.

"Why are you worrying about me? Aren't there others you need to worry about? How about Roberto or Poppi? Or Shawn? Worry about them Dom, not about me. I can take care of myself."

"Sadie, please give me a chance to explain."

"I think I'm tired of your explanations your apologies, your not trusting me and your hurting me."

"Are you saying you're tired of me?"

"Yeah, that's exactly what I'm saying. I'm tired of you." The moment the words were out Sadie realized they were true. She was tired of coming behind his long list of concerns. He was her priority but she'd allowed herself to become his option. That wasn't going to work.

"Who were you with, Sadie?"

"Not now. I need to take a shower and get some sleep. If we continue this way, I'm going to say things in a way I'll regret. I understand that you have things bothering you. But that doesn't mean I want to be treated like this. It's gone on too long. Just leave me alone okay."

"I told Poppi that you know he's not my real father."

Sadie stared at him wondering what it was he wanted. He'd not told his father anything because of her, but because Roberto had found out. She wanted to be sympathetic, to find out how he was feeling. But to be truthful she wasn't feeling in a really sympathetic mood toward him. She shook her head and worried her lip. Then she turned from him without speaking and walked up the stairs to shower. When she was done she pulled a gown over her head and went to bed.

***

The sound of the clock ticking brought Dominic out of his reverie. Had Sadie really not asked him how it had gone with his parents? Could she possibly be that angry with him? He blew out a breath in disgust knowing she had every reason to be. Going to the bar he poured a drink. *Not the way to handle the problem,* he thought as he downed the liquid fire and poured another. Where had Sadie been? Who had she been with? How had she gotten home? Did she no longer love him?

Two drinks later and he was ready to do as Sadie asked, wait until the morning. He didn't want to fight. His nerves were on edge. Still he needed to talk. He needed a friendly voice. Pulling his cell from his pocket he pushed Roberto's number.

"Why the hell are you calling me at this time of morning hombre?"

"I need to talk."

"Not now you don't. I talked to Poppi. He should have given you to your father the second you were born. You're ungrateful."

"Berto, did you know?"

"Of course I knew. Take a good look in the mirror, Dominic. The whole family knew. Everyone pretended because Poppi would get so pissed."

"I still need to talk to you. You're still my brother. I don't want things to be strained between us."

"Skip the brother routine. Talk to Sadie, or try your new brother." The phone call disconnected and Dominic sighed. Then he dialed Shawn.

"You okay, Dominic?"

Shawn's easy answer startled him. Neither Sadie nor Roberto had asked about him. "Are you still at the hospital?"

"No, Ryan is doing so well that Katie and I came home to rest. Mom and Dad are staying the night with Ryan. So tell me, what's up with you?"

"I'm going a little crazy here."

"Where's Sadie?"

"In bed." He paused then said, "She just got in a little while ago. I talked to my parents. I told Sadie, but she said nothing with the exception that she was tired of me." A chuckle was not what he'd expected.

"How was it?"

"A hell of a lot worse than I ever expected. A lot of old hurts and insecurities came up. I'm grateful to your mother for showing me how wrong I'd been on the things I'd assumed about my...Michael. It made it a hell of a lot easier knowing that the things Poppi said were lies. I was never, not wanted, nor was I the bastard child. I don't know exactly what I was but...Shawn, I don't want to talk about them right now. I'm more concerned about Sadie. A lifetime has gone into making me the man that I am. It's not going to be that easy to change. I don't have any idea how long the transition will take and I don't think she's going to stick around until I figure it out. Hell, if I don't get my act together I'll more than likely find myself without a job."

"Are you trying to get fired?"

"Honestly, I don't know. Could be. But am I also trying to get Sadie to leave me?"

"Do you want her to leave you?"

Dominic thought about it. A hell of a lot had happened to them and to him. "Sometimes I think it would be best if she did. But that's for her not for me. She's been trying so hard to be patient with me."

"And it pisses you off right?"

Dominic laughed. "How'd you guess?"

"It's not that hard. When you're in the wrong you want to be called on your shit so you can have a fair fight. You don't want the other person being nice to you. It makes you feel like hell."

Again Dominic laughed. "If only Sadie could understand that. She's fighting my battles for me, treating me as though I'm an invalid. Granted I've been behaving as an invalid for a long time now.

"What is it you want from her?"

"I don't know. I want my old kick-ass-take-no-shit Sadie back. I don't want to feel so responsible for hurting her. I know I have a lot to sort out. I think I need to spend some time with Michael."

"He'd love that."

"Maybe not so much."

"You're still angry with him?"

"All of that's not going to go away in a night. My name for thirty-three years has been Dominic Santiago. Tonight Poppi told me not to use his name anymore. So who the hell am I?" he sighed. "I wish to God I had settled this before I ever met Sadie. I wish she'd never had to deal with any of this."

"Come on, Dominic. You know Sadie loves you. But if you thought she wasn't going to be pissed after you left her, and didn't even call her then you're crazy. Man, if you'd just called her, I think it would have been so much easier with her."

"I think she may have stopped loving me, Shawn."

"No, she loved you when she was here at the hospital. Love takes longer than that to destroy."

"Yeah how about a year? I've been hurting her for almost that long." This time Shawn didn't chuckle, he was silent.

"You think I have reason to worry don't you?"

"I hate to say it but yes, you have reason to worry."

"Do you know where Sadie went tonight?"

"I didn't have her followed if that's what you're asking me."

"What am I doing, Shawn? I'm going crazy. The person I love most in the world I've been pushing away for so long now I can't really blame her if she doesn't love me anymore. But God, if she stopped, it would kill me."

"What are you doing now?"

"Talking to you."

"What else?"

"I'm drinking."

"You're not a big drinker."

"Not usually but tonight it seems to call for it."

"Why don't you go and wake Sadie, talk to her."

"I'm afraid to hear what she's going to say. I think I already know who she was with and I can't take hearing it tonight."

"You think she's cheating on you?"

"I think she's thinking about it. And I think she wants to make me hurt the way I've been hurting her. What better way than to go out with Paul?"

"When she left the hospital she was heading home."

"Yet she didn't make it home until a few minutes ago." Silence was the only thing that the men had for a long moment.

"My appearance in your life has fucked it up hasn't it little brother?"

Dominic thought about what Shawn had said then he took in a deep breath and groaned. "I'm too damn old to be feeling so sorry for myself. But I don't blame you for any of this. I've always known there was an important part of my life that didn't make sense. Connecting with you has filled that void. Yeah I'm worried about what's going to happen with Sadie, but like you said she does love me. I'm going to grovel, and I'm going to stop crapping all over her and grow the hell up."

"Good choice," Shawn laughed.

"Shawn, I want you in my life. My only regret is that we've missed so many years."

"Do you think Sadie will be okay with this?"

"Are you kidding? She told me from the beginning that I had a right to know all of you."

"Does that include Dad?"

"Don't push that one okay."

"He's really a very decent man."

"I know, Shawn, but....just let me fix one problem at a time. I've never seen Sadie like this. I've got to fix it."

"Good luck," Shawn said.

Dominic filled the now empty glass before he answered. "Good night."

"Stop drinking, it's not the answer."

"For now it is," Dominic answered hanging the phone up and slowly sipped his drink. What a life he thought. His impossibly perfect life had suddenly become so fucking imperfect that it was as though he had a cloud hanging over him.

Two hours later the only thing he knew for sure was that he was not getting drunk. In fact it appeared the more he drank the clearer his thinking became. *When had he completely lost his mind?* Placing the near empty bottle on the coffee table Dominic made his way up the stairs to Sadie. He stood for a long moment watching her as she slept fitfully. This was doing neither of them any good. He'd come to a decision, he needed to set Sadie free for both their sakes. He needed to be free to deal with his problems without worrying what it was doing to her. And she needed to be lifted from that burden. He had no idea how he'd go about doing it. If he told her it was over she'd be hurt. Somehow she needed to be the one to make that decision. Perhaps he could find a way to arrange that.

As he continued watching Sadie he could only feel the pain of losing her. If the loss was to be permanent then he wanted to love her while there was still time. Selfish yes, but he loved her and needed her right now for what lay ahead.

Stripping away his clothes he slid between the sheets and began caressing Sadie's smooth body, kissing her soft skin, feeling himself harden at the mere thought of having her. She moaned a little and he smiled turning her toward him so he could lave her breast with kisses. It had been too long since he'd touched her, what a fool.

"Sadie," he purred in her ear. "Wake up baby." Pulling the lobe of her right ear into his mouth he bit down lightly. "Wake up, Sadie," he pleaded. He found the hollow between her shoulder blade that always sent her over the edge even in her sleep. It didn't fail, he felt her tremble and she whispered. "Dominic, we need to talk."

"No baby, we need to make love. I know you were with Paul, and no, my brother wasn't spying on you. In my heart I know it. I know you're ready to give up on us and I can't let you. Sadie. The nonsense is over. I have no intention of losing you. I don't need you to tell me what happened or didn't happen tonight. I just need to know you're still my woman and I'm still your man."

He couldn't help but wonder what happened to the plan to let her go. His traitorous heart knew it was the right thing to do. Selfish, selfish, selfish. He was. He'd admit it. She was his weakness.

"Dom, I'm not in the mood to make love. Leave me alone."

His hand went between her thighs and he probed her nether regions with his finger. "Please, Sadie."

"Dom, you're not playing fair and you know it."

Smiling he laved her nipple with his tongue suckling with an urgent need. He added another finger to her heat touching her in the way she loved, listening to her moans, making him harder. "I love you, Sadie." He waited a half a heartbeat noticing she didn't repeat the sentiment. "Te Amo, Sadie." Again nothing. "Te amo, Sadie."

"I love you, Dominic, you know that."

"You want to get the 'buts' out. I know that baby. We have time to fight later. I need to feel your hands on me, your lips. I need you, Sadie. Would you deny me of the pleasure and the need? Besides, as angry as you are with me right now there is no way in hell I'll ever believe you no longer love me. In the morning I promise you can scream and yell and be angry as much as you want. But for now, I'm holding you to the promise we made. We'll never use withholding sex as a weapon, remember."

Her hand moved to cover his length and she gave him a harder than desired squeeze, but he sucked it up until her touch gentled and the heat flowed from him into her.

***

Vanilla and cinnamon roused Dominic from his sleep. His hand reached out to cradle Sadie but her side of the bed was empty. Moving a little too quickly the effects of the drinking the night before drummed through his brain. He hoped Sadie had made coffee to go with whatever she'd cooked.

"Sadie," he yelled as he brought his long legs from the side of the bed. Standing was a bit difficult, along with the yelling. He shook his head softly; maybe a shower would clear things up. It was then he saw the open bag on the bench filled with Sadie's clothes. "What the hell," he thought his heart lurching until reason took hold. More than likely Sadie was being sent out of town by the firm and hadn't had a chance to tell him. *Yeah that had to be it.*

Taking the stairs two at a time his headache was all but forgotten, "Sadie," he called as he entered the kitchen. She turned toward him then went to the cabinet removed his mug and poured coffee for him. There was no smile in her eyes. Something was wrong. "Baby, what's going on where are you going?"

"I'm going to go and stay with my parents for a few days. I need some time alone."

"But last night…"

"Last night was about me not refusing you. You've almost broken me and I can't allow that to happen."

"I'm over that. I told you."

"You've been telling me that for months but you're not doing anything differently. Maybe I've been making it too easy for you, Dom. I'm not sure."

His arms went around her and he pulled her close. How was it possible that the very words he'd spoken to Shawn a few hours before had come to fruition? Had Sadie heard him? Had she decided to do what he'd said in order to not be hurt? But no, he knew Sadie would not have eavesdropped on his conversation. And if she'd had an inkling he was planning to leave her she would not have made love to him. Whether it was good for her or not, he wasn't ready to be without her. "Sadie, without you here I don't know how I'm going to get through this.

"I can't stay and let you continue beating up on me. You haven't been treating me with respect as your woman. I'm starting to lose respect for myself and that just isn't an option. You no longer trust me…" pausing Sadie licked her lips. "Maybe you have reasons to not trust me. Regardless, I can't watch our love turn into something that I never imagined."

"Are we still engaged?"

"No. But then again I don't think we ever were."

"Are we officially breaking up?"

"We can call it a period of adjustment, or a timeout, whatever works for you."

"So Paul is finally getting what he wants."

"Do you really and truly want to go there with me right now?" Sadie glared. "That right there is what I mean. And it's why I need to get away from you for a while. Either you totally forget I exist because you're so absorbed in your problems, or you're acting like a jealous buffoon. I have grown tired of the uncertainty of our lives."

"Tell me I have nothing to worry about."

"I can't do that because that would be a lie."

"Sadie?" His mouth formed an 'o' of surprise. "You promised you would have my back."

"That promise stands. If you ever need me, night or day, you're always welcome at my parents. But I don't need to be here to watch you self-destruct or to get caught in the avalanche."

A desperate sigh from Dominic filled the room. "Aren't you even going to ask me what happened with Poppi?"

"With an end to the money train in sight I can imagine how things went. I'll take it you're not welcome to use his name any longer."

"Damn, Sadie, how did you know?"

"I'm sorry Dom, but Poppi isn't that hard to figure out. I think the friction we've had since we met has enabled me to see him clearly. Are you okay?"

"Not really. Are you sure you've got time to hear?"

Trying for a smile Sadie took plates from the cabinet. "Do I look as though I'm intending to run out? We're going to have breakfast and we're going to remain civilized about this. This has nothing to do with my loving you but everything to do with my loving me. I think you need to remember just how much you love me." She gave him a crooked smile. "I think in our case perhaps absence will make the heart grow fonder. At least I'm hoping it will."

"Baby, I love you."

"Lately it's been more lip service than proof, Dom. Come on, sit down and eat, and tell me how it went."

There was nothing left to do but sit. Sadie was determined to leave. She wasn't throwing a fit, crying or any of the other things she could have done. She wasn't manipulating him that was for sure. She was calm, determined. What had he expected?

Picking up one piece of the buttered cinnamon toast Sadie had placed in front of him he slathered on strawberry jam. Taking a look around the kitchen and a second bite of the toast he was surprised. "You broke out the bread machine to bake fresh bread and then leave me. What's up with that, Sadie? You only cook on special occasions and you rarely bake bread. Don't tell me you are now trying to tell me your leaving me is a reason to celebrate."

"You don't get it do you, Dominic. All of this," she said holding her arms out as though to encompass the entire table, "is so you know just how important you are to me."

"Important enough that you're leaving me alone when I need you most."

"You know where I'll be. I've already told you I'll never turn you away. Anytime you want me come to my parents' and I'll be there for you. I can't spend another night here alone waiting and wondering if you're coming home, and if you do what kind of mood you're going to be in."

"What about everything that's going on now? My brother, my new brother, and my entire new family? Poppi has disowned me. Roberto isn't talking to me, and now you, Sadie."

"I'm not, not talking to you. I'm not even, not seeing you. I'm just not going to live with you for a while."

"You planning on dating?"

"God!!" Sadie closed her eyes and took a breath. "If I chose to date I will. Look you're not a stupid man. Strike that, you are a damn stupid man. But you're not unintelligent. I'm laying it out on the table for you. I love you. I always have. I want you. I want to be your wife, for us to have the family we've talked about."

"But?"

"But it's coming up on a year and our relationship is going to hell. My intent is to save you. Save me. Save us, Dom."

"And for that you need to leave our home?"

'It seems like I do. I will not allow myself to be your option while you're my priority. I've been waiting for months for you to work this out. You haven't and it doesn't look as though you're going to. Now with what's going on, my hope is slim to none. I'm not going to allow you to treat me as though I'm not important to you. It's enough already, Dom. Grow the hell up and deal with the problems. You're a man, my man, now act like it."

For one long moment Dominic held Sadie's glare her eyes fiery, then he sighed as he glimpsed the worry and the love. There was tension around the curve of her lips, tension he'd put there. His hand reached up to cradle her face and she leaned into it kissing his palm letting him know how very much she loved him.

"By the way, Paul brought my car home. I saw it parked in the drive. He really let me have it yesterday. He said I was taking advantage of his feelings for me and not doing my job. He's right, I haven't been. That stops now. You've also not been doing your job. But you're an adult. I'm leaving it up to you to either get fired or go to work being the lawyer you were meant to be. Just so you know I worked in your office yesterday because your secretary called with an immediate problem. A lawyer was needed ASAP. What the hell? You were needed. But you were unavailable and failed to tell her that. So I took care of the problem and called Paul to come to Woodridge to work on our case. He was pissed that he had to lug the files to me when I should have been in the office."

"What's the big deal?"

"The big deal is that he's not getting paid to do my work. I'm a partner now, Dominic. I need to behave like one. This weekend we will enjoy. Monday I'm going back downtown, to work."

"When are you moving out?"

"Monday, when I come home from work."

"You loved your ring yet you gave it back. You love this house and you think nothing of abandoning it. You love me and yet you're leaving me. What am I supposed to think?"

"That you need to do a hell of a lot better."

Dominic opened his mouth to protest, to plead his case but knew that when Sadie set her mind to something she wasn't going to change it. She was moving out and there wasn't a damn thing he could do about it.

He'd do his damnedest to win her back.

Chapter Twenty-One

Sadie walked slowly through the rooms of their rented home. She was doing her best not to cry. There would be other houses to be turned into a home. Walking into the master bath a tear slipped. The room was so pretty. It spoke of home and family, kids. It spoke of love, moving toward the curtains on the window she ran a finger down the material. The curtains were the first thing Dominic had bought on his own for the house. They had not matched anything in the bathroom so they'd repainted the walls, and bought everything to match the curtains. It was a sign to her that he loved the house as much as she did. Now the chances of them turning it into their permanent home were slipping away.

"You don't have to leave you know."

"Will you bring my bag when you pick me up from the train station and take me to my parents?"

"You're leaving me and I'm supposed to participate."

Sadie laughed then as tears ran down her cheeks. "How else am I to get there? God, look at the two of us. You'd think someone had died. "

"It feels like it."

"Dom, take this time to do what you need to do without worrying about me."

"You promise you're not doing this to punish me?"

"No, baby, I need to do this for me. I hope you understand. I haven't been myself in months. I need to figure out what happened while you figure out what you're going to do. My mom's making dinner for us, so don't bother putting anything into the crock pot."

She was trying to pretend it was a normal day but her heart was breaking and Dominic's as well. The pain in his eyes, the look of betrayal was slaying her. He didn't understand why she had to leave and it was tearing him apart. But she knew why she had to go. She didn't like who she'd become in the months since the partnership. She didn't like knowing that a part of her was so determined to get Dominic to marry her that she'd betrayed him in the worst ways possible. If they truly loved each other, then they'd both have to fight for them.

The smile remained pasted on her face as he drove her to the Lisle train station. She kept it there as she kissed him quickly and boarded the train. But she dropped the smile when she found her seat. It didn't reappear until she walked into the prestigious law firm. She wanted to cry for her life, but she was a professional. Walking toward the office she listened to the click of her five inch heels. She smoothed a hand over her hair, her power bun Dom called it, and she checked out her reflection in the mirrored tiles that lined the wall leading to her office. It didn't matter that her heart was shattered into a million pieces she was looking and behaving every inch the professional.

A knock on her office door and she gave a cheery, 'come in,' knowing it was Paul. His eyes scanned her. She wondered what he'd been expecting when he scrutinized her from head toe. There was no way in hell she would have walked into the firm looking like a hag. Not that she thought she'd looked like a hag on Friday at the Woodridge office. But she'd admit she went through pains to win Paul's approval today. When he smiled allowing the twinkle to light his eyes she was satisfied.

"Good morning, Paul. Are you ready to work?" She slid a chart to the edge of the desk and grinned up at Paul.

"You okay, Sadie?" Paul questioned.

"Never better. Thank you for everything you've done to help me, the wakeup call, having dinner with me and returning my car. I promise I'm back ready to work and will never take advantage of you again."

"Sadie, I didn't mean—"

"Let's forget it and get back to work.

For the next eight hours Sadie worked with barely a break. Demons were chasing her. She had to make up for all the work she hadn't put in. By the time Dominic had picked her up from the train her face was hurting from smiling. When they arrived at her parents, her head was pounding. She wondered if it was as hard for Dominic as it was for her. She wanted to ask but was afraid she wouldn't be able to follow through on her plan if she had to witness the same raw ache in him that she was feeling. So she pretended that this was a great adventure and hid her tears inside. She followed behind Dominic as he carried her bag to her old bedroom. *Don't cry Sadie,* she consoled herself. *It's only for a little while.* But she didn't know that. She didn't know that at all.

***

Sadness overwhelmed him and constricted his throat making breathing damn near impossible. Dominic had to concentrate just to remember to inhale. *It would be okay.* He had to remember that. Sadie had told him it would. Only when he placed her luggage on her childhood bed and she opened it and began putting away her clothes he couldn't bear it.

He began shaking his head before he could find the words. "No, Sadie, don't unpack." She glanced at him, opened her mouth to protest then nodded. She was having as hard a time as he was talking. "Baby, I can't watch you unpack. I'm trying to hold it together, but to watch, that would be the last straw. Don't ask that of me okay?"

God, Dominic thought. Their gazes held. He licked his lips as tears shimmered in the depths of Sadie's eyes. Opening his arms to her he waited a span of a breath before she filled his arms. Crushing her to him he wanted to plead with her not to do this. But she was right. He'd ignored the one person that made his heart beat stronger, that made his wants reality. And she was right: his problems had begun months before Shawn showed up in his life. He had so many things to take care of. This incompleteness was not what he wanted to offer Sadie. This battle was his alone. He could only pray that when it was over he would be victorious and that Sadie would be waiting for him.

"I can't leave you," he said instead breathing in her
essence.

"Then don't, Dom. I'm not banning you from my life.
Dinner is ready. Let's eat. You're more than welcome to stay
the night.

"But am I wanted?"

Sadie couldn't stop the tears and she couldn't answer
Dominic. She could only hold him. She sent up a prayer of
thanks to God when her father yelled that dinner was ready.

***

Being with Sadie's parents was the thing he needed,
probably what they both needed. Dominic had always enjoyed
a good relationship with them. They loved him and he loved
them. The dinner as usual was fantastic causing him to tease
Sadie about not being able to cook like her mother. When he
casually mentioned he would be staying the night Sadie's
father grinned and said that was the way it should be. Dominic
hadn't quite known what he'd expected but her father's answer
made him feel wanted. He couldn't stop grinning.

Later when they were ready for bed a smile broke out
on his face and he marched hurriedly across Sadie's old
bedroom locking the door and turning out the light. Making his
way back to Sadie he wrapped her in his arms pulling on the
lope of an ear suckling it, caressing her shoulder, kissing,
tasting, licking, peeling away her blouse, slowly unhooking her
bra, sucking her nipples until they were hard pebbled peaks,
then he allowed the garment to drop to the floor. She was
shivering and not because she was cold. He unzipped her pants
and fell down on his knees to worship her, peeling away her
panties with his teeth. The scent of her arousal hit him and he
pressed his face against her. Dominic was fast losing it. Every
inner demon he'd ever imagined was facing him. Now he fully
understood why he'd always felt a bit intimidated by Sadie's
complete and utter love for him. He'd never felt he deserved it.
And now he knew the reason why. If only parents knew how
much they could mess up a kid with their actions maybe they
would make wiser choices.

Sadie's arms came around to cradle his head. He heard
her soft sobs. She didn't want to leave him, not really, he knew

that. But she was right. She had to save herself. Right now she wanted to love him and he wanted to let her. When he slid first her pants then her panties down the length of her legs she threw her legs around him and held on tight so he could crawl with her upward into the bed. Spreading her thighs he used his tongue to love her and when she was done he entered her, crooning to her, telling her how much he loved her, wanting to beg her not to leave him, but not giving in to that temptation. It was wrong and he damn well knew it.

When morning came they made love again, slowly, then they showered together and made love while doing so. All through breakfast it felt more as though they were on vacation than separated. It seemed Sadie and her parents' were all in extremely good moods. Whatever it was, his soul required it. It wasn't until Sadie was kissing him goodbye and telling him that her father would pick her up after work that it hit him. This was real. And it occurred to him that from the moment he'd picked her up from the train the day before until he was dropping her off that he'd not once thought to call any family member. Sadie was his only concern. How long had it been since she was his main focus? Too damn long he knew. He pulled out his cell to call her father. Dominic would be the one picking Sadie up from the train station. He laughed wondering if Sadie had thought their separation would go like this. He sure hadn't, but this he could deal with. He had Sadie.

For the rest of the week that was how it went. He'd pick Sadie up and they'd both go to her parents for the night. They'd eat, enjoy the company of her parents and make glorious love. On Saturday Dominic decided to take them all out, his way of thanking them for their hospitality. On Sunday he went to the market and grilled up a feast for them. On Monday morning when he dropped Sadie off for the train he realized he'd moved in with her parents. When he picked her up he knew it was time to start their separation.

Pulling into the drive of her parents' home Dominic opened the door for Sadie, went inside and spoke to her parents, kissing her mother and shaking hands with her father. "I won't be staying for dinner," he said. "I guess it's time that Sadie and I start our separation."

"Sadie," both her parents yelled.

"No, it wasn't Sadie. I've been avoiding it." He shrugged his shoulders. "Sadie said she needed time alone and I haven't given it to her. Instead I moved in on you."

"Dominic, you know you're welcome here. Please don't feel you're an intrusion. You're family, we were glad you stayed. You know we love you."

"I know. I love you too. And I thank you for your hospitality. But the deal was never for both of us to move in with you. Besides, I think this may not have been what Sadie had in mind. It's time I start listening to what she wants." He turned toward Sadie trying to read the look in her eyes. Was it relief or sadness?

"Dom, you can have dinner," Sadie said.

Was that his answer? She hadn't said he could stay yet he knew she wouldn't refuse him. "No, baby. I've imposed enough. I'll grab a bite or order a pizza."

"You'll do no such thing."

Sadie's mother rushed to the kitchen to make a plate for him to take home. He felt strange. Sadie didn't belong here in this house. She belonged in their own home, with him, in their bed. She'd been more than generous with him. He could come to her, but for now he had to do as she'd asked more than a week ago and let her go.

With his dinner in his hand he walked to the car Sadie trailing behind. "Do you want me to take you home to get your car or would you like for me to pick you up in the morning?" he asked.

"No that's okay. I'll get my dad to take me to the station. You okay?"

He smiled in answer. Then kissed her. "I'll talk to you later."

***

Two pairs of eyes were burning her back. With a sigh of resignation Sadie prepared to turn to face the inquisition from her parents. It had been obvious from the moment she'd asked if she could crash with them for a few days that they thought she was wrong to abandon Dominic.

"Daddy, don't look at me like that, please."

"How am I looking at you?" Her father came to stand closer to her.

"Accusation, disappointment. You're thinking I'm making a mistake."

"I'm thinking you're in love with Dominic and that he's having a real hard time right now. He needs you now more than he ever has, probably more than he will in the future. If you can't weather this little rain how are you ever going to weather a storm? I think you shouldn't have left him baby, I really don't."

Her father's words hurt because she wasn't altogether sure if she should have left him. Leaving Dominic was the last thing in the world she wanted to do. It was the last thing she ever thought she'd do.

"Daddy, do you think I wanted to leave? My leaving him is hurting me as much as it's hurting him, if not more. I have done everything in my power to help him. He loves me, I know that. I know how important I am to him, but he's forgetting that, Daddy. He can't treat me as a convenience. He has to come to terms with what's going on and deal with it. But he has to do that while loving me. He can't keep putting me in the corner and wanting me to stay there until he wants me to make him feel better."

"Dominic and I talked about what led up to your decision. Do you think it's wise to date Paul right now?"

She should have been ready for that one. "I see Dom has been filling you in." With a sigh and taking in one breath after the other she turned to face her parents. "I haven't done anything wrong," she said feeling guilty because she wasn't being totally truthful. She couldn't hold her father's gaze so she turned to her mother.

"Mom, I did go out with Paul. I needed someone who…" She stopped unable to go on, it all seemed so petty. Her man was dealing with issues of betrayal from everyone he'd ever known and here she was whining about not being the center of his world.

But she didn't want her parents' opinion of her colored by half-truths and she could tell Dominic had not filled them in on why she'd been with Paul. She told them and winced when the looks in their eyes didn't change. Apparently Dominic could do no wrong.

With a sigh Sadie tried again. "I don't want to be away from Dom but things between us haven't been good since Christmas." Her parents were looking away as though they'd made up their minds and she was the one at fault. "Please, she pleaded.

"Baby, we know you two have been having a hard time. We've been praying for you. Neither of us could figure out why it affected him so much about you getting the partnership, but with what you've told us, it makes sense. Think about it, Sadie. It's like a huge puzzle. He's had missing pieces for his entire life."

"You still think I was wrong don't you?"

"I don't want to say you were wrong if this is what you feel is best for you," her father said with a frown. "But I don't think your decision is going to be good for Dominic. He's a strong man and he's breaking. It's not easy for any man to break, but for one like Dominic, I'm just afraid for him."

Didn't her father know she was afraid for him? "You don't have any worries about me?" Sadie asked sadly.

The sudden knot of tension in her shoulders had her thinking of the portable massager Dom had bought for her. Wanting the respect of their fathers was one of the many things her and Dominic had in common. Most of her life decisions had been made with her wondering if her father would approve. But like Dom she now found herself having to grow up and do what was right for her, with or without her father's approval.

"Daddy, you have to listen to me and understand my side of it. This decision wasn't easy. It's the hardest thing I've ever done. I feel guilty, selfish and scared to death. I'm so worried about Dominic that I'm sick. I am. I'm afraid of what's going to happen to him."

She shook her head. "But I hurt too much watching him self- destruct. This isn't going to work, the two of us if he doesn't fight for us too. I've been doing all of the fighting. I can't help the timing, but it's time for him to fight for us. If I'm as important to his life as I believe I am, he'll fight. If not...." She sucked away the sobs. "Then I'll know won't I? You seem to forget, I'm strong, but I'm breaking too."

***

Walking in the house knowing Sadie would not be coming home was much harder than he'd imagined. With a sigh of regret he sat the dinner in the microwave to warm and poured himself a glass of wine. He had no intention of drinking himself into a stupor but he could definitely use something more than water. For an entire week he'd put off trying to make sense of his life. He'd worked finding purpose in that. Not having a job wasn't the way to win Sadie back.

There were things to be taken care of like calling his sisters who thankfully weren't as cold as Roberto. He couldn't believe the hostility there. Sure they'd never shared a close relationship, but since he'd passed the bar they'd at least reached an understanding and on occasion even enjoyed a beer together. Now his brother had nothing to say to him. He was treating him once again as though he'd never been wanted. It hurt but he would continue to try.

If he'd thought Berto was cold, talking to his mother was like an arctic blast chilling his spirit. At first he'd thought Poppi was home and that was the reason she was talking to him in the manner that she was. But she kept saying he'd ruined her life. He was silent when she added he'd ruined it the same as he had thirty three years before. He knew it was time to end the call. He'd never stop loving his parents but he couldn't keep begging them either.

He wanted to talk to Sadie but he'd behaved as a punk with her for an entire week. If she wanted him, she knew where he was. He'd wait for her to call him. Why he felt such a sense of urgency for human contact was obvious. He was losing the people he cared about. He thought about Shawn and dialed his brother as he ate his dinner. He told him quickly what was going on and that he'd finally accepted the separation.

"I thought that was a funny way of a couple splitting up. I couldn't believe it when you moved into her parents' home with her."

"Hell neither could I. It took me a week to figure out that was what I'd done,"

"Do you want me to drive out?"

"Probably, but Ryan's only been home a couple of days. You need to be with your family."

"You're my family also."

"And you see where I am because of family." Dominic tried to laugh. "Stay home with Katie and Ryan. I'll talk to you tomorrow."

Finishing his late bite Dominic took the plate to the sink and rinsed it, thought of refilling his wine decided against it and headed instead for the shower. When the phone rang the moment he stepped out he smiled. Shawn treated him like a kid. He didn't altogether hate it.

"Hey, Shawn, I thought I told you I was okay and I'd call you tomorrow."

"It's not Shawn. But I'm glad you're okay. I just wanted to tell you good night."

"How about a little phone sex?" he laughed as he took the phone to bed. When Sadie laughed his spirit lightened. At least he'd make it through the first night in the house without her.

***

The next two weeks passed easier than he'd expected. He'd had dinner twice a week with Sadie and her parents and stayed over and made love to her. Once a week he'd made Sadie dinner at their home, they'd made love and she'd gotten up and returned to her parents' home. He'd sucked it up. He'd even accepted that she was working on another case with Paul, not a discrimination case, but working with him just the same. And he'd barely said a word when she'd had to remain at work late into the evening to work with him on it. He was getting through it. Life did go on.

The only thing that marred his days was the relationship with his family. Roberto had not thawed, neither had his parents. And his sisters were a bit chillier to him. Sadie and Shawn had advised him to talk to them. He'd tried but it seemed he wasn't the only family member who'd lived their lives in fear of Poppi.

On the bright side, he'd forged a strong bond with Shawn, Ryan, and Katie. Sadie had been right about that also.

Their separation was giving him a chance to get to know his brother without putting further strain on his relationship with Sadie. No, he didn't like that they were no longer living in the same house, waking up in the same bed and preparing for their future but he wasn't in control of that, Sadie was. She was calling the shots. But there was a beacon of light and he was holding fast to that.

The middle of the third week brought about a drastic change. Waiting in his office for a client he stood and smiled when the secretary showed the client in. When the man pulled an envelope from his pocket, Dominic didn't hesitate to accept it.

"You've been served."

"Excuse me." *This had to be a joke.* Before Dominic could ask one single question the man turned and left and he tore into the sealed envelope. His eyes rapidly scanned the document.

The words of the document ran together. BLAH, BLAH, BLAH, the bastard son of my wife. I want the return of my name. Those were the only words that mattered. What lawyer in his or her right mind had prepared such nonsense for Poppi? This wasn't something he could hope to win. Rage tore through him followed by the most unbelievable stabbing pain. This was just for him. Poppi wanted to kill him. This was in essence a death blow. But why and why now? Dominic had hoped that in time he could be a part of two families.

He'd hoped foolishly that at least for some period of time he'd actually been a part of Poppi. That it had not all been about money. Logic told him differently.

Just three days before he'd mailed off the two thousand dollars he'd been sending his parents for the last few years. He'd not wanted to just end the money not knowing for sure if they truly counted on it. He'd not wanted to cause them any hardship. His plan had been to institute a gradual decrease until he was no longer giving anything. He'd planned to talk all of that over with his parents when they'd listen to him. Now this. What the hell?

He called each of his three sisters. None would speak to him. He couldn't help but feel an immense sadness. Then he called Roberto and wished he hadn't.

"Berto, did you know Poppi wants me to give back my name?"

"It's not your name. You're not a Santiago."

"I have been Santiago since I was born."

"Not really."

"I can't believe you're in agreement with this. You're my brother."

"If you'd thought so much of me and my advice why didn't you tell me about Shawn when he first made contact?"

"Why didn't you tell me you'd known my entire life?"

"Poppi needed the money."

Roberto's words were like a sucker punch to his guts. Hard, sure and swift. "Are you saying I was just a paycheck to him?"

"Don't you feel that? Why are you always trying to outdo the rest of us, to show us up, the fancy cars, buying them a house and whatever else they want?

"Berto, I was never trying to outdo you. Is that what this is about?"

"Like hell you weren't. I'll never make the kind of money you make. I have to depend on Maria to help pay our bills and you bitch because Sadie made partner and more money. You don't think you wanted to lord it over me how much better you were?"

"That's not true."

"Right. The two thousand a month you've been doling out to Poppi. Hell you couldn't even marry Sadie because of that money coming out of your pocket. The most important person in your life was Poppi and you paid for that privilege. Now he no longer wants you to use his name. So what?"

"What about us?"

"What about us?" Roberto asked.

"We're brothers, Berto. We're blood. Doesn't that mean anything to you?"

"You have a brother. If you had not broken your promise to Poppi you'd have a family. But the rest of us came with the package. At least now you can stop paying to be the favorite son."

"That's stupid. How could I have been the favorite if you say it was all about the money?"

"Because we all had to kowtow to your wants for years."

What the hell was going on? No one had ever favored him. No one had ever done things because he'd wanted to do them. This was crazy.

"Berto, can you come to the house tonight and tell me what you're talking about? I don't want this between us."

"Sorry bro, it's too late. Hey, here's an idea, call Shawn." Then he clicked the phone.

For several minutes Dominic simply stared into space. He'd long known his life was a complete fabrication, but his entire life, his siblings apparently hating him. It was crazy. He'd done the things he had for his parents because he loved them. His throat closed with restricted tears. And because he felt that he had to, he was grateful to Poppi. Yes, he'd tried to buy his affections. But he'd never meant to have that be a slam on his siblings. Had he?

He had to call Sadie. When his call went to voice mail his heart sank. Checking his watch he realized she was more than likely in court with Paul. He needed her and she wasn't there. And just like that his thoughts took a darker turn. This wasn't Sadie's fault but it didn't keep him from being upset with her nevertheless.

Suddenly the office was stifling. He was determined to hold on, to not allow the lawsuit or his conversation with Berto to push him over the edge. *Calm down*, he cautioned himself, be professional.

"Lillian," he called poking his head through the door. "Are there any more clients?" When she said no he told her he was going out to talk with a possible client and that she could leave also. What the hell, there were only a couple of hours left in the day.

Every ten minutes he called Sadie becoming more and more upset as the calls continued to go to voice mail. He'd thought being in their home would do it but it was having the opposite effect. Sadie should be there with him. He should not have to go through this alone. She was his woman and was supposed to have his back. She said she loved him. She should not have left him. They should be married. They should start their own family, his own children.

He wanted to get married now, today, no later than tomorrow. They could fly to Vegas tonight and be married in a matter of hours. For a moment he wondered if Sadie would go for that. If she truly loved him, if her words weren't lies she would. It should not be about a ceremony. She could even invite her parents, he wouldn't mind. He'd invite Shawn and his family; they'd make a night of it. She could call in tomorrow. Paul could handle whatever court case they had. He'd call in and let Lillian know he'd not be in. *Good*, he thought as his breathing slowed to more even tones. It was all arranged. Picking up the phone he called the one brother who wouldn't hang up on him.

"Shawn, how would you and your family like to go to Vegas tonight? Sadie and I are getting married."

"When did this happen?"

"I just thought of it."

"You? Did you tell this to Sadie?"

"No, but why should she object?"

"Aren't you still technically separated?"

"So what? I want to be married."

Shawn took a deep breath. "Dominic, this isn't just about you. Sadie has a say in it. You're sounding a bit irrational and I don't think it has a thing to do with Sadie. Tell me what's happened."

"Nothing, if you don't want to come, forget it." Dominic slammed the phone down. His brother didn't deserve this rude treatment. But he was trying to stop the pain, not add to it. Dominic was dying inside and he needed Sadie. Where the hell was she?

***

Sadie sat in the courtroom next to Paul waiting impatiently. Her cell had been constantly vibrating for over an hour. She was praying it wasn't a medical emergency. She thought of her parents, wondering if they were okay, she thought of Dominic. She wanted badly to run from the courtroom and check her phone. *Please*, she pleaded silently as she glanced at her watch and Paul glanced at her, *please come on*. When the judge finally dismissed court she barely mumbled an explanation to Paul. "My phone has been blasting off the hook. Something's wrong."

"I hope it's nothing serious. I could hear it."

"Say a prayer okay." Sadie. said and practically ran from the courtroom and to the nearest ladies room. She needed privacy. If something had happened to her parents or Dominic she wanted to be alone to hear it.

Slamming the door to the stall she finally had the nerve to check her phone. All the calls were from Dominic. Her heart was racing as she called him back. "Dom, baby, are you okay? She rushed the words out the moment he answered the phone.

"I'm going to pick you up from the train station, we're getting married tonight. We're going to Vegas."

"What?" Her head was spinning. He hadn't said he'd been hit by a train, had fallen, that someone had died. He'd said they were getting married. In Vegas. "Dom, slow down. What's going on?"

"I'm tired of our living apart. I want us back together. I want us to get married now, tonight. I love you, Sadie."

At first her heart was happy. He wanted to marry her this very night. A thrill shot through her, she wanted to marry him. But something was wrong. He wasn't his usual self. He was working on panic mode. This wasn't her man. What the hell had happened to him now?

"Dominic, baby, tell me what's going on. What happened?"

"Where have you been all day. I've been calling you."

"I told you I was going to be in court. I couldn't leave and answer the phone."

"What if I was dying? What's more important, your career or me?"

She'd let that one slide it must be something big to have him acting so insane. "What happened, Dom?"

"I tell you I want to marry you and you think something's wrong. You've done everything in your power to get me to marry you and now when I say let's go for it you're questioning me?"

"Do something for me, Dominic. Listen to your words, listen to how you're talking to me. Slow down and tell me what's wrong with you. Tell me what I can do to help."

"Marry me. Tell your parents we're taking them with us."

"Dom, slow down."

"Marry me tonight, Sadie, or it's over. I'm not a kid and I'm tired of this."

What was happening? Her head felt as though it were about to explode. "You don't mean that."

"I mean every word. You're supposed to be there for me when I need you. Yet you're never around. And if you are around you're betraying me. You've made me do things I'd promised for twenty years I wouldn't do. I have lost my entire family and I've lost you too. You just threw me out like an unwanted pair of shoes of yours. I'm a man, Sadie. I have feelings and needs, same as you. You can't just treat me like crap and expect me to keep taking it. I won't do it. Do you understand?"

Her treating him like crap? Was he kidding? "Pick me up in Lisle and I'll come home so we can talk."

"Are we getting married tonight?"

"We need to talk."

"Will you marry me tonight?"

"Not like this, Dominic. Don't give me an ultimatum."

"It's been given."

"I have a feeling that something very bad happened to you today so I'm going to remain calm. I'll do my best to help you with whatever's going on. But no, you can't demand I marry you because you're angry with someone, or even with me. I love you and yes, someday when things are right, I still have hope we'll be together. But I'm not as desperate to marry you as you might think. Like I once told you, I don't have a gun to your head. I've never wanted to force you to marry me and I don't now. And I won't marry you because of an ultimatum. So if this is how you want our relationship to end then it's on you. But I'm asking again. Give me a chance to help you. Tell me what happened."

"Fuck you, Sadie," Dominic said and slammed the phone shut.

Sadie stood deathly still for several long moments. She took a breath then another. There were no tears. She was in shock, she couldn't even think to cry. What was going on? What was wrong with Dominic? This was the second time he'd cursed her. She would not accept a third. Anger flared beneath the surface. .She wanted to say screw him and allow their relationship to just fade. Who did he think he was to continue talking to her like that? She didn't do ultimatums. She allowed the anger to continue, to simmer as she thought about Dominic and their separation.

For three weeks they'd been heading more toward where they'd been, where they wanted to return. Something major had to have happened to make him go so completely insane. She didn't know but decided to put her own feelings on the back burner and find out what had happened. She needed to compose herself, walk out of the bathroom as though nothing had happened. Knowing Paul he'd be there waiting to check on her. He was a good friend and he was concerned. Sure enough Paul was waiting for her.

"You okay, Sadie?" he asked.

"Yes, my…" she'd started to lie but didn't really want to. "I have no idea what's going on but I need to go home now. I can come in early tomorrow or do some work alone tonight on the case. I'm not trying to run out on you again, or to get you to do my work."

Paul cut her off. "I'm sorry for the things I said to you before. Go home and I'll work on the case tonight. Tomorrow we can pick things up again."

When her father picked her up she gave the briefest explanation telling him only that something was wrong with Dominic and she needed to borrow his car to go and check on him.

"Do you want me to go with you, Sadie?"

"Daddy, I need to go alone. But if you're willing to drop me off and not come in then I'd love it if you'd take me home. I miss having my own car to drive anyway."

Part of her wanted to call to let Dominic know she was on her way home, at least temporarily, but his mood was so foul she didn't know what he'd do. Face to face she thought she stood a better chance.

Chapter Twenty-Two

Pacing back and forth Dominic refused to think clearly. He wanted to be angry and he wanted more than anything to be angry with Sadie. She loved him, he knew that. But she should have not left their home. She should have not waited an hour to call him back. She should not have refused to marry him tonight. And she should be here with him now being his sounding board listening to him, holding him, telling him he wasn't wrong. She should be there packing a bag to head for Vegas.

When he heard the door open he didn't rush toward Sadie. Knowing her and her stubbornness she wasn't there to pack a bag. She hurried toward him her arms outstretched and he backed away narrowing his eyes.

"Why are you here?"

"Something is wrong with you and I needed to see for myself that you're okay."

"Have you changed your mind about our getting married tonight?"

"If you're asking me if I want to run away with you like we're two kids without family, who's decided to go against family out to prove something to someone, then no, I haven't changed my mind. I'm not the answer to whatever happened today." She again walked toward him and again he moved away. She was now almost reaching panic mode. *What could have happened?* "Dominic, won't you please tell me what happened?"

"You're not my mother, Sadie. I don't need you here to comfort me. I'm a big boy."

"You're a big boy who's hurting. I know you and I know something's wrong. That's why I came."

"You came because I said it's over." He paused and glared at her. "I'm surprised you haven't said anything about my cursing at you. You said if I ever did it again it would be over. I did it again. It's over, Sadie."

"Dominic."

"Listen, I'm not sitting around waiting for you. I'm going to start dating and you can do likewise. Now you can go after Paul and not continue lying to me about what's going on with the two of you."

"Dominic."

"Fuck you, Sadie."

She wanted to slap him so hard that his head would spin. "Don't say that to me again. I've warned you. I'm not here to take abuse from you. Think before you speak to me. Are you sure this is what you want? Do you really and truly want me out of your life?"

"Fuck you, Sadie."

Enough. It was enough. "No more, Dom," she whispered. "After things calm down we can decide what to do with the house, the apartment and everything else. We have two leases. We have to take care of them." He didn't answer so she went to the bedroom, packed a couple more bags and carried them out to the car. Before she'd only taken enough clothes to get her though a week, coming home for more. It hadn't felt permanent, now it did. Without a word to Dominic she walked out the door. He didn't glance once in her direction.

Whatever had happened she hadn't caused it. She was sick and tired of her father taking up for Dominic. She refused to continue being his punching bag when something went wrong in his life.

What had happened to the strong cocky confident man she'd fallen in love with? He'd said three fuck you too many for her to let it go. She loved him, but if need be she could live without him. *But can he live without you?* Her father's words floated into her mind. At the moment she didn't know and she didn't care.

For the next week there was more tension in her parents' home than there'd been with Dominic. Every single night without a word to her they'd both carried dinner to

Dominic and for once in her life her father's approval wasn't tantamount to her happiness. On this her parents were dead wrong. Dominic was wrong in the way he'd treated her and it didn't matter what had happened. He should have told her what the problem was instead of demanding she run away and marry him to soothe his battered ego.

That was not the way one should start a marriage and it was definitely not the way she'd start hers with intimidation and an ultimatum, disapproval from parents not withstanding. She was the one who'd been in love with him for almost five years, not her mother and not her father. What made them think they were the experts on helping Dominic? He hadn't treated them the way he'd treated her and still even if he had, she was supposed to be the woman he loved. He had no business talking to her in the manner that he had. She'd put up with a lot, done a lot to cause him pain and had done her best to make up for that pain. Giving him her soul wasn't an option. She'd be no good for him or herself if she did that. Considering the way her parents felt about the situation the time had come for her to look for a more permanent place to live.

"Sadie," her mother called to her as she came through the door. "We invited Dominic to dinner."

This was unfreaking believable. "Are you saying he accepted?"

"Sadie, he has no one else. He doesn't have a support system right now."

"You're wrong about that, Mom. I'm the one who doesn't have a support system. Dominic has the two of you. Give me until next weekend and I'll find a place to live."

"You don't have to go."

"I kind of think that I do. I need to go out for a little while."

Arriving home after ten, she was surprised to find Dom's car still there. She pulled away and parked several doors down waiting until he left before she entered the house. Immediate anger filled her. He had no right to come to her parents for dinner when he'd told her they were over. They should be her support system. Not his. Irrational thoughts filled her mind as she waited for him to leave

Her father looked up and glanced at her as she came in.
"You just missed Dominic."

"I know. I waited until he left." She decided to get at
least one thing off her mind. "Daddy, you're a traitor."

"And you're being silly, Sadie. That boy is hurting."

"Did he tell you what it was?"

"No.

"So how do you know he's hurting?"

"He needs you, Sadie. Can't you find it in your heart to
give in? I can't figure out what he did so wrong. He asked you
to marry him. You've wanted that for years, so what was the
big deal?

"It wasn't the right time and it wasn't a proposal. It
was a demand."

"You've always been too stubborn. I still think you're
wrong to be so hard on Dominic."

Sadie walked to stand before her father. "No, Daddy,
not this time. And you looking at me with disappointment isn't
going to work. You're as bad a Poppi. You both manipulate.
It's not working on me this time. Goodnight."

Oh yes, it was time to find a different place to live.

* * *

For the next few days Sadie realized she did have a
support system. She had Paul. He made her laugh and he
reminded her that she'd been made partner because she as a
great lawyer.

When they reached the conference room, Paul didn't
ask any questions of her. That alone made her want to cry,
confide in him, but she simply smiled.

Work was her haven although she'd admit her parents
had stopped going to visit Dominic every night. The case she
was working on with Paul was just the thing she needed, lots of
work, lots of research and lots of planning their strategy. It was
with that in mind that she'd invited him to her parents to
continue working on the case.

Home for several minutes and Sadie had still not said
the words. Being at her parents was stifling. She didn't like that
she felt she had to ask for permission to have a friend for

dinner. Consoling herself that it was their home and not hers, she took the plunge.

"I invited Paul for dinner." Sadie looked at her mother as she went to put her briefcase on the small desk tucked away in the kitchen. "I hope that's okay," she asked after her mother didn't comment. Turning, Sadie saw her father had entered the room. He looked at her with a look she didn't recognize. Then he looked at her mother and without a word to either of them he turned and left the room.

"Mom, I've already invited him."

"What if Dominic decides to stop by? You did tell him he's welcome anytime."

So that was it. Her mother thought she was bringing in Dom's replacement just like her father did. She swallowed. *And just like Dom would think.*

She shouldn't have to defend herself but she would. "Mom, Dominic broke up with me, remember? He said he was going to start dating and for me to do likewise. Besides, Paul and I aren't dating. We're working on a case together. We need to go over a few things."

"You need to do it in person, after hours?"

"Mom, it's no different than when Dominic and I were working cases together, we'd always strategize at night."

"But…"

"But no one thought about our working together because we were living together. This isn't about me trying to replace him. This is work. I'm not blowing my career because Dominic isn't caring about his," Sadie snapped and felt instant remorse.

"I'm sorry I spoke to you like that, Mom. It's just… I feel guilty enough about Dominic already, and you and Daddy, you're both making me feel as though you're ashamed of me. Dom knows what he needs to do. Let me change my clothes and I'll come back out and help you."

In less than fifteen minutes Sadie was back helping her mother trying to get up the courage to ask for one special concession for Paul. "I noticed you have a bottle of Pinot Noir. Do you mind if we serve it?"

"You don't think wine will be sending the wrong message to Paul?"

"That we want him to have a nice time and that we're going to a bit of trouble to see that he's comfortable." Sadie couldn't figure out the opposition she was getting from her usually hospitable mother. She was not really looking at her, sort of looking downward. "Mom, is something wrong?"

"What about Dominic? I mean, Sadie, if he happens to come over he'll get the wrong idea, especially if we're having wine."

As if on cue the bell rang and both mother and daughter looked at the clock then toward the door. "It's not Paul," Sadie said quietly sighing as she made her way to the door, opening it she stared in horror at the sight that greeted her.

Dominic stood there unshaven and looked as though he'd not shaved for several days. His eyes were blood shot and his hair wild. Sadie reached up and smoothed his hair with the palm of hand then she ran her hand over his cheek. Her heart lurched with renewed guilt. What had happened to their lives? They should have been living a perfect life, not this. She stepped back to allow him room to enter.

He glanced around. "I need to talk to you, Sadie. Come on sit down," he said urging her toward the living room tapping a chair with his finger.

Finally, he's going to tell me what the hell's been going on with him. Then she noticed the small bulge in the pocket of his pant, about the size of a jewelry box. She groaned inwardly knowing what was coming and knowing her answer would be no. "Dom, let's go in my room," she whispered trying to prevent from hurting him farther.

"No, Sadie, I need to do this now. Come on and sit down."

Sadie sat and terror filled her as she saw her mother smiling going toward the back of the house for her father. *Oh God, why is he doing this?* Why now?

"I'm so sorry for the things I said to you, for the way I've been treating you. I'm especially sorry for cursing at you. I promise it will never happen again."

"You said that before, yet you did do it again. I no longer trust you, Dom."

"Sadie, I love you. My life is incomplete without you." He held out her ring. "Baby will you marry me? This time I'm asking, not demanding, not giving you an ultimatum. We can go downtown to the courthouse and do it tomorrow, or we can get someone to come here and marry us immediately. We've planned this for so long, I think it's time we do it. Will you marry me, Sadie?"

"You broke up with me. Or don't you remember that?"

"You know I didn't mean it." He attempted to put the ring on her finger, but when she refused he placed it in her palm.

Sadie took the ring that she'd once kissed every night and every day and replaced it in the velvet jewelry box, closed the box and tried to return it to Dominic. He wouldn't accept it so she laid it on the table beside her.

"You need to eat and you need to rest. When was the last time you slept?"

"Three, four days," he shrugged his shoulders. "I'm not sure. I can't sleep without you beside me."

"And you couldn't shower?"

Shame colored his face and she wished she'd not said it but it was true. "You're staying here tonight. Come on you have time to shower before dinner is ready." Taking his hand she led him to her private bath. Anger filled her and she didn't know if it was because of her guilt over leaving him to fall apart, or that he'd fallen apart.

"You're pissed aren't you? Why?"

"Take off your clothes and get in the shower," Sadie replied. "I have one of your shirts and jeans."

"What am I going to do for underwear?"

She didn't know why but that remark was the match, as she remembered his words to her less than two weeks ago. She glared.

"Do I look like your mother?" The hurt appeared in his eyes but it did nothing to soften her stance as she marched to her dresser and pulled out a pair of his boxers that she wore as pajamas. "Clean yourself up," she ordered then marched out of the room.

Shaking her head in frustration she held up her hand to prevent her parents from questioning her then she pulled out her phone and called Paul."

The moment she was done with her call her father was questioning her. "I guess that means you're not accepting his proposal."

Turning on her father Sadie ordered herself to control her emotions. "If anyone thinks I'm accepting a proposal given like that, with him looking like that, they're crazy. No way."

"What about your work?" her mother asked. "I thought you really needed to go over your case with Paul."

"I do. But I guess I need to take care of Dominic even more." She went back to her room trying to calm down. Going to the bathroom she opened the door enough to be heard over the spray of the water.

"Did you go to work like that?"

"I haven't been to work."

Just as she'd thought. Closing her eyes Sadie sighed again in frustration. "Is it too much to hope that you at least called?"

"Stop talking to me as though I'm an idiot. I called and said I'd be out of the office for a few days."

"Does Mr. Secret Know?"

"I didn't feel a need to tell him."

"Try, he's your boss. God, Dominic, what the hell's wrong with you?"

"My life is falling apart."

"I know that. But I never expected for you to act so weak." She watched as he turned off the water ran his hand through his hair and peered out at her.

"You think I'm weak."

She didn't answer.

"Sadie?"

Dominic wondered if something similar had happened with his mother and Poppi. Had she accused him of being weak? Had she went to Michael because of Poppi's weakness? Would Sadie turn to Paul because of his? "I've lost everything, Sadie. Don't I get time to mourn?"

"You haven't lost everything, but you're going to. When you finish mourning you're going to wake up and see that."

She went for the tee shirt of his and handed it to him, watching him as he dried his body with the thick fluffy towel. This was the first time ever she'd looked at his nude body and not felt desire. This was a bad sign. She caressed the shorts before handing them over.

"So you want me to leave?"

"And worry all night that you've totally gone over the bend and done something crazy. No, you're not going anywhere."

Dominic took the jeans from the bed and slid them over his hips. He tilted his head to stare at Sadie. "I shouldn't have come here."

"Why did you?"

"For the last three days I've sat at home thinking about us, wanting to fix it, wanting you with me, trying to think of a way to get you to come back to me."

"And this is how you thought to do it, to come here reeking, unkempt and ask me to marry you? You know me better than anyone else, better than my parents. You damn well knew I wasn't going to accept that kind of a proposal from you. You're trying to manipulate me and it's not going to work. I didn't banish you from my life. You banished me from yours. You could have been here every day for dinner and every night in my bed. You didn't come and that was your choice. You broke up with me, told me to find myself someone else. And that was also your choice. What's the matter you couldn't find a woman looking the way that you are now?"

"I always thought I could count on you." He shrugged. "I guess I can't."

That did it. Before Sadie could contemplate her actions she moved quickly and slapped him. Hard. Then she moved away. Sadie didn't believe in hitting for either gender but Dominic had pushed her past what she could bear.

"And I thought I could trust you to always treat me with respect. I don't have to guess about that one. I know I can't count on it. You've disrespected me once too often. Snap. Out. Of. It." she ordered, biting off each word.

"Until you get your head together don't even utter the word marriage to me. You know what you need to do to fix it. I suggest you do it because I'm fast losing patience with you."

"You're so cold, Sadie."

"Yeah I know. But for all of these months I've taken your crap, playing the supportive role, and I've felt like hell. Well, it's too damn bad if things have changed and you're now the one feeling like hell. Get your shit together before you really do lose me. Now come on, let's go have dinner."

Inwardly Sadie was seething, at her parents and at Dom. He shouldn't be sitting at her parents table. That lame ass apology he'd given her for cursing at her was unacceptable. But she found herself forced to accept it because she could tell her parents were right about Dominic. He was hurting. For the first few minutes during dinner it was strained then Dominic put down his fork and spoke.

"I'm sorry for coming over, looking the way I did. I shouldn't have."

Then he told Sadie's parents everything that had been going on. Sadie saw the way they looked at her. Her mother got up to give Dominic the hug Sadie had yet to give him. Then their gazes shifted to her. They both thought she was wrong. In her treatment of Dominic she knew that this time in their lives was important. It would define for them how it would be. She had no intention of living her life with a man who fell apart when his life was upside down. She wasn't helping him if she did that. Whatever fire was left inside him, he had to find and fight his way back to her and find himself.

With three pair of eyes trained on her, she ate her dinner, forcing every bite down. She would not be blackmailed by love. She sat through the rest of dinner with her parents tending to Dominic, telling him how they understood.

Good for them! They weren't the ones in love with him and she didn't understand any of it, not the months that had come before and not now. It was as though someone else had invaded her man's body. She was aware what he needed to do. But it would have to come from him. He needed to have it out with his biological father. He needed to talk to his brother Roberto and the rest of his family. Then he needed to be the man she knew he was. In short he needed to handle his business and quickly.

***

"How much longer are you going to give me the cold shoulder?" Dominic asked coming up behind Sadie and wrapping his arms around her, holding her tighter when she tried to move away. "And don't think I haven't noticed that you've been avoiding talking to me or touching me. You haven't even kissed me," he said spinning her around quickly until she was facing him. "Tell me something, the hitting, when did it start? I wasn't aware that we'd started hitting."

"We haven't. I did." After a moment Sadie dropped her gaze. "I'm sorry. Even though you deserved it I had no right to hit you."

"It hurt. Damn, Sadie, that was as hard as a punch." he grinned and rubbed his cheek.

When Dominic grinned it was the first time Sadie had felt her heart melting since she'd opened the door to find him standing there.

"So you don't hate me?"

Sadie let out an exasperated breath. "You know better than that."

"But you're still pissed."

Sadie shook her head letting out a sigh. "That was a dirty trick you pulled coming here in that condition trying to play on my sympathies."

"It didn't work so why are you angry?"

"I'm angry that you tried something like that. First off you shouldn't have ever talked to me the way you did. You shouldn't have given me an ultimatum. And if you hadn't meant it you shouldn't have broken up with me and then expected that all you had to do was change your mind and I'd be okay with that. To top it off you definitely shouldn't have come here without first making up and giving me a sincere apology. Of course it worked with my parents. They think I'm the worst person in the world. If you allow yourself to become a bum I'll never forgive you."

"And you'll stop loving me?"

"I'll never stop loving you. But there is a possibility I will stop being in love with you. I won't be with you if you go down the path you seem hell bent to go down. You're not Poppi and his life is not yours. You have options, Dominic. It looks as though you are deliberately trying to ruin your life. I'm trying to understand the effect Poppi has had on you your entire life. God knows my dad has the same control over me. And though you shared some of what's going on with my parents I'm aware you haven't told them everything. There's more. You still haven't told me what set you off. Don't you think you should?"

"I was thinking perhaps we could make love first."

"I'm really not in a mood to make love."

She waited but he was giving her a look as though...as though he didn't believe her she realized. He slid the jeans down his hips slower than was necessary and gave her a sly grin before taking her in his arms.

"Dom, I've told you I'll never use sex as a weapon and I won't. But before this goes any further, there's something I need to tell you." She took a deep breath. "If we make love right now I'm going to feel used. And if I feel used I'm going to resent you and be angry at myself for allowing my body and my love for you to be used, for allowing you to manipulate me." She felt his grip loosen but he didn't take his arms from around her.

"Can I at least hold you?"

That did it. No matter how hard she wanted to be, the sadness in his voice got to her big time.

"Baby, please let me help you. Let's go away for a few days," she urged, wrapping her arms around him, pressing her lips into his neck. "You need a break, you need to..." she wanted to tell him he needed her, needed to reaffirm their love, but this wasn't about them. Of course on many levels and for her it was. But she knew for Dominic it was about Poppi and his family.

Shudders were racing rapidly through his body making Sadie reconsider her decision. Maybe her leaving him had been the last straw. Shouldn't she have his back if she were stronger at the moment? Was there a time when you simply gave up on the one you loved? If not, it wasn't a good thing she'd done, and she shouldn't be battling with him. Her parents were right.

She was being selfish. If anything happened to him she'd never forgive herself.

"I'm sorry, you're hurting. I want to help you. Let me help you, Dom. Talk to me," she pleaded massaging his shoulders, trying to take away his pain. "Dom... I..I..."

She wanted badly to tell him she'd come home, but she couldn't force the words out. Her man was hurting, she loved him with her whole heart and she believed she had the power to take away some of his pain. So why couldn't she do it? Why couldn't she say the words? *Fear,* she realized. Nothing had changed. In fact if anything he was worse. He was an emotional wreck. He had nothing to give her. And as selfish as it might be she still needed him in spite of his pain.

With a loud groan he moved his arms from around her. "The way I've been behaving, this isn't me. It's confusing that I would behave in this manner."

Dominic pulled away from Sadie as he reached for the pillows, punched them softly several times then leaned into the hollow he'd made. His mind was beginning to clear. There were some things he was angry about. The fact that Sadie left him in his darkest hour was tops among them.

"I am too damn old to be acting like a punk, yet that's what's been going on with me. Do you want me to tell you why I haven't slept? I've been going over and over all of my relationships, trying to see where I'd screwed up, what I could have done to make things better. And my conclusion: I did nothing wrong, with perhaps the exception of the way I talked to you. You didn't deserve that." On the last note of that word he turned on the bedside lamp to stare at Sadie.

"I did nothing wrong. Not even with you, Sadie." He witnessed the disbelief that crossed Sadie's face and saw the instant the first signs of annoyance sprung to life. Sadie would not run away from him. Tonight he would have his say.

"From the day I met you, I have never lied to you. I have loved you with each and every breath I've taken. I have not stabbed you in the heart. I've not plotted with the boss against you and I have not taken a new lover. Sadie, maybe you haven't slept with Paul yet, but it's not far off. I can see it in your eyes. You think you're justified. You're not justified to have treated me the way you have for almost an entire year.

"Take tonight for instance. I came to your door remembering that you said you would never turn me away and yet you looked at me with disgust. You didn't show concern, but anger. You stayed away from me all night, not touching me, not kissing, not even a hug. And I needed your touch when I came here so badly. So what if I was not presentable? So what if I smelled foul? I would not have done the same to you. I would have opened my arms and pulled you into them.

"Another thing: Paul should not have been coming here, not when you told me that I was always welcome. I don't give a damn that you needed to work with him. Since we're putting our cards on the table I thought you should know of my disgust with your actions."

Dominic was getting a bit worked up and could no longer stay in the bed. "Then to tell me if I made love to you you'd feel used. What kind of shit is that to tell your man, Sadie?"

Sadie was quietly listening to Dominic's rant tapping her fingers on her cheeks. She was giving credence to his words wanting to be fair, to see if she'd treated him unfairly and then she heard words he shouldn't have spoken. How the hell did he know she would be working with Paul? Had his little break down been planned?

"Okay, I get it, my father called and told you if you wanted your woman you'd better get your ass over here, that Paul was coming over to work with me. And I'm hoping that you said you'd needed to clean up." She gave him a look and shook her head. "I've got it. But you said you were no longer my man. You said you were going to start dating and I should do likewise."

"You knew I wasn't going to date anyone. You knew I was letting off steam because I was furious with you."

"We're going to take this point by point. Some things you've said are true. I've done things to hurt our relationship maybe..." then she stopped. This wasn't going to be a tit for tat talk.

"Dominic, tonight was strictly about working. I'm not using Paul to hurt you. I didn't assign him to work cases with me and I'm not about to ask for anyone to replace him. Paul's a damn good lawyer and we both know that. My making such a request wouldn't be fair to him. I won't have anyone doubting his abilities or mine."

She tilted her head a bit and narrowed her eyes. "And I won't have them pitying you or me. Everyone would know I'd made the request because you can't deal with my working with Paul. That would make us both appear weak. And we would be."

Taking a deep breath Sadie let it out. "Lately I have enjoyed being around Paul a hell of a lot more than I've enjoyed being around you. I'm not saying that to hurt you. I want you to be aware of what's going on. I'm human. I'm a woman and I need certain things. Lately, you have been in no condition to give those things to me. Granted, you've been dealing with a lot. But I'm not going to give you a free pass to screw me over. So if you're thinking you're getting that from me think again. You're not going to make me feel guilty, Dom. It's not going to work. You're a grown ass man. You're my man and lately you're making me ashamed to admit that fact."

The words were out before she'd even thought about it. Never once in all of her thoughts had she ever thought those words. But the moment they were out between them Sadie knew she'd meant them. She stared hard at Dominic and held his gaze.

Oh God, she thought, she shouldn't have said that. She needed to do something quickly. Moving from the bed she went to the desk in the corner and removed pen and paper. "Let's figure out a way to get our relationship back on track, let's do it together."

She wrote down, *stop hurting each other*, in bold letters and underlined it, then showed it to Dominic.

"Want to add anything?" she asked holding the pad out to him. When he only stared as her as though she'd lost her mind she pulled the tablet back toward her and wrote a second item.

Start from this moment with a clean slate. Once again she held the tablet out and once again he ignored it. Okay Sadie thought, I've hurt him beyond repair. Then she scribbled some more.

Talk, neither of us are mind readers. We must tell the other one what we need. She held the tablet out to him.

"Dominic, tell me what you need from me."

"I need you to remove your dagger from my heart."

Deep sobs came from her throat and Sadie covered her face. *We're not going to make it,* she thought. *Dominic and I are in trouble.*

Dominic sat in a chair in the opposite corner of the room steeling himself against Sadie's tears. He swallowed several times not uttering a word, waiting for her to finish.

"Why are you trying so hard to push me away?" Sadie asked scrubbing at her eyes looking at Dom through a teary haze. There was the slightest flicker in his eyes. He blinked rapidly trying to recover and she suddenly knew what he'd been doing all along. Rushing from the bed she fell to her knees between his thighs and wrapped her arms around him.

"You're such a fool. What nonsense is this that you've decided to push me away?"

His hand touched her hair and for a moment they lingered then he attempted to push her from him just as he'd been doing emotionally. Only this time she was aware of his ploy.

"Sangana," she whispered. "You stupid jackass. How dare you set out deliberately to destroy us? You don't have that right. And if you were testing me you didn't have the right to do that either. Sangana," she said again then stood and held her hand out to him. "Come back to bed. Show me how much you really love me."

"I thought you said you'd feel used if I made love to you."

"That was then. This is now. Now there is a need for us to make love. We need that connection. I'm not giving up on us just yet."

"It's just sex, Sadie," Dominic replied sadly.

"Right. It's never been just about sex with us and you damn well know it. That's why we made the promise never to use it as a weapon and that's why I said what I did earlier. If it had been just about the sex, I wouldn't have said a word. But it's about us, and what we mean to each other. It's how we communicate honestly with each other even though our hearts are breaking."

She crawled into the bed refusing to let go of Dominic's hand, kissing him until he had no recourse but to kiss her in return. Right now he needed her more than she needed to make him do things he clearly wasn't ready to do. He'd decided to not only, not fight for them, but in essence to let her go. Now that she knew what was going on she wasn't having it. He was too important to her. And she was too important to him. So she sat about to kiss away his pains, if only momentarily. His arms cradled her and he moaned her name so achingly tender with a beseeching tone of heartbreak.

"We're going to make a plan, Dom, and we're going to fix this. We're going to go away and recapture all that we've lost. I love you baby and I know you love me. We've got to work together and find something that works for both of us."

His hands began a slow tour of her hips as though he were tracing the shape of her to be stored for future use. The thought stilled her, scaring her that perhaps she'd miscalculated. Perhaps they'd already gone past the point of no return. Once again the thought that they were in trouble came to mind. Their loving was different. She was loving him with passion and he was touching her as though he was doing it for the last time.

"Dominic, stop doing that," she pleaded. "Whatever is going on in your mind, let it go and love me."

Still he continued kissing her leisurely, touching her with reverence, slowly, over and over each inch of her body. With intent Sadie began caressing him, kissing him all over, sliding downward until he pulled her up and flipped her over onto her back. He looked at her so long and so tenderly that she trembled, but she trembled with uneasiness.

"Dom, stop looking at me, okay?" He gave her a half smile scaring the hell out of her. "I'll come home," she said, "I'll spend the weekend with you."

"Not good enough," he answered and took one of her nipples into his mouth.

"It's a start."

His head lifted and he smiled again. "Starting, Sadie? We've been together almost five years. We should be starting a family. What kind of start are you talking about?"

"Starting again before all the things that have split us apart began happening."

"You mean before you made junior partner?" Dominic asked, once again taking her nipple into his mouth. He waited a moment, paused then looked at her. "Sadie, don't you know the problems we're having started before I was born?"

"And you're going to allow it to destroy us. Please, Dominic, please don't. Let me help you, please."

"You are helping me, Sadie. You're making love to me. And you're allowing me to make love to you. That's the best help I could hope for."

He began worshiping her body drowning out her words and her quiet tears with his loving of her. Sadie was right. Things had changed. How could he not have expected to lose Sadie when he'd lost himself?

"Then I'll come home for good. If that's what it takes, I'll come home." Sadie had no choice. It no longer mattered if she was his option. Something had destroyed him. She couldn't let things go any farther. She couldn't allow him to lose himself.

"No, you're not ready and you don't really want to."

"But, I'll come."

"Tell me you want to."

As he thrust into her Sadie moaned and pressed her lips against his throat. It wasn't lust that drove them but desperation and sadness. With each stroke Sadie clung to Dominic, pleading with her body. He ignored her words for him to not love her in the manner he was doing. It was so exquisite; each stroke brought her joy and pain.

He was preparing to let her go and she was preparing to let him. Oh God, that couldn't be right She couldn't let him leave her. She had to say something, do something, but what? Sadie clung to Dominic wondering if she gave him the words he wanted to hear, if he'd stop stroking her so slowly that he was driving her and himself insane.

"Te Amo, Sadie."

"You're scaring me."

"I tell you I love you and that scares you."

"Don't leave me, Dom."

"You left me remember?"

"I left our home, Dom. I didn't leave you."

Pulling partway out of Sadie's heat he plunged back in hard, fast, and raised her hips so he could go deeper. Stroke after stroke he increased the pace as though the ghosts he'd been running from were catching up with him.

"It sure as hell feels like you've left me. I sleep alone. I eat along...if it walks like a man alone and talks like a man alone then, Sadie, baby isn't a man alone, a man who's been left by the woman he loves."

Then Dominic stopped talking and rode Sadie hard, pressing her legs tighter around his body. He'd told the truth when he'd told her he needed her. He did. And with each stroke he was drawing strength from her. He drove into to her repeatedly stopping when either of them were on the brink, not wanting it to end. At last feeling his body claimed by the tremors of Sadie's release, he lifted her up so they were both in a position for maximum pleasure and took possession of her body, swallowing her scream with a brutal kiss, burying his pain in his loving of her body. Allowing himself to at last gain relief he reveled in it, letting it take him over completely, clutching tightly to Sadie he stroked even after he was spent. Sadie's cries and soft pleas were lost on him. He held her tightly, turning to reposition her on top, knowing they would both finally fall asleep like that.

Chapter Twenty-Three

For a long moment Sadie stood watching Dominic as he slept. Even in sleep he appeared to be exhausted. His making love to her had done what nothing else could. It was making her reverse her decision to give them some time apart time for him to remember that he needed to help her protect their relationship. He'd made love to her with the intent that it would be the last time. She wasn't having that. Despite her wanting him to snap out of it she had no choice but to move back home.

Resentment over the most potent emotional blackmail he could have used simmered beneath the surface but losing Dominic when her moving back home could be what it would take to allow him to heal, she felt she didn't have a choice. She loved him. Accepting his newest proposal would still have to be something to be dealt with later but she'd conceded this point. She would return home.

The beginning of a plan formulated. They needed their jobs and had to find a way to ensure they'd keep them. Right now Dominic was skating on very thin ice, and if she wasn't careful she would be right there beside him. Love was one thing but you couldn't pay your bills with love.

First things first, Dom needed time off. She would go to Mr. Secret and ask if she could fill in for him. The cases she was working on with Paul were but the briefest of thoughts. She was really enjoying the case but it couldn't be helped. She'd talk to him and finish up the one case, then work in the Woodridge office until Dominic could handle it.

Now if she could come up with a good enough excuse, something that wouldn't come back to bite either her or Dom in the butt. She was being quiet wanting to let him sleep, but he called out to her as her hand touched the knob of the door.

"Sadie, where are you going?" Dominic asked sleepily.

"Home."

"Home?"

"Yes, home. There are some things I need to do. I'll be back in a little while and we can make plans. Go back to sleep and when I return I'll make you a big breakfast." She turned made her way to the bed and kissed him absentmindedly on the forehead, tucking the covers around him, then she walked to the door, blew him a kiss and left.

"Breakfast is ready." her mom called to her. "Where's Dominic?"

'He's sleeping. I'm going to go home to take care of a couple of things. I'll be back in a couple of hours. I'll make him breakfast when I return."

"I have it all ready."

"I know, Mom but you shouldn't be taking care of him. That's my job. Besides, I'm going to make his favorites."

"Your way of apologizing for the way you treated him last night?"

Pressing her lips together Sadie turned to face her father knowing soon she'd have to question him for once again betraying her by calling Dominic to come over. "I hadn't thought of making him breakfast as an apology but," she hunched her shoulder. "Whatever."

"Are you going to marry him?"

"One day I hope I will. But if you're asking me again about accepting that proposal he gave last night the answer is still no. But, I am going home with him. Thanks for letting me stay while I sorted things out."

With that Sadie decided it was best to leave before she started bawling. Any other time she would have kissed her father but now she really didn't want to. She knew how much he liked Dom but still he hadn't even tried to understand her feelings. No one had, except maybe Paul. She cringed at having thought about him. She'd have to give him a call when she went to the house so that she could at least let him know she wouldn't be coming to the office. *Could her life get any worse?* she wondered.

***

Dominic listened to the muffled sounds coming behind the closed door. He couldn't tell what was going on but he could just imagine. Disbelief that Sadie had actually tucked him in set off something inside of him. Did she now think he was a child? The thought got lost. Sadie was right, he was exhausted he acknowledged, and fell back to sleep

***

"Please, Paul," Sadie pleaded. "Cover for me and don't mention to anyone that I wasn't in court."

"What the hell is going on with you, Sadie? I can't believe that you'd jeopardize your career like this. What kind of man is Santiago that he'd allow this nonsense?"

"Paul, it's just a case. I'll be there in a couple of days and I'll close, I promise. What's the big deal?"

"Could the big deal be that we needed to work on this case last night. We need to work on it today and you're giving me no idea when you plan to return. You won't even tell me what's going on."

'I can't."

"That just makes it worse. Now you're using my feelings for you to do something that you shouldn't. We both know you're going about all of this in the wrong way. I'm very disappointed in you."

For a moment there was silence.

"I'm sorry, Paul," Sadie said softly. "I'm in a real jam and I wouldn't have asked if it weren't so important. That's okay, you're right. I don't want to presume on our friendship. I'll call the office."

"Sadie," Paul said and sighed. "We both know I'm going to cover for you."

"Thanks, Paul."

"My God, Sadie, Santiago is becoming an albatross. You're going to be forced to make a decision soon."

"I've made my decision, Paul, thanks."

Hanging up the phone Sadie took a look at the house and began cleaning. She wasn't in a hurry to return to her parents or to see Dom. Yes, she was returning home. Yes, she loved him. But something about her giving in like this left a bad taste in her mouth. She didn't like compromising herself or losing Paul's respect. If she wasn't convinced that Dominic would do something crazy she'd kick his behind to the curb.

***

She needed to take a breath of air before she walked into the house. Dom could read her like no one else and she darn well knew he was going to be observing her. She said a quick prayer that he'd still be sleeping as she walked inside.

The stop in conversation wasn't a total surprise but it hurt. This was her home, these were her parents. Dom was her man, but they were all treating her as an intruder, as though she'd walked in on their private conversation. She stared at them all thinking it would be a good thing to just let it go.

"Looks like I should have called, or made more noise before coming in."

She stood for a moment staring at the three of them, feeling like an outsider. Letting out a breath she walked quickly to Dominic and gave him a quick peck on the forehead and turned away. He grabbed her arm, spun her around and stood up looking deep into her eyes.

He whispered. "What you just did was akin to taking my temperature. I don't have a fever," he said softly, wrapping her in his arms and plunging his tongue into her mouth giving her a passion filled kissed. He was not about to allow her to treat him as her pet project.

When he released her, she stumbled a bit and he grinned at her. "I don't need a nurse, Sadie." He picked up his mug and sipped his coffee sitting down to the table.

"Considering that you've cooked a grand total of seven times in the almost five years we've been together I can't wait to see what you plan to make for me."

Sadie was looking at him strangely; so many emotions flitted across her face in rapid succession. It told him so much more than her words. She was confused, worried for him, scared for them and she loved him.

But beneath all of that he sensed residual anger toward him. He couldn't blame her. He'd put her through hell the past year. She was right to still be angry. His most precious treasure was her love, and he'd allowed it to sit unattended gathering dust. And he knew she was, wondering if he loved her still if he was willing to walk away from her.

Watching her trying to cook was amusing, watching her trying to cook in a kitchen that was not her own was hilarious. She knew where nothing was. It didn't matter what final concoction she placed before him he'd eat it and ask for seconds.

As touched as he was by her culinary attempts he recognized with that action that Sadie had changed the status quo. He cooked for her, worried about her, cared for her, earned the living. He cringed. Seemed like he did still have an issue or two to work out. But he wouldn't do it here. Sadie was trying so damn hard he'd not make it any harder.

He glanced suspiciously at the plate of food she put before him and leaned both elbows on the table supporting his chin on his hand. He knew he'd promised to eat whatever Sadie cooked but at least he needed to know what it was intended to be.

"Sadie, what is this?" he asked.

At first disappointment lit her eyes then amusement.

"Breakfast, now eat it."

Dipping his fork into the mixture on his plate he noticed Sadie opted for yogurt, a sure sign that maybe he should also. But no, he ate it and darn if he didn't enjoy it and ask for seconds glad that he had when Sadie beamed at him. It was the first real smile he'd seen on her face in months. The knowledge sickened Dominic. What the hell had he done to them? He had to fix things. He was Sadie's man, the man she was going to marry. He had to be that for her.

Ten seconds after he'd cleaned his plate Sadie plopped into the chair beside him and opened up a notebook and began writing on the legal pads. She was planning his life while he barely listened. She was talking of making an appointment for him for therapy. He couldn't believe it. Sadie wanted him to take drugs to deal with his problems.

"I'll call in and ask for a medical leave for you. Then I'll ask to come to Woodridge and work until you're able to return."

"What about the cases you're working with Paul? How are you going to do your work and mine?"

He was watching her closely, his mind in a tailspin. This was all too fucking insane. He wasn't a kid, why the hell was Sadie talking about taking over his life like that? Did she think a week of his having lost it meant he didn't have cohoonies?

Blinking several times he was trying his best not to lose his temper. On some level he was aware that Sadie was trying to help, trying to have his back, but this was not the way it was supposed to be and not the way he would allow it to remain.

Frowning Dominic remembered why he'd received the urgent call from Sadie's father in the first place. Sadie had invited Paul to dinner, to work on a case her father had said. He'd insisted Dominic come immediately. When he'd tried to tell him he needed to shower and change Sadie's father had insisted that he had no time, telling him not to bother with a shower.

Dominic had driven over on pure adrenaline ready to pulverize Paul, expecting to find them in a hot and heavy embrace. He'd been crazed and made even more so by Sadie's father dire warning, the look on Sadie's face when she's seen him unkempt was never a look he wanted to see from her again. Their perfect life had long ago degenerated into a dung heap. If it had been so important that Sadie needed to work with Paul the night before why was she sitting in her mother's kitchen with him making plans to take care of him as though he were an invalid? Why wasn't she dressing to go work on her important case with Paul?

"Sadie," Dominic interrupted her plans for them. "Why aren't you at work?" She blinked a couple of times and he was aware she was thinking of a lie, something they'd never done a year before. But now it seemed lying to each other was becoming the norm. "Sadie, baby, don't sugar coat it. Why aren't you at work?"

"You need me, Dom."

Another stab into his heart. Closing his eyes tightly he shook his head slowly from side to side and worried his lips chewing on them. He had to stop this.

"Sadie, you're supposed to be working on a case with Paul. You thought it was so important that you invited him here for dinner last night." A brief flicker of anger as Sadie's head snapped up and she cast a glare toward the area where her father had disappeared some time before. She was still angry with him that much was obvious.

"What did you do, Sadie?"

"I asked Paul to cover for me."

"God!" Dominic groaned. "What did you tell him?"

"That we had a family emergency and I couldn't come in."

"What did he say?"

"That the case was important, that I was jeopardizing my career." Sadie was worrying her lips with her teeth before she finished. "I don't care, Dom, about any of it. You're more important to me."

"But you should care, Sadie. Do you think you're going to just pick up a junior partnership like that? What the hell is wrong with you? Why are you doing this?"

"I have to make things right for us."

"Guilt, Sadie?"

"Love, Dom."

"You sure there's no guilt?"

"Maybe a little. How could there not be when you haven't forgiven me. But mostly it's about my loving you and my doing anything in my power to save you."

"Save me?" Dom snapped.

"To save us, Dom. We've come so far in the opposite direction that I barely recognize us anymore. I don't like where we are."

"And where is that?"

"At a crossroad. For you to have to even ask me that question tells me how far apart we've become."

"It has nothing to do with you wanting out of this relationship, that you want to leave a sinking ship and a drowning man?" Her forehead wrinkled in puzzlement. "Sorry. Shawn told me I was behaving like a drowning man with not enough sense to reach out and grasp the life preserver being thrown to me."

'What are you talking about?" Sadie asked not bothering to hid her confusion.

"The bio. Michael." Sadie was staring at him as though he'd gone completely insane. He had to explain at least some of it. "Shawn wants to know why I don't get to know Michael. That if Poppi no longer wants to be my father that I have a biological father wanting to get to know me. I'm not a little kid, Sadie. It's not like I've been searching for a father. I already had one."

Seeing the immense sadness for him in Sadie's beautiful eyes he became angry. "I wish I'd never told you how it was for me growing up. I wish I'd done as Poppi asked and kept the promise I made to him. I never should have said a word. You haven't looked at me the same since then." He thought over the past months. "You haven't looked at me the same since you made partner."

***

Sorrow pure and simple filled her veins and she was breathing hard, not speaking in order to control it. She was determined not to allow Dominic to get to her. Perhaps Dominic was still attempting to push her away. It was true that being made a junior partner had been the beginning of their problems. But that initial catalyst was not her fault or her doing. How could something that was going to be the beginning of their living their dreams if Dominic had gotten it be so wrong when she was given the title?

Dominic was staring at her with something she couldn't read in his gaze. She remembered the way he'd made love to her the night before, the letting her go and she stilled her resentment at him, herself and the situation. If only his mother had not had an affair. If only he truly were Poppi's son. Then he wouldn't be sitting looking at her so broken, so willing to give up on them, to throw her love away.

"I think this is a talk we should have at home." She swallowed

"Then what do you recommend after we get home and work it out?"

He was being sarcastic. She was going to let it go. "I think I'll call a couple of travel agents and see what kind of deals we can get right now. Maybe a cruise," she tried to smile but he wasn't smiling back so she stopped.

"Te amo, Dom."

"I know you do baby. I love you too. You ready to go home?" He gave a snort. "Unless you think I'm too disgusting to leave here. If so I'll shower now."

Why was he doing this?" he wondered when she was trying so hard to make things right. She'd agreed to return home when in his heart he knew she wasn't ready. She didn't want to return home just yet and he shouldn't want her to, not until she really wanted it.

Love. Their love had become not only tainted but unrecognizable. There was no way for Dominic to fix what was wrong between him and Sadie until he fixed what was wrong with himself. The ghost had found a home in his spirit. And like it or not, it was time he dealt with it like a man.

***

He remained quiet, listening to Sadie making calls to the office, talking to their boss, then to the travel agents saying she'd go pick up brochures. They'd yet to talk. He'd not told her that Poppi was suing him for the return of his name. She was feeling sorry enough for him already.

"Tell you what," Dominic volunteered. "I want to go by the Woodridge office and take care of a couple of things. I'll pick up the travel brochures. Don't make lunch," he said. "When I return, I'll take you out."

He ran the pad of his thumb over Sadie's face, gazing at her, loving her, then he kissed her, releasing her.

"Dom?"

"Don't worry, baby. You have tried telling me the things I need to do in order not to lose you. Well, there are things I need to do in order not to lose me. I'm going to do those things for both of us. I need to check on a couple of things then I'll leave." He gave her another kiss. "I love you Sadie." Walking into his bedroom he pretended to be on the phone, anything to make sure Sadie gave him some privacy. Then he scribbled a hasty letter to Sadie and placed it in his underwear drawer along with the court papers served on him by Poppi, knowing eventually she'd do the laundry and find it. When he walked out the door he made sure to leave his cell on the dresser in their bedroom.

**

Ringing the bell of his parents' home Dominic waited. Things had not been left in a good way after he'd gone there after being served with the papers. He'd given his parents time to digest what they were doing to him. He didn't want to end their relationship. He was hoping they could talk reasonably now.

Hell, no one had given him time to digest the information when he was ten. No, his father had merely beaten the hell out of him and that was the end of the matter. Then of course there was the matter of that ridiculous promise he'd forced a ten year old to make. Since leaving Sadie he no longer blamed her for his wanting to unload on her. He should have told her straight away about the things that were important to him.

As he rang the bell several more times after not getting an answer he sighed in disgust. There was no way to know what would happen if they allowed him in, but the knowledge that he had to confront his parents before things could ever be made right with him and Sadie was paramount on his list. The door opened and his mother with a frown on her face looked at him with something close to hatred in her eyes. It was so vivid, it made him cringe.

"What are you doing here, Dominic?"

This coldness coming her had to be part of a bad dream. "I think we need to talk about all of this."

"No need for talking. Your father doesn't want you here. You got the papers so you know. You're not welcome."

"Are you serious? I'm not welcome in the home I bought for you?"

His mother shrugged her shoulder and looked away from him before she turned back to glare angrily at him. "You've made trouble for us. Your father and I were happy. We've been fighting for a month. It's all your fault."

Whatever else may have happened Dominic knew this mess was not of his making. His relationship with Sadie, now that he'd accept the blame for. But not this. "Mom, I did not go behind my father's back and sleep with another man. I did not have a baby and not bother to tell the kid who the father was. I did not raise that kid in a home where he felt different, unwanted, unloved, always having to prove himself. I did not beat the hell out of a kid when he was ten because he'd taken a bike ride with his brother. And I didn't lie to him for his entire life that his father hadn't wanted him."

"Your father—"

"No, not Poppi. It's clear not much has changed on how he feels about me. I regret that. I love him and always will whether or not he loves me. I'm talking about Michael, my biological father. I believe him because I know the two you didn't make the kind of money that came into the house. When I was a kid I'd never thought about it. But I've had time to put two and two together. I believe he loved me because he has proof and I've seen his love for me in his eyes, something I've never seen in Poppi's eyes."

"So you've made your decision?"

Poppi must have been behind the door because he was not there one second then the next he was. Dominic blinked.

"Poppi why do you think if I have a relationship with my brother and his family and yes, even with my biological father, that it has to take away from what we have?"

"You are no longer my son, Dominic. I wish you had never carried my name You don't deserve it. You're not Hispanic, you're a gringo, a half breed. I will fight to make sure your name is changed."

This was going too far. He'd thought all that was needed was a little time for Poppi to get over his anger. Dominic Santiago was his name. What would he do if Poppi followed through on his threat to have his name changed? He tried to think, could he legally do that? He should have researched it. He should have asked for Sadie's help in researching it. She was the best damn researcher around. But the bigger issue remained. Did Dominic even want a name his father didn't want him to have?

He decided to try again. "Poppi, can't we talk about this? We can work out something, I'm sure. I'm not trying to replace you. I promise."

"Your promises are no good, Dominic."

That stopped him cold in his tracks. Sadie had told him the same thing. His control snapped and he glared back at the father who was glaring at him.

"And whose fault is that Poppi? When you teach children to be dishonest they become dishonest with other people. You and mom taught me to be dishonest. You think I'm dishonoring you by trying to know people who make up the other part of me. Maybe if things had been different..." Dominic stopped. "I'm thirty-three in little more than a month I'll be thirty-four. To be that old and still worried about what my parents think is pretty dam sad. I should have searched for my biological family long ago. I didn't because of not wanting to hurt you, some stupid promise you forced a kid to give."

The rage was building in him as he thought of the things he'd given up for this family. Damn it, he and Sadie were having the hardest period of their relationship because of his hunger to be Poppi's obedient son. Sadie had seen through the manipulation and Poppi was aware of it. That was the reason for the animosity between them. He stopped talking to his father and turned toward his mother. "Is this the way you feel about it too?"

"Yes, Dominic," she answered him, holding his gaze without fear of repercussion from her husband. She was truly angry with Dominic.

"Listen, you think because she is your mother her answer would be different. You owe your life to me, Dominic. Your mother wanted to kill you. I stopped her." Poppi laughed out loud for several seconds then he stood there smiling.

The smile on Poppi's face was more sinister than anything Dominic had ever seen in his life. It would be wise to leave before the words that would really destroy him could come out. But he didn't move. He couldn't. A look of horror filled his mother's eyes and she pulled on Poppi's sleeve. "Don't," she pleaded.

"No," Poppi laughed. He thinks because he's a lawyer he's so damn smart. Let me show you, Dominic, just how smart I am. I knew from the beginning you were worth a lot. And I'm not talking about you becoming a lawyer. I knew your mother's mistake would profit us. I knew her lover would pay and he did. We made him pay dearly. He was so taken through the years with my wife that all she had to do was cry a little, tell him how very afraid she was and he'd give her anything she wanted. Sure he threatened many times to take you, but she'd meet him, cry and tell him how she couldn't live without you, that you were part of him and if he'd ever loved her and loved you he wouldn't take her child. He never did."

"He's as soft as you, Dominic. And you're as big a fool as he is. You've been free to leave my home and search for your father since you were eighteen, and look at you, you're here begging a man who never wanted you to remain your father. And you've been stupid enough to fall in love with Sadie a woman who's haughty, too proud, and thinks she's a man. A woman who took your job, make more money than you do and screws around on you." Then he laughed emitting a harsh and brutal sound. "You are truly your father's son. Get the hell away from this house, Dominic, you have no family here."

"Then I guess there is nothing more for me to say is there? I'm not casting the two of you out of my life. But the Dominic gravy train has come to end. Because I am who I am, I will not do it so abruptly. Next month you will receive fifteen hundred dollars, the next month, one thousand, then finally five hundred. That will be the last payment. The name you no longer want me to use, for your information, I've paid for the use of that name and so has my father. And, Poppi, in case you think that makes me stupid, I have my own reason for not just cutting you off. You want me, you know where to find me."

Dominic walked away feeling empty. He didn't know what he'd expected, but surely not the ice cold reception from his mother. He'd also not expected to be told in such a brutal way that he'd been nothing more than a means to bring more money into Poppi's pocket even before he was born. As for his mother, he wanted badly to believe his mother was behaving the way she was because of Poppi, but it wasn't true. His mother's actions were her own. He sighed. There was one more member of his family that he had to see, Roberto. He'd told his sisters but would wait until later to see them face to face. He couldn't do all that needed doing in one day. But he needed to talk to Roberto. Taking a quick glance at his watch he knew his brother was still at work. In thoughtful concentration he chewed on his lips intending to go to Roberto's job to talk to him since he'd adamantly told him he wasn't welcome in his home.

Thirty minutes later Dominic's was sitting in his car wondering what would be his next move.   His brother's attitude had been the same as his parents but he'd gone even a step further ordering him not to bother any other family member with his nonsense, telling him none of them wanted anything else to do with him, making Dominic feel more and more like the bastard Poppi had screamed that he was. It didn't appear he was really welcome anywhere.

Then he thought of Shawn, the brother who'd been watching over him for so many years, who'd craved a relationship with him. He reached into his pocket for his phone but remembered he'd left it home so Sadie wouldn't be able to reach him. He'd never just dropped in on Shawn. He wondered if he should, and decided no time like the present. If Shawn really meant the standing invitation he'd given, telling him he was welcome anytime, now was the time to put that to the test.

***

It was now or never, do or die, Dominic thought as he made his way to the front door of his brother's home. Glancing around taking note of the upscale neighborhood and professional landscaping he knew Sadie would be happy living in this neighborhood. Once again he wondered what line of work his brother was in. Whatever it was, it sure as hell paid well. He rang the bell thinking of his wish to provide Sadie with the kinds of luxuries his brother provided for his family. He wanted to provide those things for Sadie without her help.

Katie opened the door and smiled at him moving in to hug him. That was one thing he wasn't sure if he'd ever get used to. They were definitely a bunch of touch feely people always hugging him. He hugged her back admitting reluctantly to himself that he rather liked it.

"I want to apologize," Dominic began, "for just barging over like this without calling to ask if it were okay."

By that time Shawn had come to the door and both he and Katie were looking at him strangely.

"Why do you think you'd need to call first?" Shawn asked. "You're my brother; you're welcome here anytime day or night, no call necessary."

"I don't have my cell with me." Dominic hunched his shoulders still not moving across the threshold.

"Dominic, get in here," Shawn laughed pulling him through the door. "What do you want to drink?"

"I'm good." He couldn't help wondering if this reception was because of the newness of the relationship. Whatever it was he sure wished that at least Berto had welcomed him. His visit here, with his brother was to make peace with his past. He wanted to become better acquainted with his brother and he wanted to finally accept the hand that his father had offered. Dominic stood staring at Shawn and Katie, wondering at what point he'd come to think of his biological father as more than the bio. Hell Poppi had disowned him. Maybe it was time to elevate his bio just a bit in his life.

"Why the heck are you standing there looking so uncomfortable?" Shawn asked. "Come on in and relax and tell me what the heck's going on. It's obvious you want to talk."

"Sadie came home."

Tilting his head to the side Shawn studied him. "That's a good thing right?"

"I thought it would be," he answered glancing at Katie. "She's not back for the right reasons." He ran his hand over his face and sawed his bottom lip with his teeth.

Seeing Dominic hesitance to talk, Shawn turned to his wife. "Honey, could you make us a snack please?" He waited until his wife was safely out of the room then he lead Dominic to the back of the house to his office. He closed the door.

"Spill it little brother."

A smile lit Dominic's face. "You do think of me like that don't you?"

"I always have. Just be glad that I've stopped calling you my baby brother. What's going on, Dominic?"

"It's my life, my damn imperfect life. My parents have both disowned me. They're suing me for the return of the Santiago name. Berto wants nothing to do with me. And apparently neither does any other member of my family. Then there's Sadie. She didn't want to come back. But she's afraid I'm going to kill myself. She's worried about me."

"Does she have reason to worry?"

Dominic gave a halfhearted smile. "I'm not thinking of killing myself if that's what you're asking me."

"In that case why is Sadie worried that you're thinking it?"

Dominic lifted his eyes to stare at his brother. "I've been acting like it for a week, not going to work, not sleeping, just not giving a damn."

"And?"

"And I allowed Sadie's father to get me riled up when I was in that state. He called me to warn me." Dominic stopped and laughed. "He wanted me to interrupt Sadie's plans she'd made with Paul."

"She's dating him now?"

"No. But she invited him for dinner at her parents." He shook his head. "I did tell you she was staying with them, right?" When Shawn nodded in the affirmative he sighed again before continuing. "It was a business thing. But Sadie looked at me with such disappointment and disgust when I showed up at the door."

"Were you raging like the jealous fiancé we both know you are?"

"Not fiancé any longer. I didn't tell you, but Sadie called off the engagement after some nasty things I said."

"This just keeps getting better doesn't it?"

For a long moment there was nothing but silence. Before Dominic asked, "Do you want me to continue or what? I hadn't been bothering to shower or change and it pissed Sadie off that I was wallowing in self-pity. I got down on my knees and proposed to her again and she said, 'no way in hell."

Dominic ignored the way Shawn raised his brows in disbelief at him. He wasn't there, he hadn't seen Sadie's face, and he wasn't the one who'd made love to her as she cried.

"So when did she decide to return home?"

"Sometime during the middle of the night. She left this morning, kissed me on the forehead and tucked me in."

His mouth fell open and he opened his eyes wide. "Can you believe it? She really tucked me in like I was her son. Then she came back and made me breakfast. Sadie rarely cooks. Actually, that's a good thing because she's a horrible cook."

He couldn't help the way his lips quirked upwards into a smile. But thoughts of Sadie's cooking efforts always made him smile. Shaking his head to clear it he sighed and continued.

"She pulled out her legal pad while I was eating and made plans for my life, about how I was going to pull myself together. Then she called Paul, told him she wasn't coming to work and began calling travel agents for a vacation for the two of us."

"What's so wrong with that, Dominic?"

"It's the look I glimpsed in her eyes."

"She loves you."

"That I know, but I don't want her to pity me, to see me as less than a man. She moved home out of worry and pity, not love, not because she can't get along without me. She can Shawn. I've found that out, that she can do very well without me. She can do a lot better without me than I can do without her."

"So what are you going to do?"

"Pick up the pieces of my life and continue. I hope I haven't fucked up my job."

"What about your relationship with Sadie?"

"If I were done hurting her I wouldn't be here with you. I'm not going home for a while."

"You're back to punishing her?"

"I have no desire to punish Sadie. I am saddened and disappointed in her just as she is in me. I was hurt that she was more worried about my appearance instead of my state of mind."

"Ah, so you did leave home to punish her."

"That's not it at all. There's something I need to do and I really don't want to tell Sadie right now."

"Hmm."

Dominic stared at Shawn. "It was no accident that I didn't have a phone to call you. I left it home so Sadie wouldn't be able to reach me."

'Do you still love her, Dom?"

"With all my heart."

"Then why the hell are you doing your best to screw things up with her? She's at the breaking point, has been for some time and now you want to do more. Why can't you tell her your plans?"

"I'm afraid I don't really know my plans. Besides if I had taken the time to tell her, I know she would have been hurt. I've given her enough hurt to last a lifetime. If I'd seen the slightest flicker of hurt in her eyes I would have chickened out."

Shawn got up and began pacing stopping every few steps to narrow his eyes as he stared at his brother. "You're being rather vague but I believe you know more than what you're telling me. What are you planning?"

"I want to talk to your father and get to know him. I'm wondering if he'll go away for a few days with me so we can become acquainted."

"My father?"

"I don't know what to call him. I'm too damn old to call another man Poppi, Dad, or anything like that. I don't know him and I'm thinking maybe I really do need to get to know him. I want to repair things that have been wrong in my life for a very long time. I want to start with him."

"Where does Sadie think you are?"

"I was supposed to be picking up brochures at the travel agent."

"How long ago?"

Taking a look at his watch Dominic let out a low whistle. "It's been a few hours. But I haven't been idle. I drove downtown and went to talk to my boss. I'm not going to allow Sadie to clean up my mess. Then I went to my Woodridge office and gave them an explanation. It may have been lame but at least it came from me. I also went to see my parents and Berto. They didn't have much use for me, so I came here."

"To lick you wounds?" Shawn gave a laugh. "Dominic you have no idea how many years I wanted to be the brother you came to. I couldn't do a hell of a lot for you when you were a kid, but you can be damn sure I'll be here for you, whenever you need me."

Memories of the letters and cards he'd received through the years came with a rush to the forefront of Dominic's mind.

"That's not true, Shawn. Sometimes your words of encouragement were the only thing that kept me going. You influenced my life more than you know. I haven't said it to you yet but I want to do so now. Thank you for being a brother to me."

Closing his eyes Dominic nearly choked on a hard sob. He wasn't a punk, not a little boy, but, right now he was fragile and felt as though he'd break. He needed Sadie. He needed to feel her arms around him. But he wasn't going home to what he needed. He'd wait until he'd regained a sense of self. If he couldn't be made whole then he had no plans to return for Sadie.

It was as though his brother truly had a psychic link with him because before he'd finished the thought about Sadie comforting him, Shawn was hugging him tightly. Dominic heard the sob his brother did not try to hide. When Shawn was done hugging him he gave him a light punch in the shoulder.

"That's for making me cry," Shawn said and grinned as he wiped his eyes.

"Do you think your father will go?"

Shawn laughed. "Are you kidding me? He'll jump at the chance."

"What about your mother?"

"Are you inviting her?"

The first real smile appeared on both brothers lips as a soft knock sounded on the door. Katie came in with burgers, fries and beer on a wooden tray. "You two okay in here?" she asked.

"Yeah, Dominic is going to stay the night."

Katie frowned before speaking. "I thought you said Sadie came home." She stared first at Dominic then turned toward her husband.

Neither man would answer her and looked only at each other.

"Dominic, are you going to call Sadie?"

For a long moment Dominic wished he'd put more thought into his plan. He should have known Katie would question him. Women believed in fixing the world's problem. Well, Katie couldn't solve his problems and neither could Sadie. He found he had to clear his throat before answering his brother's wife. As it was his nerves were on edge. He didn't have the patience to walk on eggshells. He really only wanted to talk with Shawn.

"Katie, I have some things I need to do. I can't go home right now. Listen, if you'd rather I didn't stay," Dominic said quietly.

"Nonsense," Katie rushed forward wrapping her arms around him. "You're going through a lot. I know how much you love Sadie. I just don't want you to mess things up with her."

"You might say I'm doing this for her. I haven't dealt with my parentage and it's time I do." He sat back down and reached for the plate. "Thanks for the lunch, it looks delicious," he said as he took a healthy bite. "It tastes as good as it look," he complimented around a mouth full of burger. "Maybe you can give Sadie cooking lessons," he teased halfheartedly.

Shawn took a bite of his own burger before asking what was uppermost in his mind. "Are you calling Dad tonight?"

"Not tonight, I need to sleep on the idea."

"And you're not calling Sadie."

"Not tonight."

Dominic glanced from Shawn to Katie, then back to Shawn. "Listen, Shawn, like I said I'm not in need of a babysitter, okay? I really can't talk to Sadie right now or I'm not going to follow through with things. I need to do this."

"I'm sorry to butt in," Katie interrupted. She stopped when Shawn gave her a look and spoke.

"Dominic, I have to take care of something okay. Katie, will you keep him entertained until I get back?"

"Shawn, don't call him."

"I won't. That's something I agree with you about. You need to do it and you need to do it cold. If it were me, that's how I'd want it, no one paving the way for me. I promise I won't call. But I do have to take care of something," he said and left the room.

There was a moment of uncertainty between Dominic and Katie and Dominic laughed softly. "Your husband isn't very subtle. I know what he's doing." He waited until Shawn returned. The brothers stared at each other, both with amusement.

"Did you check everything thoroughly?"

"Yeah. You have to admit you're behaving a bit strangely. You don't have any emotional ties to him. But I happen to love him and think he's a pretty good guy."

Stretching out his legs in front of him Dominic shook his head slowly. "I don't blame you for thinking I'd try to harm him."

"What are you two talking about?" Katie demanded. "What is this about?"

"Your husband checked out my car to make sure I hadn't stashed any weapons. I'm going to ask his… I'm going to ask Shawn's father if he'd like to go somewhere with me for a few days so we can get to know each other."

Before he could finish the words Katie was hugging him again and this time she was crying.

"Oh my God! Dominic, you're giving him the gift he's wanted ever since I've known him. He was beginning to think it would never happen. Thank you, so much. You've given my husband and son their dreams, now to do this for my father-in-law. We all owe you. There is nothing that you could want that we wouldn't do for you."

"Don't tell Sadie."

"Maybe except for that. Dominic, you have to tell her if you're planning on leaving town. As it is she's going to be going crazy with worry when you don't come home tonight or even call her. She should know you're here with us, and safe. To not tell her, it's not right."

"But, Kathie, can't you understand? I'm going to feel so guilty if I call her. I should be working on us. And she's going to see it like that. Sure, she wants me to have a relationship with all of you. But she's going to think I'm putting this first, that I think it's more important than her. She's not going to look at it as my trying to make things right between the two of us."

"I don't think you have a right to make decisions for her that will have her up all night calling hospitals, police stations, and your family. I don't think you should stay away all night and not tell her. Just tell her you're okay."

"No, I'm sorry," Dominic said quietly.

"Then let me tell her."

"Katie, I know Sadie. If you call her you're going to make it worse. I can promise you that. Later she'll be able to forgive me, but not if you call her and I don't."

"I don't feel right about this."

Shawn stood in the middle of the room looking from his wife to his brother. He heaved out a breath before placing both hands behind his head and emitting a low growl.

"Katie, leave it alone. It's really not your business. Dominic's a big boy. Sadie is his concern. If he wants to fuck up his life, that's his business."

Dominic wasn't falling for this. He was a bit annoyed that so soon into their budding relationship they were trying to tell him what to do. He'd tired of people telling him what to do and in a way that included Sadie. But that bit of information they didn't need to know.

"This was a bad idea my coming here." He stood and took two steps toward the door when his brother stopped him.

"Don't leave, Dominic. I can promise you my wife will not call Sadie." Shawn gave his wife a no nonsense look. "Let it go," he said in a commanding voice.

Causing tension in his brother's home was definitely not in his plans. "I know what the two of you are trying to do. I'm serious about this and I don't care what reason you have. I've been betrayed my entire life. If either of you go behind my back and call Sadie I will know that I can't have a relationship with you.'" His gaze landed on his brother. "I really want to have a relationship with you, Shawn. I want to trust you. Don't screw me over, okay."

"No one in this house will ever betray you. That's a promise. Hey, if you want to fuck up your life, I'll stand behind you. I'm proud of you though for deciding to get to know Dad."

"Listen, I haven't even asked... him yet. He may say no."

"Damn, Dominic, you really don't know what to call him do you? Just call him Michael. And I can guarantee he's going to jump at the chance."

"We'll see." Shaking his head he laughed as his brother moved to hug him again, then Katie.

***

Frantic with worry Sadie called every person Dominic knew and almost wished she hadn't. Not only wasn't his family worried because she was looking for him, they attempted to give her foul messages which she would never repeat to him even if she'd understood it. Apparently they'd all forgotten she didn't speak fluent Spanish. The bottom line: He was not welcome in their homes. He was not a part of their family. And finally she heard, 'yes' he'd been there. No, they didn't know where he was heading and didn't give a damn.

Hospitals and police had been no help, not when she was worried that he'd been attacked somewhere and lying on the side of the road bleeding to death or worse. On a hunch she called her parents. He loved them. But no he wasn't there.

"Sadie, I told you he was breaking." Her father said angrily.

"I know Dad. I know."

God please let him call, please let him be okay. For the rest of the night and into the morning that was Sadie's prayer. "Te amo Dominic."

Chapter Twenty-Four

Perspiration lined Dominic's lips. He kept clasping and unclasping his hands out of nervousness before he made the call. Finally he could put it off no longer. Accepting the number from Shawn he dialed and asked the question.

Within an hour the plans were made. Michael was going to rent an RV and meet at Shawn's the following day. Dominic was going shopping for clothes since he had no plans to return home for any. And Shawn was going to go with him. Whether he was making sure he didn't change his mind or taking this big brother thing a bit far Dominic wasn't sure. He glimpsed the big cheesy grin on his brother's face as he looked at him and knew the reason. His brother was simply happy to spend time with him.

"I'll bet Sadie has been up all night calling the hospitals and...." Katie's voice trailed off.

Dominic's head snapped up. Katie was right. He should have called Sadie, another selfish act added to his growing list of sins toward her. He pictured her, tears in her eyes and confusion on her face. She wouldn't go to work without hearing from him. But if he called her now she wouldn't be any good at work anyway. She'd be furious. It was an excuse for not having done things the right way and he was aware of it.

"Katie," Shawn and Dominic called her name at the same instant.

"No, Shawn. Katie's right. Tomorrow, once we're on the road I'll call and tell her what I'm doing."

He was being a coward and he knew it but if he heard Sadie's voice right now he just might not be able to do what needed doing. Sadie was a part of his present, Poppi, his mother, and Roberto. They all expected certain things from him. He was Dominic Santiago to all of them. For the most part that persona had worked, but when the hypocrisy hit, the cover had blown apart like so much rice paper. He needed intense ground work from the frame outward and the best way he knew how to do it was to see who he really was. As much as he wanted to be Dominic Santiago, had tried to be him, when all was said and done he wasn't. It was time to see what this Dominic was without Poppi, Roberto and the rest of his family in his life.

"That's another twenty-four hour for her to worry needlessly," Katie said in a soft voice.

"I know I'm being a jerk." Sucking in a breath he momentarily closed his eyes as he thought of Sadie. "Katie, I'm aware my not calling her is cruel. That's not my intent. I'm trying to protect her. I want to give her back the man she fell in love with. If I can't find that man I'm not going to return to her. I love Sadie with all my heart. I promise you I will call her tomorrow."

"Dominic, would you mind if I call Sadie after you? Perhaps talking to a woman might help you with her later."

Katie had a long on her face like she'd crossed an unseen boundary and Shawn's look was almost identical. They were so worried about offending him. He laughed to show them he wasn't upset by Katie's request. "Sure, Katie, you can call her. Give it a couple of hours after we take off. It shouldn't take me longer than that to get the courage to call her."

When he saw relief wash over their faces, he grinned, and walked over to look out of the window, wondering how things would go with his father.

Dominic's attention was captured by Shawn and his wife whispering. When he caught their gazes they both looked at him embarrassed then Shawn smiled and Dominic knew what the whispering had been about.

"Shawn, you know I want you to come. I didn't want to ask you…your son….he hasn't been home long."

"I'll check in often with Katie, twice a day."

"Shawn, do you really want to come?"

"If you don't mind."

"You're sure this isn't about making certain I don't have a dastardly plan involving your father?" Dominic was teasing him and it felt good to know that his brother was aware of it.

This was too good to be true. When Shawn moved to give him a pound on his back this time it was Dominic who reached out and gave his brother a hug and released him quickly. He watched him while he ran up the stairs to pack his bag, taking the stairs two at a time as excited as a little kid.

The little twosome had become a threesome and the moment Dominic heard Ryan asking his father where he was going and couldn't he go he knew it was going to be a family affair. Though Shawn tried to remain hard and tell the boy the trip was only for adults, when the boy came down the stairs and looked so sad there was no way in hell Dominic was going to take the child's father from him.

Grinning, he looked at Shawn. "Why not?" The grins on the faces of the entire family was so bright that he didn't regret it for a second. He shushed their attempts to tell him he didn't have to have all of them barging in on his planned trip, but Ryan was running up the stairs to pack, not giving his parents or his uncle a chance to say no.

"Dominic... I... I... we shouldn't."

"This is perfect. Besides, I wanted to spend some time with you also. Do you think the way your son was looking at you I was going to be the one to break his heart? Dominic laughed. "I don't think so."

***

Hanging up the phone Sadie prayed for Dom's safety as she'd done for two days. Her parents attempted to console her with the knowledge that he wasn't at any hospital. Finally she'd given up and called Roberto again. He'd told her Dominic was a big boy to stop worrying about him. How could she stop worrying about him? No one but her had seen him the night before when he'd made love to her. She could not just do nothing.

She'd found his cell on his nightstand along with the jewelry box containing her engagement ring. She had a reason for worrying. When the phone finally rang a loud sob came out and she snatched the phone up calling Dom's name.

"No, it's not Dominic." It was a female voice speaking slowly and hesitantly. "I'm Katie, Shawn's wife."

Fear ricocheted across Sadie's body. "Dom, is he…"

"He's okay. I mean he's alive and well… uninjured, but…didn't he call you—"

"Where is he?" Sadie interrupted.

"He's gone on a road trip with my husband, son and my father-in- law. I have no idea where they're going or when they're coming back. They're going to bond. They rented an Rv."

Sadness was rapidly replacing her relief at knowing that Dominic had done nothing to injure himself.

"So he asked you to call me?"

"He said that I could."

Sadie got the message. The woman's unfinished words told her all that she needed to know. She'd had to argue for Sadie to even know the man she loved was alive. Dom hadn't cared enough to let her know he was okay. At that moment something in her died. He'd finally managed to kill a part of her.

"Thanks, Katie, whenever you talk to Dominic please tell him for me that I hope he finds what he's looking for."

"Sadie, I was supposed to wait until he had called you. He said he was going to. I'm sorry I called before he had a chance to. I had thought you might need someone to talk to. Now it looks like I've messed things up. I don't know you, but I do know how much he loves you. Don't give up on him now."

"How would you like it if Shawn were treating you this way? You shouldn't have been the one to call me. That's utterly disrespectful. I have spent the last two days on the phone in a panic. He was supposed to be going to the travel agent. He deliberately left his cell phone so I couldn't reach him. A couple of seconds would have been all it would have taken for him to let me know he was alive. He's known you people a few weeks. We've been in love almost five years. Wouldn't you be upset?"

Silence.

"Again I want to thank you for calling. I was worried about Dominic. At least now I can stop and begin rebuilding my own life."

"You're breaking up with him aren't you?"

"Whatever I'm going to do I'll tell Dominic when I talk to him. By the way I'm very glad to hear your son was well enough to make the trip. Have a nice day," Sadie said and disconnected the call without waiting for a response.

As she showered her mind became clearer. It was over. It was really over. Now she had to concentrate on her job. Going over to the nightstand she picked up Dominic's cell phone and rubbed it then she replaced it on the nightstand. Lifting the lid on the box containing her engagement ring she shook her head not feeling as broken as she thought she'd be.

"It's over," she said aloud. At least she wouldn't miss another day of work staying home to worry about him.

***

For the first hour of their road trip they'd had no idea where they were heading. Dominic had not thought out his plan so his father had just started driving. Then Ryan had solved the problem of where they were going.

"I want to go to the Dells," he'd piped in.

"This isn't your call," Shawn scolded. "Any complaints and we'll turn around and take you back home. This is your uncle's trip with grandpa. We're horning in."

Dominic laughed. "You know I didn't even think where to go. I don't mind going to the Dells."

"We have a cabin that's only a couple of miles from there," Michael had added. "But are you sure, Dominic? We want to do whatever will make you happy."

For a long moment Dominic gazed at his biological father. "Thank you, Michael. Let's do the Dells."

For a nano second it seemed as if his father was going to say something then he smiled and changed lanes.

Guilt was setting in though. He needed to talk to Sadie. It had been two days since he'd left home without a word. She was going to be pissed and hurt but he couldn't hide from that forever. Asking his brother to borrow his phone he took in a deep breath then allowed it to escape as he prepared to beg. He cringed thinking what a jerk he was to have made her worry.

"Sadie, just let me explain." But he didn't get a chance she was screaming at him through her sobs. There were only three words he heard. "It's over, Dominic." Then she slammed the phone off.

He tried redialing, knowing she wouldn't answer. When he heard Ryan asking Shawn why his uncle didn't wait until Sadie was no longer angry he laughed to himself. *Because Sadie could stay angry for a very long time.* But this he didn't say to his newly acquired family. He merely closed the phone and returned it to Shawn. He'd known having Katie call Sadie was the worst idea possible. Glancing at his watch he was surprised to see they'd been on the road for nearly three hours. He'd told Katie she could make her call after two. This mess too was his fault. He'd have to give Sadie time to cool off enough to talk to him.

Still the trip to the Dells was a lot of fun. They talked, sang and kept it light. Mostly Dominic listened to them and for the first time in years he wished that he had known this family, that he'd been a part of their lives. He'd missed out on so much. A sudden lump formed in his throat and he closed his eyes. When he opened them his father was watching him.

"It's okay Dominic. I'm feeling the same things."

When Shawn pulled up to 'the cabin' Dominic's mouth opened wide. This was the little cabin his father had been talking about. The place was beautiful, huge and very rustic with a wraparound porch. A wave of loneliness hit him. Sadie's one dream was that they'd someday have a porch like this. It didn't feel right to be enjoying even a little part of her dream without her there. "You okay?" Shawn asked.

"Yeah, just thinking of Sadie." Shawn handed him his cell phone and Dominic didn't refuse it. He attempted calling Sadie at home, her cell and the office. Her secretary said she was in court.

With a sigh he returned the phone to Shawn wondering if he'd done the right thing by coming on this trip.

"Dominic, your bedroom's the third one on the left," Michael said not pausing in his getting bags from the car, but a look passed between Michael and Shawn. He took his belonging to the room he'd been assigned. What the heck? Just like in Michael's home this bedroom was his literally.

He spotted a photo-shopped picture of him with Ryan, Shawn and Michael, holding a huge fish and he laughed out loud and went to help with the rest of the luggage.

How the hell was he going to tell his father that he'd not been there for him when his entire life proved that to be wrong? His father had loved him, provided for him and had done what he'd thought best for his son. And he'd somehow found a way to include Dominic in his life. This was a strange family he'd gotten himself into.

***

The jury came back and Sadie stared hard at Paul with worry creasing her brow. The decision went against their client. After talking with their client and instructing him on the next steps she gave a slight nod to Paul to take over. She sat back at the table until the client left the courtroom and Paul returned. She glanced at him and held his gaze. "I should have let you close."

"You did a good job."

"We both know it takes a fantastic job to win. I've taken too many days off and left everything on you. I'm so sorry, Paul"

"What are you worrying about, Sadie?"

"Who said I'm worried about anything?"

"I've known you for almost five years now. And I know that you're worried. You're trying to pull it off, but it isn't working. Let me hazard a guess and say it has something to do with Santiago. You know I do like him."

Sadie raised her brow.

A small chuckle followed and Paul laughed out loud. "Okay, so we're rivals, so what? We both wanted the same woman and we both lusted after the same job. That doesn't mean I hate the guy."

"No, but you know how to push his buttons and you do it every chance you get. You have made him crazy from the moment I met you."

"I was making Dominic crazy long before you came to work. He's too easy, Sadie. He becomes too emotional. He takes everything so seriously. Hell, I didn't even know he could smile until the day you walked into the office. Then his face lit up as though he'd just seen an angel."

"Wow, an angel," Sadie teased. "How do you know that's the vision Dominic had in his head?"

"Because it was what I was thinking." He took in a deep breath and let it out slowly. "It's still what I think."

Sadie began gathering her papers shoving them back into her brief case. "Don't go there, Paul, okay. Right now I'm feeling a bit more than vulnerable and I don't need you giving me compliments."

"For almost a year you've been unhappy, Sadie. This time I'm not kidding. I'm going to say this once and only once. When you get tired of Dominic you'll know where to find me. But let me be clear in this. At the moment I have not found anyone else. It may not always be that way."

"Paul, stop it. I'm never going to be over Dominic. Don't you get it? I'm not just in love with him. I love him. Come on, cut it out. I enjoy spending time with you. Talking with you makes me feel good. You make me laugh but you also make me feel guilty that perhaps we've gone farther than I ever intended and by doing so I hurt Dom in the process. I've flirted with you, encouraged you and perhaps even..." She blinked several times and stopped.

"Wanted things you shouldn't?" Paul asked.

Reaching for her briefcase Sadie picked it up and walked away only stopping when Paul called her name. Turning she looked over her shoulder. "Perhaps, Paul, but that would be taking you on the rebound. I think much too highly of you to ever do that. You're much too good a man to ever settle for being a woman's second choice." She stood there until Paul grinned at her and came to stand alongside her. "Why the grin?" she asked.

"I'm trying to think how I will rework your words to make Dominic wonder." He moved away as she swatted at him.

Sadie stopped herself from asking Paul not to say anything to Dominic. He was just kidding and a few short months ago she would have thought nothing of it. Things had changed she realized. How she wished she could go back in time and change them back. She slipped her hand through the crook in Paul's arm and walked away with him, trying to laugh, trying to pretend that this was a normal day and they were just two friends goofing around.

She felt Paul's thumb brush across her hand. Or maybe things weren't as innocent as she wanted to believe. Perhaps it was time to take Dominic's calls. She wasn't a saint and being angry with Dominic and entertained by Paul were definitely two powder kegs. Better to deal with her life and leave Paul out of the rubble.

***

For an entire week Dominic enjoyed the time he spent with his father, brother and nephew. He'd decided to give them real memories rather than the photo shopped pictures Shawn had provided. To be honest it wasn't that hard, they were fun and their enjoyment was real. The only thing he didn't like was they pandered to him. He wanted to make them stop, to stop apologizing for things they couldn't change. That was one of the reason he'd provoked a fight one night with his father. Ryan had been sleeping at least an hour and they were on the porch enjoying a beer and conversation. When Dominic started in on his father, he would have continued until Shawn broke in, angry at the way Dominic was treating Michael. Thank God.

"You've got a real convenient memory, Dominic," Shawn shouted, standing over his brother. "Dad has been taking this crap off of you because frankly we all told him it was part of the process you'd have to go through in order to allow him into your life. But frankly, I've gotten a bit tired of your sanctimonious attitude. And yeah, I've gotten tired of the way you're treating my father, our father, little brother. I've gotten tired of you beating up on him. Hell, I don't care if you don't want to acknowledge it right now, but we're out in the middle of nowhere, your choice little brother, remember? And I'm damn well going to have my say.

"Our father may not be perfect but who the hell is? Look at how you've fucked up your life and your relationship with Sadie in the last year. Who could blame her if she's in bed with Paul? Tell me, what would you do if that happens? We all know you love her and she loves you. It still doesn't mean things don't happen. No, our father had no right to sleep with another man's wife. But your mother is just as guilty as he is. He didn't rape her, Dominic. And he didn't abandon you. But I think you already know that. Now you need to be a big enough man and admit it."

"Shawn," Michael's voice was stern as he stared at first his eldest son then his youngest. "Let it go. He's doing the best he can under the circumstances."

"No, Dad we've both tried to tell him how things were. I think we've been too damn easy on him."

"But Ryan, we'll wake him. I don't want him hearing us fighting."

"Dad, Ryan's not going to hear us, and believe me, this need to be said. Dominic is not a little kid anymore. He's an adult. It's time you stopped feeling guilty for him thinking you didn't give a damn, that you abandoned him."

Shawn took in a breath, turned to his brother and sighed. "And it's high time Dominic stopped thinking you didn't love him."

"Listen, Dominic, this is the last time I will tell you this. Our father has loved you from the beginning. He loved you so much that he allowed your parents to blackmail him into paying for a trip to Disneyland for your entire family. As for me, you already know I got into surveillance because of you."

Dominic turned to Michael. "You paid for that Disney trip?" Dominic rubbed his fingers across his forehead as long forgotten memories rolled over him. He blinked. "You contacted me several times when I first went away to college."

"And you told him to go to hell, that you didn't want anything to do with him ever, that you had a father and wasn't in need of another."

Dominic looked at the two of them. "I did say that didn't I?"

"You did," Shawn agreed. "We still paid all of your bills and we intruded into your life as little as possible. That wasn't abandonment, Dominic. That was love."

Things were becoming a bit clearer. And it was that clarity that was allowing Dominic to remember the emotional scene between him and Poppi when he was going away to college. It was the first time Poppi had told him he loved him and was proud of him. It was what Dominic had always wanted. Then he remembered something else. Poppi had frantically begged him to not renounce him telling him that his biological father would more than likely try and contact him, that he should have nothing to do with the man. He made him promise again. Thinking he finally had Poppi's love, he'd wanted to be loyal to him. He'd worked eighteen years for his love and he wasn't going to give that up.

It was hard to admit that the man who'd raised you had done it only for the money. Swallowing Dominick knew his brother was telling the truth. Poppi had never loved him. He'd simply used him, holding him hostage to obtain money from his biological father. And when he could have reached out to his Michael at last, Poppi had assured he wouldn't by binding Dominic to him with a renewed promise.

"Michael, I'm sorry. The one thing I wanted for most of my life was a father. I didn't get that until I was eighteen. But looking back on everything, I see I didn't get it even then. I made a vow that kept out all of the people who loved me, you two, and Sadie."

He held out his hand to his father. "Shawn is right. I haven't done the best that I can and to be honest with you, our fighting tonight wasn't really necessary. I've seen the evidence of your love." He grinned.

"But if we didn't slug it out how am I to tell Sadie that it took this long for us to get to the point that I like you. She's going to think we took a trip without her just for fun. If I told her I liked you before we came on this trip she's going to hand me my ass on a platter." Shawn and his father were both staring at him in total shock.

"Are you serious?" Michael asked.

"Yes. I'm very serious. I would very much like to have you in my life. But you two have got to stop making me the center of attention, trying to please me. You don't have to try so hard. Okay. To tell you the truth I'm not used to all of this attention and its beginning to make me a bit uncomfortable. This is a family trip. I'd say for the rest of it we all concentrate on making sure Ryan has the time of his life. As for me, I'm enjoying being with the three of you."

His father took his hand and gave him a strong shake, then Dominic laughed knowing what was coming next. But before his father could make the first move Dominic hugged him and when his father's embrace tightened so did his.

"So would you prefer if I call you Michael or Dad?"

"The fact that you want to call me at all is a gift. I won't quibble. Thank you for giving me a chance. Like you said you already had a father and was not in need of another."

Tilting his chin upward Dominic studied the man standing in front of him showing him what he would look like in thirty years. He'd been wrong. He'd never had a father. "You're welcome, Dad," he grinned.

He decided he'd fill his father in on all that had happened in his life, not for revenge, to make him angry or for him to feel guilty. He wanted him to understand why he'd so stubbornly refused his love. And he'd not leave any of it out. It would be hard for his father to hear but he was sure his father and brother could handle it.

"I promise before we leave we'll have another talk, one without the yelling." Then it hit him what his brother had said. He could have finally pushed Sadie into Paul's arms.

"Listen, we can talk later, right now I need to hear Sadie's voice. God!! I really do have a lot of making up to do to her. He turned to walk away from the cabin accepting the cell phone lying in Shawn's outstretched hand. "Thanks, Shawn," he said softly to his brother. "Michael, thank you, for never giving up on me."

"How could I, Dominic? You're my son and I love you."

"Yeah I know," Dominic said. "Thanks for that also." He walked away to share the new information with Sadie. Damn how could he have been so blind? Sadie had tried to tell him repeatedly that Poppi was using him and he'd not listened.

Now that everything was out in the open he could hear just fine.

***

Ten days and she hadn't spoken to Dominic. It wasn't for his lack of trying though. She hadn't been ready to hear anything he had to say. The idea that he'd left town, left it to someone else, a virtual stranger to tell her he was alive burned her like nothing else. Sadie's intentions to ignore what it meant that he'd not called her first pulled at her. Sure Katie had said Dominic had promised to call her. And yes, he'd called eventually, but after Katie. That was not the way it should have happened.

She felt adrift. Her parents had merely shaken their heads when she told them of the latest development. She wondered how they could so easily understand his motives for leaving her without a word. Though she was grateful that Shawn's wife had called she considered it an insult that Katie would be privy to information about her man that she didn't have. It didn't matter that her parents thought she was being petty; her feelings were every bit as valid as Dominic.

The only person that seemed to acknowledge that Sadie had any right to be hurt or angry with Dominic was Paul. And yes, she'd be a fool if she didn't know that he had his own reasons. But it felt good to have at least one person who didn't think she was a selfish, evil monster. Which was why she was having dinner with Paul tonight. He'd asked if he could make dinner for her and she'd accepted.

Paul's home was made for comfort from his butter soft leather furniture to the bowls of fresh fruit that scented the air. His home wasn't heavily masculine, more like masculine waiting for a woman to soften the edges, and she rather liked that. That he'd literally hand fed her a lobster that was a big as her arm was no surprise, nor were the crab legs that he dipped in the melted butter before feeding it to her. It had been a long time since Dominic had pampered her in that way. She refused to complain about the amount of rich food he was serving, each course was better than the next. When he brought out steaks that melted in her mouth she was ready to lie down and call it a night but he only laughed insisting she had to have deserts. So she sat in one of his huge recliners as he fed her crème Brule. She tried not to think of the meals Dominic made for them.

"What happened, Sadie? Why are you here with me tonight?"

"I broke up with Dominic."

"Oh."

"You don't sound too surprised."

"I'm only surprised it took so long. So what am I going to be, your rebound guy?"

Before she knew what was happening Sadie burst into tears. Her heart was aching. She couldn't believe it, there was no more her and Dom and she was mourning. And just as suddenly she was in Paul's arms and he was comforting her holding her tightly to his chest, kissing her brow repeatedly pleading with her not to cry, to tell him what was wrong. And all she could do was cry until she no longer had any tears and no voice.

"Sadie, what the hell's going on?" Paul pleaded. "You're scaring me half to death. Nothing can be nearly as bad as you think it is."

"Poppi is not Dominic's biological father. A few weeks ago he met his biological father. Since then things have been really crazy. Dominic isn't handling it well at all. He's so lost. I've tried my best to be there for him, to be understanding but he keeps pushing me further away."

"That's the reason you broke up with him?"

"It was the catalyst. He and I were planning a trip then he went off with his biological father and brother without telling me. He left it up to his new sister-in-law to call me."

Sadie held tearful eyes up to Paul. "I was so worried. I thought he had done something crazy. I was terrified he was lying dead in a ditch. For two days there was no word from him and then to have a stranger call me, one who had to beg him to let me know he was alive..." She stopped and cried some more. "That was the last straw. I couldn't take any more."

When she'd told the whole story she expected Paul to take her side, to at least tell her he understood why she was so upset. But he didn't, he pulled back and studied her.

"Now I see why Dominic is the way he is. That's why he was so angry with you a few months back for not siding with him on that case that he was willing to work pro bono. Sadie, you're not adopted, nor were you handed news that could destroy your entire self-image.

From everything you've told me Dominic has been dealing with a heavy load. I can't tell you what's harder, to know you're not who you're supposed to be and have the parental approval and love jerked away every time you do something wrong, like in Dominic's case. Or to find out when you're an adult and find your birth parents are dead, when there's nothing you can do about it, no amends to be made, nothing, no relationship to be formed, no chance to be made whole."

"Are your birth parents dead?"

'I'm not sure. But so far I can't find anything on them. But right now this isn't about me and I'm not going to allow you to switch the subject. Look at me, Sadie." He gently turned her head back to him.

"Sadie, it's not that Dominic no longer loves or values you. He's being driven by something more primitive than you can imagine. I think he's pretty confident that when all is said and done you love him enough to listen and forgive him. Right now, Sadie, he's searching for himself. As much as I'd like to lie and tell you what a bum he is and how inconsiderate he was of your feelings, I won't do that. I understand what he's going through somewhat. I can't imagine a kid being put through that. To think your parents don't love you for whatever reason, and then to find out they don't. Sadie," Paul stopped. "I feel for the guy."

"Why couldn't he have said all of this to me? Why did he take off without telling me what he wanted to do?"

"That's something Santiago will have to tell you. But I suspect it was one of the hardest things he's ever done. All his life, he's been trying to pretend he was someone else, this big macho Latino guy, and think about it, now, he's not even that."

"But none of this has changed an iota of how I feel about him. I still love him, Paul. For the past week I've been determined to put him out of my heart. He's hurt me so much in the past year that I no longer want to forgive him. I'm angry, hurt and confused, but I can't stop loving him."

Chuckling softly Paul gave Sadie a friendly hug. "If you stopped loving Santiago so quickly then you wouldn't be the woman I thought you were."

"So you've given up on the idea of the two of us."

"I've fought for lost causes all my life. But even I'm not a masochist for love. You are in love with Dominic Santiago or whatever the hell name he decides to use. It's the man you love, not the name. And when he figures this out he knows you're going to continue loving him. Until he comes home though I don't see a reason why I can't keep you company."

"He probably has his spies watching us," Sadie said and rolled her eyes. "I can just imagine him blowing his top when he finds out."

"And you don't care? You dumped him. Right?" Taking a deep breath Paul sighed and laid Sadie's head on his chest. "I will always love you, Sadie, but I've decided it's time for me to stop being in love with you and find someone who's unattached. What do you think?"

"I think maybe you're right, Paul. Thanks for being a good friend to me. I really appreciate it."

"Enough for one last kiss?"

For long moments their gazes locked then they each smiled and pressed their lips together, when it deepened into something more than friendship, more like passion, they continued cautiously. When lust invaded the kiss they stopped.

"We really would have been good together, Sadie."

"Yeah, I know. You're a fantastic kisser and an even better friend. That really was the last kiss. You're too much of a temptation for me to do this anymore."

"You feel guilty?"

"No. For what I've endured the past year I think I'm entitled to a kiss. Besides, right now Dominic and I are officially broken up aren't we? So I didn't actually cheat on him did I?"

Booming laughter erupted. Paul laughed. "If you ask me I'd say we could go in my room and make love and it will all be fine, that it doesn't matter. But if you'd ask Santiago he'd say if you smile at me it's cheating. And since it's him you're in love with I guess we'd better call a halt to the kissing."

***

Screaming was out of the question so was kicking or hitting. Neither action would accomplish anything. And right now Sadie needed to accomplish one thing to remain sane. She had to talk to Dominic. Sure she was still angry and hurt but it wasn't getting her anyplace. It wasn't until her mother had reminded her of the hurts she'd inflicted on Dominic in the past year that her guilt pushed her into action. It was time to listen to his explanation.

With a sigh of irritation she scanned the saved numbers in her caller ID and dialed the number she was looking for. With another sigh she waited. "Katie, this is Sadie. I need to talk to Dominic. Would you mind giving me Shawn's number so I can call him please?" Ignoring the tears in Katie's voice Sadie thanked her. She didn't need anything more trying to sway her in one direction of the other.

This was the most important call she would ever make, no wonder her hands were shaking a bit as she punched in the numbers. Trying to curb her temper at having been reduced to going through such measures to reach Dominic Sadie bit back the angry words when Shawn answered the phone.

"Shawn, this is Sadie. Would you mind letting me talk to Dominic please?'

"Sadie…"Shawn stumbled, "Sure, just a second," he said.

***

"It's Sadie," Shawn said holding out his cell to Dominic.

An instant light ignited Dominic's soul. He'd waited for this moment. It had been two weeks since they'd last spoken. Sadie had refused his nightly calls that he'd made from Shawn's cell.

"Sadie,"

"If you're ready to talk, Dominic, I'm ready to listen."
And she was.

"Sadie, I've come home," Dominic said as he moved
away from his family. "All my life I have been searching for
something. I never knew what it was. I've been a real bastard
to my father."

"Your father, not your bio?"

"No, to my father. He didn't have to take my crap but
he did. And the crazy thing, Sadie, he didn't blame me. We've
gone off a few times by ourselves and slugged it out. Now it's
as though we've been a part of each other lives always."

"You fought?"

"No, baby," Dominic laughed. "I'm talking
figuratively. Shawn needed time with his son and I needed time
with my father. Then we needed time as a family, the men of
the family. Sadie, Ryan's the cutest kid. I hope we have a
dozen just like him."

Silence.

"Sadie."

"You know I'm happy for you right?"

"I know."

"And you do know you're not out of trouble right?"

"Yeah baby, I know."

"I'm not making you any promises."

"Then I'll make you one. You're going to be getting the
man you always thought I was. And, Sadie, I promise no more
stunts, no more running off and not telling you where I'm
going."

"You've got a lot of ground to cover with me, Dom. I
almost didn't call you. It felt too much like begging to have to
ask two people to put me into contact with you. First off you
know what you need to do immediately."

"I'll get a new phone today." There was something
amiss. Sadie hadn't mentioned anything about the note he'd
left her. It hit him. She'd never seen it. No wonder she was still
so angry with him.

"Sadie, did you do the laundry?"

"Excuse me."

"Did you do the laundry?" When she didn't answer he
laughed and rephrased the question. "Did you do my laundry?"

"Dominic…"

"Go look in my underwear drawer. I left something in there for you." He waited as she rumbled through the drawer and while she read the note. He heard her, *Ohh*, of surprise knowing things had just improved for him.

"You still should have called me before Katie."

"I know. And I was going to. But I didn't just leave and not tell you. That's why I left you the note."

"You should have left the note out some place where I would have seen it. Actually, you should have told me and not left a note. But I'm glad to know you at least thought about me."

It was a dig, one he deserved and one he'd take. Connecting with his family was what he'd needed. Reconnecting with Sadie was what his heart required. "So what have you been doing without me?"

"I'm spending a lot of time with Paul. I've told him everything that's been going on and I do mean everything. This time you should be thanking him. Paul's adopted and only learned of it a few years ago. He understands what you're going through and explained a lot of it to me from his perspective. But I shouldn't have had to hear those words from him. I should have heard them from you."

"You're right." Dominic filled her in on every single moment that had transpired since he'd left. He'd shushed her when she cried for him. And she'd not commented about his plan to gradually decrease giving money to Poppi each month. But he was aware she'd know what it meant for them.

They'd both said the things that needed to be said. The hurt wasn't quite as stark. The anguish a little less. So they talked for hours, Dominic trying to mend fences, trying to assure Sadie that he loved her, that he'd made himself whole for the two of them. When he got ready to end the call she gave him hope.

"Dom, I think you were right to make peace with your past. I'm glad you've invited your family to be a part of your life. You sound good."

It wasn't the, 'I love you,' he'd hoped to hear in answer to his own vows of love, but she was melting a little, wanting to forgive him almost as much as she wanted to kill him. That he could take. They were going to be okay if he didn't screw things up again. And he had no plans on screwing his life up any more than he already had. He walked back toward his family thinking how right that sounded, his family.

Holding the phone out to Shawn he shrugged sheepishly. "I need to go and get a phone pronto. Sorry, but I think you need to recharge your phone."

"How are things with you and Sadie?"

"Better than I anticipated. I never expected for her to call me. When she's pissed...," he stopped looked at his nephew and changed directions. "When Sadie is ticked I wait until she's not. She's happy that I found what I needed."

***

Each day spent with his family was made better with his morning call to Sadie. The knowing he would begin and end his day with her voice was the cherry on top of his not so imperfect life. Admitting that Poppi had never loved him was perhaps the hardest thing he'd ever done.

Falling in love with Sadie had prepared him for being able to deal with the hurt and rejection of his family. He'd known from the beginning that Sadie was the link to his soul. It had been her ability to see through Poppi's manipulation and present it to him in a way he could acknowledge. She'd been the one who'd prepared him to meet his biological family, to finally feel the acceptance he'd craved. And it had been Sadie whom Dom had ultimately blamed for his breaking Poppi's trust, for starting his world crumbling. But somewhere along the way his heart had known that he'd needed to get rid of the façade he'd lived in, finally turning his imperfect life into a much better one.

No life would ever be perfect but it sure as hell would be nothing without Sadie at his side. Yeah he had a lot of making up to her for the way he'd treated her this past year. And every day he'd thank God for keeping her by his side.

***

Now the male bonding was over, or at least they had come far enough along in the process that they could return home. And to think it had only taken a couple of months to find a family and have them firmly entrenched in his life.

It was time to make things right with Sadie. He was heading home and he had a surprise for her. Thankful that Sadie's parents loved him and were more than happy to assist him in his surprise was a plus. Having made a half dozen calls and several more stops for essentials he needed to implement his plans before their little caravan pulled up outside her parents' home he called to ready them.

***

"Shouldn't we at least give Sadie a bit of warning that Dominic's coming? I mean she's looking a mess. She's going to be mortified."

Sadie's father laughed and shook his head. "We're not going to tell her. She needs a good dose of her own medicine. I still remember the look on Dominic's face when he came here and she looked at him as though he was something she wouldn't touch with a ten foot pole. My baby girl needs to be brought down a peg."

"But honey, Dominic's not coming here alone. If we don't tell her that will be kind of mean."

"Maybe, but she'll see the way she should have acted with Dominic. He's not going to give a damn about how she looks. That boy loves her so much I doubt if he'll even see the goop on her face. She needs to know that honey. She needs to believe he loves her unconditionally. He's hurt her and I think that will go a long way to repair some of that hurt. His complete acceptance of her will enable her to accept his flaws. Let's not tell her okay." Then he leaned over and kissed his wife into submission and sat back to wait for their daughter's surprise.

***

When the phone rang it has been answered so quickly that both of Sadie's parents laughed. Sure it was Dominic they were determined not to let Sadie's answering the phone give anything away. Her father opened the door as quietly as he could and allowed Dominic and his party to enter. Once they'd all filed into the house Sadie's mother called out to her.

"Mom, I'm giving myself a pedicure. I can't come now."

"Sadie, get out here. I need you. I could care less what you're doing."

Trying to keep from messing up her nail polish Sadie duck waddled into the living room to see what her mother needed so urgently. She came into the room took one look at the crowd gathered there and gasped. Her hair was set in huge roller, her face covered with a green mask, and she had on a Tower of Terror tee shirt that had so many holes that it truly couldn't be called anything but a rag. And there were dividers between her toes. When a male voice called out, "Hi, Sadie," she saw it was Paul. With a shriek she attempted to run but was hindered by the dividers. Dominic laughed and followed behind her.

"Sadie," he called to her. "Come here."

Sadie's heart was pounding. Dominic was home. She'd never been able to resist him calling to her in the manner he'd just done, his voice low, sensual and heart stopping. She turned slowly saw his family and hers watching her and turned away again.

"Sadie," Dominic called again and once again she turned toward him. He gave her a look snagged her gaze and smiled. Then he made a beeline for her, his walk confident, his mind clear. Things were as they should be.

Suddenly Sadie threw herself in his arms and he planted himself to catch her, holding her tightly, then kissing her until his thirst was slaked. "Sadie, you and I both know I love you. I know I've hurt you. I know also there is no logical reason for you to forgive me. But then again love isn't logical is it?" He paused and dropped down on his knees. "How much time do you need to plan a wedding?"

"At least six months, maybe a year," Sadie replied without thinking. Dom smiled and she closed her eyes. It wasn't supposed to be this easy for him. She'd planned to make him suffer just a bit for hurting her.

"Paul's a great kisser," she blurted out. Making sure to keep her voice pitched low so only Dominic could hear her.

"He kept me entertained when I was going out of my mind with worry over you."

"Is there anything else Paul's good at?"

"He's a great lawyer."

"And?"

"A wonderful friend."

"Was this intended as a confession?"

"Sort of. I don't want any secrets between us. He likes you."

"I know. I talked to him. He's not a bad guy."

"That's what he said about you?"

"Am I forgiven?"

"Not yet."

"Are you going to marry me?"

"Yes."

Dominic grinned like a fool and pulled Sadie down with him. "She said yes," he yelled to their families, and then he slipped the new ring he'd bought for her on her finger. "Since we're starting over I figured you needed something that didn't have bad memories. I think it's time I did something else. I'm leaving the firm."

"Dom, don't..."

"No baby, it's okay. I'm opening up a new firm and I've taken on a partner already."

"Me....but, Dom."

"Not you, Sadie, Paul. He's a good lawyer. Besides, I decided maybe I need to keep him close to me."

"Don't you want me at your new firm?"

"No, not just yet. You stay where you are. You've earned that partnership. Besides I think it's better for our marriage if we don't work together. It's going to take a while to make a go of this"

"I think we have more than enough money."

"Money's not an issue here. Michael...My father," Dominic said slowly, weighing the sound on his tongue. "He's been putting money away for me since my birth. At first I wasn't going to accept it. But Shawn convinced me. It was Shawn who suggested I open a firm of my own. In the long run I think we'll all be a lot happier. That way Mr. Secret will no longer have to worry about me going crazy and neither will you. My brother and father have already gotten busy getting us clients. Paul and I have decided to buy the Woodridge office from the firm. We only have to tie up a few legal ends and we'll be on our way."

"Are you saying the things that happened with Paul you forgive me for?"

"I'm saying I love you and I'm grateful that you didn't stop loving me. I'm also grateful that it was Paul you turned to. He loves you enough not to take advantage of the situation. The amazing thing is we've talked and believe it or not the chance for a real friendship is in the working. Katie plans on introducing him to her friend Brenda. I hope that doesn't upset you. But we're all planning on finding a woman for Paul to replace you."

A grin was Sadie's answer before Dominic closed her in the safety of his arms. Our lives are what me make of them Sadie, neither perfect or imperfect, just us living each day as it comes and trying our best. He kissed her again deep and hard. When he let go Sadie whispered, "Welcome home, Dominic Santiago Donavan."

Lifting Sadie in his arms he carried her to her bedroom and helped her to clean up in record time.

Walking back out to properly greet Dominic's family and Paul Sadie stopped in shock seeing the transformation of her parents' home. Flowers were everywhere. She spotted a camera set on a tripod and then she noticed Paul standing there grinning at her. Her heart nearly seized when she spotted an altar and a man she was sure was a minister standing beside it in a flowing, royal blue robe. "Dominic," she whispered. "What's going on?"

"I knew you were going to take much longer than I wanted to get a wedding together so I took the liberty of doing it for you." He grinned. "This isn't an ultimatum baby, this is a plea. Will you marry me right here and right now? We can still do your big wedding later. I promise. But if we get married today I have the best spot in the world picked out for our honeymoon. It has a wraparound porch." He saw the gleam in Sadie's eyes. "Will you marry me baby?"

"What about a license?'

"I have it. Now, are we getting married today?"

Taking a look around at all of the expectant faces she brought her gaze back to the only one that mattered. "Yes, Dominic I'll marry you right this moment."

"Good, then before we begin the ceremony let me do something I should have done already. Then he took her hand and properly introduced her to his family. When he got to Michael, Dominic smiled broadly feeling pride in what he was going to say.

"This is what I should have been man enough to do when you came to the hospital to be with me. Sadie, this is my father, Michael Donovan." He turned toward his father. "Michael this is the woman who's going to be my wife."

Then Dominic pulled Paul to the front and introduced him to his family. When he turned to look at Sadie he knew all was right. The look she'd always given Poppi wasn't there. She liked Michael. She had a sixth sense about people. It was apparent that she trusted Michael to be a true father to him, so did he. It appeared one was never too old to need the love of a parent.

He introduced Sadie and Paul to Ryan and Kellie Donovan. Then he'd released Sadie from his embrace to give her a moment to talk to Paul. He smiled as he watched his new family talking to Sadie's parents. He noted the approval in the eyes of both their families.

Dominic stood with Shawn while they watched Sadie talking to Paul then giving him a hug. "Are you okay with that?" Shawn asked. "You don't have the urge to rip Paul's throat out?"

"Not anymore big brother. Only I can stop Sadie from loving me and I have no desire to do that." At that moment Sadie turned to him and his heart burst with love for her. Her smile was brighter than he could ever remember seeing it. The hurt that had haunted her for almost a year was gone. He held out his hand to her and she took it. They were getting married.

"Te amo, Sadie," Dominic whispered.

The doorbell rang and as Sadie's father went to answer it Dominic stared in surprise as his sisters and Maria, Roberto's wife entered the house. His gaze connected with Mr. Hawkins

and he smiled and went to his family. He wanted to introduce
them to the other half of who he was.

***

Standing to the side Sadie watched Dominic as he
talked with his sisters and sister-in- law. Tears formed in her
eyes. "Thanks, Daddy, for what you've done for Dominic."

"You're wrong this time, Sadie. This I did for you. I'm
glad he found his biological family. But he's going to need at
least some of his old family in his life. You can't be
everything to Dominic. I didn't want you to start your marriage
with that hanging over you. I knew having them here would
help you and Dominic. I called all of them and reminded them
that they are his family. I jogged their memory recapping all
the times he's been there for them. It's more than the finances
he's helped them with. I don't know if his parents will ever
come around. They've mistreated that boy. But that's on them.
As for Roberto, he's always been jealous of Dominic and
blamed him for the things that happened with their parents. But
he may come around eventually."

"Daddy, how do you know all of this?"

"I figured it out when I was talking to Roberto. I didn't
know if any of them would show up but I'm glad to see at least
his sisters and Maria came."

"So am I," Sadie replied. "Thanks Daddy. By the way, I
forgive you for betraying me to Dominic. I'm glad you were
looking out for him."

"Sadie,'" Dominic called to her. "The minister is ready.
Let's get married."

The End

Author's Information:

Dyanne Davis is an award winning author. She lives in a Chicago suburb with her husband Bill, and their son Bill Jr. An avid reader her love of the written word turned into a desire to write. She retired from nursing more than a decade ago to pursue her lifelong dream.

Dyanne has been a presenter of numerous workshops. She has a local cable show, *The Art of Writing,* in her hometown to give writing tips to aspiring writers.

When not writing you can find her with a book in her hands, her greatest passion next to spending time with her husband Bill and son Bill Jr. Whenever possible she loves getting together with friends and family

A member of Romance writers of American she served in many capacities for her local chapter, Windy City, including two terms as president.

Dyanne Davis loves to hear from her readers. You can reach her at davisdyanne@aol.com.